D1266666

AGATHA CHRISTIE

Collected Works

AGATHA CHRISTIE

At Bertram's Hotel

A Caribbean Mystery

Distributed by
Omniprose Ltd., Scarborough, Ontario

Published by arrangement with
William Collins Sons & Co. Ltd.

Original illustrations by
ETTICE DE LOACHE &
SILVIE DAUSSET

I.S.B.N.: 84-599-0313-3

13 097 04

At Bertram's Hotel

For Harry Smith
because I appreciate the scientific way
he reads my books

CONTENTS

CONTENTS

Printed in Italy

CHAPTER I

In the heart of the West End, there are many quiet pockets, unknown to almost all but taxi drivers who traverse them with expert knowledge, and arrive triumphantly thereby at Park Lane, Berkeley Square or South Audley Street.

If you turn off an unpretentious street from the Park, and turn left and right once or twice, you will find yourself in a quiet street with Bertram's Hotel on the right hand side. Bertram's Hotel has been there a long time. During the war, houses were demolished on the right of it, and a little farther down on the left of it, but Bertram's itself remained unscathed. Naturally it could not escape being, as house agents would say, scratched, bruised and marked, but by the expenditure of only a reasonable amount of money it was restored to its original condition. By 1955 it looked precisely as it had looked in 1939—dignified, unostentatious, and quietly expensive.

Such was Bertram's, patronized over a long stretch of years by the higher echelons of the clergy, dowager ladies of the aristocracy up from the country, girls on their way home for the holidays from expensive finishing schools. ('So few places where a girl can stay alone in London but of course it is *quite* all right at Bertram's. We have stayed there for *years*.')

There had, of course, been many other hotels on the model of Bertram's. Some still existed, but nearly all had felt the wind of change. They had had necessarily to modernize themselves, to cater for a different clientele. Bertram's, too, had had to change, but it had been done so cleverly that it was not at all apparent at the first casual glance.

Outside the steps that led up to the big swing doors stood what at first sight appeared to be no less than a Field-Marshal. Gold braid and medal ribbons adorned a broad and manly chest. His deportment was perfect. He received you with tender concern as you emerged with rheumatic difficulty from a taxi or a car, guided you carefully up the steps and piloted you through the silently swinging doorway.

Inside, if this was the first time you had visited Bertram's, you felt, almost with alarm, that you had re-entered a vanished world. Time had gone back. You were in Edwardian England once more.

There was, of course, central heating, but it was not apparent. As there had always been, in the big central lounge, there were two magnificent coal fires; beside them big brass coal scuttles shone in the way they used to shine when Edwardian housemaids polished them, and they were filled with exactly the right sized lumps of coal. There was a general appearance of rich red velvet and plushy cosiness. The arm-chairs were not of this time and age. They were well above the level of the floor, so that rheumatic old ladies had not to struggle in an undignified manner in order to get to their feet. The seats of the chairs did not, as in so many modern high-priced arm-chairs, stop half-way between the thigh and the knee, thereby inflicting agony on those suffering from arthritis and sciatica; and they were not all of a pattern. There were straight backs and reclining backs, different widths to accommodate the slender and the obese. People of almost any dimension could find a comfortable chair at Bertram's.

Since it was now the tea hour, the lounge hall was full. Not that the lounge hall was the only place where you could have tea. There was a drawing-room (chintzy), a smoking-room, (by some hidden influence reserved for gentlemen only) where the vast chairs were of fine leather, two writing-rooms, where you could take a special friend and have a cosy little gossip in a quiet corner—and even write a letter if you wanted to. Besides these amenities of the Edwardian age, there were other retreats, not in any way publicized, but known to those who wanted them. There was a double bar, with two bar attendants, an American barman to make the Americans feel at home and to provide them with bourbon, rye, and every kind of cocktail, and an English one to deal with sherries and Pimms No. 1, and to talk knowledgeably about the runners at Ascot and Newbury to the middle-aged men who stayed at Bertram's for the more serious race meetings. There was also, tucked down a passage, in a secretive way, a television room for those who asked for it.

But the big entrance lounge was the favourite place for the afternoon tea drinking. The elderly ladies enjoyed seeing who came in and out, recognizing old friends, and commenting unfavourably on how these had aged. There were also American visitors fascinated by seeing the titled English really getting down to their traditional afternoon tea. For afternoon tea was quite a feature of Bertram's.

It was nothing less than splendid. Presiding over the ritual was Henry, a large and magnificent figure, a ripe fifty, avuncular, sympathetic, and with the courtly manners of that long-vanished species: the perfect butler. Slim youths performed the actual work under Henry's austere direction. There were large crested silver trays, and Georgian silver teapots. The china, if not actually Rockingham and Davenport, looked like it. The Blind Earl services were particular favourites. The tea was the best Indian, Ceylon, Darjeeling, Lapsang, etc. As for eatables, you could ask for anything you liked—and get it!

On this particular day, November the 17th, Lady Selina Hazy, sixty-five, up from Leicestershire, was eating delicious well-buttered muffins with all an elderly lady's relish.

Her absorption with muffins, however, was not so great that she failed to look up sharply every time the inner pair of swing doors opened to admit a newcomer.

So it was that she smiled and nodded to welcome Colonel Luscombe—erect, soldierly, race glasses hanging round his neck. Like the old autocrat that she was, she beckoned imperiously and in a minute or two, Luscombe came over to her.

'Hallo, Selina, what brings you up to Town?'

'Dentist,' said Lady Selina, rather indistinctly, owing to muffin. 'And I thought as I *was* up, I might as well go and see that man in Harley Street about my arthritis. You know whom I mean.'

Although Harley Street contained several hundreds of fashionable practitioners for all and every ailment, Luscombe did know whom she meant.

'Do you any good?' he asked.

'I rather think he did,' said Lady Selina grudgingly. 'Extraordinary fellow. Took me by the neck when I wasn't expecting it, and wrung it like a chicken.' She moved her neck gingerly.

'Hurt you?'

'It must have done, twisting it like that, but really I hadn't time to know.' She continued to move her neck gingerly. 'Feels all right. Can look over my right shoulder for the first time in years.'

She put this to a practical test and exclaimed.

'Why I do believe that's old Jane Marple. Thought she was dead years ago. Looks a hundred.'

Colonel Luscombe threw a glance in the direction of Jane Marple thus resurrected, but without much interest: Bertram's always had a sprinkling of what he called fluffy old pussies.

Lady Selina was continuing.

'Only place in London you can still get muffins. Real muffins. Do you know when I went to America last year they had something *called* muffins on the breakfast menu. Not real muffins at all. Kind of teacake with raisins in them. I mean, why call them muffins?'

She pushed in the last buttery morsel and looked round vaguely. Henry materialized immediately. Not quickly or hurriedly. It seemed that, just suddenly, he was there.

'Anything further I can get you, my lady? Cake of any kind?'

'Cake?' Lady Selina thought about it, was doubtful.

'We are serving very good seed cake, my lady. I can recommend it.'

'Seed cake? I haven't eaten seed cake for *years*. It is *real* seed cake?'

'Oh yes, my lady. The cook has had the receipt for years. You'll enjoy it, I'm sure.'

Henry gave a glance at one of his retinue, and the lad departed in search of seed cake.

'I suppose you've been at Newbury, Derek?'

'Yes. Darned cold, I didn't wait for the last two races. Disastrous day. That filly of Harry's was no good at all.'

'Didn't think she would be. What about Swanhilda?'

'Finished fourth.' Luscombe rose. 'Got to see about my room.'

He walked across the lounge to the reception desk. As he went he noted the tables and their occupants. Astonishing number of people having tea here. Quite like old days. Tea as a meal had rather gone out of fashion since the war. But evidently not at Bertram's. Who *were* all these people? Two Canons and the Dean of Chislehampton. Yes, and another pair of gaitered legs over in the corner, a Bishop, no less! Mere Vicars were scarce. 'Have to be at least a Canon to afford Bertram's,' he thought. The rank and file of the clergy certainly couldn't, poor devils. As far as that went, he wondered how on earth people like old Selina Hazy could. She'd only got twopence or so a year to bless herself with. And there was old Lady Berry, and Mrs Posselthwaite from Somerset, and Sybil Kerr—all poor as church mice.

Still thinking about this he arrived at the desk and was pleasantly greeted by Miss Gorringe the receptionist. Miss Gorringe was an old friend. She knew every one of the clientele and, like Royalty, never forgot a face. She looked frumpy but respectable. Frizzled yellowish hair (old-fashioned tongs, it suggested), black silk dress, a high bosom on which reposed a large gold locket and a cameo brooch.

'Number fourteen,' said Miss Gorringe. 'I think you had fourteen last time, Colonel Luscombe, and liked it. It's quiet.'

'How you always manage to remember these things, I can't imagine, Miss Gorringe.'

'We like to make our old friends comfortable.'

'Takes me back a long way, coming in here. Nothing seems to have changed.'

He broke off as Mr Humfries came out from an inner sanctum to greet him.

Mr Humfries was often taken by the uninitiated to be Mr Bertram in person. Who the actual Mr Bertram was, or indeed, if there ever *had* been a Mr Bertram was now lost in the mists of antiquity. Bertram's had existed since about 1840, but nobody had taken any interest in tracing its past history. It was just there, solid, a fact. When addressed as Mr Bertram, Mr Humfries never corrected the impression. If they wanted him to be Mr Bertram he would be Mr Bertram. Colonel Luscombe knew his name, though he didn't know if Humfries was the manager or the owner. He rather fancied the latter.

Mr Humfries was a man of about fifty. He had very good manners, and the presence of a Junior Minister. He could, at any moment, be all things to all people. He could talk racing shop, cricket, foreign politics, tell anecdotes of Royalty, give Motor Show information, knew the most interesting plays on at present—advise on places Americans ought to see in England however short their stay. He had knowledgeable information about where it would suit persons of all incomes and tastes to dine. With all this, he did not make himself too cheap. He was not on tap all the time. Miss Gorringe had all the same facts at her fingertips and could retail them efficiently. At brief intervals Mr Humfries, like the sun, made his appearance above the horizon and flattered someone by his personal attention.

This time it was Colonel Luscombe who was so honoured. They exchanged a few racing platitudes, but Colonel Luscombe was absorbed by his problem. And here was the man who could give him the answer.

'Tell me, Humfries, how do all these old dears manage to come and stay here?'

'Oh, you've been wondering about that?' Mr Humfries seemed amused. 'Well, the answer's simple. They couldn't afford it. Unless—'

He paused.

'Unless you make special prices for them? Is that it?'

'More or less. They don't know, usually, that they *are* special prices, or if they do realize it, they think it's because they're old customers.'

'And it isn't just that?'

'Well, Colonel Luscombe, I *am* running a hotel. I couldn't afford actually to lose money.'

'But how can that pay you?'

'It's a question of atmosphere . . . Strangers coming to this country (Americans, in particular, because they are the ones who have the money) have their own rather queer ideas of what England is like. I'm not talking, you understand, of the rich business tycoons who are always crossing the Atlantic. They usually go to the Savoy or the Dorchester. They want modern décor, American food, all the things that will make them feel at home. But there are a lot of people who come abroad at rare intervals and who expect this country to be—well, I won't go back as far as Dickens, but they've read *Cranford* and Henry James, and they don't want to find this country just the same as their own! So they go back home afterwards and say: "There's a wonderful place in London: Bertram's Hotel, it's called. It's just like stepping back a hundred years. It just *is* old England! And the people who stay there! People you'd never come across anywhere else. Wonderful old Duchesses. They serve all the old English dishes, there's a marvellous old-fashioned beafsteak pudding! You've never tasted anything like it; and great sirloins of beef and saddles of mutton, and an old-fashioned English tea and a wonderful English breakfast. And of course all the usual things as well. And it's wonderfully comfortable. *And* warm. Great log fires.' "

Mr Humfries ceased his impersonation and permitted himself something nearly approaching a grin.

'I see,' said Luscombe thoughtfully. 'These people; decayed aristocrats, impoverished members of the old County families, they are all so much *mise en scène*?'

Mr Humfries nodded agreement.

'I really wonder no one else has thought of it. Of course I found Bertram's ready made, so to speak. All it needed was some rather expensive restoration. All the people who come here think it's something that they've discovered for themselves, that no one else knows about.'

'I suppose,' said Luscombe, 'that the restoration *was* quite expensive?'

'Oh yes. The place has got to *look* Edwardian, but it's got to have the modern comforts that we take for granted in these days. Our old dears—if you will forgive me referring to them as that—have got to feel that nothing has changed since the turn of the century, and our travelling clients have got to feel they can have period surroundings, and still have what they are used to having at home, and can't really live without!'

'Bit difficult sometimes?' suggested Luscombe.

'Not really. Take central heating for instance. Americans require—need, I should say—at least ten degrees Fahrenheit higher than English people do. We actually have two quite different sets of bedrooms. The English we put in one lot, the Americans in the other. The rooms all look alike, but they are full of actual differences—electric razors, and showers as well as tubs in some of the bathrooms, and if you want an American breakfast, it's there—cereals and iced orange juice and all—or if you prefer you can have the English breakfast.'

'Eggs and bacon?'

'As you say—but a good deal more than that if you want it. Kippers, kidney and bacon, cold grouse, York ham. Oxford marmalade.'

'I must remember all that tomorrow morning. Don't get that sort of thing any more at home.'

Humfries smiled.

'Most gentlemen only ask for eggs and bacon. They've—well, they've got out of the way of thinking about the things there used to be.'

'Yes, yes . . . I remember when I was a child . . . Sideboards groaning with hot dishes. Yes, it was a luxurious way of life.'

'We endeavour to give people anything they ask for.'

'Including seed cake and muffins—yes, I see. To each according to his need—I see . . . Quite Marxian.'

'I beg your pardon?'

'Just a thought, Humfries. Extremes meet.'

Colonel Luscombe turned away, taking the key Miss Gorringe offered him. A page-boy sprang to attention and conducted him to the lift. He saw in passing that Lady Selina Hazy was now sitting with her friend Jane Something or other.

CHAPTER II

'AND I suppose you're still living at that dear St Mary Mead?' Lady Selina was asking. 'Such a sweet unspoilt village. I often think about it. Just the same as ever, I suppose?'

'Well, not quite.' Miss Marple reflected on certain aspects of her place of residence. The new Building Estate. The additions to the Village Hall, the altered appearance of the High Street with its up-to-date shop fronts— She sighed. 'One has to accept change, I suppose.'

'Progress,' said Lady Selina vaguely. 'Though it often seems to me that it isn't progress. All these smart plumbing fixtures they have nowadays. Every shade of colour and superb what they call "finish"—but do any of them really *pull*? Or *push*, when they're that kind. Every time you go to a friend's house, you find some kind of a notice in the Loo— "Press sharply and release," "Pull to the *left*," "Release *quickly*." But in the old days, one just pulled up a handle *any* kind of way, and cataracts of water came *at once*— There's the dear Bishop of Medmenham,' Lady Selina broke off to say, as a handsome, elderly cleric passed by. 'Practically quite blind, I believe. But such a splendid *militant* priest.'

A little clerical talk was indulged in, interspersed by Lady Selina's recognition of various friends and acquaintances, many of whom were not the people she thought they were.

She and Miss Marple talked a little of 'old days', though Miss Marple's upbringing, of course, had been quite different from Lady Selina's, and their reminiscences were mainly confined to the few years when Lady Selina, a recent widow of severely straitened means, had taken a small house in the village of St Mary Mead during the time her second son had been stationed at an airfield near-by.

'Do you always stay here when you come up, Jane? Odd I haven't seen you here before.'

'Oh no, indeed. I couldn't afford to, and anyway, I hardly ever leave home these days. No, it was a very kind niece of mine who thought it would be a treat for me to have a short visit to London. Joan is a very kind girl—at least perhaps hardly a girl.' Miss Marple reflected with a qualm that Joan must now be close on fifty. 'She is a painter, you know. Quite a well-known painter. Joan West. She had an exhibition not long ago.'

Lady Selina had little interest in painters, or indeed in anything artistic. She regarded writers, artists and musicians as a species of clever performing animals; she was prepared to feel indulgent towards them, but to wonder privately why they wanted to do what they did.

'This modern stuff, I suppose,' she said, her eyes wandering. 'There's Cicely Longhurst—dyed her hair again, I see.'

'I'm afraid dear Joan *is* rather modern.'

Here Miss Marple was quite wrong. Joan West had been modern about twenty years ago, but was now regarded by the young *arriviste* artists as completely old-fashioned.

Casting a brief glance at Cicely Longhurst's hair, Miss Marple relapsed into a pleasant remembrance of how kind Joan had been. Joan had actually said to her husband, 'I wish we could do something for poor old Aunt Jane. She never gets away from home. Do you think she'd like to go to Bournemouth for a week or two?'

'Good idea,' said Raymond West. His last book was doing very well indeed, and he felt in a generous mood.

'She enjoyed her trip to the West Indies, I think, though it was a pity she had to get mixed up in a murder case. Quite the wrong thing at her age.'

'That sort of thing seems to happen to her.'

Raymond was very fond of his old aunt and was constantly devising treats for her, and sending her books that he thought might interest her. He was surprised when she often politely declined the treats, and though she always said the books were 'so interesting' he sometimes suspected that she had not read them. But then, of course, her eyes were failing.

In this last he was wrong. Miss Marple had remarkable eyesight for her age, and was at this moment taking in everything that was going on round her with keen interest and pleasure.

To Joan's proffer of a week or two at one of Bournemouth's best hotels, she had hesitated, murmured, 'It's very, very kind of you, my dear, but I really don't think—'

'But it's *good* for you, Aunt Jane. Good to get away from home sometimes. It gives you new ideas, and new things to think about.'

'Oh yes, you are quite right there, and I *would* like a little visit somewhere for a change. Not, perhaps, Bournemouth.'

Joan was slightly surprised. She had thought Bournemouth would have been Aunt Jane's Mecca.

'Eastbourne? Or Torquay?'

'What I would really like—' Miss Marple hesitated.

'Yes?'

'I dare say you will think it rather silly of me.'

'No, I'm sure I shan't.' (Where *did* the old dear want to go?)

'I would really like to go to Bertram's Hotel—in London.'

'Bertram's Hotel?' The name was vaguely familiar.

Words came from Miss Marple in a rush.

'I stayed there once—when I was fourteen. With my uncle and aunt, Uncle Thomas, that was, he was Canon of Ely. And I've never forgotten it. If I could stay there—a week would be quite enough—two weeks might be too expensive.'

'Oh, that's all right. Of course you shall go. I ought to have thought that you might want to go to London—the shops and everything. We'll fix it up—if Bertram's Hotel still exists. So many hotels have vanished, sometimes bombed in the war and sometimes just given up.'

'No, I happen to know Bertram's Hotel is still going. I had a letter from there—from my American friend Amy McAllister of Boston. She and her husband were staying there.'

'Good, then I'll go ahead and fix it up.' She added gently, 'I'm afraid you may find it's changed a good deal from the days when you knew it. So don't be disappointed.'

But Bertram's Hotel had not changed. It was just as it had always been. Quite miraculously so, in Miss Marple's opinion. In fact, she wondered . . .

It really seemed too good to be true. She knew quite well with her usual clear-eyed common sense, that what she wanted was simply to refurbish her memories of the past in their old original colours. Much of her life had, perforce, to be spent recalling past pleasures. If you could find someone to remember them with, that was indeed happiness. Nowadays that was not easy to do; she had outlived most of her contemporaries. But she still sat and remembered. In a queer way, it made her come to life again—Jane Marple, that pink and white eager young girl . . . Such a silly girl in many ways . . . now who was that very unsuitable young man whose name—oh dear, she couldn't even remember it now! How wise her mother had been to nip that friendship so firmly in the bud. She had come across him years later—and really he was quite dreadful! At the time she had cried herself to sleep for at least a week!

Nowadays, of course—she considered nowadays . . . These poor young things. Some of them had mothers, but never mothers who seemed to be any good—mothers who were quite incapable of protecting their daughters from silly affairs, illegitimate babies, and early and unfortunate marriages. It was all very sad.

Her friend's voice interrupted these meditations.

'Well, I never. Is it—yes, it is—Bess Sedgwick over there! Of all the unlikely places—'

Miss Marple had been listening with only half an ear to Lady Selina's comments on her surroundings. She and Miss Marple moved in entirely different circles, so that Miss Marple had been unable to exchange scandalous titbits about the various friends or acquaintances that Lady Selina recognized or thought she recognized.

But Bess Sedgwick was different. Bess Sedgwick was a name that almost everyone in England knew. For over thirty years now, Bess Sedgwick had been reported by the Press as doing this or that outrageous or extraordinary thing. For a good part of the war she had been a member of the French Resistance, and was said to have six notches on her gun representing dead Germans. She had flown solo across the Atlantic years ago, had ridden on horseback across Europe and fetched up at Lake Van. She had driven racing cars, had once saved two children from a burning house, had several marriages to her credit and discredit and was said to be the second best-dressed woman in Europe. It was also said that she had successfully smuggled herself on board a nuclear submarine on its test voyage.

It was therefore with the most intense interest that Miss Marple sat up and indulged in a frankly avid stare.

Whatever she had expected of Bertram's Hotel, it was not to find Bess Sedgwick there. An expensive night club, or a lorry drivers' pull up—either of those would be quite in keeping with Bess Sedgwick's range of interests. But this highly respectable and old world hostelry seemed strangely alien.

Still there she was—no doubt of it. Hardly a month passed without Bess Sedgwick's face appearing in the fashion magazines or the popular Press. Here she was in the flesh, smoking a cigarette in a quite impatient manner and looking in a surprised way at the large tea tray in front of her as though she had never seen one before. She had ordered—Miss Marple screwed up her eyes and peered—it was rather far away—yes, *doughnuts*. Very interesting.

As she watched, Bess Sedgwick stubbed out her cigarette in her saucer, lifted a doughnut and took an immense bite. Rich red real strawberry jam gushed out over her chin. Bess threw back her head and laughed, one of the loudest and gayest sounds to have been heard in the lounge of Bertram's Hotel for some time.

Henry was immediately beside her, a small delicate napkin proffered. She took it, scrubbed her chin with the vigour of a schoolboy, exclaiming: 'That's what I call a *real* doughnut. Gorgeous.'

She dropped the napkin on the tray and stood up. As usual every eye was on her. She was used to that. Perhaps she liked it, perhaps she no longer noticed it. She was worth looking at—a striking woman rather than a beautiful one. The palest of platinum hair fell sleek and smooth to her shoulders. The bones of her head and face were exquisite. Her nose was faintly aquiline, her eyes deep set and a real grey in colour. She had the wide mouth of a natural comedian. Her dress was of such simplicity that it puzzled most men. It looked like the coarsest kind of sacking, had no ornamentation of any kind, and no apparent fastening or seams. But women knew better. Even the provincial old dears in Bertram's knew, quite certainly, that it had cost the earth!

Striding across the lounge towards the lift, she passed quite close to Lady Selina and Miss Marple, and she nodded to the former.

'Hallo, Lady Selina. Haven't seen you since Crufts. How are the Borzois?'

'What on earth are you doing here, Bess?'

'Just staying here. I've just driven up from Land's End. Four hours and three quarters. Not bad.'

'You'll kill yourself one of these days. Or someone else.'

'Oh I hope not.'

'But why are you staying *here*?'

Bess Sedgwick threw a swift glance round. She seemed to see the point and acknowledged it with an ironic smile.

'Someone told me I ought to try it. I think they're right. I've just had the most marvellous doughnut.'

'My dear, they have *real* muffins too.'

'Muffins,' said Lady Sedgwick thoughtfully. 'Yes . . .' She seemed to concede the point. 'Muffins!'

She nodded and went on towards the lift.

'Extraordinary girl,' said Lady Selina. To her, like to Miss Marple, every woman under sixty was a girl. 'Known her ever since she was a child. Nobody could do anything with her. Ran away with an Irish groom when she was sixteen. They managed to get her back in time—or perhaps not in time. Anyway they bought him off and got her safely married to old Coniston—thirty years older than she was, awful old rip, quite dotty about her. *That* didn't last long. She went off with Johnnie Sedgwick. That *might* have stuck if he hadn't broken his neck steeplechasing. After that she married Ridgway Becker, an American yacht owner. He divorced her three years ago and I hear she's taken up with some Racing Motor Driver—a Pole or something. I don't know whether she's actually married him or not. After the American divorce she went back to calling herself Sedgwick. She goes about with *the* most extraordinary people. They *say* she takes drugs. . . . I don't know, I'm sure.'

'One wonders if she is happy,' said Miss Marple.

Lady Selina, who had clearly never wondered anything of the kind, looked rather startled.

'She's got packets of money, I suppose,' she said doubtfully. 'Alimony and all that. Of course that isn't everything . . .'

'No, indeed.'

'And she's usually got a man—or several men—in tow.'

'Yes?'

'Of course when some women get to that age, that's all they want . . . But somehow—'

She paused.

'No,' said Miss Marple. '*I* don't think so either.'

There were people who would have smiled in gentle derision at this pronouncement on the part of an old-fashioned old lady who could hardly be expected to be an authority on nymphomania, and indeed it was not a word that Miss Marple would have used—her own phrase would have been 'always too fond of men.' But Lady Selina accepted her opinion as a confirmation of her own.

'There have been a lot of men in her life,' she pointed out.

'Oh yes, but I should say, wouldn't you, that men were an adventure to her, not a need?'

And would any woman, Miss Marple wondered, come to Bertram's Hotel for an assignation with a man? Bertram's was very definitely not that sort of place. But possibly that could be, to someone of Bess Sedgwick's disposition, the very reason for choosing it.

She sighed, looked up at the handsome grandfather clock decorously ticking in the corner, and rose with the careful effort of the rheumatic to her feet. She walked slowly towards the lift. Lady Selina cast a glance around her and pounced upon an elderly gentleman of military appearance who was reading the *Spectator*.

'How nice to see you again. Er—it is General Arlington, isn't it?'

But with great courtesy the old gentleman declined being General Arlington. Lady Selina apologized, but was not unduly discomposed. She combined short sight with optimism and since the thing she enjoyed most was meeting old friends and acquaintances, she was always making this kind of mistake. Many other people did the same, since the lights were pleasantly dim and heavily shaded. But nobody ever took offence—usually indeed it seemed to give them pleasure.

Miss Marple smiled to herself as she waited for the lift to come down. So like Selina! Always convinced that she knew everybody. She herself could not compete. Her solitary achievement in that line had been the handsome and well-gaitered Bishop of Westchester whom she had addressed affectionately as 'dear Robbie' and who had responded with equal affection and with memories of himself as a child in a Hampshire village calling out lustily 'Be a crocodile now, Aunty Jane. Be a crocodile and eat me.'

The lift came down, the uniformed middle-aged man threw open the door. Rather to Miss Marple's surprise the alighting passenger was Bess Sedgwick whom she had seen go up only a minute or two before.

And then, one foot poised, Bess Sedgwick stopped dead, with a suddenness that surprised Miss Marple and made her own forward step falter. Bess Sedgwick was staring over Miss Marple's shoulder with such concentration that the old lady turned her own head.

The commissionaire had just pushed open the two swing doors of the entrance and was holding them to let two women pass through into the lounge. One of them was a fussy looking middle-aged lady wearing a rather unfortunate flowered violet hat, the other was a tall, simply but smartly dressed, girl of perhaps seventeen or eighteen with long straight flaxen hair.

Bess Sedgwick pulled herself together, wheeled round abruptly and re-entered the lift. As Miss Marple followed her in, she turned to her and apologized.

'I'm so sorry. I nearly ran into you.' She had a warm, friendly voice. 'I just remembered I'd forgotten something

—which sounds nonsense but isn't really.'

'Second floor?' said the operator. Miss Marple smiled and nodded in acknowledgement of the apology, got out and walked slowly along to her room, pleasurably turning over sundry little unimportant problems in her mind as was so often her custom.

For instance what Lady Sedgwick had said wasn't true. She had only just gone up to her room, and it must have been then that she 'remembered she had forgotten something' (if there had been any truth in that statement at all) and had come down to find it. Or had she perhaps come down to meet someone or look for someone? But if so, what she had seen as the lift door opened had startled and upset her, and she had immediately swung round into the lift again and gone up so as *not* to meet whoever it was she had seen.

It must have been the two newcomers. The middle-aged woman and the girl. Mother and daughter? No, Miss Marple thought, *not* mother and daughter.

Even at Bertram's, thought Miss Marple, happily, interesting things could happen . . .

CHAPTER III

'Er—is Colonel Luscombe—?'

The woman in the violet hat was at the desk. Miss Gorringe smiled in a welcoming manner and a page, who had been standing at the ready, was immediately dispatched but had no need to fulfil his errand, as Colonel Luscombe himself entered the lounge at that moment and came quickly across to the desk.

'How do you do, Mrs Carpenter.' He shook hands politely, then turned to the girl. 'My dear Elvira.' He took both her hands affectionately in his. 'Well, well, this *is* nice. Splendid—splendid. Come and let's sit down.' He led them to chairs, established them. 'Well, well,' he repeated, 'this is nice.'

The effort he made was somewhat palpable as was his lack of ease. He could hardly go on saying how nice this was. The two ladies were not very helpful. Elvira smiled very sweetly. Mrs Carpenter gave a meaningless little laugh, and smoothed her gloves.

'A good journey, eh?'

'Yes, thank you,' said Elvira.

'No fog. Nothing like that?'

'Oh no.'

'Our flight was five minutes ahead of time,' said Mrs Carpenter.

'Yes, yes. Good, very good.' He took a pull upon himself.

'I hope this place will be all right for you?'

'Oh, I'm sure it's *very* nice,' said Mrs Carpenter warmly, glancing round her. 'Very comfortable.'

'Rather old-fashioned, I'm afraid,' said the Colonel apologetically. 'Rather a lot of old fogies. No—er—dancing, anything like that.'

'No, I suppose not,' agreed Elvira.

She glanced round in an expressionless manner. It certainly seemed impossible to connect Bertram's with dancing.

'Lot of old fogies here, I'm afraid,' said Colonel Luscombe, repeating himself. 'Ought, perhaps, to have taken you somewhere more modern. Not very well up in these things, you see.'

'This is very nice,' said Elvira politely.

'It's only for a couple of nights,' went on Colonel Luscombe. 'I thought we'd go to a show this evening. A musical—' he said the word rather doubtfully, as though not sure he was using the right term. '*Let Down Your Hair Girls*. I hope that will be all right?'

'How delightful,' exclaimed Mrs Carpenter. 'That will be a treat, won't it, Elvira?'

'Lovely,' said Elvira, tonelessly.

'And then supper afterwards? At the Savoy?'

Fresh exclamations from Mrs Carpenter. Colonel Luscombe, stealing a glance at Elvira, cheered up a little. He thought that Elvira was pleased, though quite determined to express nothing more than polite approval in front of Mrs Carpenter. 'And I don't blame her,' he said to himself.

He said to Mrs Carpenter,

'Perhaps you'd like to see your rooms—see they're all right and all that—'

'Oh, I'm sure they will be.'

'Well, if there's anything you don't like about them, we'll make them change it. They know me here very well.'

Miss Gorringe, in charge at the desk, was pleasantly welcoming. Nos. 28 and 29 on the second floor with an adjoining bathroom.

'I'll go up and get things unpacked,' said Mrs Carpenter. 'Perhaps, Elvira, you and Colonel Luscombe would like to have a little gossip.'

Tact, thought Colonel Luscombe. A bit obvious, perhaps, but anyway it would get rid of her for a bit. Though what he was going to gossip about to Elvira, he really didn't know. A very nice-mannered girl, but he wasn't used to girls. His wife had died in childbirth and the baby, a boy, had been brought up by his wife's family whilst an elder sister had come to keep house for him. His son had married and gone to live in Kenya, and his grandchildren were eleven, five and two and a half and had been entertained on their last visit by football and space science talk, electric trains, and a ride on his foot. Easy! But young girls!

He asked Elvira if she would like a drink. He was about to propose a bitter lemon, ginger ale, or orangeade, but Elvira forestalled him.

'Thank you. I should like a gin and vermouth.'

Colonel Luscombe looked at her rather doubtfully. He supposed girls of—what was she?—sixteen? seventeen?—did drink gin and vermouth. But he reassured himself that Elvira knew, so to speak, correct Greenwich social time. He ordered a gin and vermouth and a dry sherry.

He cleared his throat and asked:

'How was Italy?'

'Very nice, thank you.'

'And that place you were at, the Contessa what's-her-name? Not too grim?'

'She is rather strict. But I didn't let that worry me.'

He looked at her, not quite sure whether the reply was not slightly ambiguous.

He said, stammering a little, but with a more natural manner than he had been able to manage before:

'I'm afraid we don't know each other as well as we ought to, seeing I'm your guardian as well as your godfather. Difficult for me, you know—difficult for a man who's an old buffer like me—to know what a girl wants—at least—I mean to know what a girl ought to have. Schools and then after schools—what they used to call finishing in my day. But now, I suppose it's all more serious. Careers eh? Jobs? All that? We'll have to have a talk about all that sometime. Anything in particular you want to do?'

'I suppose I shall take a secretarial course,' said Elvira without enthusiasm.

'Oh. You want to be a secretary?'

'Not particularly.'

'Oh—well, then—'

'It's just what you start with,' Elvira explained.

Colonel Luscombe had an odd feeling of being relegated to his place.

'These cousins of mine, the Melfords. You think you'll like living with them? If not—'

'Oh I think so. I like Nancy quite well. And Cousin Mildred is rather a dear.'

'That's all right then?'

'Quite, for the present.'

Luscombe did not know what to say to that. Whilst he was considering what next to say, Elvira spoke. Her words were simple and direct.

'Have I any money?'

Again he took his time before answering, studying her thoughtfully. Then he said:

'Yes. You've got quite a lot of money. That is to say, you will have when you are twenty-one.'

'Who has got it now?'

He smiled. 'It's held in trust for you; a certain amount is deducted each year from the income to pay for your maintenance and education.'

'And you are the trustee?'

'One of them. There are three.'

'What happens if I die?'

'Come, come, Elvira, you're not going to die. What nonsense!'

'I hope not—but one never knows, does one? An airliner crashed only last week and everyone was killed.'

'Well, it's not going to happen to you,' said Luscombe firmly.

'You can't really know that,' said Elvira. 'I was just wondering who would get my money if I died?'

'I haven't the least idea,' said the Colonel irritably. 'Why do you ask?'

'It might be interesting,' said Elvira thoughtfully. 'I wondered if it would be worth anyone's while to kill me.'

'Really, Elvira! This is a most unprofitable conversation. I can't understand why your mind dwells on such things.'

'Oh, just ideas. One wants to know what the facts really are.'

'You're not thinking of the *Mafia*—or something like that?'

'Oh no. That would be silly. Who would get my money if I was married?'

'Your husband, I suppose. But really—'

'Are you sure of that?'

'No, I'm not in the least sure. It depends on the wording of the Trust. But you're not married, so why worry?'

Elvira did not reply. She seemed lost in thought. Finally she came out of her trance and asked:

'Do you ever see my mother?'

'Sometimes. Not very often.'

'Where is she now?'

'Oh—abroad.'

'Where abroad?'

'France—Portugal. I don't really know.'

'Does she ever want to see me?'

Her limpid gaze met his. He didn't know what to reply. Was this a moment for truth? Or for vagueness? Or for a good thumping lie? What could you say to a girl who asked a question of such simplicity, when the answer was of great complexity? He said unhappily,

'I don't know.'

Her eyes searched him gravely. Luscombe felt thoroughly ill at ease. He was making a mess of this. The girl must wonder—clearly was wondering. Any girl would.

He said, 'You mustn't think—I mean it's difficult to explain. Your mother is, well, rather different from—' Elvira was nodding energetically.

'I know. I'm always reading about her in the papers. She's something rather special, isn't she? In fact, she's rather a wonderful person.'

'Yes,' agreed the Colonel. 'That's exactly right. She's a wonderful person.' He paused and then went on. 'But a wonderful person is very often—' He stopped and started again—'it's not always a happy thing to have a wonderful person for a mother. You can take that from me because it's the truth.'

'You don't like speaking the truth very much, do you? But I think what you've just said *is* the truth.'

They both sat staring towards the big brass-bound swing doors that led to the world outside.

Suddenly the doors were pushed open with violence—a violence quite unusual in Bertram's Hotel—and a young man strode in and went straight across to the desk. He wore a black leather jacket. His vitality was such that Bertram's Hotel took on the atmosphere of a museum by way of contrast. The people were the dust encrusted relics of a past age. He bent towards Miss Gorringe and asked,

'Is Lady Sedgwick staying here?'

Miss Gorringe on this occasion had no welcoming smile. Her eyes were flinty. She said,

'Yes.' Then, with definite unwillingness, she stretched out her hand towards the telephone. 'Do you want to—?'

'No,' said the young man. 'I just wanted to leave a note for her.'

He produced it from a pocket of his leather coat and slid it across the mahogany counter.

'I only wanted to be sure this was the right hotel.'

There might have been some slight incredulity in his voice as he looked round him, then turned back towards the entrance. His eyes passed indifferently over the people sitting round him. They passed over Luscombe and Elvira in the same way, and Luscombe felt a sudden unsuspected anger. 'Dammit all,' he thought to himself, 'Elvira's a pretty girl. When I was a young chap I'd have noticed a pretty girl, especially among all these fossils.' But the young man seemed to have no interested eyes to spare for pretty girls.

He turned back to the desk and asked, raising his voice slightly as though to call Miss Gorringe's attention,

'What's the telephone number here? 1129 isn't it?'

'No,' said Miss Gorringe, '3925.'

'Regent?'

'No. Mayfair.'

He nodded. Then swiftly he strode across to the door and passed out, swinging the doors to behind him with something of the same explosive quality he had shown on entering.

Everybody seemed to draw a deep breath; to find difficulty in resuming their interrupted conversations.

'Well,' said Colonel Luscombe, rather inadequately, as if at a loss for words. 'Well, really! These young fellows nowadays . . .'

Elvira was smiling.

'You recognized him, didn't you?' she said. 'You know who he is?' She spoke in a slightly awed voice. She proceeded to enlighten him. 'Ladislaus Malinowski.'

'Oh, that chap.' The name was indeed faintly familiar to Colonel Luscombe. 'Racing driver.'

'Yes. He was world champion two years running. He had a bad crash a year ago. Broke lots of things. But I believe he's driving again now.' She raised her head to listen. 'That's a racing car he's driving now.'

The roar of the engine had penetrated through to Bertram's Hotel from the street outside. Colonel Luscombe perceived that Ladislaus Malinowski was one of Elvira's heroes. 'Well,' he thought to himself, 'better that than one of those pop singers or crooners or long-haired Beatles or whatever they call themselves.' Luscombe was old-fashioned in his views of young men.

The swing doors opened again. Both Elvira and Colonel Luscombe looked at them expectantly but Bertram's Hotel had reverted to normal. It was merely a white-haired elderly cleric who came in. He stood for a moment looking round him with a slightly puzzled air as of one who fails to understand where he was or how he had come there. Such an experience was no novelty to Canon Pennyfather. It came to him in trains when he did not remember where he had come from, where he was going, or why! It came to him when he was walking along the street, it came to him when he found himself sitting on a committee. It had come to him before now when he was in his cathedral stall, and did not know whether he had already preached his sermon or was about to do so.

'I believe I know that old boy,' said Luscombe, peering at him. 'Who is he now? Stays here fairly often, I believe. Abercrombie? Archdeacon Abercrombie—no, it's not Abercrombie, though he's rather like Abercrombie.'

Elvira glanced round at Canon Pennyfather without interest. Compared with a racing driver he had no appeal at all. She was not interested in ecclesiastics of any kind although, since being in Italy, she admitted to a mild admiration for Cardinals whom she considered as at any rate properly picturesque.

Canon Pennyfather's face cleared and he nodded his head appreciatively. He had recognized where he was. In Bertram's Hotel, of course; where he was going to spend the night on his way to—now where was he on his way to? Chadminster? No, no, he had just *come* from Chadminster. He was going to—of course—to the Congress at Lucerne. He stepped forward, beaming, to the reception desk and was greeted warmly by Miss Gorringe.

'So glad to see you, Canon Pennyfather. How well you are looking.'

'Thank you—thank you—I had a severe cold last week but I've got over it now. You have a room for me. I *did* write?'

Miss Gorringe reassured him.

'Oh yes, Canon Pennyfather, we got your letter. We've reserved No. 19 for you, the room you had last time.'

'Thank you—thank you. For—let me see—I shall want it for four days. Actually I am going to Lucerne and shall be away for one night, but please keep the room. I shall leave most of my things here and only take a small bag to Switzerland. There won't be any difficulty over that?'

Again Miss Gorringe reassured him.

'Everything's going to be quite all right. You explained very clearly in your letter.'

Other people might not have used the word 'clearly'. 'Fully' would have been better, since he had certainly written at length.

All anxieties set at rest, Canon Pennyfather breathed a sigh of relief and was conveyed, together with his baggage, to Room 19.

In Room 28 Mrs Carpenter had removed her crown of violets from her head and was carefully adjusting her nightdress on the pillow of her bed. She looked up as Elvira entered.

'Ah, there you are, my dear. Would you like me to help you with your unpacking?'

'No, thank you,' said Elvira politely. 'I shan't unpack very much, you know.'

'Which of the bedrooms would you like to have? The bathroom is between them. I told them to put your luggage in the far one. I thought this room might be a little noisy.'

'That was very kind of you,' said Elvira in her expressionless voice.

'You're sure you wouldn't like me to help you?'

'No, thanks, really I wouldn't. I think I might perhaps have a bath.'

'Yes, I think that's a very good idea. Would you like to have the first bath? I'd rather finish putting my things away.'

Elvira nodded. She went into the adjoining bathroom, shut the door behind her and pushed the bolts across. She went into her own room, opened her suitcase and flung a few things on the bed. Then she undressed, put on a dressing-gown, went into the bathroom and turned the taps on. She went back into her own room and sat down on the bed by the telephone. She listened a moment or two in case of interruptions, then lifted the receiver.

'This is Room 29. Can you give me Regent 1129 please?'

CHAPTER IV

WITHIN the confines of Scotland Yard a conference was in progress. It was by way of being an informal conference. Six or seven men were sitting easily around a table and each of those six men was a man of some importance in his own line. The subject that occupied the attention of these guardians of the law was a subject that had grown terrifically in importance during the last two or three years. It concerned a branch of crime whose success had been overwhelmingly disquieting. Robbery on a big scale was increasing. Bank hold-ups, snatches of pay-rolls, thefts of consignments of jewels sent through the mail, train robberies. Hardly a month passed but some daring and stupendous coup was attempted and brought off successfully.

Sir Ronald Graves, Assistant Commissioner of Scotland Yard, was presiding at the head of the table. According to his usual custom he did more listening than talking. No formal reports were being presented on this occasion. All that belonged to the ordinary routine of CID work. This was a high level consultation, a general pooling of ideas between men looking at affairs from slightly different points of view. Sir Ronald Graves's eyes went slowly round his little group, then he nodded his head to a man at the end of the table.

'Well, Father,' he said, 'let's hear a few homely wisecracks from you.'

The man addressed as 'Father' was Chief-Inspector Fred Davy. His retirement lay not long ahead and he appeared to be even more elderly than he was. Hence his nickname of 'Father'. He had a comfortable spreading presence, and such a benign and kindly manner that many criminals had been disagreeably surprised to find him a less genial and gullible man that he had seemed to be.

'Yes, Father, let's hear your views,' said another Chief-Inspector.

'It's big,' said Chief-Inspector Davy with a deep sigh. 'Yes, it's big. Maybe it's growing.'

'When you say big, do you mean numerically?'

'Yes, I do.'

Another man, Comstock, with a sharp, foxy face and alert eyes, broke in to say,

'Would you say that was an advantage to them?'

'Yes and no,' said Father. 'It *could* be a disaster. But so far, devil take it, they've got it all well under control.'

Superintendent Andrews, a fair, slight, dreamy-looking man, said thoughtfully,

'I've always thought there's a lot more to size than people realize. Take a little one-man business. If that's well run and if it's the right size, it's a sure and certain winner. Branch out, make it bigger, increase personnel, and perhaps you'll get it suddenly to the *wrong* size and down the hill it goes. The same way with a great big chain of stores. An empire in industry. If that's *big* enough it will succeed. If it's *not* big enough it just won't manage it. Everything has got its right size. When it is its right size and well run it's the tops.'

'How big do you think this show is?' Sir Ronald barked.

'Bigger than we thought at first,' said Comstock.

A tough looking man, Inspector McNeill, said,

'It's growing, I'd say. Father's right. Growing all the time.'

'That may be a good thing,' said Davy. 'It may grow a bit *too* fast, and then it'll get out of hand.'

'The question is, Sir Ronald,' said McNeill, 'who we pull in and when?'

'There's a round dozen or so we could pull in,' said Comstock. 'The Harris lot are mixed up in it, we know that. There's a nice little pocket down Luton way. There's a garage at Epsom, there's a pub near Maidenhead, and there's a farm on the Great North Road.'

'Any of them worth pulling in?'

'I don't think so. Small fry all of them. Links. Just links here and there in the chain. A spot where cars are converted, and turned over quickly; a respectable pub where messages get passed; a second-hand clothes shop where appearance can be altered, a theatrical costumier in the East End, also very useful. They're paid, these people. Quite well paid but they don't really *know* anything!'

The dreamy Superintendent Andrews said again,

'We're up against some good brains. We haven't got near them yet. We know some of their affiliations and that's all. As I say, the Harris crowd are in it and Marks is in on the financial end. The foreign contacts are in touch with Weber but he's only an agent. We've nothing actually *on* any of these people. We know that they all have ways of maintaining contact with each other, and with the different branches of the concern, but we don't know exactly how they do it. We watch them and follow them, and they know we're watching them. *Somewhere* there's a great central exchange. What we want to get at is the planners.'

Comstock said,

'It's like a giant network. I agree that there must be an operational headquarters somewhere. A place where each operation is planned and detailed and dovetailed completely. Somewhere, someone plots it all, and produces a working blueprint of Operation Mailbag or Operation Payroll. Those are the people we're out to get.'

'Possibly they are not even in this country,' said Father quietly.

'No, I dare say that's true. Perhaps they're in an igloo somewhere, or in a tent in Morocco or in a chalet in Switzerland.'

'I don't believe in these master-minds,' said McNeill, shaking his head. 'they sound all right in a story. There's got to *be* a head, of course, but I don't believe in a Master Criminal. I'd say there was a very clever little Board of Directors behind this. Centrally planned, with a Chairman. They've got on to something good, and they're improving their technique all the time. All the same—'

'Yes?' said Sir Ronald encouragingly.

'Even in a right tight little team, there are probably expendables. What I call the Russian Sledge principle. From time to time, if they think we might be getting hot on the scent, they throw off one of them, the one they think they can best afford.'

'Would they dare to do that? Wouldn't it be rather risky?'

'I dare say it could be done in such a way that whoever it was wouldn't even know he *had* been pushed off the sledge. He'd just think he'd fallen off. He'd keep quiet because he'd think it was worth his while to keep quiet. So it would be, of course. They've got plenty of money to play with, and they can afford to be generous. Family looked after, if he's got one, whilst he's in prison. Possibly an escape engineered.'

'There's been too much of that,' said Comstock.

'I think, you know,' said Sir Ronald, 'that it's not much good going over and over our speculations again. We always say much the same thing.'

McNeill laughed.

'What is it you really wanted us for, sir?'

'Well—' Sir Ronald thought a moment, 'we're all agreed on the main things,' he said slowly. 'We're agreed on our main policy, on what we're trying to do. I think it *might* be profitable to have a look around for some of the small things, the things that don't matter much, that are just a bit out of the usual run. It's hard to explain what I mean, but like that business some years ago in the Culver case. An ink stain. Do you remember? An ink stain round a mouse-hole. Now why on earth should a man empty a bottle of ink into a mouse-hole? It didn't seem important. It was hard to get at the answer. But when we did hit on the answer, it led somewhere. That's—roughly—the sort of thing I was thinking about. Odd things. Don't mind saying if you come across something that strikes you as a bit out of the usual. Petty if you like, but irritating, because it doesn't quite fit in. I see Father's nodding his head.'

'Couldn't agree with you more,' said Chief-Inspector Davy. 'Come on, boys, try to come up with something. Even if it's only a man wearing a funny hat.'

There was no immediate response. Everyone looked a little uncertain and doubtful.

'Come on,' said Father. 'I'll stick my neck out first. It's just a funny story, really, but you might as well have it for what it's worth. The London and Metropolitan Bank hold-up. Carmolly Street Branch. Remember it? A whole list of car numbers and car colours and makes. We appealed to people to come forward and they responded—how they responded! About a hundred and fifty pieces of misleading information! Got it sorted out in the end to about seven cars that had been seen in the neighbourhood, any one of which *might* have been concerned in the robbery.'

'Yes,' said Sir Ronald, 'go on.'

'There were one or two we couldn't get tags on. Looked as though the numbers might have been changed. Nothing out of the way in that. It's often done. Most of them got tracked down in the end. I'll just bring up one instance. Morris Oxford, black saloon, number CMG 256, reported by a probation officer. He said it was being driven by Mr Justice Ludgrove.'

He looked round. They were listening to him, but without any manifest interest.

'I know,' he said, 'wrong as usual. Mr Justice Ludgrove is a rather noticeable old boy, ugly as sin for one thing. Well, it wasn't Mr Justice Ludgrove because at that exact time he was actually in Court. He *has* got a Morris Oxford, but its number isn't CMG 256.' He looked round. 'All right. All right. So there's no point in it, you'll say. But do you know what the number *was*? CMG 265. Near enough, eh? Just the sort of mistake one does make when you're trying to remember a car number.'

'I'm sorry,' said Sir Ronald, 'I don't quite see—'

'No,' said Chief-Inspector Davy, 'there's nothing *to* see

really, is there? Only—it was very like the actual car number, wasn't it? 265—256 CMG. Really rather a coincidence that there should be a Morris Oxford car of the right colour with the number just one digit wrong, and with a man in it closely resembling the owner of the car.'

'Do you mean—?'

'Just one little digit difference. Today's "deliberate mistake." It almost seems like that.'

'Sorry, Davy. I still don't get it.'

'Oh, I don't suppose there's anything *to* get. There's a Morris Oxford car, CMG 265, proceeding along the street two and a half minutes after the bank snatch. In it, the probation officer recognizes Mr Justice Ludgrove.'

'Are you suggesting it really *was* Mr Justice Ludgrove? Come now, Davy.'

'No, I'm not suggesting that it was Mr Justice Ludgrove and that he was mixed up in a bank robbery. He was staying at Bertram's Hotel in Pond Street, and he was at the Law Courts at that exact time. All proved up to the hilt. I'm saying the car number and make and the identification by a probation officer who knows old Ludgrove quite well by sight is the kind of coincidence that *ought* to mean something. Apparently it doesn't. Too bad.'

Comstock stirred uneasily.

'There was another case a bit like that in connection with the Jewellery business at Brighton. Some old Admiral or other. I've forgotten his name now. Some woman identified him most positively as having been on the scene.'

'And he wasn't?'

'No, he'd been in London that night. Went up for some naval dinner or other, I think.'

'Staying at his club?'

'No, he was staying at a hotel—I believe it was that one you mentioned just now, Father, Bertram's, isn't it? Quiet place. A lot of old service geezers go there, I believe.'

'Bertram's Hotel,' said Chief-Inspector Davy, thoughtfully.

CHAPTER V

MISS MARPLE awoke early because she always woke early. She was appreciative of her bed. Most comfortable.

She pattered across to the window and pulled the curtains, admitting a little pallid London daylight. As yet, however, she did not try to dispense with the electric light. A very nice bedroom they had given her, again quite in the tradition of Bertram's. A rose-flowered wallpaper, a large well-polished mahogany chest of drawers—a dressing-table to correspond. Two upright chairs, one easy chair of a reasonable height from the ground. A connecting door led to a bathroom which was modern but which had a tiled wallpaper of roses and so avoided any suggestion of over-frigid hygiene.

Miss Marple got back into bed, plumped her pillows up, glanced at her clock, half-past seven, picked up the small devotional book that always accompanied her, and read as usual the page and a half allotted to the day. Then she picked up her knitting and began to knit, slowly at first, since her fingers were stiff and rheumatic when she first awoke, but very soon her pace grew faster, and her fingers lost their painful stiffness.

'Another day,' said Miss Marple to herself, greeting the fact with her usual gentle pleasure. Another day—and who knew what it might bring forth?

She relaxed, and abandoning her knitting, let thoughts pass in an idle stream through her head . . . Selina Hazy . . . what a pretty cottage she had had in St Mary Mead's—and now someone had put on that ugly green roof . . . Muffins . . . very wasteful in butter . . . but very good . . . And fancy serving old-fashioned seed cake! She had never expected, not for a moment, that things would be as much like they used to be . . . because, after all, Time didn't stand still . . . And to have made it stand still in this way must really have cost a lot of money . . . Not a bit of plastic in the place! . . . It must pay them, she supposed. The out-of-date returns in due course as the picturesque . . . Look how people wanted old-fashioned roses now, and scorned hybrid teas! . . . None of this place seemed real at all . . . well, why should it? . . . It was fifty—no, nearer sixty years since she had stayed here. And it didn't seem real to her because she was now acclimatized in this present year of Our Lord—Really, the whole thing opened up a very interesting set of problems . . . The atmosphere and the *people* . . . Miss Marple's fingers pushed her knitting farther away from her.

'Pockets,' she said aloud . . . 'Pockets, I suppose . . . And quite difficult to find . . .'

Would that account for that curious feeling of uneasiness she had had last night? That feeling that something was wrong . . .

All those elderly people—really very much like those she remembered when she had stayed here fifty years ago. They had been natural then—but they weren't very natural now. Elderly people nowadays weren't like elderly people then—they had that worried harried look of domestic anxieties with which they are too tired to cope, or they rushed around to committees and tried to appear bustling and competent, or they dyed their hair gentian blue, or wore wigs, and their hands were not the hands she remembered, tapering, delicate hands—they were harsh from washing up and detergents . . .

And so—well, so these people didn't look real. But the point was that they *were* real. Selina Hazy was real. And that rather handsome old military man in the corner was real—she had met him once, although she did not recall his name—and the Bishop (dear Robbie!) was dead.

Miss Marple glanced at her little clock. It was eight-thirty. Time for her breakfast.

She examined the instructions given by the hotel—Splendid big print so that it wasn't necessary to put one's spectacles on.

Meals could be ordered through the telephone by asking for Room Service, or you could press the bell labelled Chambermaid.

Miss Marple did the latter. Talking to Room Service always flustered her.

The result was excellent. In no time at all there was a tap on the door and a highly satisfactory chambermaid appeared. A real chambermaid looking unreal, wearing a striped lavender print dress and actually a *cap*, a freshly laundered cap. A smiling, rosy, positively *countrified* face. (Where did they *find* these people?)

Miss Marple ordered her breakfast. Tea, poached eggs, fresh rolls. So adept was the chambermaid that she did not even mention cereals or orange juice.

Five minutes later breakfast came. A comfortable tray with a big pot-bellied teapot, creamy-looking milk, a silver hot water jug. Two beautifully poached eggs on toast, poached the proper way, not little round hard bullets shaped in tin cups, a good-sized round of butter stamped with a thistle. Marmalade, honey and strawberry jam. Delicious-looking rolls, not the hard kind with papery interiors—they *smelt* of fresh bread (the most delicious smell in the world!). There were also an apple, a pear and a banana.

Miss Marple inserted a knife gingerly but with confidence. She was not disappointed. Rich deep yellow yolk oozed out, thick and creamy. *Proper* eggs!

Everything piping hot. A *real* breakfast. She could have cooked it herself but she hadn't had to! It was brought to her as if—no, not as though she were a queen—as though she were a middle-aged lady staying in a good but not unduly expensive hotel. In fact—back to 1909. Miss Marple expressed appreciation to the chambermaid who replied smiling,

'Oh, yes, Madam, the Chef is very particular about his breakfasts.'

Miss Marple studied her appraisingly. Bertram's Hotel could certainly produce marvels. A *real* housemaid. She pinched her left arm surreptitiously.

'Have you been here long?' she asked.

'Just over three years, Madam.'

'And before that?'

'I was in a hotel at Eastbourne. Very modern and up-to-date—but I prefer an old-fashioned place like this.'

Miss Marple took a sip of tea. She found herself humming in a vague way—words fitting themselves to a long forgotten song.

'Oh where have you been all my life . . .'

The chambermaid was looking slightly startled.

'I was just remembering an old song,' twittered Miss

Marple apologetically. 'Very popular at one time.'

Again she sang softly. 'Oh where have you been all my life . . .'

'Perhaps you know it?' she asked.

'Well—' The chambermaid looked rather apologetic.

'Too long ago for you,' said Miss Marple. 'Ah well, one gets to remembering things—in a place like this.'

'Yes, Madam, a lot of the ladies who stay here feel like that, I think.'

'It's partly why they come, I expect,' said Miss Marple.

The chambermaid went out. She was obviously used to old ladies who twittered and reminisced.

Miss Marple finished her breakfast, and got up in a pleasant leisurely fashion. She had a plan ready made for a delightful morning of shopping. Not too much—to overtire herself. Oxford Street today, perhaps. And tomorrow Knightsbridge. She planned ahead happily.

It was about ten o'clock when she emerged from her room fully equipped: hat, gloves, umbrella—just in case, though it looked fine—handbag—her smartest shopping bag—

The door next but one on the corridor opened sharply and someone looked out. It was Bess Sedgwick. She withdrew back into the room and closed the door sharply.

Miss Marple wondered as she went down the stairs. She preferred the stairs to the lift first thing in the morning. It limbered her up. Her steps grew slower and slower . . . she stopped.

II

As Colonel Luscombe strode along the passage from his

room, a door at the top of the stairs opened sharply and Lady Sedgwick spoke to him.

'There you are at last! I've been on the look-out for you —waiting to pounce. Where can we go and talk? That is to say without falling over some old pussy every second.'

'Well, really, Bess, I'm not quite sure—I think on the mezzanine floor there's a sort of writing-room.'

'You'd better come in here. Quick now, before the chambermaid gets peculiar ideas about us.'

Rather unwillingly, Colonel Luscombe stepped across the threshold and had the door shut firmly behind him.

'I'd no idea you would be staying here, Bess, I hadn't the faintest idea of it.'

'I don't suppose you had.'

'I mean—I would never have brought Elvira here. I *have* got Elvira here, you know?'

'Yes, I saw her with you last night.'

'But I really didn't know that you were here. It seemed such an unlikely place for you.'

'I don't see why,' said Bess Sedgwick, coldly. 'It's far and away the most comfortable hotel in London. Why shouldn't I stay here?'

'You must understand that I hadn't any idea of . . . I mean—'

She looked at him and laughed. She was dressed ready to go out in a well cut dark suit and a shirt of bright emerald green. She looked gay and very much alive. Beside her, Colonel Luscombe looked rather old and faded.

'Darling Derek, don't look so worried. I'm not accusing you of trying to stage a mother and daughter sentimental meeting. It's just one of those things that happen; where people meet each other in unsuspected places. But you *must* get Elvira out of here, Derek. You must get her out of it at once—today.'

'Oh, she's going. I mean, I only brought her here just for a couple of nights. Do a show—that sort of thing. She's going down to the Melfords tomorrow.'

'Poor girl, that'll be boring for her.'

Luscombe looked at her with concern. 'Do you think she will be very bored?'

Bess took pity on him.

'Probably not after duress in Italy. She might even think it wildly thrilling.'

Luscombe took his courage in both hands.

'Look here, Bess, I was startled to find you here, but don't you think it—well, you know, it might be *meant* in a way. I mean that it might be an opportunity—I don't think you really know how—well, how the girl might feel.'

'What are you trying to say, Derek?'

'Well, you *are* her mother, you know.'

'Of course I'm her mother. She's my daughter. And what good has that fact ever been to either of us, or ever will be?'

'You can't be sure. I think—I think she feels it.'

'What gives you that idea?' said Bess Sedgwick sharply.

'Something she said yesterday. She asked where you were, what you were doing.'

Bess Sedgwick walked across the room to the window. She stood there a moment tapping on the pane.

'You're so nice, Derek,' she said. 'You have such nice ideas. But they don't work, my poor angel. That's what you've got to say to yourself. They don't work and they might be dangerous.'

'Oh come now, Bess. Dangerous?'

'Yes, yes, yes. Dangerous. *I'm* dangerous. I've always

been dangerous.'

'When I think of some of the things you've done,' said Colonel Luscombe.

'That's my own business,' said Bess Sedgwick. 'Running into danger has become a kind of habit with me. No, I wouldn't say habit. More an addiction. Like a drug. Like that nice little dollop of heroin addicts have to have every so often to make life seem bright coloured and worth living. Well, that's all right. That's my funeral—or not—as the case may be. I've never taken drugs—never needed them—Danger has been my drug. But people who live as I do can be a source of harm to others. Now don't be an obstinate old fool, Derek. You keep that girl well away from me. I can do her no good. Only harm. If possible, don't even let her know I was staying in the same hotel. Ring up the Melfords and take her down there *today*. Make some excuse about a sudden emergency—'

Colonel Luscombe hesitated, pulling his moustache.

'I think you're making a mistake, Bess.' He sighed. 'She asked where you were. I told her you were abroad.'

'Well, I shall be in another twelve hours, so that all fits very nicely.'

She came up to him, kissed him on the point of his chin, turned him smartly around as though they were about to play Blind Man's Buff, opened the door, gave him a gentle little propelling shove out of it. As the door shut behind him, Colonel Luscombe noticed an old lady turning the corner from the stairs. She was muttering to herself as she looked into her handbag. 'Dear, dear me. I suppose I must have left it in my room. Oh dear.'

She passed Colonel Luscombe without paying much attention to him apparently, but as he went on down the stairs Miss Marple paused by her room door and directed a piercing glance after him. Then she looked towards Bess Sedgwick's door. 'So that's who she was waiting for,' said Miss Marple to herself. 'I wonder why.'

III

Canon Pennyfather, fortified by breakfast, wandered across the lounge, remembered to leave his key at the desk, pushed his way through the swinging doors, and was neatly inserted into a taxi by the Irish commissionaire who existed for this purpose.

'Where to, sir?'

'Oh dear,' said Canon Pennyfather in sudden dismay. 'Now let me see—where *was* I going?'

The traffic in Pond Street was held up for some minutes whilst Canon Pennyfather and the commissionaire debated this knotty point.

Finally Canon Pennyfather had a brainwave and the taxi was directed to go to the British Museum.

The commissionaire was left on the pavement with a broad grin on his face, and since no other exits seemed to be taking place, he strolled a little way along the façade of the hotel whistling an old tune in a muted manner.

One of the windows on the ground floor of Bertram's was flung up—but the commissionaire did not even turn his head until a voice spoke unexpectedly through the open window.

'So this is where you've landed up, Micky. What on earth brought you to this place?'

He swung round, startled—and stared.

Lady Sedgwick thrust her head through the open window. 'Don't you know me?' she demanded.

A sudden gleam of recognition came across the man's face.

'Why, if it isn't little Bessie now! Fancy that! After all these years. Little Bessie.'

'Nobody but you ever called me Bessie. It's a revolting name. What have you been doing all these years?'

'This and that,' said Micky with some reserve. 'I've not been in the news like you have. I've read of your doings in the paper time and again.'

Bess Sedgwick laughed. 'Anyway, I've worn better than you have,' she said. 'You drink too much. You always did.'

'You've worn well because you've always been in the money.'

'Money wouldn't have done you any good. You'd have drunk even more and gone to the dogs completely. Oh yes, you would! What brought you *here*? That's what I want to know. How did you ever get taken on at this place?'

'I wanted a job. I had these—' his hand flicked over the row of medals.

'Yes, I see.' She was thoughtful. 'All genuine too, aren't they?'

'Sure they're genuine. Why shouldn't they be?'

'Oh I believe you. You always had courage. You've always been a good fighter. Yes, the army suited you. I'm sure of that.'

'The army's all right in time of war, but it's no good in peace time.'

'So you took to this stuff. I hadn't the least idea—' she stopped.

'You hadn't the least idea what, Bessie?'

'Nothing. It's queer seeing you again after all these years.'

'*I* haven't forgotten,' said the man. 'I've never forgotten you, little Bessie. Ah! a lovely girl you were! A lovely slip of a girl.'

'A damn' fool of a girl, that's what I was,' said Lady Sedgwick.

'That's true now. You hadn't much sense. If you had, you wouldn't have taken up with me. What hands you had for a horse. Do you remember that mare—what was her name now?—Molly O'Flynn. Ah, she was a wicked devil that one was.'

'You were the only one that could ride her,' said Lady Sedgwick.

'She'd have had me off if she could! When she found she couldn't, she gave in. Ah, she was a beauty, now. But talking of sitting a horse, there wasn't one lady in those parts better than you. A lovely seat you had, lovely hands. Never any fear in you, not for a minute! And it's been the same ever since, so I judge. Aeroplanes, racing cars.'

Bess Sedgwick laughed.

'I must get on with my letters.'

She drew back from the window.

Micky leaned over the railing. 'I've not forgotten Ballygowlan,' he said with meaning. 'Sometimes I've thought of writing to you—'

Bess Sedgwick's voice came out harshly.

'And what do you mean by that, Mick Gorman?'

'I was just saying as I haven't forgotten—anything. I was just—reminding you like.'

Bess Sedgwick's voice still held its harsh note.

'If you mean what I think you mean, I'll give you a piece

of advice. Any trouble from you, and I'd shoot you as easily as I'd shoot a rat. I've shot men before—'

'In foreign parts, maybe—'

'Foreign parts or here—it's all the same to me.'

'Ah, good lord, now, and I believe you would do just that!' His voice held admiration. 'In Ballygowlan—'

'In Ballygowlan,' she cut in, 'they paid you to keep your mouth shut and paid you well. You took the money. You'll get no more from me so don't think it.'

'It would be a nice romantic story for the Sunday papers . . .'

'You heard what I said.'

'Ah,' he laughed, 'I'm not serious. I was just joking. I'd never do anything to hurt my little Bessie. I'll keep my mouth shut.'

'Mind you do,' said Lady Sedgwick.

She shut down the window. Staring down at the desk in front of her she looked at her unfinished letter on the blotting paper. She picked it up, looked at it, crumpled it into a ball and slung it into the waste-paper basket. Then abruptly she got up from her seat and walked out of the room. She did not even cast a glance around her before she went.

The smaller writing-rooms at Bertram's often had an appearance of being empty even when they were not. Two well-appointed desks stood in the windows, there was a table on the right that held a few magazines, on the left were two very high-backed arm-chairs turned towards the fire. These were favourite spots in the afternoon for elderly military or naval gentlemen to ensconce themselves and fall happily asleep until tea-time. Anyone coming in to write a letter did not usually even notice them. The chairs were not so much in demand during the morning.

As it happened, however, they were on this particular morning both occupied. An old lady was in one and a young girl in the other. The young girl rose to her feet. She stood a moment looking uncertainly towards the door through which Lady Sedgwick had passed out, then she moved slowly towards it. Elvira Blake's face was deadly pale.

It was another five minutes before the old lady moved. Then Miss Marple decided that the little rest which she always took after dressing and coming downstairs had lasted quite long enough. It was time to go out and enjoy the pleasures of London. She might walk as far as Piccadilly, and take a No. 9 bus to High Street, Kensington, or she might walk along to Bond Street and take a 25 bus to Marshall & Snelgrove's or she might take a 25 the other way which as far as she remembered would land her up at the Army & Navy Stores. Passing through the swing doors she was still savouring these delights in her mind. The Irish commissionaire, back on duty, made up her mind for her.

'You'll be wanting a taxi, Ma'am,' he said with firmness.

'I don't think I do,' said Miss Marple. 'I think there's a 25 bus I could take quite near here—or a 2 from Park Lane.'

'You'll not be wanting a bus,' said the commissionaire firmly. 'It's very dangerous springing on a bus when you're getting on in life. The way they start and stop and go on again. Jerk you off your feet, they do. No heart at all, these fellows, nowadays. I'll whistle you along a taxi and you'll go to wherever you want to like a queen.'

Miss Marple considered and fell.

'Very well then,' she said, 'perhaps I *had* better have a taxi.'

The commissionaire had no need even to whistle. He merely clicked his thumb and a taxi appeared like magic. Miss Marple was helped into it with every possible care and decided on the spur of the moment to go to Robinson & Cleaver's and look at their splendid offer of real linen sheets. She sat happily in her taxi feeling indeed as the commissionaire had promised her, just like a queen. Her mind was filled with pleasurable anticipation of linen sheets, linen pillow cases and proper glass- and kitchen-cloths without pictures of bananas, figs or performing dogs and other pictorial distractions to annoy you when you were washing up.

Lady Sedgwick came up to the Reception desk.

'Mr Humfries in his office?'

'Yes, Lady Sedgwick.' Miss Gorringe looked startled.

Lady Sedgwick passed behind the desk, tapped on the door and went in without waiting for any response.

Mr Humfries looked up startled.

'What—?'

'Who engaged that man Michael Gorman?'

Mr Humfries spluttered a little.

'Parfitt left—he had a car accident a month ago. We had to replace him quickly. This man seemed all right. References OK—ex-army—quite good record—Not very bright perhaps—but that's all the better sometimes—you don't know anything against him, do you?'

'Enough not to want him here.'

'If you insist,' Humfries said slowly, 'we'll give him his notice—'

'No,' said Lady Sedgwick slowly. 'No—it's too late for that— Never mind.'

CHAPTER VI

'ELVIRA.'

'Hallo, Bridget.'

The Hon. Elvira Blake pushed her way through the front door of 180 Onslow Square, which her friend Bridget had rushed down to open for her, having been watching through the window.

'Let's go upstairs,' said Elvira.

'Yes, we'd better. Otherwise we'll get entangled by Mummy.'

The two girls rushed up the stairs, thereby circumventing Bridget's mother, who came out on to the landing from her own bedroom just too late.

'You really are lucky not to have a mother,' said Bridget, rather breathlessly, as she took her friend into her bedroom and shut the door firmly. 'I mean, Mummy's quite a pet and all that, but the *questions* she asks! Morning, noon and night. Where are you going, and who have you met? And are they cousins of somebody else of the same name in Yorkshire? I mean, the *futility* of it all.'

'I suppose they have nothing else to think about,' said Elvira vaguely. 'Look here, Bridget, there's something terribly important I've got to do, and you've got to help me.'

'Well, I will if I can. What is it—a man?'

'No, it isn't, as a matter of fact.' Bridget looked disappointed. 'I've got to get away to Ireland for twenty-four hours or perhaps longer, and you've got to cover up for me.'

'To Ireland? Why?'

'I can't tell you all about it now. There's no time. I've got to meet my guardian, Colonel Luscombe, at Prunier's for lunch at half-past one.'

'What have you done with the Carpenter?'

'Gave her the slip in Debenham's.'

Bridget giggled.

'And after lunch they're taking me down to the Melfords. I'm going to live with them until I'm twenty-one.'

'How ghastly!'

'I expect I shall manage. Cousin Mildred is fearfully easy to deceive. It's arranged I'm to come up for classes and things. There's a place called World of Today. They take you to lectures and to Museums and to Picture Galleries and the House of Lords, and all that. The whole point is that nobody will know whether you're where you ought to be or not! We'll manage lots of things.'

'I expect we will.' Bridget giggled. 'We managed in Italy, didn't we? Old Macaroni thought she was so strict. Little did she know what we got up to when we tried.'

Both girls laughed in the pleasant consciousness of successful wickedness.

'Still, it did need a lot of planning,' said Elvira.

'And some splendid lying,' said Bridget. 'Have you heard from Guido?'

'Oh yes, he wrote me a long letter signed Ginevra as though he was a girl-friend. But I do wish you'd stop talking so much, Bridget. We've got a lot to do and only about an hour and a half to do it in. Now first of all just *listen*. I'm coming up tomorrow for an appointment with the dentist. That's easy, I can put it off by telephone—or you can from here. Then, about midday, you can ring up the Melfords pretending to be your mother and explain that the dentist wants to see me again the next day and so I'm staying over with you here.'

'That ought to go down all right. They'll say how very kind and gush. But supposing you're *not* back the next day?'

'Then you'll have to do some more ringing up.'

Bridget looked doubtful.

'We'll have lots of time to think up something before then,' said Elvira impatiently. 'What's worrying me now is *money*. You haven't got any, I suppose?' Elvira spoke without much hope.

'Only about two pounds.'

'That's no good. I've got to buy my air ticket. I've looked up the flights. It only takes about two hours. A lot depends upon how long it takes me when I get there.'

'Can't you tell me what you're going to do?'

'No, I can't. But it's terribly, terribly important.'

Elvira's voice was so different that Bridget looked at her in some surprise.

'Is anything really the matter, Elvira?'

'Yes, it is.'

'Is it something nobody's got to know about?'

'Yes, that's the sort of thing. It's frightfully, frightfully secret. I've got to find out if something is really true or not. It's a bore about the money. What's maddening is that I'm really quite rich. My guardian told me so. But all they give me is a measly dress allowance. And that seems to go as soon as I get it.'

'Wouldn't your guardian—Colonel Thingummybob lend you some money?'

'That wouldn't do at all. He'd ask a lot of questions and want to know what I wanted it for.'

'Oh dear, I suppose he would. I can't think why everybody wants to ask so many questions. Do you know that if somebody rings me up, Mummy has to ask *who it is*? When it really is *no* business of hers!'

Elvira agreed, but her mind was on another tack.

'Have you ever pawned anything, Bridget?'

'Never. I don't think I'd know how to.'

'It's quite easy, I believe,' said Elvira. 'You go to the sort of jeweller who has three balls over the door, isn't that right?'

'I don't think I've got anything that would be any good taking to a pawnbroker,' said Bridget.

'Hasn't your mother got some jewellery somewhere?'

'I don't think we'd better ask her to help.'

'No, perhaps not— But we could pinch something perhaps.'

'Oh, I don't think we could do that,' said Bridget, shocked.

'No? Well, perhaps you're right. But I bet she wouldn't notice. We could get it back before she missed it. *I* know. We'll go to Mr Bollard.'

'Who's Mr Bollard?'

'Oh, he's a sort of family jeweller. I take my watch there always to have it mended. He's known me ever since I was six. Come on, Bridget, we'll go there right away. We'll just have time.'

'We'd better go out the back way,' said Bridget, 'and then Mummy won't ask us where we're going.'

Outside the old established business of Bollard and Whitley in Bond Street the two girls made their final arrangements.

'Are you sure you understand, Bridget?'

'I think so,' said Bridget in a far from happy voice.

'First,' said Elvira, 'we synchronize our watches.'

Bridget brightened up a little. This familiar literary phrase had a heartening effect. They solemnly synchronized their watches, Bridget adjusting hers by one minute.

'Zero hour will be twenty-five past exactly,' said Elvira. 'That will give me plenty of time. Perhaps even more than I need, but it's better that way about.'

'But supposing—?' began Bridget.

'Supposing what?' asked Elvira.

'Well, I mean, supposing I *really* got run over?'

'Of course you won't get run over,' said Elvira. 'You know how nippy you are on your feet, and all London traffic is used to pulling up suddenly. It'll be all right.'

Bridget looked far from convinced.

'You won't let me down, Bridget, will you?'

'All right,' said Bridget, 'I won't let you down.'

'Good,' said Elvira.

Bridget crossed to the other side of Bond Street and Elvira pushed open the doors of Messrs Bollard and Whitley, old established jewellers and watchmakers. Inside there was a beautiful and hushed atmosphere. A frock-coated nobleman came forward and asked Elvira what he could do for her.

'Could I see Mr Bollard?'

'Mr Bollard. What name shall I say?'

'Miss Elvira Blake.'

The nobleman disappeared and Elvira drifted to a counter

where, below plate glass, brooches, rings and bracelets showed off their jewelled proportions against suitable shades of velvet. In a very few moments Mr Bollard made his appearance. He was the senior partner of the firm, an elderly man of sixty odd. He greeted Elvira with warm friendliness.

'Ah, Miss Blake, so you are in London. It's a great pleasure to see you. Now what can I do for you?'

Elvira produced a dainty little evening wrist-watch.

'This watch doesn't go properly,' said Elvira. 'Could you do something to it?'

'Oh yes, of course. There's no difficulty about *that.*' Mr Bollard took it from her. 'What address shall I send it to?'

Elvira gave the address.

'And there's another thing,' she said. 'My guardian—Colonel Luscombe you know—'

'Yes, yes of course.'

'He asked me what I'd like for a Christmas present,' said Elvira. 'He suggested I should come in here and look at some different things. He said would I like him to come with me, and I said I'd rather come along first—because I always think it's rather embarrassing, don't you? I mean, prices and all that.'

'Well, that's certainly one aspect,' said Mr Bollard, beaming in an avuncular manner. 'Now what had you in mind, Miss Blake? A brooch, bracelet—a ring?'

'I think really brooches are more useful,' said Elvira. 'But I wonder—could I look at a *lot* of things?' She looked up at him appealingly. He smiled sympathetically.

'Of course, of course. No pleasure at all if one has to make up one's mind too quickly, is it?'

The next five or six minutes were spent very agreeably.

Nothing was too much trouble for Mr Bollard. He fetched things from one case and another, brooches and bracelets piled up on the piece of velvet spread in front of Elvira. Occasionally she turned aside to look at herself in a mirror, trying the effect of a brooch or a pendant. Finally, rather uncertainly, a pretty little bangle, a small diamond wrist-watch and two brooches were laid aside.

'We'll make a note of these,' said Mr Bollard, 'and then when Colonel Luscombe is in London next, perhaps he'll come in and see what he decides himself he'd like to give you.'

'I think that way will be very nice,' said Elvira. 'Then he'll feel more that he's chosen my present himself, won't he?' Her limpid blue gaze was raised to the jeweller's face. That same blue gaze had registered a moment earlier that the time was now exactly twenty five minutes past the hour.

Outside there was the squealing of brakes and a girl's loud scream. Inevitably the eyes of everyone in the shop turned towards the windows of the shop giving on Bond Street. The movement of Elvira's hand on the counter in front of her and then to the pocket of her neat tailor-made coat and skirt was so rapid and unobtrusive as to be almost unnoticeable, even if anybody had been looking.

'Tcha, tcha,' said Mr Bollard, turning back from where he had been peering out into the street. 'Very nearly an accident. Silly girl! Rushing across the road like that.'

Elvira was already moving towards the door. She looked at her wrist-watch and uttered an exclamation.

'Oh dear, I've been far too long in here. I shall miss my train back to the country. Thank you *so* much, Mr Bollard, and you won't forget which the four things are, will you?'

In another minute she was out of the door. Turning

rapidly to the left and then to the left again, she stopped in the arcade of a shoe shop until Bridget, rather breathless, rejoined her.

'Oh,' said Bridget, 'I was terrified. I thought I was going to be killed. And I've torn a hole in my stocking, too.'

'Never mind,' said Elvira and walked her friend rapidly along the street and round yet another corner to the right. 'Come on.'

'Is it—was it—all right?'

Elvira's hand slipped into her pocket and out again, showing the diamond and sapphire bracelet in her palm.

'Oh, Elvira, how you dared!'

'Now, Bridget, you've got to get along to that pawnshop we marked down. Go in and see how much you can get for this. Ask for a hundred.'

'Do you think—supposing they say—I mean—I mean, it might be on a list of stolen things—'

'Don't be silly. How could it be on a list so soon? They haven't even noticed it's gone yet.'

'But Elvira, when they *do* notice it's gone, they'll think—perhaps they'll know—that you must have taken it.'

'They *might* think so—if they discover it soon.'

'Well, then they'll go to the police and—'

She stopped as Elvira shook her head slowly, her pale yellow hair swinging to and fro and a faint enigmatic smile curving up the corners of her mouth.

'They won't go to the police, Bridget. Certainly not if they think *I* took it.'

'Why—you mean—?'

'As I told you, I'm going to have a lot of money when I'm twenty-one. I shall be able to buy lots of jewels from them. *They* won't make a scandal. Go on and get the money quick. Then go to Aer Lingus and book the ticket—I must take a taxi to Prunier's. I'm already ten minutes late. I'll be with you tomorrow morning by half-past ten.'

'Oh Elvira, I wish you wouldn't take such frightful risks,' moaned Bridget.

But Elvira had hailed a taxi.

II

Miss Marple had a very enjoyable time at Robinson & Cleaver's. Besides purchasing expensive but delicious sheets—she loved linen sheets with their texture and their coolness—she also indulged in a purchase of good quality red-bordered glass-cloths. Really the difficulty in getting proper glass-cloths nowadays! Instead, you were offered things that might as well have been ornamental table-cloths, decorated with radishes or lobsters or the *Tour Eiffel* or Trafalgar Square, or else littered with lemons and oranges. Having given her address in St Mary Mead, Miss Marple found a convenient bus which took her to the Army & Navy Stores.

The Army & Navy Stores had been a haunt of Miss Marple's aunt in days long gone. It was not, of course, quite the same nowadays. Miss Marple cast her thoughts back to Aunt Helen seeking out her own special man in the grocery department, settling herself comfortably in a chair, wearing a bonnet and what she always called her 'black poplin' mantle. Then there would ensue a long hour with nobody in a hurry and Aunt Helen thinking of every conceivable grocery that could be purchased and stored up for future use. Christmas was provided for, and there was even a far-off look towards Easter. The young Jane had fidgeted somewhat, and had been told to go and look at the glass department by way of amusement.

Having finished her purchases, Aunt Helen would then proceed to lengthy inquiries about her chosen shop-assistant's mother, wife, second boy and crippled sister-in-law. Having had a thoroughly pleasant morning, Aunt Helen would say in the playful manner of those times, 'And how would a little girl feel about some luncheon?' Whereupon they went up in the lift to the fourth floor and had luncheon which always finished with a strawberry ice. After that, they bought half a pound of coffee chocolate creams and went to a matinée in a four wheeler.

Of course, the Army & Navy Stores had had a good many face lifts since those days. In fact, it was now quite unrecognizable from the old times. It was gayer and much brighter. Miss Marple, though throwing a kindly and indulgent smile at the past, did not object to the amenities of the present. There was still a restaurant, and there she repaired to order her lunch.

As she was looking carefully down the menu and deciding what to have, she looked across the room and her eyebrows went up a little. How extraordinary coincidence was! Here was a woman she had never seen till the day before, though she had seen plenty of newspaper photographs of her—at race meetings, in Bermuda, or standing by her own plane or car. Yesterday, for the first time, she had seen her in the flesh. And now, as was so often the case, there was the coincidence of running into her again in a most unlikely place. For somehow she did not connect lunch at the Army

& Navy Stores with Bess Sedgwick. She would not have been surprised to see Bess Sedgwick emerging from a den in Soho, or stepping out of Covent Garden Opera House in evening dress with a diamond tiara on her head. But somehow, not in the Army & Navy Stores which in Miss Marple's mind was, and always would be, connected with the armed forces, their wives, daughters, aunts and grandmothers. Still, there Bess Sedgwick was, looking as usual very smart, in her dark suit and her emerald shirt, lunching at a table with a man. A young man with a lean hawklike face, wearing a black leather jacket. They were leaning forward talking earnestly together, forking in mouthfuls of food as though they were quite unaware what they were eating.

An assignation, perhaps? Yes, probably an assignation. The man must be fifteen or twenty years younger than she was—but Bess Sedgwick was a magnetically attractive woman.

Miss Marple looked at the young man consideringly and decided that he was what she called a 'handsome fellow'. She also decided that she didn't like him very much. 'Just like Harry Russell,' said Miss Marple to herself, dredging up a prototype as usual from the past. 'Never up to any good. Never did any woman who had anything to do with him any good either.'

'She wouldn't take advice from me,' thought Miss Marple, 'but I could give her some.' However, other people's love affairs were no concern of hers, and Bess Sedgwick, by all accounts, could take care of herself very well when it came to love affairs.

Miss Marple sighed, ate her lunch, and meditated a visit to the stationery department.

Curiosity, or what she preferred herself to call 'taking an interest' in other people's affairs, was undoubtedly one of Miss Marple's characteristics.

Deliberately leaving her gloves on the table, she rose and crossed the floor to the cash desk, taking a route that passed close to Lady Sedgwick's table. Having paid her bill she 'discovered' the absence of her gloves and returned to get them—unfortunately dropping her handbag on the return route. It came open and spilled various oddments. A waitress rushed to assist her in picking them up, and Miss Marple was forced to show a great shakiness and dropped coppers and keys a second time.

She did not get very much by these subterfuges but they were not entirely in vain—and it was interesting that neither of the two objects of her curiosity spared as much as a glance for the dithery old lady who kept dropping things.

As Miss Marple waited for the lift down she memorized such scraps as she had heard.

'*What about the weather forecast?*'

'*OK. No fog.*'

'*All set for Lucerne?*'

'*Yes. Plane leaves* 9.40.'

That was all she had got the first time. On the way back it had lasted a little longer.

Bess Sedgwick had been speaking angrily.

'*What possessed you to come to Bertram's yesterday—you shouldn't have come near the place.*'

'*It's all right. I asked if you were staying there and everyone knows we're close friends—*'

'*That's not the point. Bertram's is all right for me— Not for you. You stick out like a sore thumb. Everyone stares at you.*'

'Let them!'

'You really are an idiot. Why—why? What reasons did you have? You had *a reason—I know you . . .'*

'Calm down, Bess.'

'You're such a liar!'

That was all she had been able to hear. She found it interesting.

CHAPTER VII

On the evening of 19th November Canon Pennyfather had finished an early dinner at the Athenæum, he had nodded to one or two friends, had had a pleasant acrimonious discussion on some crucial points of the dating of the Dead Sea scrolls and now, glancing at his watch, saw that it was time to leave to catch his plane to Lucerne. As he passed through the hall he was greeted by one more friend: Dr Whittaker, of the SOAS, who said cheerfully:

'How are you, Pennyfather? Haven't seen you for a long time. How did you get on at the Congress? Any points of interest come up?'

'I am sure there will be.'

'Just come back from it, haven't you?'

'No, no, I am on my way there. I'm catching a plane this evening.'

'Oh I see.' Whittaker looked slightly puzzled. 'Somehow or other I thought the Congress was today.'

'No, no. Tomorrow, the 19th.'

Canon Pennyfather passed out through the door while his friend, looking after him, was just saying,

'But my dear chap, *today* is the 19th, isn't it?'

Canon Pennyfather, however, had gone beyond earshot. He picked up a taxi in Pall Mall, and was driven to the air terminal in Kensington. There was quite a fair crowd this evening. Presenting himself at the desk it at last came to his turn. He managed to produce ticket and passport and other necessities for the journey. The girl behind the desk, about to stamp these credentials, paused abruptly.

'I beg your pardon, sir, this seems to be the wrong ticket.'

'The wrong ticket? No, no, that is quite right. Flight one hundred and—well, I can't really read without my glasses—one hundred and something to Lucerne.'

'It's the date, sir. This is dated Wednesday the 18th.'

'No, no, surely. At least—I mean—today is Wednesday the 18th.'

'I'm sorry, sir. Today is the 19th.'

'The 19th!' The Canon was dismayed. He fished out a small diary, turning the pages eagerly. In the end he had to be convinced. Today *was* the 19th. The plane he had meant to catch had gone yesterday.

'Then that means—that means—dear me, it means the Congress at Lucerne has taken place *today.*'

He stared in deep dismay across the counter; but there were many others travelling; the Canon and his perplexities were elbowed aside. He stood sadly, holding the useless ticket in his hand. His mind ranged over various possibilities. Perhaps his ticket could be changed? But that would be no use—no indeed—what time was it now? Going on for 9 o'clock? The conference had actually taken place; starting at 10 o'clock this morning. Of course, that was what Whittaker had meant at the Athenæum. He thought Canon Pennyfather had already *been* to the Congress.

'Oh dear, oh dear,' said Canon Pennyfather, to himself. '*What* a muddle I have made of it all!' He wandered sadly and silently into the Cromwell Road, not at its best a very cheerful place.

He walked slowly along the street carrying his bag and revolving perplexities in his mind. When at last he had worked out to his satisfaction the various reasons for which he had made a mistake in the day, he shook his head sadly.

'Now, I suppose,' he said to himself, 'I suppose—let me see, it's after nine o'clock, yes, I suppose I had better have something to eat.'

It was curious, he thought, that he did not feel hungry.

Wandering disconsolately along the Cromwell Road he finally settled upon a small restaurant which served Indian curries. It seemed to him that though he was not quite as hungry as he ought to be, he had better keep his spirits up by having a meal, and after that he must find a hotel and —but no, there was no need to do *that*. He had a hotel! Of course. He was staying at Bertram's; and had reserved his room for four days. What a piece of luck! What a splendid piece of luck! So his room was there, waiting for him. He had only to ask for his key at the desk and—here another reminiscence assailed him. Something heavy in his pocket?

He dipped his hand in and brought out one of those large and solid keys with which hotels try and discourage their vaguer guests from taking them away in their pockets. It had not prevented the Canon from doing so!

'No. 19,' said the Canon, in happy recognition. 'That's right. It's very fortunate that I haven't got to go and find a room in a hotel. They say they're very crowded just now. Yes, Edmunds was saying so at the Athenæum this evening. He had a terrible job finding a room.'

Somewhat pleased with himself and the care he had taken over his travelling arrangements by booking a hotel beforehand, the Canon abandoned his curry, remembered to pay for it, and strode out once more into the Cromwell Road.

It seemed a little tame to go home just like this when he ought to have been dining in Lucerne and talking about all sorts of interesting and fascinating problems. His eye was caught by a cinema. *Walls of Jericho*. It seemed an eminently suitable title. It would be interesting to see if biblical accuracy had been preserved.

He bought himself a seat and stumbled into the darkness. He enjoyed the film, though it seemed to him to have no relationship to the biblical story whatsoever. Even Joshua seemed to have been left out. The walls of Jericho seemed to be a symbolical way of referring to a certain lady's marriage vows. When they had tumbled down several times, the beautiful star met the dour and uncouth hero whom she had secretly loved all along and between them they proposed to build up the walls in a way that would stand the test of time better. It was not a film destined particularly to appeal to an elderly clergyman; but Canon Pennyfather enjoyed it very much. It was not the sort of film he often saw and he felt it was enlarging his knowledge of life. The film ended, the lights went up, the National Anthem was played and Canon Pennyfather stumbled out into the lights of London, slightly consoled for the sad events of earlier in the evening.

It was a fine night and he walked home to Bertram's Hotel after first getting into a bus which took him in the opposite direction. It was midnight when he got in and Bertram's Hotel at midnight usually preserved a decorous appearance of everyone having gone to bed. The lift was on a higher floor so the Canon walked up the stairs. He came to his room, inserted the key in the lock, threw the door open and entered!

Good gracious, was he seeing things? But who—how—he saw the upraised arm too late . . .

Stars exploded in a kind of Guy Fawkes' display within his head . . .

CHAPTER VIII

THE IRISH MAIL rushed through the night. Or, more correctly through the darkness of the early morning hours.

At intervals the diesel engine gave its weird banshee warning cry. It was travelling at well over eighty miles an hour. It was on time.

Then, with some suddenness, the pace slackened as the brakes came on. The wheels screamed as they gripped the metals. Slower . . . slower . . . The guard put his head out of the window, noting the red signal ahead as the train came to a final halt. Some of the passengers woke up. Most did not.

One elderly lady, alarmed by the suddenness of the deceleration, opened the door and looked out along the corridor. A little way along one of the doors to the line was open. An elderly cleric with a thatch of thick white hair was climbing up from the permanent way. She presumed he had previously climbed down to the line to investigate.

The morning air was distinctly chilly. Someone at the end of the corridor said : 'Only a signal.' The elderly lady withdrew into her compartment and tried to go to sleep again.

Farther up the line, a man waving a lantern was running towards the train from a signal box. The fireman climbed down from the engine. The guard who had descended from the train came along to join him. The man with the lantern arrived, rather short of breath, and spoke in a series of gasps.

'Bad crash ahead . . . Goods train derailed . . .'

The engine driver looked out of his cab, then climbed down also to join the others.

At the rear of the train, six men who had just climbed up the embankment boarded the train through a door left open for them in the last coach. Six passengers from different coaches met them. With well rehearsed speed, they proceeded to take charge of the postal van, isolating it from the rest of the train. Two men in Balaclava helmets at front and rear of the compartment stood on guard, coshes in hand.

A man in railway uniform went forward along the corridor of the stationary train, uttering explanations to such as demanded them.

'Block on the line ahead. Ten minutes' delay, maybe, not much more . . .' It sounded friendly and reassuring.

By the engine, the driver and the fireman lay neatly gagged and trussed up. The man with the lantern called out:

'Everything OK here.'

The guard lay by the embankment, similarly gagged and tied.

The expert cracksmen in the postal van had done their work. Two more neatly trussed bodies lay on the floor. The special mailbags sailed out to where other men on the embankment awaited them.

In their compartments, passengers grumbled to each other that the railways were not what they used to be.

Then, as they settled themselves to sleep again, there

came through the darkness the roar of an exhaust.

'Goodness,' murmured a woman. 'Is that a jet plane?'

'Racing car, I should say.'

The roar died away.

On the Bedhampton Motorway, nine miles away, a steady stream of night lorries was grinding its way north. A big white racing car flashed past them.

Ten minutes later, it turned off the motorway.

The garage on the corner of the B road bore the sign CLOSED. But the big doors swung open and the white car was driven straight in, the doors closing again behind it. Three men worked at lightning speed. A fresh set of number plates were attached. The driver changed his coat and cap. He had worn white sheepskin before. Now he wore black leather. He drove out again. Three minutes after his departure, an old Morris Oxford, driven by a clergyman, chugged out on to the road and proceeded to take a route through various turning and twisting country lanes.

A station wagon, driven along a country road, slowed up as it came upon an old Morris Oxford stationary by the hedge, with an elderly man standing over it.

The driver of the station wagon put out a head.

'Having trouble? Can I help?'

'Very good of you. It's my lights.'

The two drivers approached each other—listened. 'All clear.'

Various expensive American-style cases were transferred from the Morris Oxford to the station wagon.

A mile or two farther on, the station wagon turned off on what looked like a rough track but which presently turned out to be the back way to a large and opulent mansion. In what had been a stableyard, a big white Mercedes car was standing. The driver of the station wagon opened its boot with a key, transferred the cases to the boot, and drove away again in the station wagon.

In a near-by farmyard a cock crowed noisily.

CHAPTER IX

ELVIRA BLAKE looked up at the sky, noted that it was a fine morning and went into a telephone box. She dialled Bridget's number in Onslow Square. Satisfied by the response, she said,

'Hallo? Bridget?'

'Oh Elvira, is that you?' Bridget's voice sounded agitated.

'Yes. Has everything been all right?'

'Oh no. It's been *awful*. Your cousin, Mrs Melford, rang up Mummy yesterday afternoon.'

'What, about me?'

'Yes. I thought I'd done it so well when I rang her up at lunch-time. But it seems she got worried about your teeth. Thought there might be something really wrong with them. Abscesses or something. So she rang up the dentist herself and found, of course, that you'd never been there at all. So then she rang up Mummy and unfortunately Mummy was right there by the telephone. So I couldn't get there first. And naturally Mummy said *she* didn't know anything about it, and that you certainly weren't staying *here*. I didn't know *what* to do.'

'What *did* you do?'

'Pretended I knew nothing about it. I did say that I thought you'd said something about going to see some friends at Wimbledon.'

'Why Wimbledon?'

'It was the first place came into my head.'

Elvira sighed. 'Oh well, I suppose I'll have to cook up something. An old governess, perhaps, who lives at Wimbledon. All this fussing does make things so *complicated*. I hope Cousin Mildred doesn't make a real fool of herself and ring up the police or something like that?'

'Are you going down there now?'

'Not till this evening. I've got a lot to do first.'

'You got to Ireland. Was it—all right?'

'I found out what I wanted to know.'

'You sound—sort of grim.'

'I'm feeling grim.'

'Can't I help you, Elvira? Do anything?'

'Nobody can help me really . . . It's a thing I have to do myself. I hoped something wasn't true, but it *is* true. I don't know quite what to do about it.'

'Are you in danger, Elvira?'

'Don't be melodramatic, Bridget. I'll have to be careful that's all. I'll have to be very careful.'

'Then you *are* in danger.'

Elvira said after a moment's pause, 'I expect I'm just imagining things, that's all.'

'Elvira, what are you going to do about that bracelet?'

'Oh, that's all right. I've arranged to get some money from someone, so I can go and—what's the word?—redeem it. Then just take it back to Bollards.'

'D'you think they'll be all right about it?— No, Mummy, it's just the laundry. They say we never sent that sheet. Yes, Mummy, yes, I'll tell the manageress. All right then.'

At the other end of the line Elvira grinned and put down the receiver. She opened her purse, sorted through her money, counted out the coins she needed and arranged them in front of her and proceeded to put through a call. When she got the number she wanted she put in the necessary coins, pressed Button A and spoke in a small rather breathless voice.

'Hallo, Cousin Mildred. Yes, it's me . . . I'm terribly sorry . . . Yes, I know . . . well I was going to . . . yes it was dear old Maddy, you know our old Mademoiselle . . . yes I wrote a postcard, then I forgot to post it. It's still in my pocket now . . . well, you see she was ill and there was no one to look after her and so I just stopped to see she was all right. Yes, I *was* going to Bridget's but this changed things . . . I don't understand about the message you got. Someone must have jumbled it up . . . Yes, I'll explain it all to you when I get back . . . yes, this afternoon. No, I shall just wait and see the nurse who's coming to look after old Maddy—well, not really a nurse. You know one of those—er—practical aid nurses or something like that. No, she would hate to go to hospital . . . But I *am* sorry, Cousin Mildred, I really am very, very sorry.' She put down the receiver and sighed in an exasperated manner. 'If only,' she murmured to herself, 'one didn't have to tell so many lies to everybody.'

She came out of the telephone box, noting as she did so the big newspaper placards—BIG TRAIN ROBBERY. IRISH MAIL ATTACKED BY BANDITS.

II

Mr Bollard was serving a customer when the shop door opened. He looked up to see the Honourable Elvira Blake entering.

'No,' she said to an assistant who came forward to her. 'I'd rather wait until Mr Bollard is free.'

Presently Mr Bollard's customer's business was concluded and Elvira moved into the vacant place.

'Good morning, Mr Bollard,' she said.

'I'm afraid your watch isn't done quite as soon as this, Miss Elvira,' said Mr Bollard.

'Oh, it's not the watch,' said Elvira. 'I've come to apologize. A dreadful thing happened.' She opened her bag and took out a small box. From it she extracted the sapphire and diamond bracelet. 'You will remember when I came in with my watch to be repaired that I was looking at things for a Christmas present and there was an accident outside in the street. Somebody was run over I think, or nearly run over. I suppose I must have had the bracelet in my hand and put it into the pocket of my suit without thinking, although I only found it this morning. So I rushed along *at once* to bring it back. I'm so terribly sorry, Mr Bollard, I don't know how I came to do such an idiotic thing.'

'Why, that's quite all right, Miss Elvira,' said Mr Bollard, slowly.

'I suppose you thought someone had stolen it,' said Elvira. Her limpid blue eyes met his.

'We *had* discovered its loss,' said Mr Bollard. 'Thank you very much, Miss Elvira, for bringing it back so promptly.'

'I felt simply awful about it when I found it,' said Elvira. 'Well, thank you very much, Mr Bollard, for being so nice about it.'

'A lot of strange mistakes do occur,' said Mr Bollard. He smiled at her in an avuncular manner. 'We won't think of it any more. But don't do it again, though.' He laughed with the air of one making a genial little joke.

'Oh no,' said Elvira, 'I shall be terribly careful in future.'

She smiled at him, turned and left the shop.

'Now I wonder,' said Mr Bollard to himself, 'I really do wonder . . .'

One of his partners, who had been standing near, moved nearer to him.

'So she *did* take it?' he said.

'Yes. She took it all right,' said Mr Bollard.

'But she brought it back,' his partner pointed out.

'She brought it back,' agreed Mr Bollard. 'I didn't actually expect that.'

'You mean you didn't expect her to bring it back?'

'No, not if it was she who'd taken it.'

'Do you think her story is true?' his partner inquired curiously. 'I mean, that she slipped it into her pocket by accident?'

'I suppose it's possible,' said Bollard, thoughtfully.

'Or it *could* be kleptomania, I suppose.'

'Or it could be kleptomania,' agreed Bollard. 'It's more likely that she took it on purpose . . . But if so, why did she bring it back so soon? It's curious—'

'Just as well we didn't notify the police. I admit *I* wanted to.'

'I know, I know. You haven't got as much experience as I have. In this case, it was definitely better not.' He added softly to himself, 'The thing's interesting, though. Quite interesting. I wonder how old she is? Seventeen or eighteen I suppose. She might have got herself in a jam of some kind.'

'I thought you said she was rolling in money.'

'You may be an heiress and rolling in money,' said Bollard, 'but at seventeen you can't always get your hands on it. The funny thing is, you know, they keep heiresses much shorter of cash than they keep the more impecunious. It's not always a good idea. Well, I don't suppose we shall ever know the truth of it.'

He put the bracelet back in its place in the display case and shut down the lid.

CHAPTER X

THE OFFICES of Egerton, Forbes & Willborough were in Bloomsbury, in one of those imposing and dignified squares which have as yet not felt the wind of change. Their brass plate was suitably worn down to illegibility. The firm had been going for over a hundred years and a good proportion of the landed gentry of England were their clients. There was no Forbes in the firm any more and no Willborough. Instead there were Atkinsons, father and son, and a Welsh Lloyd and a Scottish MacAllister. There was, however, still an Egerton, descendant of the original Egerton. This particular Egerton was a man of fifty-two and he was adviser to several families which had in their day been advised by his grandfather, his uncle, and his father.

At this moment he was sitting behind a large mahogany desk in his handsome room on the first floor, speaking kindly but firmly to a dejected looking client. Richard Egerton was a handsome man, tall, dark with a touch of grey at the temples and very shrewd grey eyes. His advice was always good advice, but he seldom minced his words.

'Quite frankly you haven't got a leg to stand upon, Freddie,' he was saying. 'Not with those letters you've written.'

'You don't think—' Freddie murmured dejectedly.

'No, I don't,' said Egerton. 'The only hope is to settle out of court. It might even be held that you've rendered yourself liable to criminal prosecution.'

'Oh look here, Richard, that's carrying things a bit far.'

There was a small discreet buzz on Egerton's desk. He picked up the telephone receiver with a frown.

'I thought I said I wasn't to be disturbed.'

There was a murmur at the other end. Egerton said, 'Oh. Yes— Yes, I see. Ask her to wait, will you.'

He replaced the receiver and turned once more to his unhappy looking client.

'Look here, Freddie,' he said, 'I know the law and you don't. You're in a nasty jam. I'll do my best to get you out of it, but it's going to cost you a bit. I doubt if they'd settle for less than twelve thousand.'

'Twelve thousand!' The unfortunate Freddie was aghast. 'Oh, I say! I haven't got it, Richard.'

'Well, you'll have to raise it then. There are always ways and means. If she'll settle for twelve thousand, you'll be lucky, and if you fight the case it'll cost you a lot more.'

'You lawyers!' said Freddie. 'Sharks, all of you!'

He rose to his feet. 'Well,' he said, 'do your bloody best for me, Richard old boy.'

He took his departure, shaking his head sadly. Richard Egerton put Freddie and his affairs out of his mind, and thought about his next client. He said softly to himself, 'The Honourable Elvira Blake. I wonder what she's like . . .' He lifted the receiver. 'Lord Frederick's gone. Send up Miss Blake, will you.'

As he waited he made little calculations on his desk pad. How many years since—? She must be fifteen—seventeen —perhaps even more than that. Time went so fast. 'Coniston's daughter,' he thought, 'and Bess's daughter. I wonder which of them she takes after?'

The door opened, the clerk announced Miss Elvira Blake and the girl walked into the room. Egerton rose from his chair and came towards her. In appearance, he thought, she did not resemble either of her parents. Tall, slim, very fair, Bess's colouring but none of Bess's vitality, with an old-fashioned air about her; though that was difficult to be sure of, since the fashion in dress happened at the moment to be ruffles and baby bodices.

'Well, well,' he said, as he shook hands with her. 'This is a surprise. Last time I saw you, you were eleven years old. Come and sit here.' He pulled forward a chair and she sat down.

'I suppose,' said Elvira, a little uncertainly, 'that I ought to have written first. Written and made an appointment. Something like that, but I really made up my mind very suddenly and it seemed an opportunity, since I was in London.'

'And what are you doing in London?'

'Having my teeth seen to.'

'Beastly things, teeth,' said Egerton. 'Give us trouble from the cradle to the grave. But I am grateful for the teeth, if it gives me an opportunity of seeing you. Let me see now; you've been in Italy, haven't you, finishing your education there at one of these places all girls go to nowadays?'

'Yes,' said Elvira, 'the Contessa Martinelli. But I've left there now for good. I'm living with the Melfords in Kent until I make up my mind if there's anything I'd like to do.'

'Well, I hope you'll find something satisfactory. You're not thinking of a university or anything like that?'

'No,' said Elvira, 'I don't think I'd be clever enough for that.' She paused before saying, 'I suppose *you*'d have to agree to anything if I did want to do it?'

Egerton's keen eyes focused sharply.

'I am one of your guardians, and a trustee under your father's will, yes,' he said. 'Therefore, you have a perfect right to approach me at any time.'

Elvira said 'Thank you' politely. Egerton asked:

'Is there anything worrying you?'

'No. Not really. But you see, I don't *know* anything. Nobody's ever told me things. One doesn't always like to ask.'

He looked at her attentively.

'You mean things about yourself?'

'Yes,' said Elvira. 'It's kind of you to understand. Uncle Derek—' she hesitated.

'Derek Luscombe, you mean?'

'Yes. I've always called him uncle.'

'I see."

'He's very kind,' said Elvira, 'but he's not the sort of person who ever tells you anything. He just arranges things, and looks a little worried in case they mightn't be what I'd like. Of course he listens to a lot of people—women, I mean —who tell him things. Like Contessa Martinelli. He arranges for me to go to schools or to finishing places.'

'And they haven't been where you wanted to go?'

'No, I didn't mean that. They've been quite all right. I mean they've been more or less where everyone else goes.'

'I see.'

'But I don't know anything about *myself*. I mean what money I've got, and how much, and what I could do with it if I wanted.'

'In fact,' said Egerton, with his attractive smile, 'you want to talk business. Is that it? Well, I think you're quite right. Let's see. How old are you? Sixteen—seventeen?'

'I'm nearly twenty.'

'Oh dear. I'd no idea.'

'You see,' explained Elvira, 'I feel all the time that I'm being shielded and sheltered. It's nice in a way, but it can get very irritating.'

'It's an attitude that's gone out of date,' agreed Egerton, 'but I can quite see that it would appeal to Derek Luscombe.'

'He's a dear,' said Elvira, 'but very difficult, somehow, to talk to seriously.'

'Yes, I can see that that might be so. Well, how much *do* you know about yourself, Elvira? About your family circumstances?'

'I know that my father died when I was five and that my mother had run away from him with someone when I was about two, I don't remember her at all. I barely remember my father. He was very old and had his leg up on a chair. He used to swear. I was rather scared of him. After he died I lived first with an aunt or a cousin or something of my father's, until *she* died, and then I lived with Uncle Derek and his sister. But then she died and I went to Italy. Uncle Derek has arranged for me, now, to live with the Melfords, who are his cousins, and very kind and nice and have two daughters about my age.'

'You're happy there?'

'I don't know yet. I've barely got there. They're all very dull. I really wanted to know how much money I've got.'

'So it's financial information you really want?'

'Yes,' said Elvira. 'I've got *some* money, I know. Is it a lot?'

Egerton was serious now.

'Yes,' he said. 'You've got a lot of money. Your father

was a very rich man. You were his only child. When he died, the title and the estate went to a cousin. He didn't like the cousin, so he left all his personal property, which was considerable, to his daughter—to you, Elvira. You're a very rich woman, or will be, when you are twenty-one.'

'You mean I am not rich *now*?'

'Yes,' said Egerton, 'you're rich now, but the money is not yours to dispose of until you are twenty-one or marry. Until that time it is in the hands of your trustees. Luscombe, myself and another.' He smiled at her. 'We haven't embezzled it or anything like that. It's still there. In fact, we've increased your capital considerably by investments.'

'How much will I have?'

'At the age of twenty-one or upon your marriage, you will come into a sum which at a rough estimate would amount to six or seven hundred thousand pounds.'

'That *is* a lot,' said Elvira, impressed.

'Yes, it is a lot. Probably it is because it is such a lot that nobody has ever talked to you about it much.'

He watched her as she reflected upon this. Quite an interesting girl, he thought. Looked an unbelievably milk-and-water Miss, but she was more than that. A good deal more. He said, with a faintly ironic smile:

'Does that satisfy you?'

She gave him a sudden smile.

'It ought to, oughtn't it?'

'Rather better than winning the pools,' he suggested.

She nodded, but her mind was elsewhere. Then she came out abruptly with a question.

'Who gets it if I die?'

'As things stand now, it would go to your next of kin.'

'I mean—I couldn't make a will now, could I? Not until

I was twenty-one. That's what someone told me.'

'They were quite right.'

'That's really rather annoying. If I was married and died I suppose my husband would get the money?'

'Yes.'

'And if I wasn't married my mother would be my next of kin and get it. I really seem to have very few relations—I don't even know my mother. What is she like?'

'She's a very remarkable woman,' said Egerton shortly. 'Everybody would agree to that.'

'Didn't she ever *want* to see me?'

'She may have done . . . I think it's very possible that she did. But having made—in certain ways—rather a mess of her own life, she may have thought that it was better for you that you should be brought up quite apart from her.'

'Do you actually *know* that she thinks that?'

'No. I don't really know anything about it.'

Elvira got up.

'Thank you,' she said. 'It's very kind of you to tell me all this.'

'I think perhaps you ought to have been told more about things before,' said Egerton.

'It's rather humiliating *not* to know things,' said Elvira. 'Uncle Derek, of course, thinks I'm just a *child*.'

'Well, he's not a very young man himself. He and I, you know, are well advanced in years. You must make allowances for us when we look at things from the point of view of our advanced age.'

Elvira stood looking at him for a moment or two.

'But *you* don't think I'm really a child, do you?' she said shrewdly, and added, 'I expect you know rather more about girls than Uncle Derek does. He just lived with his sister.'

Then she stretched out her hand and said, very prettily, 'Thank you so much. I hope I haven't interrupted some important work you had to do,' and went out.

Egerton stood looking at the door that had closed behind her. He pursed up his lips, whistled a moment, shook his head and sat down again, picked up a pen and tapped thoughtfully on his desk. He drew some papers towards him, then thrust them back and picked up his telephone.

'Miss Cordell, get me Colonel Luscombe, will you? Try his club first. And then the Shropshire address.'

He put back the receiver. Again he drew his papers towards him and started reading them but his mind was not on what he was doing. Presently his buzzer went.

'Colonel Luscombe is on the wire now, Mr Egerton.'

'Right. Put him through. Hallo, Derek. Richard Egerton here. How are you? I've just been having a visit from someone you know. A visit from your ward.'

'From Elvira?' Derek Luscombe sounded very surprised.

'Yes.'

'But why—what on earth—what did she come to you for? Not in any trouble?'

'No, I wouldn't say so. On the contrary, she seemed rather—well, pleased with herself. She wanted to know all about her financial position.'

'You didn't tell her, I hope?' said Colonel Luscombe, in alarm.

'Why not? What's the point of secrecy?'

'Well, I can't help feeling it's a little unwise for a girl to know that she is going to come into such a large amount of money.'

'Somebody else will tell her that, if we don't. She's got to be prepared, you know. Money is a responsibility.'

'Yes, but she's so much of a child still.'

'Are you sure of that?'

'What do you mean? Of course she's a child.'

'I wouldn't describe her as such. Who's the boy-friend?'

'I beg your pardon.'

'I said who's the boy-friend? There *is* a boy-friend in the offing, isn't there?'

'No, indeed. Nothing of the sort. What on earth makes you think that?'

'Nothing that she actually said. But I've got some experience, you know. I think you'll find there *is* a boy friend.'

'Well, I can assure you you're quite wrong. I mean, she's been most carefully brought up, she's been at very strict schools, she's been in a very select finishing establishment in Italy. I should know if there was anything of that kind going on. I dare say she's met one or two pleasant young fellows and all that, but I'm sure there's been nothing of the kind you suggest.'

'Well, my diagnosis is a boy friend—and probably an undesirable one.'

'But why, Richard, why? What do *you* know about young girls?'

'Quite a lot,' said Egerton dryly. 'I've had three clients in the last year, two of whom were made wards of court and the third one managed to bully her parents into agreeing to an almost certainly disastrous marriage. Girls don't get looked after the way they used to be. Conditions are such that it's very difficult to look after them at all—'

'But I assure you Elvira has been most carefully looked after.'

'The ingenuity of the young female of the species is beyond anything you could conjecture! You keep an eye on her, Derek. Make a few inquiries as to what she's been up to.'

'Nonsense. She's just a sweet simple girl.'

'What you don't know about sweet simple girls would fill an album! Her mother ran away and caused a scandal—remember?—when she was younger than Elvira is today. As for old Coniston, he was one of the worst rips in England.'

'You upset me, Richard. You upset me very much.'

'You might as well be warned. What I didn't quite like was one of her other questions. Why is she so anxious to know who'd inherit her money if she dies?'

'It's queer your saying that, because she asked me that same question.'

'Did she now? Why should her mind run on early death? She asked me about her mother, by the way.'

Colonel Luscombe's voice sounded worried as he said: 'I wish Bess would get in touch with the girl.'

'Have you been talking to her on the subject—to Bess, I mean?'

'Well, yes . . . Yes I did. I ran across her by chance. We were staying in the same hotel, as a matter of fact. I urged Bess to make some arrangements to see the girl.'

'What did she say?' asked Egerton curiously.

'Refused point blank. She more or less said that she wasn't a safe person for the girl to know.'

'Looked at from one point of view I don't suppose she is,' said Egerton. 'She's mixed up with that racing fellow, isn't she?'

'I've heard rumours.'

'Yes, I've heard them too. I don't know if there's much in it really. There might be, I suppose. That could be why she feels as she does. Bess's friends are strong meat from time to time! But what a woman she is, eh Derek? What a woman.'

'Always been her own worst enemy,' said Derek Luscombe, gruffly.

'A really nice conventional remark,' said Egerton. 'Well, sorry I bothered you, Derek, but keep a look-out for undesirables in the background. Don't say you haven't been warned.'

He replaced the receiver and drew the pages on his desk towards him once more. This time he was able to put his whole attention on what he was doing.

CHAPTER XI

Mrs McCrae, Canon Pennyfather's housekeeper, had ordered a Dover sole for the evening of his return. The advantages attached to a good Dover sole were manifold. It need not be introduced to the grill or frying pan until the Canon was safely in the house. It could be kept until the next day if necessary. Canon Pennyfather was fond of Dover sole; and, if a telephone call or telegram arrived saying that the Canon would after all be elsewhere on this particular evening, Mrs McCrae was fond of a good Dover sole herself. All therefore was in good trim for the Canon's return. The Dover sole would be followed by pancakes. The sole sat on the kitchen table, the batter for the pancakes was ready in a bowl. All was in readiness. The brass shone, the silver sparkled, not a minuscule of dust showed anywhere. There was only one thing lacking. The Canon himself.

The Canon was scheduled to return on the train arriving at 6.30 from London.

At 7 o'clock he had not returned. No doubt the train was late. At 7.30 he still had not returned. Mrs McCrae gave a sigh of vexation. She suspected that this was going to be another of these things. Eight o'clock came and no Canon. Mrs McCrae gave a long, exasperated sigh. Soon, no doubt, she would get a telephone call, though it was quite within the bounds of possibility that there would not be even a telephone call. He might have written to her. No doubt he had written, but he had probably omitted to post the letter.

'Dear, dear!' said Mrs McCrae.

At 9 o'clock she made herself three pancakes with the pancake batter. The sole she put carefully away in the Frigidaire. 'I wonder where the good man's got to now,' she said to herself. She knew by experience that he might be anywhere. The odds were that he would discover his mistake in time to telegraph her or telephone her before she retired to bed. 'I shall sit up until 11 o'clock but no longer,' said Mrs McCrae. Ten-thirty was her bed-time, and extension to eleven she considered her duty, but if at eleven there was nothing, no word from the Canon, then Mrs McCrae would duly lock up the house and betake herself to bed.

It cannot be said that she was worried. This sort of thing had happened before. There was nothing to be done but wait for news of some kind. The possibilities were numerous. Canon Pennyfather might have got on the wrong train and failed to discover his mistake until he was at Land's End or John o' Groats, or he might still be in London having made some mistake in the date, and was therefore convinced he was not returning until tomorrow. He might have met a friend or friends at this foreign conference he was going to and been induced to stay out there perhaps over the week-end. He would have meant to let her know but had entirely forgotten to do so. So, as has been already said, she was not worried. The day after tomorrow his old friend, Archdeacon Simmons, was coming to stay. That was the sort of thing the Canon *did* remember, so no doubt he himself or a telegram from him would arrive tomorrow and at latest he would be home on the day after, or there would be a letter.

The morning of the day after, however, arrived without a word from him. For the first time Mrs McCrae began to be uneasy. Between 9 a.m. and 1 p.m. she eyed the telephone in a doubtful manner. Mrs McCrae had her own fixed views about the telephone. She used it and recognized its convenience but she was not fond of the telephone. Some of her household shopping was done by telephone, though she much preferred to do it in person owing to a fixed belief that if you did not see what you were being given, a shopkeeper was sure to try and cheat you. Still, telephones were useful for domestic matters. She occasionally, though rarely, telephoned her friends or relations in the near neighbourhood. To make a call of any distance, or a London call, upset her severely. It was a shameful waste of money. Nevertheless, she began to meditate facing that problem.

Finally, when yet another day dawned without any news of him she decided to act. She knew where the Canon was staying in London. Bertram's Hotel. A nice old-fashioned place. It might be as well, perhaps, if she rang up and made certain inquiries. They would probably know where the Canon was. It was not an ordinary hotel. She would ask to be put through to Miss Gorringe. Miss Gorringe was always efficient and thoughtful. The Canon might, of course, return by the twelve-thirty. If so he would be here any minute now.

But the minutes passed and there was no Canon. Mrs McCrae took a deep breath, nerved herself and asked for a call to London. She waited, biting her lips and holding the receiver clamped firmly to her ear.

'Bertram's Hotel, at your service,' said a voice.

'I would like, if you please, to speak to Miss Gorringe,' said Mrs McCrae.

'Just a moment. What name shall I say?'

'It's Canon Pennyfather's housekeeper. Mrs McCrae.'

'Just a moment please.'

Presently the calm and efficient voice of Miss Gorringe came through.

'Miss Gorringe here. Did you say Canon Pennyfather's housekeeper?'

'That's right. Mrs McCrae.'

'Oh yes. Of course. What can I do for you, Mrs McCrae?'

'Is Canon Pennyfather staying at the hotel still?'

'I'm glad you've rung up,' said Miss Gorringe. 'We have been rather worried as to what exactly to do.'

'Do you mean something's happened to Canon Pennyfather? Has he had an accident?'

'No, no, nothing of that kind. But we expected him back from Lucerne on Friday or Saturday.'

'Eh—that'd be right.'

'But he didn't arrive. Well, of course that wasn't really surprising. He had booked his room on—booked it, that is, until yesterday. He didn't come back yesterday or send any word and his things are still here. The major part of his baggage. We hadn't been quite sure what to do about it. Of course,' Miss Gorringe went on hastily, 'we know the Canon is, well—somewhat forgetful sometimes.'

'You may well say that!'

'It makes it a little difficult for us. We are so fully booked up. His room is actually booked for another guest.' She added: 'You have no idea where he is?'

With bitterness Mrs McCrae said,

'The man might be anywhere!' She pulled herself together. 'Well, thank you, Miss Gorringe.'

'Anything I can do—' Miss Gorringe suggested helpfully.

'I dare say I'll hear soon enough,' said Mrs McCrae. She thanked Miss Gorringe again and rang off.

She sat by the telephone, looking upset. She did not fear for the Canon's personal safety. If he had had an accident she would by now have been notified. She felt sure of that. On the whole the Canon was not what one would call accident prone. He was what Mrs McCrae called to herself 'one of the scatty ones', and the scatty ones seemed always to be looked after by a special providence. Whilst taking no care or thought, they could still survive even a Panda crossing. No, she did not visualize Canon Pennyfather as lying groaning in a hospital. He was *somewhere*, no doubt innocently and happily prattling with some friend or other. Maybe he was abroad still. The difficulty was that Archdeacon Simmons would expect to find a host to receive him. She couldn't put Archdeacon Simmons off because she didn't know where he was. It was all very difficult, but it had, like most difficulties, its bright spot. Its bright spot was Archdeacon Simmons. Archdeacon Simmons would know what to do. She would place the matter in his hands.

Archdeacon Simmons was a complete contrast to her employer. He knew where he was going, and what he was doing, and was always cheerfully sure of knowing the right thing to be done and doing it. A confident cleric. Archdeacon Simmons, when he arrived, to be met by Mrs McCrae's explanations, apologies and perturbation, was a tower of strength. He, too, was not alarmed.

'Now don't you worry, Mrs McCrae,' he said in his genial fashion, as he sat down to the meal she had prepared for his arrival. 'We'll hunt the absent-minded fellow down. Ever heard that story about Chesterton? G. K. Chesterton, you know, the writer. Wired to his wife when he'd gone on a lecture tour "Am at Crewe Station. Where ought I to be?" '

He laughed. Mrs McCrae smiled dutifully. She did not

think it was very funny because it was so exactly the sort of thing that Canon Pennyfather might have done.

'Ah,' said Archdeacon Simmons, with appreciation, 'one of your excellent veal cutlets! You're a marvellous cook, Mrs McCrae. I hope my old friend appreciates you.'

Veal cutlets having been succeeded by some small castle puddings with a blackberry sauce which Mrs McCrae had remembered was one of the Archdeacon's favourite sweets, the good man applied himself in earnest to the tracking down of his missing friend. He addressed himself to the telephone with vigour and a complete disregard for expense, which made Mrs McCrae purse her lips anxiously, although not really disapproving, because definitely her master had got to be tracked down.

Having first dutifully tried the Canon's sister who took little notice of her brother's goings and comings and as usual had not the faintest idea where he was or might be, the Archdeacon spread his net farther afield. He addressed himself once more to Bertram's Hotel and got details as precisely as possible. The Canon had definitely left there on the early evening of the 19th. He had with him a small BEA handbag, but his other luggage had remained behind in his room, which he had duly retained. He had mentioned that he was going to a conference of some kind at Lucerne. He had not gone direct to the airport from the hotel. The commissionaire, who knew him well by sight, had put him into a taxi and had directed it, as told by the Canon, to the Athenæum Club. That was the last time that anyone at Bertram's Hotel had seen Canon Pennyfather. Oh yes, a small detail—he had omitted to leave his key behind but had taken it with him. It was not the first time that that had happened.

Archdeacon Simmons paused for a few minutes' consideration before the next call. He could ring up the air station in London. That would no doubt take some time. There might be a short cut. He rang up Dr Weissgarten, a learned Hebrew scholar who was almost certain to have been at the conference.

Dr Weissgarten was at his home. As soon as he heard who was speaking to him he launched out into a torrent of verbiage consisting mostly of disparaging criticism of two papers that had been read at the conference in Lucerne.

'Most unsound, that fellow Hogarov,' he said, 'most unsound. How he gets away with it I don't know! Fellow isn't a scholar at all. Do you know what he actually said?'

The Archdeacon sighed and had to be firm with him. Otherwise there was a good chance that the rest of the evening would be spent in listening to criticism of fellow scholars at the Lucerne Conference. With some reluctance Dr Weissgarten was pinned down to more personal matters.

'Pennyfather?' he said, 'Pennyfather? He ought to have been there. Can't think why he wasn't there. Said he was going. Told me so only a week before when I saw him in the Athenæum.'

'You mean he wasn't at the conference at all?'

'That's what I've just said. He *ought* to have been there.'

'Do you know *why* he wasn't there? Did he send an excuse?'

'How should I know? He certainly talked about being there. Yes, now I remember. He was expected. Several people remarked on his absence. Thought he might have had a chill or something. Very treacherous weather.' He was about to revert to his criticisms of his fellow scholars but Archdeacon Simmons rang off.

He had got a fact but it was a fact that for the first time awoke in him an uneasy feeling. Canon Pennyfather had not been at the Lucerne Conference. He had meant to go to that conference. It seemed very extraordinary to the Archdeacon that he had not been there. He might, of course, have taken the wrong plane, though on the whole BEA were pretty careful of you and shepherded you away from such possibilities. Could Canon Pennyfather have forgotten the actual day that he was going to the conference? It was always possible, he supposed. But if so where had he gone instead?

He addressed himself now to the air terminal. It involved a great deal of patient waiting and being transferred from department to department. In the end he got a definite fact. Canon Pennyfather had booked as a passenger on the 21.40 plane to Lucerne on the 18th but he had not been on the plane.

'We're getting on,' said Archdeacon Simmons to Mrs McCrae, who was hovering in the background. 'Now, let me see. Who shall I try next?'

'All this telephoning will cost a fearful lot of money,' said Mrs McCrae.

'I'm afraid so. I'm afraid so,' said Archdeacon Simmons. 'But we've got to get on his track, you know. He's not a very young man.'

'Oh, sir, you don't think there's anything could really have happened to him?'

'Well I hope not . . . I don't think so, because I think you'd have heard if so. He—er—always had his name and address on him, didn't he?'

'Oh yes, sir, he had cards on him. He'd have letters too, and all sorts of things in his wallet.'

'Well, I don't think he's in a hospital then,' said the Archdeacon. 'Let me see. When he left the hotel he took a taxi to the Athenæum. I'll ring them up next.'

Here he got some definite information. Canon Pennyfather, who was well known there, had dined there at seven thirty on the evening of the 19th. It was then that the Archdeacon was struck by something he had overlooked until then. The aeroplane ticket had been for the 18th but the Canon had left Bertram's Hotel by taxi to the Athenæum, having mentioned he was going to the Lucerne Conference, on the 19th. Light began to break. 'Silly old ass,' thought Archdeacon Simmons to himself, but careful not to say it aloud in front of Mrs McCrae. 'Got his dates wrong. The conference was on the 19th. I'm sure of it. He must have thought that he was leaving on the 18th. He was one day wrong.'

He went over the next bit carefully. The Canon would have gone to the Athenæum, he would have dined, he would have gone on to Kensington Air Station. There, no doubt, it would have been pointed out to him that his ticket was for the day before and he would then have realized that the conference he was going to attend was now over.

'That's what happened,' said Archdeacon Simmons, 'depend upon it.' He explained it to Mrs McCrae, who agreed that it was likely enough. 'Then what would he do?'

'Go back to his hotel,' said Mrs McCrae.

'He wouldn't have come straight down here—gone straight to the station, I mean.'

'Not if his luggage was at the hotel. At any rate, he would have called there for his luggage.'

'True enough,' said Simmons. 'All right. We'll think of it like this. He left the airport with his little bag and he went back to the hotel, or started for the hotel at all events. He might have had dinner perhaps—no, he'd dined at the Athenæum. All right, he went back to the hotel. *But* he never arrived there.' He paused a moment or two and then said doubtfully, 'Or did he? Nobody seems to have seen him there. So what happened to him on the way?'

'He could have met someone,' said Mrs McCrae, doubtfully.

'Yes. Of course that's perfectly possible. Some old friend he hadn't seen for a long time . . . He could have gone off with a friend to the friend's hotel or the friend's house, but he wouldn't have stayed there three days, would he? He wouldn't have forgotten for three whole days that his luggage was at the hotel. He'd have rung up about it, he'd have called for it, or in a supreme fit of absent-mindedness he might have come straight home. Three days' silence. That's what's so inexplicable.'

'If he had an accident—'

'Yes, Mrs McCrae, of course that's possible. We can try the hospitals. You say he had plenty of papers on him to identify him? Hm—I think there's only one thing for it.'

Mrs McCrae looked at him apprehensively.

'I think, you know,' said the Archdeacon gently, 'that we've got to go to the police.'

CHAPTER XII

MISS MARPLE had found no difficulty in enjoying her stay in London. She did a lot of the things that she had not had the time to do in her hitherto brief visits to the capital. It has to be regretfully noted that she did not avail herself of the wide cultural activities that would have been possible to her. She visited no picture galleries and no museums. The idea of patronizing a dress show of any kind would not even have occurred to her. What she did visit were the glass and china departments of the large stores, and the household linen departments, and she also availed herself of some marked down lines in furnishing fabrics. Having spent what she considered a reasonable sum upon these household investments, she indulged in various excursions of her own. She went to places and shops she remembered from her young days, sometimes merely with the curiosity of seeing whether they were still there. It was not a pursuit that she had ever had time for before, and she enjoyed it very much. After a nice little nap after lunch, she would go out, and, avoiding the attentions of the commissionaire if possible, because he was so firmly imbued with the idea that a lady of her age and frailty should always go in a taxi, she walked towards a bus stop, or tube station. She had bought a small guide to buses and their routes—and an Underground Transport Map; and she would plan her excursion carefully. One afternoon she could be seen walking happily and nostalgically round Evelyn Gardens or Onslow Square murmuring softly, 'Yes, that was Mrs Van Dylan's house. Of course it looks *quite* different now. They seem to have remodelled it. Dear me, I see it's got four bells. Four flats, I suppose. Such a nice old-fashioned square this always was.'

Rather shamefacedly she paid a visit to Madame Tussaud's, a well-remembered delight of her childhood. In Westbourne Grove she looked in vain for Bradley's. Aunt Helen had always gone to Bradley's about her sealskin jacket.

Window shopping in the general sense did not interest Miss Marple, but she had a splendid time rounding up knitting patterns, new varieties of knitting wool, and suchlike delights. She made a special expedition to Richmond to see the house that had been occupied by Great-Uncle Thomas, the retired admiral. The handsome terrace was still there but here again each house seemed to be turned into flats. Much more painful was the house in Lowndes Square where a distant cousin, Lady Merridew, had lived in some style. Here a vast skyscraper building of modernistic design appeared to have arisen. Miss Marple shook her head sadly and said firmly to herself, 'There must *be* progress I suppose. If Cousin Ethel knew, she'd turn in her grave, I'm sure.'

It was on one particularly mild and pleasant afternoon that Miss Marple embarked on a bus that took her over Battersea Bridge. She was going to combine the double pleasure of taking a sentimental look at Princes Terrace Mansions where an old governess of hers had once lived, and visiting Battersea Park. The first part of her quest was abortive. Miss Ledbury's former home had vanished without trace and had been replaced by a great deal of gleaming concrete. Miss Marple turned into Battersea Park. She had always been a good walker but had to admit that nowadays her walking powers were not what they were. Half a mile was quite enough to tire her. She could manage, she thought, to cross the Park and go out over Chelsea Bridge and find herself once more on a convenient bus route, but her steps grew gradually slower and slower, and she was pleased to come upon a tea enclosure situated on the edge of the lake.

Teas were still being served there in spite of the autumn chill. There were not many people today, a certain amount of mothers and prams, and a few pairs of young lovers. Miss Marple collected a tray with tea and two sponge cakes. She carried her tray carefully to a table and sat down. The tea was just what she needed. Hot, strong and very reviving. Revived, she looked round her, and her eyes stopping suddenly at a particular table, she sat up very straight in her chair. Really, a very strange coincidence, very strange indeed! First the Army & Navy Stores and now here. Very unusual places those particular two people chose! But no! She was wrong. Miss Marple took a second and stronger pair of glasses from her bag. Yes, she had been mistaken. There was a certain similarity, of course. That long straight blonde hair; but this was not Bess Sedgwick. It was someone years younger. Of course! It was the daughter! The young girl who had come into Bertram's with Lady Selina Hazy's friend, Colonel Luscombe. But the man was the same man who had been lunching with Lady Sedgwick in the Army & Navy Stores. No doubt about it, the same handsome, hawk-like look, the same leanness, the same predatory toughness and—yes, the same strong virile attraction.

'Bad!' said Miss Marple. 'Bad all through! Cruel! Unscrupulous. I don't *like* seeing this. First the mother, now the daughter. What does it mean?'

It meant no good. Miss Marple was sure of that. Miss Marple seldom gave anyone the benefit of the doubt; she invariably thought the worst, and nine times out of ten, so she insisted, she was right in so doing. Both these meetings, she was sure, were more or less secret meetings. She observed now the way these two bent forward over the table until their heads nearly touched; and the earnestness with which they talked. The girl's face—Miss Marple took off her spectacles, rubbed the lenses carefully, then put them on again. Yes, this girl was in love. Desperately in love, as only the young can be in love. But what were her guardians about to let her run about London and have these clandestine assignments in Battersea Park? A nicely brought up, well-behaved girl like that. *Too* nicely brought up, no doubt! Her people probably believed her to be in some quite other spot. She had to tell lies.

On her way out Miss Marple passed the table where they were sitting, slowing down as much as she could without its being too obvious. Unfortunately, their voices were so low that she could not hear what they said. The man was speaking, the girl was listening, half pleased, half afraid. 'Planning to run away together, perhaps?' thought Miss Marple. 'She's still under age.'

Miss Marple passed through the small gate in the fence that led to the side-walk of the park. There were cars parked along there and presently she stopped beside one particular car. Miss Marple was not particularly knowledgeable over cars but such cars as this one did not come her way very often, so she had noted and remembered it. She had acquired a little information about cars of this style from an enthusiastic great-nephew. It was a racing car. Some foreign make—she couldn't remember the name now. Not only that, she had seen this car or one exactly like it, seen it only yesterday in a side street close to Bertram's Hotel. She had noticed it not only because of its size and its powerful and unusual appearance but because the number had awakened some vague memory, some trace of association in her memory. FAN 2266. It had made her think of her cousin Fanny Godfrey. Poor Fanny who stuttered, who had said 'I have got t-t-t-wo s-s-s-potz . . .'

She walked along and looked at the number of this car. Yes, she was quite right. FAN 2266. It was the same car. Miss Marple, her footsteps growing more painful every moment, arrived deep in thought at the other side of Chelsea Bridge and by then was so exhausted that she hailed the first taxi she saw with decision. She was worried by the feeling that there was something she ought to do about things. But what things and what to do about them? It was all so indefinite. She fixed her eyes absently on some news-boards.

'Sensational developments in train robbery,' they ran. 'Engine driver's story,' said another one. Really! Miss Marple thought to herself, every day there seemed to be a bank hold-up or a train robbery or a wage pay snatch.

Crime seemed to have got above itself.

CHAPTER XIII

VAGUELY reminiscent of a large bumble bee, Chief-Inspector Fred Davy wandered around the confines of the Criminal Investigation Department, humming to himself. It was a well-known idiosyncrasy of his, and caused no particular notice except to give rise to the remark that 'Father was on the prowl again.'

His prowling led him at last to the room where Inspector Campbell was sitting behind a desk with a bored expression. Inspector Campbell was an ambitious young man and he found much of his occupation tedious in the extreme. Nevertheless, he coped with the duties appointed to him and achieved a very fair measure of success in so doing. The powers that be approved of him, thought he should do well and doled out from time to time a few words of encouraging commendation.

'Good morning, sir,' said Inspector Campbell, respectfully, when Father entered his domain. Naturally he called Chief-Inspector Davy 'Father' behind his back as everyone else did; but he was not yet of sufficient seniority to do such a thing to his face.

'Anything I can do for you, sir?' he inquired.

'La, la, boom, boom,' hummed the Chief-Inspector, slightly off key. 'Why must they call me Mary when my name's Miss Gibbs?' After this rather unexpected resurrection of a by-gone musical comedy, he drew up a chair and sat down.

'Busy?' he asked.

'Moderately so.'

'Got some disappearance case or other on, haven't you, to do with some hotel or other. What's the name of it now? Bertram's. Is that it?'

'Yes, that's right, sir. Bertram's Hotel.'

'Contravening the licensing hours? Call girls?'

'Oh no, sir,' said Inspector Campbell, slightly shocked at hearing Bertram's Hotel being referred to in such a connection. 'Very nice, quiet, old-fashioned place.'

'Is it now?' said Father. 'Yes, is it now? Well, that's interesting, really.'

Inspector Campbell wondered why it was interesting. He did not like to ask, as tempers in the upper hierarchy were notoriously short since the mail train robbery which had been a spectacular success for the criminals. He looked at Father's large, heavy, bovine face and wondered as he had once or twice wondered before, how Chief-Inspector Davy had reached his present rank and why he was so highly thought of in the department. 'All right in his day, I suppose,' thought Inspector Campbell, 'but there are plenty of go-ahead chaps about who could do with some promotion, once the deadwood is cleared away.' But the deadwood had begun another song, partly hummed, with an occasional word or two here and there.

'*Tell me, gentle stranger, are there any more at home like you?*' intoned Father and then in a sudden falsetto, '*A few, kind sir, and nicer girls you never knew*. No, let's see, I've got the sexes mixed up. *Floradora.* That was a good show, too.'

'I believe I've heard of it, sir,' said Inspector Campbell.

'Your mother sang you to sleep in the cradle with it, I expect,' said Chief-Inspector Davy. 'Now then, what's been going on at Bertram's Hotel? Who has disappeared and how and why?'

'A Canon Pennyfather, sir. Elderly clergyman.'

'Dull case, eh?'

Inspector Campbell smiled.

'Yes, sir, it *is* rather dull in a way.'

'What did he look like?'

'Canon Pennyfather?'

'Yes—you've got a description, I suppose?'

'Of course.' Campbell shuffled papers and read: 'Height 5 ft. 8. Large thatch of white hair—stoops . . .'

'And he disappeared from Bertram's Hotel—when?'

'About a week ago—November 19th.'

'And they've just reported it. Took their time about it, didn't they?'

'Well, I think there was a general idea that he'd turn up.'

'Any idea what's behind it?' asked Father. 'Has a decent God-fearing man suddenly gone off with one of the church-wardens' wives? Or does he do a bit of secret drinking, or has he embezzled the church funds? Or is he the sort of absent-minded old chap who goes in for this sort of thing?'

'Well, from all I can hear, sir, I should say the latter. He's done it before.'

'What—disappeared from a respectable West End hotel?'

'No, not exactly that, but he's not always returned home when he was expected. Occasionally he's turned up to stay with friends on a day when they haven't asked him, or not turned up on the date when they *had* asked him. That sort of thing.'

'Yes,' said Father. 'Yes. Well, that sounds very nice and natural and according to plan, doesn't it? When exactly did you say he disappeared?'

'Thursday. November 19th. He was supposed to be attending a congress at—' He bent down and studied some papers on his desk. '—Oh yes, Lucerne. Society of Biblical Historical Studies. That's the English translation of it. I think it's actually a German society.'

'And it was held at Lucerne? The old boy—I suppose he *is* an old boy?'

'Sixty-three, sir, I understand.'

'The old boy didn't turn up, is that it?'

Inspector Campbell drew his papers towards him and gave Father the ascertainable facts in so far as they had been ascertained.

'Doesn't sound as if he'd gone off with a choirboy,' observed Chief-Inspector Davy.

'I expect he'll turn up all right,' said Campbell, 'but we're looking into it, of course. Are you—er—particularly interested in the case, sir?' He could hardly restrain his curiosity on this point.

'No,' said Davy thoughtfully. 'No, I'm not interested in the *case*. I don't see anything to be interested about in it.'

There was a pause, a pause which clearly contained the words 'Well, then?' with a question mark after it from Inspector Campbell, which he was too well trained to utter in audible tones.

'What I'm *really* interested in,' said Father, 'is the date. And Bertram's Hotel, of course.'

'It's always been very well conducted, sir. No trouble there.'

'That's very nice, I'm sure,' said Father. He added

thoughtfully, 'I'd rather like to have a look at the place.'

'Of course, sir,' said Inspector Campbell. 'Any time you like. I was thinking of going round there myself.'

'I might as well come along with you,' said Father. 'Not to butt in, nothing like that. But I'd just rather like to have a look at the place, and this disappearing Archdeacon of yours, or whatever he is, makes rather a good excuse. No need to call me "sir" when we're there—you throw your weight about. I'll just be your stooge.'

Inspector Campbell became interested.

'Do you think there's something that might tie in there, sir, something that might tie in with something else?'

'There's no reason to believe so, so far,' said Father. 'But you know how it is. One gets—I don't know what to call them—whims, do you think? Bertram's Hotel, somehow, sounds almost too good to be true.'

He resumed his impersonation of a bumble bee with a rendering of 'Let's All Go Down the Strand.'

The two detective officers went off together, Campbell looking smart in a lounge suit, (he had an excellent figure), and Chief-Inspector Davy carrying with him a tweedy air of being up from the country. They fitted in quite well. Only the astute eye of Miss Gorringe, as she raised it from her ledgers, singled them out and appreciated them for what they were. Since she had reported the disappearance of Canon Pennyfather herself and had already had a word with a lesser personage in the police force, she had been expecting something of this kind.

A faint murmur to the earnest-looking girl assistant whom she kept handy in the background enabled the latter to come forward and deal with any ordinary inquiries or services while Miss Gorringe gently shifted herself a little farther along the counter and looked up at the two men. Inspector Campbell laid down his card on the desk in front of her and she nodded. Looking past him to the large tweed-coated figure behind him, she noted that he had turned slightly sideways, and was observing the lounge and its occupants with an apparently naïve pleasure at beholding such a well bred, upper-class world in action.

'Would you like to come into the office?' said Miss Gorringe. 'We can talk better there perhaps.'

'Yes, I think that would be best.'

'Nice place you've got here,' said the large, fat, bovine-looking man, turning his head back towards her. 'Comfortable,' he added, looking approvingly at the large fire. 'Good old-fashioned comfort.'

Miss Gorringe smiled with an air of pleasure.

'Yes indeed. We pride ourselves on making our visitors comfortable,' she said. She turned to her assistant. 'Will you carry on, Alice? There is the ledger. Lady Jocelyn will be arriving quite soon. She is sure to want to change her room as soon as she sees it but you must explain to her we are really full up. If necessary, you can show her number 340 on the third floor and offer her that instead. It's not a very pleasant room and I'm sure she will be content with her present one as soon as she sees that.'

'Yes, Miss Gorringe. I'll do just that, Miss Gorringe.'

'And remind Colonel Mortimer that his field glasses are here. He asked me to keep them for him this morning. Don't let him go off without them.'

'No, Miss Gorringe.'

These duties accomplished, Miss Gorringe looked at the two men, came out from behind the desk and walked along to a plain mahogany door with no legend on it. Miss Gorringe opened it and they went into a small, rather sad-looking office. All three sat down.

'The missing man is Canon Pennyfather, I understand,' said Inspector Campbell. He looked at his notes. 'I've got Sergeant Wadell's report. Perhaps you'll tell me in your own words just what occurred.'

'I don't think that Canon Pennyfather has really disappeared in the sense in which one would usually use that word,' said Miss Gorringe. 'I think, you know, that he's just met someone somewhere, some old friend or something like that, and has perhaps gone off with him to some scholarly meeting or reunion or something of that kind, on the Continent— He is so very vague.'

'You've known him for a long time?'

'Oh yes, he's been coming here to stay for—let me see—oh five or six years at least, I should think.'

'You've been here some time yourself, ma'am,' said Chief-Inspector Davy, suddenly putting in a word.

'I have been here, let me think, fourteen years,' said Miss Gorringe.

'It's a nice place,' repeated Davy again. 'And Canon Pennyfather usually stayed here when he was in London? Is that right?'

'Yes. He always came to us. He wrote well beforehand to retain his room. He was much less vague on paper than he was in real life. He asked for a room from the 17th to the 21st. During that time he expected to be away for one or two nights, and he explained that he wished to keep his room on while he was away. He quite often did that.'

'When did you begin to get worried about him?' asked Campbell.

'Well, I didn't really. Of course it was awkward. You see,

his room was let on from the 23rd and when I realized—I didn't at first—that he hadn't come back from Lugano—'

'I've got Lucerne here in my notes,' said Campbell.

'Yes, yes, I think it *was* Lucerne. Some Archæological Congress or other. Anyway, when I realized he hadn't come back here and that his baggage was still here waiting in his room, it made things rather awkward. You see, we are very booked up at this time of year and I had someone else coming into his room. The Honourable Mrs Saunders, who lives at Lyme Regis. She always has that room. And then his housekeeper rang up. She was worried.'

'The housekeeper's name is Mrs McCrae, so I understand from Archdeacon Simmons. Do you know her?'

'Not personally, no, but I have spoken to her on the telephone once or twice. She is, I think, a very reliable woman and has been with Canon Pennyfather for some years. She was worried naturally. I believe she and Archdeacon Simmons got in touch with near friends and relations but they knew nothing of Canon Pennyfather's movements. And since he was expecting the Archdeacon to stay with him it certainly seemed very odd—in fact it still does—that the Canon should not have returned home.'

'Is this Canon usually as absent-minded as that?' asked Father.

Miss Gorringe ignored him. This large man, presumably the accompanying sergeant, seemed to her to be pushing himself forward a little too much.

'And now I understand,' continued Miss Gorringe, in an annoyed voice, 'and now I understand from Archdeacon Simmons that the Canon never even went to this conference in Lucerne.'

'Did he send any message to say he wouldn't go?'

'I don't think so—not from here. No telegram or anything like that. I really know nothing about Lucerne—I am really only concerned with *our* side of the matter. It has got into the evening papers, I see—the fact that he is missing, I mean. They haven't mentioned he was staying *here*. I hope they won't. We don't want the Press here, our visitors wouldn't like that at all. If you can keep them off us, Inspector Campbell, we should be very grateful. I mean it's not as if he had disappeared from *here*.'

'His luggage is still here?'

'Yes. In the baggage room. If he didn't go to Lucerne, have you considered the possibility of his being run over? Something like that?'

'Nothing like that has happened to him.'

'It really does seem very, very curious,' said Miss Gorringe, a faint flicker of interest appearing in her manner, to replace the annoyance. 'I mean, it does make one wonder where he *could* have gone and why?'

Father looked at her comprehendingly.

'Of course,' he said. 'You've only been thinking of it from the hotel angle. Very natural.'

'I understand,' said Inspector Campbell, referring once more to his notes, that Canon Pennyfather left here about six-thirty on the evening of Thursday the 19th. He had with him a small overnight bag and he left here in a taxi, directing the commissionaire to tell the driver to drive to the Athenæum Club.'

Miss Gorringe nodded her head.

'Yes, he dined at the Athenæum Club—Archdeacon Simmons told me that *that* was the place he was last seen.'

There was a firmness in Miss Gorringe's voice as she transferred the responsibility of seeing the Canon last from

Bertram's Hotel to the Athenæum Club.

'Well, it's nice to get the facts straight,' said Father in a gentle rumbling voice. 'We've got 'em straight now. He went off with his little blue BOAC bag or whatever he'd got with him—it *was* a blue BOAC bag, yes? He went off and he didn't come back, and that's that.'

'So you see, really I cannot help you,' said Miss Gorringe, showing a disposition to rise to her feet and get back to work.

'It doesn't *seem* as if you could help us,' said Father, 'but someone else might be able to,' he added.

'Someone else?'

'Why, yes,' said Father. 'One of the staff perhaps.'

'I don't think anyone knows *anything*; or they would certainly have reported it to me.'

'Well, perhaps they might. Perhaps they mightn't. What I mean is, they'd have told you if they'd distinctly *known* anything. But I was thinking more of something he might have *said*.'

'What sort of thing?' said Miss Gorringe, looking perplexed.

'Oh, just some chance word that might give one a clue. Something like "I'm going to see an old friend tonight that I haven't seen since we met in Arizona." Something like that. Or "I'm going to stay next week with a niece of mine for her daughter's confirmation." With absent-minded people, you know, clues like that are a great help. They show what was in the person's mind. It may be that after his dinner at the Athenæum, he gets into a taxi and thinks "Now where am I going?" and having got—say—the confirmation in his mind—thinks he's going off there.'

'Well, I see what you mean,' said Miss Gorringe doubtfully. 'It seems a little unlikely.'

'Oh, one never knows one's luck,' said Father cheerfully. 'There are the various guests here. I suppose Canon Pennyfather knew some of them since he came here fairly often.'

'Oh yes,' said Miss Gorringe. 'Let me see now. I've seen him talking to—yes, Lady Selina Hazy. Then there was the Bishop of Norwich. They're old friends, I believe. They were at Oxford together. And Mrs Jameson and her daughters. They come from the same part of the world. Oh yes, quite a lot of people.'

'You see,' said Father, 'he might have talked to one of *them*. He might have just mentioned some little thing that would give us a clue. Is there anyone staying here now that the Canon knew fairly well?'

Miss Gorringe frowned in thought.

'Well, I think General Radley is here still. And there's an old lady who came up from the country—who used to stay here as a girl, so she told me. Let me see, I can't remember her name at the moment, but I can find it for you. Oh yes, Miss Marple, that's her name. I believe she knew him.'

'Well, we could make a start with those two. And there'd be a chambermaid, I suppose.'

'Oh yes,' said Miss Gorringe. 'But she has been interviewed already by Sergeant Wadell.'

'I know. But not perhaps from this angle. What about the waiter who attended on his table. Or the head waiter?'

'There's Henry, of course,' said Miss Gorringe.

'Who's Henry?' asked Father.

Miss Gorringe looked almost shocked. It was to her impossible that anyone should not know Henry.

'Henry has been here for more years than I can say,' she said. 'You must have noticed him serving teas as you came in.'

'Kind of personality,' said Davy. 'I remember noticing him.'

'I don't know what we should do without Henry,' said Miss Gorringe with feeling. 'He really is wonderful. He sets the tone of the place, you know.'

'Perhaps he might like to serve some tea to me,' said Chief-Inspector Davy. 'Muffins, I saw he'd got there. I'd like a good muffin again.'

'Certainly if you like,' said Miss Gorringe, rather coldly. 'Shall I order two teas to be served to you in the lounge?' she added, turning to Inspector Campbell.

'That would—' the inspector began, when suddenly the door opened and Mr Humfries appeared in his Olympian manner.

He looked slightly taken aback, then looked inquiringly at Miss Gorringe. Miss Gorringe explained.

'These are two gentlemen from Scotland Yard, Mr Humfries,' she said.

'Detective-Inspector Campbell,' said Campbell.

'Oh yes. Yes, of course,' said Mr Humfries. 'The matter of Canon Pennyfather, I suppose? Most extraordinary business. I hope nothing's happened to him, poor old chap.'

'So do I,' said Miss Gorringe. 'Such a dear old man.'

'One of the old school,' said Mr Humfries approvingly.

'You seem to have quite a lot of the old school here,' observed Chief-Inspector Davy.

'I suppose we do, I suppose we do,' said Mr Humfries. 'Yes, in many ways we are quite a survival.'

'We have our regulars you know,' said Miss Gorringe.

She spoke proudly. 'The same people come back year after year. We have a lot of Americans. People from Boston, and Washington. Very quiet, nice people.'

'They like our English atmosphere,' said Mr Humfries, showing his very white teeth in a smile.

Father looked at him thoughtfully. Inspector Campbell said,

'You're quite sure that no message came here from the Canon? I mean it might have been taken by someone who forgot to write it down or to pass it on.'

'Telephone messages are always taken down *most* carefully,' said Miss Gorringe with ice in her voice. 'I cannot conceive it possible that a message would not have been passed on to me or to the appropriate person on duty.'

She glared at him.

Inspector Campbell looked momentarily taken aback.

'We've really answered all these questions before, you know,' said Mr Humfries, also with a touch of ice in his voice. 'We gave all the information at our disposal to your sergeant—I can't remember his name for the moment.'

Father stirred a little and said, in a kind of homely way,

'Well you see, things have begun to look rather more serious. It looks like a bit more than absent-mindedness. That's why, I think, it would be a good thing if we could have a word or two with those two people you mentioned —General Radley and Miss Marple.'

'You want me to—to arrange an interview with them?' Mr Humfries looked rather unhappy. 'General Radley's very deaf.'

'I don't think it will be necessary to make it too formal,' said Chief-Inspector Davy. 'We don't want to worry people. You can leave it quite safely to us. Just point out those two you mentioned. There is just a chance, you know, that Canon Pennyfather *might* have mentioned some plan of his, or some person he was going to meet at Lucerne or who was going with him to Lucerne. Anyway, it's worth trying.'

Mr Humfries looked somewhat relieved.

'Nothing more we can do for you?' he asked. 'I'm sure you understand that we wish to help you in every way, only you do understand how we feel about any Press publicity.'

'Quite,' said Inspector Campbell.

'And I'll just have a word with the chambermaid,' said Father.

'Certainly, if you like. I doubt very much whether she can tell you anything.'

'Probably not. But there might be some detail—some remark the Canon made about a letter or an appointment. One never knows.'

Mr Humfries glanced at his watch.

'She'll be on duty at six,' he said. 'Second floor. Perhaps, in the meantime, you'd care for tea?'

'Suits me,' said Father promptly.

They left the office together.

Miss Gorringe said, 'General Radley will be in the smoking-room. The first room down that passage on the left. He'll be in front of the fire there with *The Times*. I think,' she added discreetly, 'he might be asleep. You're sure you don't want me to—'

'No, no, I'll see to it,' said Father. 'And what about the other one—the old lady?'

'She's sitting over there, by the fireplace,' said Miss Gorringe.

'The one with white fluffy hair and the knitting?' said

Father, taking a look. 'Might almost be on the stage, mightn't she? Everybody's universal great-aunt.'

'Great-aunts aren't much like that nowadays,' said Miss Gorringe, 'nor grandmothers nor great-grandmothers, if it comes to that. We had the Marchioness of Barlowe in yesterday. She's a great-grandmother. Honestly, I didn't know her when she came in. Just back from Paris. Her face a mask of pink and white and her hair platinum blonde and I suppose an entirely false figure, but it looked wonderful.'

'Ah,' said Father, 'I prefer the old-fashioned kind myself. Well, thank you, ma'am.' He turned to Campbell. 'I'll look after it, shall I, sir? I know you've got an important appointment.'

'That's right,' said Campbell, taking his cue. 'I don't suppose anything much will come of it, but it's worth trying.'

Mr Humfries disappeared into his inner sanctum, saying as he did so:

'Miss Gorringe—just a moment, please.'

Miss Gorringe followed him in and shut the door behind her.

Humfries was walking up and down. He demanded sharply,

'What do they want to see Rose for? Wadell asked all the necessary questions.'

'I suppose it's just routine,' said Miss Gorringe, doubtfully.

'You'd better have a word with her first.'

Miss Gorringe looked a little startled.

'But surely Inspector Campbell—'

'Oh, I'm not worried about Campbell. It's the other one. Do you know who he is?'

'I don't think he gave his name. Sergeant of some kind, I suppose. He looks rather a yokel.'

'Yokel my foot,' said Mr Humfries, abandoning his elegance. 'That's Chief-Inspector Davy, an old fox if there ever was one. They think a lot of him at the Yard. I'd like to know what *he's* doing here, nosing about and playing the genial hick. I don't like it at all.'

'You can't think—'

'I don't know what to think. But I tell you I don't like it. Did he ask to see anyone else besides Rose?'

'I think he's going to have a word with Henry.'

Mr Humfries laughed. Miss Gorringe laughed too.

'We needn't worry about Henry.'

'No, indeed.'

'And the visitors who knew Canon Pennyfather?'

Mr Humfries laughed again.

'I wish him joy of old Radley. He'll have to shout the place down and then he won't get anything worth having. He's welcome to Radley and that funny old hen, Miss Marple. All the same, I don't much like his poking his nose in . . .'

CHAPTER XIV

'You know,' said Chief-Inspector Davy thoughtfully, 'I don't much like that chap Humfries.'

'Think there's something wrong with him?' asked Campbell.

'Well—' Father sounded apologetic, 'you know the sort of feeling one gets. Smarmy sort of chap. I wonder if he's the owner or only the manager.'

'I could ask him.' Campbell took a step back towards the desk.

'No, don't ask him,' said Father. 'Just find out—quietly.'

Campbell looked at him curiously.

'What's on your mind, sir?'

'Nothing in particular,' said Father. 'I just think I'd like to have a good deal more information about this place. I'd like to know who is behind it, what its financial status is. All that sort of thing.'

Campbell shook his head.

'I should have said if there was one place in London that was absolutely above suspicion—'

'I know, I know,' said Father. 'And what a useful thing it is to have that reputation!'

Campbell shook his head and left. Father went down the passage to the smoking-room. General Radley was just waking up. *The Times* had slipped from his knees and disintegrated slightly. Father picked it up and reassembled the sheets and handed it to him.

'Thank ye, sir. Very kind,' said General Radley gruffly.

'General Radley?'

'Yes.'

'You'll excuse me,' said Father, raising his voice, 'but I want to speak to you about Canon Pennyfather.'

'Eh—what's that?' The General approached a hand to his ear.

'Canon Pennyfather,' bellowed Father.

'My father? Dead years ago.'

'Canon *Penny*-father.'

'Oh. What about him? Saw him the other day. He was staying here.'

'There was an address he was going to give me. Said he'd leave it with you.'

This was rather more difficult to get over but he succeeded in the end.

'Never gave me any address. Must have mixed me up with somebody else. Muddle-headed old fool. Always was. Scholarly sort of chap, you know. They're always absent-minded.'

Father persevered for a little longer but soon decided that conversation with General Radley was practically impossible and almost certainly unprofitable. He went and sat down in the lounge at a table adjacent to that of Miss Jane Marple.

'Tea, sir?'

Father looked up. He was impressed, as everyone was impressed by Henry's personality. Though such a large and portly man he had appeared, as it were, like some vast travesty of Ariel who could materialize and vanish at will. Father ordered tea.

'Did I see you've got muffins here?' he asked.

Henry smiled benignly.

'Yes, sir. Very good indeed our muffins are, if I may say so. Everyone enjoys them. Shall I order you muffins, sir? Indian or China tea?'

'Indian,' said Father. 'Or Ceylon if you've got it.'

'Certainly we have Ceylon, sir.'

Henry made the faintest gesture with a finger and the pale young man who was his minion departed in search of Ceylon tea and muffins. Henry moved graciously elsewhere.

'You're *Someone*, you are,' thought Father. 'I wonder where they got hold of you and what they pay you. A packet, I bet, *and* you'd be worth it.' He watched Henry bending in a fatherly manner over an elderly lady. He wondered what Henry thought, if he thought anything, about Father. Father considered that he fitted into Bertram's Hotel reasonably well. He might have been a prosperous gentleman farmer or he might have been a peer of the realm with a resemblance to a bookmaker. Father knew two peers who were very like that. On the whole, he thought, he passed muster, but he also thought it possible that he had not deceived Henry. 'Yes, you're *Someone* you are,' Father thought again.

Tea came and the muffins. Father bit deeply. Butter ran down his chin. He wiped it off with a large handkerchief. He drank two cups of tea with plenty of sugar. Then he leaned forward and spoke to the lady sitting in the chair next to him.

'Excuse me,' he said, 'but aren't you Miss Jane Marple?'

Miss Marple transferred her gaze from her knitting to Chief Detective-Inspector Davy.

'Yes,' she said, 'I am Miss Marple.'

'I hope you don't mind my speaking to you. As a matter

of fact I am a police officer.'

'Indeed? Nothing seriously wrong here, I hope?'

Father hastened to reassure her in his best paternal fashion.

'Now, don't you worry, Miss Marple,' he said. 'It's not the sort of thing you mean at all. No burglary or anything like that. Just a little difficulty about an absent-minded clergyman, that's all. I think he's a friend of yours. Canon Pennyfather.'

'Oh, Canon Pennyfather. He was here only the other day. Yes, I've known him slightly for many years. As you say, he *is* very absent-minded.' She added, with some interest, 'What has he done now?'

'Well, as you might say in a manner of speaking, he's lost himself.'

'Oh dear,' said Miss Marple. 'Where ought he to be?'

'Back home in his Cathedral Close,' said Father, 'but he isn't.'

'He told *me*,' said Miss Marple, 'he was going to a conference at Lucerne. Something to do with the Dead Sea scrolls, I believe. He's a great Hebrew and Aramaic scholar, you know.'

'Yes,' said Father. 'You're quite right. That's where he—well, that's where he was supposed to be going.'

'Do you mean he didn't turn up there?'

'No,' said Father, 'he didn't turn up.'

'Oh, well,' said Miss Marple, 'I expect he got his dates wrong.'

'Very likely, very likely.'

'I'm afraid,' said Miss Marple, 'that that's not the first time that that's happened. I went to have tea with him in Chadminster once. He was actually absent from home. His housekeeper told me then how very absent-minded he was.'

'He didn't say anything to you when he was staying here that might give us a clue, I suppose?' asked Father, speaking in an easy and confidential way. 'You know the sort of thing I mean, any old friend he'd met or any plans he'd made apart from this Lucerne Conference?'

'Oh no. He just mentioned the Lucerne Conference. I think he said it was on the 19th. Is that right?'

'That was the date of the Lucerne Conference, yes.'

'I didn't notice the date particularly. I mean—' like most old ladies, Miss Marple here became slightly involved—'I *thought* he said the 19th and he *might* have said the 19th, but at the same time he might have *meant* the 19th and it might really have been the *20th*. I mean, he may have thought the 20th *was* the 19th or he may have thought the 19th was the 20th.'

'Well—' said Father, slightly dazed.

'I'm putting it badly,' said Miss Marple, 'but I mean people like Canon Pennyfather, if they say they're going somewhere on a Thursday, one is quite prepared to find that they didn't mean Thursday, it may be Wednesday or Friday they really mean. Usually they find out in time but sometimes they just don't. I thought at the time that something like that must have happened.'

Father looked slightly puzzled.

'You speak as though you knew already, Miss Marple, that Canon Pennyfather hadn't gone to Lucerne.'

'I knew he wasn't in Lucerne on *Thursday*,' said Miss Marple. 'He was here all day—or most of the day. That's why I thought, of course, that though he may have said Thursday to me, it was really Friday he meant. He certainly left here on Thursday evening carrying his BEA bag.'

'Quite so.'

'I took it he was going off to the airport then,' said Miss Marple. 'That's why I was so surprised to see he was back again.'

'I beg your pardon, what do you mean by "back again"?'

'Well, that he was back here again, I mean.'

'Now, let's get this quite clear,' said Father, careful to speak in an agreeable and reminiscent voice, and not as though it was really important. 'You saw the old idio—you saw the Canon, that is to say, leave as you thought for the airport with his overnight bag, fairly early in the evening. Is that right?'

'Yes. About half-past six, I would say, or quarter to seven.'

'But you say he came *back*.'

'Perhaps he missed the plane. That would account for it.'

'*When* did he come back?'

'Well, I don't really know. I didn't see him come back.'

'Oh,' said Father, taken aback. 'I thought you said you *did* see him.'

'Oh, I did see him *later*,' said Miss Marple, 'I meant I didn't see him actually come into the hotel.'

'You saw him later? When?'

Miss Marple thought.

'Let me see. It was about 3 a.m. I couldn't sleep very well. Something woke me up. Some sound. There are so many queer noises in London. I looked at my little clock, it was ten minutes past three. For some reason—I'm not quite sure what—I felt uneasy. Footsteps, perhaps, outside my door. Living in the country, if one hears footsteps in the middle of the night it makes one nervous. So I just opened my door and looked out. There was Canon Pennyfather leaving his room—it's next door to mine—and going off down the stairs wearing his overcoat.'

'He came out of his room wearing his overcoat and went down the stairs at 3 a.m. in the morning?'

'Yes,' said Miss Marple, and added: 'I thought it odd at the time.'

Father looked at her for some moments.

'Miss Marple,' he said, 'why haven't you told anyone this before?'

'Nobody asked me,' said Miss Marple simply.

CHAPTER XV

FATHER drew a deep breath.

'No,' he said. 'No, I suppose nobody would ask you. It's as simple as that.'

He relapsed into silence again.

'You think something has happened to him, don't you?' asked Miss Marple.

'It's over a week now,' said Father. 'He didn't have a stroke and fall down in the street. He's not in a hospital as a result of an accident. So where *is* he? His disappearance has been reported in the Press, but nobody's come forward with any information yet.'

'They may not have seen it. *I* didn't.'

'It looks—it really looks—' Father was following out his own line of thought—'as though he *meant* to disappear. Leaving this place like that in the middle of the night. You're quite sure about it, aren't you?' he demanded sharply. 'You didn't dream it?'

'I am absolutely sure,' said Miss Marple with finality.

Father heaved himself to his feet.

'I'd better go and see that chambermaid,' he said.

Father found Rose Sheldon on duty and ran an approving eye over her pleasant person.

'I'm sorry to bother you,' he said. 'I know you've seen our sergeant already. But it's about that missing gentleman,

Canon Pennyfather.'

'Oh yes, sir, a very nice gentleman. He often stays here.'

'Absent-minded,' said Father.

Rose Sheldon permitted a discreet smile to appear on her respectful mask of a face.

'Now let me see.' Father pretended to consult some notes. 'The last time you saw Canon Pennyfather—was—'

'On the Thursday morning, sir. Thursday the 19th. He told me that he would not be back that night and possibly not the next either. He was going, I think, to Geneva. Somewhere in Switzerland, anyway. He gave me two shirts he wanted washed and I said they would be ready for him on the morning of the following day.'

'And that's the last you saw of him, eh?'

'Yes, sir. You see, I'm not on duty in the afternoons. I come back again at 6 o'clock. By then he must have left, or at any rate he was downstairs. Not in his room. He had left two suitcases behind.'

'That's right,' said Father. The contents of the suitcases had been examined, but had given no useful lead. He went on: 'Did you call him the next morning?'

'Call him? No, sir, he was away.'

'What did you do ordinarily—take him early tea? Breakfast?'

'Early tea, sir. He breakfasted downstairs always.'

'So you didn't go into his room at all the next day?'

'Oh yes, sir.' Rose sounded shocked. 'I went into his room as usual. I took his shirts in for one thing. And of course I dusted the room. We dust all the rooms every day.'

'Had the bed been slept in?'

She stared at him. 'The bed, sir? Oh no.'

'Was it rumpled—creased in any way?'

She shook her head.

'What about the bathroom?'

'There was a damp hand towel, sir, that had been used, I presume that would be the evening before. He may have washed his hands last thing before going off.'

'And there was nothing to show that he had come back into the room—perhaps quite late—after midnight?'

She stared at him with an air of bewilderment. Father opened his mouth, then shut it again. Either she knew nothing about the Canon's return or she was a highly accomplished actress.

'What about his clothes—suits. Were they packed up in his suitcases?'

'No, sir, they were hanging up in the cupboards. He was keeping his room on, you see, sir.'

'Who did pack them up?'

'Miss Gorringe gave orders, sir. When the room was wanted for the new lady coming in.'

A straightforward coherent account. But if that old lady was correct in stating that she saw Canon Pennyfather leaving his room at 3 a.m. on Friday morning, then he must have come back to that room sometime. Nobody had seen him enter the hotel. Had he, for some reason, deliberately avoided being seen? He had left no traces in the room. He hadn't even lain down on the bed. Had Miss Marple dreamed the whole thing? At her age it was possible enough. An idea struck him.

'What about his airport bag?'

'I beg your pardon, sir?'

'A small bag, dark blue—a BEA or BOAC bag—you must have seen it?'

'Oh that—yes, sir. But of course he'd take that with him abroad.'

'But he didn't *go* abroad. He never went to Switzerland after all. So he must have left it behind. Or else he came back and left it here with his other luggage.'

'Yes—yes—I think—I'm not quite sure—I believe he did.'

Quite unsolicited, the thought raced into Father's mind: *They didn't brief you on that, did they?*

Rose Sheldon had been calm and competent up till now. But that question had rattled her. She hadn't known the right answer to it. *But she ought to have known.*

The Canon had taken his bag to the airport, had been turned away from the airport. If he had come back to Bertram's, the bag would have been with him. *But Miss Marple had made no mention of it when she had described the Canon leaving his room and going down the stairs.*

Presumably it was left in the bedroom, but it had not been put in the baggage room with the suitcases. Why not? *Because the Canon was supposed to have gone to Switzerland?*

He thanked Rose genially and went downstairs again.

Canon Pennyfather! Something of an enigma, Canon Pennyfather. Talked a lot about going to Switzerland, muddled up things so that he didn't go to Switzerland, came back to his hotel so secretly that nobody saw him, left it again in the early hours of the morning. (To go where? To do what?)

Could absent-mindedness account for all this?

If not, then what was Canon Pennyfather up to? And more important, where was he?

From the staircase, Father cast a jaundiced eye over the occupants of the lounge, and wondered whether *anyone* was what they seemed to be. He had got to that stage! Elderly people, middle-aged people (nobody very young), nice old-fashioned people, nearly all well-to-do, all highly respectable. Service people, lawyers, clergymen; American husband and wife near the door, a French family near the fireplace. Nobody flashy, nobody out of place; most of them enjoying an old-fashioned English afternoon tea. Could there really be anything seriously wrong with a place that served old-fashioned afternoon teas?

The Frenchman made a remark to his wife that fitted in appositively enough.

'*Le Five o'clock*,' he was saying. '*C'est bien Anglais ça, n'est-ce pas*?' He looked round him with approval.

'Le Five o'clock,' thought Davy as he passed through the swing doors to the street. 'That chap doesn't know that "le Five o'clock" is as dead as the Dodo!'

Outside, various vast American wardrobe cases and suit-cases were being loaded on to a taxi. It seemed that Mr and Mrs Elmer Cabot were on their way to the Hotel Vendôme, Paris.

Beside him on the kerb, Mrs Elmer Cabot was expressing her views to her husband.

'The Pendleburys were quite right about this place, Elmer. It just *is* old England. So beautifully Edwardian. I just feel Edward the Seventh could walk right in any moment and sit down there for his afternoon tea. I mean to come back here next year—I really do.'

'If we've got a million dollars or so to spare,' said her husband dryly.

'Now, Elmer, it wasn't as bad as all *that*.'

The baggage was loaded, the tall commissionaire helped them in, murmuring 'Thank you, sir' as Mr Cabot made the expected gesture. The taxi drove off. The commissionaire transferred his attention to Father.

'Taxi, sir?'

Father looked up at him.

Over six feet. Good-looking chap. A bit run to seed. Ex-army. Lots of medals—genuine, probably. A bit shifty? Drinks too much.

Aloud he said: 'Ex-army man?'

'Yes, sir. Irish Guards.'

'Military Medal, I see. Where did you get that?'

'Burma.'

'What's your name?'

'Michael Gorman. Sergeant.'

'Good job here?'

'It's a peaceful spot.'

'Wouldn't you prefer the Hilton?'

'I would not. I like it here. Nice people come here, and quite a lot of racing gentlemen—for Ascot and Newbury. I've had good tips from them now and again.'

'Ah, so you're an Irishman and a gambler, is that it?'

'Och! now, what would life be like without a gamble?'

'Peaceful and dull,' said Chief-Inspector Davy, 'like mine.'

'Indeed, sir?'

'Can you guess what my profession is? ' asked Father.

The Irishman grinned.

'No offence to you, sir, but if I may guess I'd say you were a cop.'

'Right first time,' said Chief-Inspector Davy. 'You remember Canon Pennyfather?'

'Canon Pennyfather now, I don't seem to mind the name—'

'Elderly clergyman.'

Michael Gorman laughed.

'Ah now, clergymen are as thick as peas in a pod in there.'

'This one disappeared from here.'

'Oh, *that* one!' The commissionaire seemed slightly taken aback.

'Did you know him?'

'I wouldn't remember him if it hadn't been for people asking me questions about him. All I know is, I put him into a taxi and he went to the Athenæum Club. That's the last I saw of him. Somebody told me he'd gone to Switzerland, but I hear he never got there. Lost himself, it seems.'

'You didn't see him later that day?'

'Later— No, indeed.'

'What time do you go off duty?'

'Eleven-thirty.'

Chief-Inspector Davy nodded, refused a taxi and moved slowly away along Pond Street. A car roared past him close to the kerb, and pulled up outside Bertram's Hotel, with a scream of brakes. Chief-Inspector Davy turned his head soberly and noted the number plate. FAN 2266. There was something reminiscent about that number, though he couldn't for the moment place it.

Slowly he retraced his steps. He had barely reached the entrance before the driver of the car, who had gone through the doors a moment or two before, came out again. He and the car matched each other. It was a racing model, white with long gleaming lines. The young man had the same eager greyhound look with a handsome face and a body with not a superfluous inch of flesh on it.

The commissionaire held the car door open, the young man jumped in, tossed a coin to the commissionaire and drove off with a burst of powerful engine.

'You know who *he* is?' said Michael Gorman to Father.

'A dangerous driver, anyway.'

'Ladislaus Malinowski. Won the Grand Prix two years ago—world champion he was. Had a bad smash last year. They say he's all right again now.'

'Don't tell me *he's* staying at Bertram's. Highly unsuitable.'

Michael Gorman grinned.

'He's not staying here, no. But a friend of his is—' He winked.

A porter in a striped apron came out with more American luxury travel equipment.

Father stood absent-mindedly watching them being ensconced in a Daimler Hire Car whilst he tried to remember what he knew about Ladislaus Malinowski. A reckless fellow—said to be tied up with some well known woman—what was her name now? Still staring at a smart wardrobe case, he was just turning away when he changed his mind and re-entered the hotel again.

He went to the desk and asked Miss Gorringe for the hotel register. Miss Gorringe was busy with departing Americans, and pushed the book along the counter towards him. He turned the pages. Lady Selina Hazy, Little Cottage, Merryfield, Hants. Mr and Mrs Hennessey King, Elderberries, Essex. Sir John Woodstock, 5 Beaumont Crescent, Cheltenham. Lady Sedgwick, Hurstings House, Northumberland. Mr and Mrs Elmer Cabot, Connecticut. General Radley, 14, The Green, Chichester. Mr and Mrs Woolmer Pickington, Marble Head, Connecticut. La Comtesse de Beauville, Les Sapins, St Germain en Laye. Miss Jane Marple, St Mary Mead, Much Benham. Colonel Luscombe, Little Green, Suffolk. Mrs Carpenter, The Hon. Elvira Blake. Canon Pennyfather, The Close, Chadminster. Mrs Holding, Miss Holding, Miss Audrey Holding, The Manor House, Carmanton. Mr and Mrs Rysville, Valley Forge, Pennsylvania. The Duke of Barnstable, Doone Castle, N. Devon . . . A cross section of the kind of people who stayed at Bertram's Hotel. They formed, he thought, a kind of pattern . . .

As he shut the book, a name on an earlier page caught his eye. Sir William Ludgrove.

Mr Justice Ludgrove who had been recognized by a probation officer near the scene of a bank robbery. Mr Justice Ludgrove—Canon Pennyfather—both patrons of Bertram's Hotel . . .

'I hope you enjoyed your tea, sir?' It was Henry, standing at his elbow. He spoke courteously, and with the slight anxiety of the perfect host.

'The best tea I've had for years,' said Chief-Inspector Davy.

He remembered he hadn't paid for it. He attempted to do so, but Henry raised a deprecating hand.

'Oh no, sir. I was given to understand that your tea was on the house. Mr Humfries' orders.'

Henry moved away. Father was left uncertain whether he ought to have offered Henry a tip or not. It was galling to think that Henry knew the answer to that social problem much better than he did!

As he moved away along the street, he stopped suddenly. He took out his note-book and put down a name and an address—no time to lose. He went into a telephone box. He was going to stick out his neck. Come hell or high water, he was going all out on a hunch.

CHAPTER XVI

IT WAS the wardrobe that worried Canon Pennyfather. It worried him before he was quite awake. Then he forgot it and he fell asleep again. But when his eyes opened once more, there the wardrobe still was in the wrong place. He was lying on his left side facing the window and the wardrobe ought to have been there between him and the window on the left wall. But it wasn't. It was on the right. It worried him. It worried him so much that it made him feel tired. He was conscious of his head aching badly, and on top of that, to have the wardrobe in the wrong place . . . At this point once more his eyes closed.

There was rather more light in the room the next time he woke. It was not daylight yet. Only the faint light of dawn. 'Dear me,' said Canon Pennyfather to himself, suddenly solving the problem of the wardrobe. 'How stupid I am! Of course, I'm not at home.'

He moved gingerly. No, this wasn't his own bed. He was away from home. He was—where was he? Oh, of course. He'd gone to London, hadn't he? He was in Bertram's Hotel and—but no, he *wasn't* in Bertram's Hotel. In Bertram's Hotel his bed was facing the window. So that was wrong, too.

'Dear me, where can I be?' said Canon Pennyfather.

Then he remembered that he was going to Lucerne. 'Of course,' he said to himself, 'I'm in Lucerne.' He began thinking about the paper he was going to read. He didn't think about it long. Thinking about his paper seemed to make his head ache so he went to sleep again.

The next time he woke his head was a great deal clearer. Also there was a good deal more light in the room. He was not at home, he was not at Bertram's Hotel and he was fairly sure that he was not in Lucerne. This wasn't a hotel bedroom at all. He studied it fairly closely. It was an entirely strange room with very little furniture in it. A kind of cupboard (what he'd taken for the wardrobe) and a window with flowered curtains through which the light came. A chair and a table and a chest of drawers. Really, that was about all.

'Dear me,' said Canon Pennyfather, 'this is *most* odd. Where am I?'

He was thinking of getting up to investigate but when he sat up in bed his headache began again so he lay down.

'I must have been ill,' decided Canon Pennyfather. 'Yes, definitely I must have been ill.' He thought a minute or two and then said to himself, 'As a matter of fact, I think perhaps I'm still ill. Influenza, perhaps?' Influenza, people often said, came on very suddenly. Perhaps—perhaps it had come on at dinner at the Athenæum. Yes, that was right. He remembered that he had dined at the Athenæum.

There were sounds of moving about in the house. Perhaps they'd taken him to a nursing home. But no, he didn't think this was a nursing home. With the increased light it showed itself as a rather shabby and ill-furnished small bedroom. Sounds of movement went on. From downstairs a voice called out, 'Goodbye, ducks. Sausage and mash this evening.'

Canon Pennyfather considered this. Sausage and mash.

The words had a faintly agreeable quality.

'I believe,' he said to himself, 'I'm *hungry*.'

The door opened. A middle-aged woman came in, went across to the curtains, pulled them back a little and turned towards the bed.

'Ah, you're awake now,' she said. 'And how are you feeling?'

'Really,' said Canon Pennyfather, rather feebly, 'I'm not quite sure.'

'Ah, I expect not. You've been quite bad, you know. Something hit you a nasty crack, so the doctor said. These motorists! Not even stopping after they'd knocked you down.'

'Have I had an accident?' said Canon Pennyfather. 'A motor accident?'

'That's right,' said the woman. 'Found you by the side of the road when we come home. Thought you was drunk at first.' She chuckled pleasantly at the reminiscence. 'Then my husband said he'd better take a look. It may have been an accident, he said. There wasn't no smell of drink or anything. No blood or anything neither. Anyway, there you was, out like a log. So my husband said "we can't leave him here lying like that" and he carried you in here. See?'

'Ah,' said Canon Pennyfather, faintly, somewhat overcome by all these revelations. 'A good Samaritan.'

'And he saw you were a clergyman so my husband said "it's all quite respectable". Then he said he'd better not call the police because being a clergyman and all that you mightn't like it. That's if you was drunk, in spite of there being no smell of drink. So then we hit upon getting Dr Stokes to come and have a look at you. We still call him Dr Stokes although he's been struck off. A very nice man he is, embittered a bit, of course, by being struck off. It was only his kind heart really, helping a lot of girls who were no better than they should be. Anyway, he's a good enough doctor and we got him to come and take a look at you. He says you've come to no real harm, says it's mild concussion. All we'd got to do was to keep you lying flat and quiet in a dark room. "Mind you," he said, "I'm not giving an opinion or anything like that. This is unofficial. I've no right to prescribe or to say anything. By rights I dare say you ought to report it to the police, but if you don't want to, why should you?" Give the poor old geezer a chance, that's what he said. Excuse me if I'm speaking disrespectful. He's a rough and ready speaker, the doctor is. Now what about a drop of soup or some hot bread and milk?'

'Either,' said Canon Pennyfather faintly, 'would be very welcome.'

He relapsed on to his pillows. An accident? So *that* was it. An accident, and he couldn't remember a thing about it! A few minutes later the good woman returned bearing a tray with a steaming bowl on it.

'You'll feel better after this,' she said. 'I'd like to have put a drop of whisky or a drop of brandy in it but the doctor said you wasn't to have nothing like that.'

'Certainly not,' said Canon Pennyfather, 'not with concussion. No. It would have been unadvisable.'

'I'll put another pillow behind your back, shall I, ducks? There, is that all right?'

Canon Pennyfather was a little startled by being addressed as 'ducks'. He told himself that it was kindly meant.

'Upsydaisy,' said the woman, 'there we are.'

'Yes, but where are we?' said Canon Pennyfather. 'I mean, where am I? Where is this place?'

'Milton St John,' said the woman. 'Didn't you know?'

'Milton St John?' said Canon Pennyfather. He shook his head. 'I never heard the name before.'

'Oh well, it's not much of a place. Only a village.'

'You have been very kind,' said Canon Pennyfather. 'May I ask your name?'

'Mrs Wheeling. Emma Wheeling.'

'You are most kind,' said Canon Pennyfather again. 'But this accident now. I simply cannot remember—'

'You put yourself outside that, luv, and you'll feel better and up to remembering things.'

'Milton St John,' said Canon Pennyfather to himself, in a tone of wonder. 'The name means nothing to me *at all*. How very extraordinary!'

CHAPTER XVII

Sir Ronald Graves drew a cat upon his blotting pad. He looked at the large portly figure of Chief-Inspector Davy sitting opposite him and drew a bulldog.

'Ladislaus Malinowski?' he said. 'Could be. Got any evidence?'

'No. He'd fit the bill, would he?'

'A daredevil. No nerves. Won the World Championship. Bad crash about a year ago. Bad reputation with women. Sources of income doubtful. Spends money here and abroad very freely. Always going to and fro to the Continent. Have you got some idea that he's the man behind these big organized robberies and hold-ups?'

'I don't think he's the planner. But I think he's in with them.'

'Why?'

'For one thing, he runs a Mercedes-Otto car. Racing model. A car answering to that description was seen near Bedhampton on the morning of the mail robbery. Different number plates—but we're used to that. And it's the same stunt—unlike, but not too unlike. FAN 2299 instead of 2266. There aren't so many Mercedes-Otto models of that type about. Lady Sedgwick has one and young Lord Merrivale.'

'You don't think Malinowski runs the show?'

'No—I think there are better brains than his at the top.

But he's in it. I've looked back over the files. Take the hold-up at the Midland and West London. Three vans happened—just happened—to block a certain street. A Mercedes-Otto that was on the scene got clear away owing to that block.'

'It was stopped later.'

'Yes. And given a clear bill of health. Especially as the people who'd reported it weren't sure of the correct number. It was reported as FAM 3366—Malinowski's registration number is FAN 2266— It's all the same picture.'

'And you persist in tying it up with Bertram's Hotel. They dug up some stuff about Bertram's for you—'

Father tapped his pocket.

'Got it here. Properly registered company. Balance—paid up capitals—directors—etcetera, etcetera, etcetera. Doesn't mean a thing! These financial shows are all the same—just a lot of snakes swallowing each other! Companies, and holding companies—makes your brain reel!'

'Come now, Father. That's just a way they have in the City. Has to do with taxation—'

'What I want is the real dope. If you'll give me a chit, sir, I'd like to go and see some top brass.'

The A.C. stared at him.

'And what exactly do you mean by top brass?'

Father mentioned a name.

The A.C. looked upset. 'I don't know about that. I hardly think we dare approach *him*.'

'It might be very helpful.'

There was a pause. The two men looked at each other. Father looked bovine, placid, and patient. The A.C. gave in.

'You're a stubborn old devil, Fred,' he said. 'Have it your own way. Go and worry the top brains behind the international financiers of Europe.'

'*He'll* know,' said Chief-Inspector Davy. 'He'll *know*. And if he doesn't, he can find out by pressing one buzzer on his desk or making one telephone call.'

'I don't know that he'll be pleased.'

'Probably not,' said Father, 'but it won't take much of his time. I've got to have authority behind me, though.'

'You're really serious about this place, Bertram's, aren't you? But what have you got to go on? It's well run, has a good respectable clientele—no trouble with the licensing laws.'

'I know—I know. No drinks, no drugs, no gambling, no accommodation for criminals. All pure as the driven snow. No beatniks, no thugs, no juvenile delinquents. Just sober Victorian-Edwardian old ladies, county families, visiting travellers from Boston and the more respectable parts of the USA. All the same, a respectable Canon of the church is seen to leave it at 3 a.m. in the morning in a somewhat surreptitious manner—'

'Who saw that?'

'An old lady.'

'How did she manage to see him? Why wasn't she in bed and asleep?'

'Old ladies are like that, sir.'

'You're not talking of—what's his name—Canon Pennyfather?'

'That's right, sir. His disappearance was reported and Campbell has been looking into it.'

'Funny coincidence—his name's just come up in connection with the mail robbery at Bedhampton.'

'Indeed? In what way, sir?'

'Another old lady—or middle-aged anyway. When the

train was stopped by that signal that had been tampered with, a good many people woke up and looked out into the corridor. This woman, who lives in Chadminster and knows Canon Pennyfather by sight, says she saw him entering the train by one of the doors. She thought he'd got out to see what was wrong and was getting in again. We were going to follow it up because of his disappearance being reported—'

'Let's see—the train was stopped at 5.30 a.m. Canon Pennyfather left Bertram's Hotel not long after 3 a.m. Yes, it could be done. If he were driven there—say—in a racing car . . .'

'So we're back again to Ladislaus Malinowski!'

The A.C. looked at his blotting pad doodles. 'What a bulldog you are, Fred,' he said.

Half an hour later Chief-Inspector Davy was entering a quiet and rather shabby office.

The large man behind the desk rose and put forward a hand.

'Chief-Inspector Davy? Do sit down,' he said. 'Do you care for a cigar?'

Chief-Inspector Davy shook his head.

'I must apologize,' he said, in his deep countryman's voice, 'for wasting your valuable time.'

Mr Robinson smiled. He was a fat man and very well dressed. He had a yellow face, his eyes were dark and sad looking and his mouth was large and generous. He frequently smiled to display over-large teeth. 'The better to eat you with,' thought Chief-Inspector Davy irrelevantly. His English was perfect and without accent but he was not an Englishman. Father wondered, as many others had wondered before him, what nationality Mr Robinson really was.

'Well, what can I do for you?'

'I'd like to know,' said Chief-Inspector Davy, 'who owns Bertram's Hotel.'

The expression on Mr Robinson's face did not change. He showed no surprise at hearing the name nor did he show recognition. He said thoughtfully,

'You want to know who owns Bertram's Hotel. That, I think, is in Pond Street, off Piccadilly.'

'Quite right, sir.'

'I have occasionally stayed there myself. A quiet place. Well run.'

'Yes,' said Father, 'particularly well run.'

'And you want to know who owns it? Surely that is easy to ascertain?'

There was a faint irony behind his smile.

'Through the usual channels, you mean? Oh yes.' Father took a small piece of paper from his pocket and read out three or four names and addresses.

'I see,' said Mr Robinson, 'someone has taken quite a lot of trouble. Interesting. And you come to me?'

'If anyone knows, you would, sir.'

'Actually I do not know. But it is true that I have ways of obtaining information. One has—' he shrugged his very large, fat shoulders—'one has contacts.'

'Yes, sir,' said Father with an impassive face.

Mr Robinson looked at him, then he picked up the telephone on his desk.

'Sonia? Get me Carlos.' He waited a minute or two then spoke again. 'Carlos?' He spoke rapidly half a dozen sentences in a foreign language. It was not a language that Father could even recognize.

Father could converse in good British French. He had a

smattering of Italian and he could make a guess at plain travellers' German. He knew the sounds of Spanish, Russian and Arabic, though he could not understand them. This language was none of those. At a faint guess he hazarded it might be Turkish or Persian or Armenian, but even of that he was by no means sure. Mr Robinson replaced the receiver.

'I do not think,' he said genially, 'that we shall have long to wait. I am interested, you know. Very much interested. I have occasionally wondered myself—'

Father looked inquiring.

'About Bertram's Hotel,' said Mr Robinson. 'Financially, you know. One wonders how it can pay. However, it has never been any of my business. And one appreciates—' He shrugged his shoulders, '—a comfortable hostelry with an unusually talented personnel and staff . . . Yes, I have wondered.' He looked at Father. 'You know how and why?'

'Not yet,' said Father, 'but I mean to.'

'There are several possibilities,' said Mr Robinson, thoughtfully. 'It is like music, you know. Only so many notes to the octave, yet one can combine them in—what is it—several million different ways? A musician told me once that you do not get the same tune twice. Most interesting.'

There was a slight buzz on his desk and he picked up the receiver once more.

'Yes? Yes, you have been very prompt. I am pleased. I see. Oh! Amsterdam, yes . . . Ah . . . Thank you . . . Yes. You will spell that? Good.'

He wrote rapidly on a pad at his elbow.

'I hope this will be useful to you,' he said, as he tore off the sheet and passed it across the table to Father, who read the name out loud. 'Wilhelm Hoffman.'

'Nationality Swiss,' said Mr Robinson. 'Though not, I would say, born in Switzerland. Has a good deal of influence in Banking circles and though keeping strictly on the right side of the law, he has been behind a great many —questionable deals. He operates solely on the Continent, not in this country.'

'Oh.'

'But he has a brother,' said Mr Robinson. 'Robert Hoffman. Living in London—a diamond merchant—most respectable business— His wife is Dutch— He also has offices in Amsterdam—Your people may know about him. As I say, he deals mainly in diamonds, but he is a very rich man, and he owns a lot of property, not usually in his own name. Yes, he is behind quite a lot of enterprises. He and his brother are the real owners of Bertram's Hotel.'

'Thank you, sir.' Chief-Inspector Davy rose to his feet. 'I needn't tell you that I'm much obliged to you. It's wonderful,' he added, allowing himself to show more enthusiasm than was normal.

'That I should know?' inquired Mr Robinson, giving one of his larger smiles. 'But that is one of my specialities. Information. I like to know. That is why you came to me, is it not?'

'Well,' said Chief-Inspector Davy, 'we do know about you. The Home Office. The Special Branch and all the rest of it.' He added almost naïvely, 'It took a bit of nerve on my part to approach you.'

Again Mr Robinson smiled.

'I find you an interesting personality, Chief-Inspector Davy,' he said. 'I wish you success in whatever you are undertaking.'

'Thank you, sir. I think I shall need it. By the way, these

two brothers, would you say they were violent men?'

'Certainly not,' said Mr Robinson. 'It would be quite against their policy. The brothers Hoffman do not apply violence in business matters. They have other methods that serve them better. Year by year, I would say, they get steadily richer, or so my information from Swiss Banking circles tells me.'

'It's a useful place, Switzerland,' said Chief-Inspector Davy.

'Yes, indeed. What we should all do without it I do not know! So much rectitude. Such a fine business sense! Yes, we business men must all be very grateful to Switzerland. I myself,' he added, 'have also a high opinion of Amsterdam.' He looked hard at Davy, then smiled again, and the Chief-Inspector left.

When he got back to headquarters again, he found a note awaiting him.

Canon Pennyfather has turned up—safe if not sound. Apparently was knocked down by a car at Milton St John and has concussion.

CHAPTER XVIII

CANON PENNYFATHER looked at Chief-Inspector Davy and Inspector Campbell, and Chief-Inspector Davy and Inspector Campbell looked at him. Canon Pennyfather was at home again. Sitting in the big arm-chair in his library, a pillow behind his head and his feet up on a pouffe, with a rug over his knees to emphasize his invalid status.

'I'm afraid,' he was saying politely, 'that I simply cannot remember anything at all.'

'You can't remember the accident when the car hit you?'

'I'm really afraid not.'

'Then how did you know a car hit you?' demanded Inspector Campbell acutely.

'The woman there, Mrs—Mrs—was her name Wheeling?—told me about it.'

'And how did she know?'

Canon Pennyfather looked puzzled.

'Dear me, you are quite right. She couldn't have known, could she? I suppose she thought it was what must have happened.'

'And you really cannot remember *anything*? How did you come to be in Milton St John?'

'I've no idea,' said Canon Pennyfather. 'Even the name is quite unfamiliar to me.'

Inspector Campbell's exasperation was mounting, but Chief-Inspector Davy said in his soothing, homely voice,

'Just tell us again the last thing you do remember, sir.'

Canon Pennyfather turned to him with relief. The inspector's dry scepticism had made him uncomfortable.

'I was going to Lucerne to a congress. I took a taxi to the airport—at least to Kensington Air Station.'

'Yes. And then?'

'That's all. I can't remember any more. The next thing I remember is the wardrobe.'

'What wardrobe?' demanded Inspector Campbell.

'It was in the wrong place.'

Inspector Campbell was tempted to go into this question of a wardrobe in the wrong place. Chief-Inspector Davy cut in.

'Do you remember arriving at the air station, sir?'

'I suppose so,' said Canon Pennyfather, with the air of one who has a great deal of doubt on the matter.

'And you duly flew to Lucerne.'

'Did I? I don't remember anything about it if so.'

'Do you remember arriving back at Bertram's Hotel that night?'

'No.'

'You do remember Bertram's Hotel?'

'Of course. I was staying there. Very comfortable. I kept my room on.'

'Do you remember travelling in a train?'

'A train? No, I can't recall a train.'

'There was a hold-up. The train was robbed. Surely, Canon Pennyfather, you can remember *that*.'

'I ought to, oughtn't I?' said Canon Pennyfather. 'But somehow—' he spoke apologetically, '—I don't.' He looked from one to the other of the officers with a bland gentle smile.

'Then your story is that you remember nothing after going in a taxi to the air station until you woke up in the Wheelings' cottage at Milton St John.'

'There is nothing unusual in that,' the Canon assured him. 'It happens quite often in cases of concussion.'

'What did you think had happened to you when you woke up?'

'I had such a headache I really couldn't think. Then of course I began to wonder where I was and Mrs Wheeling explained and brought me some excellent soup. She called me "love" and "dearie", and "ducks",' said the Canon with slight distaste, 'but she was very kind. Very kind indeed.'

'She ought to have reported the accident to the police. Then you would have been taken to hospital and properly looked after,' said Campbell.

'She looked after me very well,' the Canon protested, with spirit, 'and I understand that with concussion there is very little you *can* do except keep the patient quiet.'

'If you should remember anything more, Canon Pennyfather—'

The Canon interrupted him.

'Four whole days I seem to have lost out of my life,' he said. 'Very curious. Really very curious indeed. I wonder so much where I was and what I was doing. The doctor tells me it may all come back to me. On the other hand it may not. Possibly I shall never know what happened to me during those days.' His eyelids flickered. 'You'll excuse me. I think I am rather tired.'

'That's quite enough now,' said Mrs McCrae, who had been hovering by the door, ready to intervene if she thought it necessary. She advanced upon them. 'Doctor says he wasn't to be worried,' she said firmly.

The policemen rose and moved towards the door. Mrs McCrae shepherded them out into the hall rather in the manner of a conscientious sheepdog. The Canon murmured something and Chief-Inspector Davy who was the last to pass through the door wheeled round at once.

'What was that?' he asked, but the Canon's eyes were now closed.

'What did you think he said?' said Campbell as they left the house after refusing Mrs McCrae's lukewarm offer of refreshment.

Father said thoughtfully,

'I thought he said "the walls of Jericho".'

'What could he mean by that?'

'It sounds biblical,' said Father.

'Do you think we'll ever know,' asked Campbell, 'how that old boy got from the Cromwell Road to Milton St John?'

'It doesn't seem as if we shall get much help from him,' agreed Davy.

'That woman who says she saw him on the train after the hold-up. Can she possibly be right? Can he be mixed up in some way with these robberies? It seems impossible. He's such a thoroughly respectable old boy. Can't very well suspect a Canon of Chadminster Cathedral of being mixed up with a train robbery, can one?'

'No,' said Father thoughtfully, 'no. No more than one can imagine Mr Justice Ludgrove being mixed up with a bank hold-up.'

Inspector Campbell looked at his superior officer curiously.

The expedition to Chadminster concluded with a short and unprofitable interview with Dr Stokes.

Dr Stokes was aggressive, unco-operative and rude.

'I've known the Wheelings quite a while. They're by way of being neighbours of mine. They'd picked some old chap up off the road. Didn't know whether he was dead drunk, or ill. Asked me in to have a look. I told them he wasn't drunk—that it was concussion—'

'And you treated him for that.'

'Not at all. I didn't treat him, or prescribe for him or attend him. I'm not a doctor—I was once, but I'm not now—I told them what they ought to do was ring up the police. Whether they did or not I don't know. Not my business. They're a bit dumb, both of them—but kindly folk.'

'You didn't think of ringing up the police yourself?'

'No, I did not. I'm not a doctor. Nothing to do with me. As a human being I told them not to pour whisky down his throat and to keep him quiet and flat until the police came.'

He glared at them and, reluctantly, they had to leave it at that.

CHAPTER XIX

Mr Hoffman was a big solid-looking man. He gave the appearance of being carved out of wood—preferably teak.

His face was so expressionless as to give rise to surmise—could such a man be capable of thinking—of feeling emotion? It seemed impossible.

His manner was highly correct.

He rose, bowed, and held out a wedge-like hand.

'Chief-Inspector Davy? It is some years since I had the pleasure—you may not even remember—'

'Oh yes I do, Mr Hoffman. The Aaronberg Diamond Case. You were a witness for the Crown—a most excellent witness, let me say. The Defence was quite unable to shake you.'

'I am not easily shaken,' said Mr Hoffman gravely.

He did not look a man who would easily be shaken.

'What can I do for you?' he went on. 'No trouble, I hope —I always want to agree well with the police. I have the greatest admiration for your superb police force.'

'Oh! there is no trouble. It is just that we wanted you to confirm a little information.'

'I shall be delighted to help you in any way I can. As I say, I have the highest opinion of your London Police Force. You have such a splendid class of men. So full of integrity, so fair, so just.'

'You'll make me embarrassed,' said Father.

'I am at your service. What is it that you want to know?'

'I was just going to ask you to give me a little dope about Bertram's Hotel.'

Mr Hoffman's face did not change. It was possible that his entire attitude became for a moment or two even more static than it had been before—that was all.

'Bertram's Hotel?' he said. His voice was inquiring, slightly puzzled. It might have been that he had never heard of Bertram's Hotel or that he could not quite remember whether he knew Bertram's Hotel or not.

'You have a connection with it, have you not, Mr Hoffman?'

Mr Hoffman moved his shoulders.

'There are so many things,' he said. 'One cannot remember them all. So much business—so much—it keeps me very busy.'

'You have your fingers in a lot of pies, I know that.'

'Yes,' Mr Hoffman smiled a wooden smile. 'I pull out many plums, that is what you think? And so you believe I have a connection with this—Bertram's Hotel?'

'I shouldn't have said a connection. As a matter of fact, you own it, don't you?' said Father genially.

This time, Mr Hoffman definitely did stiffen.

'Now who told you *that*, I wonder?' he said softly.

'Well, it's true, isn't it?' said Chief-Inspector Davy, cheerfully. 'Very nice place to own, I should say. In fact, you must be quite proud of it.'

'Oh yes,' said Hoffman. 'For the moment—I could not quite remember—you see—' he smiled deprecatingly, '—I own quite a lot of property in London. It is a good investment—property. If something comes on the market in what I think is a good position, and there is a chance of snapping it up cheap, I invest.'

'And was Bertram's Hotel going cheap?'

'As a running concern, it had gone down the hill,' said Mr Hoffman, shaking his head.

'Well, it's on its feet now,' said Father. 'I was in there just the other day. I was very much struck with the atmosphere there. Nice old-fashioned clientele, comfortable, old-fashioned premises, nothing rackety about it, a lot of luxury without looking luxurious.'

'I know very little about it personally,' explained Mr Hoffman. 'It is just one of my investments—but I believe it is doing well.'

'Yes, you seem to have a first-class fellow running it. What is his name? Humfries? Yes, Humfries.'

'An excellent man,' said Mr Hoffman. 'I leave everything to him. I look at the balance sheet once a year to see that all is well.'

'The place was thick with titles,' said Father. 'Rich travelling Americans, too.' He shook his head thoughtfully. 'Wonderful combination.'

'You say you were in there the other day?' Mr Hoffman inquired. 'Not—not officially, I hope?'

'Nothing serious. Just trying to clear up a little mystery.'

'A mystery? In Bertram's Hotel?'

'So it seems. The Case of the Disappearing Clergyman, you might label it.'

'That is a joke,' Mr Hoffman said. 'That is your Sherlock Holmes language.'

'This clergyman walked out of the place one evening and was never seen again.'

'Peculiar,' said Mr Hoffman, 'but such things happen. I

remember many, many years ago now, a great sensation. Colonel—now let me think of his name—Colonel Fergusson I think, one of the equerries of Queen Mary. He walked out of his club one night and he, too, was never seen again.'

'Of course,' said Father, with a sigh, 'a lot of these disappearances are voluntary.'

'You know more about that than I do, my dear Chief Inspector,' said Mr Hoffman. He added, 'I hope they gave you every assistance at Bertram's Hotel?'

'They couldn't have been nicer,' Father assured him. 'That Miss Gorringe, she has been with you some time, I believe?'

'Possibly. I really know so very little about it. I take no *personal* interest, you understand. In fact—' he smiled disarmingly, '—I was surprised that you even knew it belonged to me.'

It was not quite a question; but once more there was a slight uneasiness in his eyes. Father noted it without seeming to.

'The ramifications that go on in the City are like a gigantic jigsaw,' he said. 'It would make my head ache if I had to deal with that side of things. I gather that a company—Mayfair Holding Trust or some name like that—is the registered owner. They're owned by another company and so on and so on. The real truth of the matter is that it belongs to *you*. Simple as that. I'm right, aren't I?'

'I and my fellow directors are what I dare say you'd call behind it, yes,' admitted Mr Hoffman rather reluctantly.

'Your fellow directors. And who might they be? Yourself and, I believe, a brother of yours?'

'My brother Wilhelm is associated with me in this venture. You must understand that Bertram's is only a part of a chain of various hotels, offices, clubs and other London properties.'

'Any other directors?'

'Lord Pomfret, Abel Isaacstein.' Hoffman's voice was suddenly edged. 'Do you really need to know all these things? Just because you are looking into the Case of the Disappearing Clergyman?'

Father shook his head and looked apologetic.

'I suppose it's really curiosity. Looking for my disappearing clergyman was what took me to Bertram's, but then I got—well, interested if you understand what I mean. One thing leads to another sometimes, doesn't it?'

'I suppose that could be so, yes. And now?' he smiled, 'your curiosity is satisfied?'

'Nothing like coming to the horse's mouth when you want information, is there?' said Father, genially. He rose to his feet. 'There's only one thing I'd really like to know—and I don't suppose you'll tell me that.'

'Yes, Chief-Inspector?' Hoffman's voice was wary.

'Where do Bertram's get hold of their staff? Wonderful! That fellow what's-his-name—Henry. The one that looks like an Archduke or an Archbishop, I'm not sure which. Anyway, he serves you tea and muffins—most wonderful muffins! An unforgettable experience.'

'You like muffins with much butter, yes?' Mr Hoffman's eyes rested for a moment on the rotundity of Father's figure with disapprobation.

'I expect you can see I do,' said Father. 'Well, I mustn't be keeping you. I expect you're pretty busy taking over take-over bids, or something like that.'

'Ah. It amuses you to pretend to be ignorant of all these things. No, I am not busy. I do not let business absorb me too much. My tastes are simple. I live simply, with leisure, with growing of roses, and my family to whom I am devoted.'

'Sounds ideal,' said Father. 'Wish I could live like that.'

Mr Hoffman smiled and rose ponderously to shake hands with him.

'I hope you will find your disappearing clergyman very soon.'

'Oh! that's all right. I'm sorry I didn't make myself clear. He's found—disappointing case, really. Had a car accident and got concussion—simple as that.'

Father went to the door, then turned and asked:

'By the way, is Lady Sedgwick a director of your company?'

'Lady Sedgwick?' Hoffman took a moment or two. 'No. Why should she be?'

'Oh well, one hears things— Just a shareholder?'

'I—yes.'

'Well, goodbye, Mr Hoffman. Thanks very much.'

Father went back to the Yard and straight to the A.C.

'The two Hoffman brothers are the ones behind Bertram's Hotel—financially.'

'What? Those scoundrels?' demanded Sir Ronald.

'Yes.'

'They've kept it very dark.'

'Yes—and Robert Hoffman didn't half like our finding it out. It was a shock to him.'

'What did he say?'

'Oh, we kept it all very formal and polite. He tried, not

too obviously, to learn how I had found out about it.'

'And you didn't oblige him with that information, I suppose.'

'I certainly did not.'

'What excuse did you give for going to see him?'

'I didn't give any,' said Father.

'Didn't he think that a bit odd?'

'I expect he did. On the whole I thought that was a good way to play it, sir.'

'If the Hoffmans are behind all this, it accounts for a lot. They're never concerned in anything crooked themselves—oh no! *They* don't organize crime—they finance it though!

'Wilhelm deals with the banking side from Switzerland. He was behind those foreign currency rackets just after the war—we knew it—but we couldn't prove it. Those two brothers control a great deal of money and they use it for backing all kinds of enterprises—some legitimate—some not. But they're careful—they know every trick of the trade. Robert's diamond broking is straightforward enough—but it makes a suggestive picture—diamonds—banking interests, and property—clubs, cultural foundations, office buildings, restaurants, hotels—all apparently owned by somebody else.'

'Do you think Hoffman is the planner of these organized robberies?'

'No, I think those two deal only with finance. No, you'll have to look elsewhere for your planner. Somewhere there's a first-class brain at work.'

CHAPTER XX

THE FOG had come down over London suddenly that evening. Chief-Inspector Davy pulled up his coat collar and turned into Pond Street. Walking slowly like a man who was thinking of something else, he did not look particularly purposeful but anyone who knew him well would realize that his mind was wholly alert. He was prowling as a cat prowls before the moment comes for it to pounce on its prey.

Pond Street was quiet tonight. There were few cars about. The fog had been patchy to begin with, had almost cleared, then had deepened again. The noise of the traffic from Park Lane was muted to the level of a suburban side road. Most of the buses had given up. Only from time to time individual cars went on their way with determined optimism. Chief-Inspector Davy turned up a cul-de-sac, went to the end of it and came back again. He turned again, aimlessly as it seemed, first one way, then the other, but he was not aimless. Actually his cat prowl was taking him in a circle round one particular building. Bertram's Hotel. He was appraising carefully just what lay to the east of it, to the west of it, to the north of it and to the south of it. He examined the cars that were parked by the pavement, he examined the cars that were in the cul-de-sac. He examined a mews with special care. One car in particular interested him and he stopped. He pursed up his lips and said softly,

'So you're here again, you beauty.' He checked the number and nodded to himself. 'FAN 2266 tonight, are you?' He bent down and ran his fingers over the number plate delicately, then nodded approval. 'Good job they made of it,' he said under his breath.

He went on, came out at the other end of the mews, turned right and right again and came out in Pond Street once more, fifty yards from the entrance of Bertram's Hotel. Once again he paused, admiring the handsome lines of yet another racing car.

'You're a beauty, too,' said Chief-Inspector Davy. 'Your number plate's the same as the last time I saw you. I rather fancy your number plate always *is* the same. And that should mean—' he broke off '—or should it?' he muttered. He looked up towards what could have been the sky. 'Fog's getting thicker,' he said to himself.

Outside the door to Bertram's, the Irish commissionaire was standing swinging his arms backwards and forwards with some violence to keep himself warm. Chief-Inspector Davy said good evening to him.

'Good evening, sir. Nasty night.'

'Yes. I shouldn't think anyone would want to go out tonight who hadn't got to.'

The swing doors were pushed open and a middle-aged lady came out and paused uncertainly on the step.

'Want a taxi, ma'am?'

'Oh dear. I meant to walk.'

'I wouldn't if I were you, ma'am. It's very nasty, this fog. Even in a taxi it won't be too easy.'

'Do you think you could find me a taxi?' said the lady doubtfully.

'I'll do my best. You go inside now, and keep warm and

I'll come in and tell you if I've got one.' His voice changed, modulated to a persuasive tone. 'Unless you *have* to, ma'am, I wouldn't go out tonight at all.'

'Oh dear. Perhaps you're right. But I'm expected at some friends in Chelsea. I don't know. It might be very difficult getting back here. What do you think?'

Michael Gorman took charge.

'If I were you, ma'am,' he said firmly, 'I'd go in and telephone to your friends. It's not nice for a lady like you to be out on a foggy night like this.'

'Well—really—yes, well, perhaps you're right.'

She went back in again.

'I have to look after them,' said Micky Gorman turning in an explanatory manner to Father. 'That kind would get her bag snatched, she would. Going out this time of night in a fog and wandering about Chelsea or West Kensington or wherever she's trying to go.'

'I suppose you've had a good deal of experience of dealing with elderly ladies?' said Davy.

'Ah yes, indeed. This place is a home from home to them, bless their ageing hearts. How about you, sir? Were you wanting a taxi?'

'Don't suppose you could get me one if I did,' said Father. 'There don't seem to be many about in this. And I don't blame them.'

'Ah, now, I might lay my hand on one for you. There's a place round the corner where there's usually a taxi driver got his cab parked, having a warm up and a drop of something to keep the cold out.'

'A taxi's no good to me,' said Father with a sigh.

He jerked his thumb towards Bertram's Hotel.

'I've got to go inside. I've got a job to do.'

'Indeed now? Would it be still the missing Canon?'

'Not exactly. He's been found.'

'Found?' The man stared at him. 'Found where?'

'Wandering about with concussion after an accident.'

'Ah, that's just what one might expect of him. Crossed the road without looking, I expect.'

'That seems to be the idea,' said Father.

He nodded, and pushed through the doors into the hotel. There were not very many people in the lounge this evening. He saw Miss Marple sitting in a chair near the fire and Miss Marple saw him. She made, however, no sign of recognition. He went towards the desk. Miss Gorringe, as usual, was behind her books. She was, he thought, faintly discomposed to see him. It was a very slight reaction, but he noted the fact.

'You remember me, Miss Gorringe,' he said. 'I came here the other day.'

'Yes, of course I remember you, Chief-Inspector. Is there anything more you want to know? Do you want to see Mr Humfries?'

'No thank you. I don't think that'll be necessary. I'd just like one more look at your register if I may.'

'Of course.' She pushed it along to him.

He opened it and looked slowly down the pages. To Miss Gorringe he gave the appearance of a man looking for one particular entry. In actuality this was not the case. Father had an accomplishment which he had learnt early in life and had developed into a highly skilled art. He could remember names and addresses with a perfect and photographic memory. That memory would remain with him for twenty-four or even forty-eight hours. He shook his head as he shut the book and returned it to her.

'Canon Pennyfather hasn't been in, I suppose?' he said in a light voice.

'Canon Pennyfather?'

'You know he's turned up again?'

'No indeed. Nobody has told *me*. Where?'

'Some place in the country. Car accident it seems. Wasn't reported to us. Some good Samaritan just picked him up and looked after him.'

'Oh! I am pleased. Yes, I really am very pleased. I was worried about him.'

'So were his friends,' said Father. 'Actually I was looking to see if one of them might be staying here now. Archdeacon —Archdeacon—I can't remember his name now, but I'd know it if I saw it.'

'Tomlinson?' said Miss Gorringe helpfully. 'He is due next week. From Salisbury.'

'No, not Tomlinson. Well, it doesn't matter.' He turned away.

It was quiet in the lounge tonight.

An ascetic looking middle-aged man was reading through a badly typed thesis, occasionally writing a comment in the margin in such small crabbed handwriting as to be almost illegible. Every time he did this, he smiled in vinegary satisfaction.

There were one or two married couples of long standing who had little need to talk to each other. Occasionally two or three people were gathered together in the name of the weather conditions, discussing anxiously how they or their families were going to get where they wanted to be.

'—I rang up and begged Susan not to come by car . . . it

means the M1 and always so dangerous in fog—'

'They say it's clearer in the Midlands . . .'

Chief-Inspector Davy noted them as he passed. Without haste, and with no seeming purpose, he arrived at his objective.

Miss Marple was sitting near the fire and observing his approach.

'So you're still here, Miss Marple. I'm glad.'

'I go tomorrow,' said Miss Marple.

That fact had, somehow, been implicit in her attitude. She had sat, not relaxed, but upright, as one sits in an airport lounge, or a railway waiting-room. Her luggage, he was sure, would be packed, only toilet things and night wear to be added.

'It is the end of my fortnight's holiday,' she explained.

'You've enjoyed it, I hope?'

Miss Marple did not answer at once.

'In a way—yes . . .' She stopped.

'And in another way, no?'

'It's difficult to explain what I mean—'

'Aren't you, perhaps, a little too near the fire? Rather hot, here. Wouldn't you like to move—into that corner perhaps.'

Miss Marple looked at the corner indicated, then she looked at Chief-Inspector Davy.

'I think you are quite right,' she said.

He gave her a hand up, carried her handbag and her book for her and established her in the quiet corner he had indicated.

'All right?'

'Quite all right.'

'You know why I suggested it?'

'You thought—very kindly—that it was too hot for me by the fire. Besides,' she added, 'our conversation cannot be overheard here.'

'Have you got something you want to tell me, Miss Marple?'

'Now why should you think that?'

'You looked as though you had,' said Davy.

'I'm sorry I showed it so plainly,' said Miss Marple. 'I didn't mean to.'

'Well, what about it?'

'I don't know if I ought to do so. I would like you to believe, Inspector, that I am not really fond of interfering. I am against interference. Though often well meant, it can cause a great deal of harm.'

'It's like that, is it? I see. Yes, it's quite a problem for you.'

'Sometimes one sees people doing things that seem to one unwise—even dangerous. But has one any right to interfere? Usually not, I think.'

'Is this Canon Pennyfather you're talking about?'

'Canon Pennyfather?' Miss Marple sounded very surprised. 'Oh no. Oh dear me no, nothing whatever to do with him. It concerns—a girl.'

'A girl, indeed? And you thought I could help?'

'I don't know,' said Miss Marple. 'I simply don't know. But I'm worried, very worried.'

Father did not press her. He sat there looking large and comfortable and rather stupid. He let her take her time. She had been willing to do her best to help him, and he was quite prepared to do anything he could to help her. He was not, perhaps, particularly interested. On the other hand, one never knew.

'One reads in the papers,' said Miss Marple in a low clear voice, 'accounts of proceedings in court, of young people, children or girls "in need of care and protection". It's just a sort of legal phrase, I suppose, but it could mean something real.'

'This girl you mentioned, you feel she is in need of care and protection?'

'Yes. Yes I do.'

'Alone in the world?'

'Oh no,' said Miss Marple. 'Very much not so, if I may put it that way. She is to all outward appearances very heavily protected and very well cared for.'

'Sounds interesting,' said Father.

'She was staying in this hotel,' said Miss Marple, 'with a Mrs Carpenter, I think. I looked in the register to see the name. The girl's name is Elvira Blake.'

Father looked up with a quick air of interest.

'She was a lovely girl. Very young, very much as I say, sheltered and protected. Her guardian was a Colonel Luscombe, a very nice man. Quite charming. Elderly of course, and I am afraid terribly innocent.'

'The guardian or the girl?'

'I meant the guardian,' said Miss Marple. 'I don't know about the girl. But I do think she is in danger. I came across her quite by chance in Battersea Park. She was sitting at a refreshment place there with a young man.'

'Oh, that's it, is it?' said Father. 'Undesirable, I suppose. Beatnik—spiv—thug—'

'A very handsome man,' said Miss Marple. 'Not so very young. Thirty-odd, the kind of man that I should say is very attractive to women, but his face is a bad face. Cruel, hawk-like, predatory.'

'He mayn't be as bad as he looks,' said Father soothingly.

'If anything he is worse than he looks,' said Miss Marple. 'I am convinced of it. He drives a large racing car.'

Father looked up quickly.

'Racing car?'

'Yes. Once or twice I've seen it standing near this hotel.'

'You don't remember the number, do you?'

'Yes, indeed I do. FAN 2266. I had a cousin who stuttered,' Miss Marple explained. 'That's how I remember it.'

Father looked puzzled.

'Do you know who he is?' demanded Miss Marple.

'As a matter of fact I do,' said Father slowly. 'Half French, half Polish. Very well known racing driver, he was world champion three years ago. His name is Ladislaus Malinowski. You're quite right in some of your views about him. He has a bad reputation where women are concerned. That is to say, he is not a suitable friend for a young girl. But it's not easy to do anything about that sort of thing. I suppose she is meeting him on the sly, is that it?'

'Almost certainly,' said Miss Marple.

'Did you approach her guardian?'

'I don't know him,' said Miss Marple. 'I've only just been introduced to him once by a mutual friend. I don't like the idea of going to him in a tale-bearing way. I wondered if perhaps in some way *you* could do something about it.'

'I can try,' said Father. 'By the way, I thought you might like to know that your friend, Canon Pennyfather, has turned up all right.'

'Indeed!' Miss Marple looked animated. 'Where?'

'A place called Milton St John.'

'How very odd. What was he doing there? Did he know?'

'*Apparently*—' Chief-Inspector Davy stressed the word.

'—He had had an accident.'

'What kind of an accident?'

'Knocked down by a car—concussed—or else, of course, he might have been conked on the head.'

'Oh! I see.' Miss Marple considered the point. 'Doesn't he know himself?'

'He *says*—' again the Chief-Inspector stressed the word, '—that he does not know anything.'

'Very remarkable.'

'Isn't it? The last thing he remembers is driving in a taxi to Kensington Air Station.'

Miss Marple shook her head perplexedly.

'I know it does happen that way in concussion,' she murmured. 'Didn't he say anything—useful?'

'He murmured something about the Walls of Jericho.'

'Joshua?' hazarded Miss Marple, 'or Archæology—excavations?—or I remember, long ago, a play—by Mr Sutro, I think.'

'And all this week north of the Thames, Gaumont Cinemas—*The Walls of Jericho*, featuring Olga Radbourne and Bart Levinne,' said Father.

Miss Marple looked at him suspiciously.

'He could have gone to that film in the Cromwell Road. He could have come out about eleven and come back here—though if so, someone ought to have seen him—it would be well before midnight—'

'Took the wrong bus,' Miss Marple suggested. 'Something like that—'

'Say he got back here *after* midnight,' Father said, '—he *could* have walked up to his room without anyone seeing him— But if so, what happened then—and why did he go out again three hours later?'

Miss Marple groped for a word.

'The only idea that occurs to me is—oh!'

She jumped as a report sounded from the street outside.

'Car backfiring,' said Father soothingly.

'I'm sorry to be so jumpy—I am nervous tonight—that feeling one has—'

'That something's going to happen? I don't think you need worry.'

'I have never liked fog.'

'I wanted to tell you,' said Chief-Inspector Davy, 'that you've given me a lot of help. The things you've noticed here—just little things—they've added up.'

'So there *was* something wrong with this place?'

'There was and is everything wrong with it.'

Miss Marple sighed.

'It seemed wonderful at first—unchanged you know—like stepping back into the past—to the part of the past that one had loved and enjoyed.'

She paused.

'But of course, it wasn't really like that. I learned (what I suppose I really knew already) that one can never go back, that one should not ever try to go back—that the essence of life is going forward. Life is really a One Way Street, isn't it?'

'Something of the sort,' agreed Father.

'I remember,' said Miss Marple, diverging from her main topic in a characteristic way, 'I remember being in Paris with my mother and my grandmother, and we went to have tea at the Elysée Hotel. And my grandmother looked round, and she said suddenly, "Clara, I do believe I am the only woman here in a *bonnet*!" And she was, too! When she got home she packed up all her bonnets, and her beaded mantles too—and sent them off—'

'To the Jumble Sale?' inquired Father, sympathetically.

'Oh no. Nobody would have wanted them at a jumble sale. She sent them to a theatrical Repertory Company. They appreciated them very much. But let me see—' Miss Marple recovered her direction. '—Where was I?'

'Summing up this place.'

'Yes. It seemed all right—but it wasn't. It was mixed up—real people and people who weren't real. One couldn't always tell them apart.'

'What do you mean by not real?'

'There were retired military men, but there were also what seemed to be military men but who had never been in the army. And clergymen who weren't clergymen. And admirals and sea captains who've never been in the navy. My friend, Selina Hazy—it amused me at first how she was always so anxious to recognize people she knew (quite natural, of course) and how often she was mistaken and they weren't the people she thought they were. But it happened too often. And so—I began to wonder. Even Rose, the chambermaid—so nice—but I began to think that perhaps *she* wasn't real, either.'

'If it interests you to know, she's an ex-actress. A good one. Gets a better salary here than she ever drew on the stage.'

'But—why?'

'Mainly, as part of the décor. Perhaps there's more than that to it.'

'I'm glad to be leaving here,' said Miss Marple. She gave a little shiver. 'Before anything happens.'

Chief-Inspector Davy looked at her curiously.

'What do you expect to happen?' he asked.

'Evil of some kind,' said Miss Marple.

'Evil is rather a big word—'

'You think it is too melodramatic? But I have some experience—I seem to have been—so often—in contact with murder.'

'Murder?' Chief-Inspector Davy shook his head. 'I'm not suspecting murder. Just a nice cosy round up of some remarkably clever criminals—'

'That's not the same thing. Murder—the wish to do murder—is something quite different. It—how shall I say—it defies God.'

He looked at her and shook his head gently and reassuringly.

'There won't be any murders,' he said.

A sharp report, louder than the former one, came from outside. It was followed by a scream and another report.

Chief-Inspector Davy was on his feet, moving with a speed surprising in such a bulky man. In a few seconds he was through the swing doors and out in the street.

II

The screaming—a woman's—was piercing the mist with a note of terror. Chief-Inspector Davy raced down Pond Street in the direction of the screams. He could dimly visualize a woman's figure backed against a railing. In a dozen strides he had reached her. She wore a long pale fur coat, and her shining blonde hair hung down each side of her face. He thought for a moment that he knew who she was, then he realized that this was only a slip of a girl. Sprawled on the pavement at her feet was the body of a man in uniform. Chief-Inspector Davy recognized him. It was Michael Gorman.

As Davy came up to the girl, she clutched at him, shivering all over, stammering out broken phrases.

'Someone tried to kill me . . . Someone . . . they shot at me . . . If it hadn't been for *him*—' she pointed down at the motionless figure at her feet. 'He pushed me back and got in front of me—and then the second shot came . . . and he fell . . . He saved my life. I think he's hurt—badly hurt . . .'

Chief-Inspector Davy went down on one knee. His torch came out. The tall Irish commissionaire had fallen like a soldier. The left hand side of his tunic showed a wet patch that was growing wetter as the blood oozed out into the cloth. Davy rolled up an eyelid, touched a wrist. He rose to his feet again.

'He's had it all right,' he said.

The girl gave a sharp cry. 'Do you mean he's *dead*? Oh no, no! He can't be *dead*.'

'Who was it shot at you?'

'I don't know . . . I'd left my car just round the corner and was feeling my way along by the railings—I was going to Bertram's Hotel. And then suddenly there was a shot—and a bullet went past my cheek and then—he—the porter from Bertram's—came running down the street towards me, and shoved me behind him, and then another shot came . . . I think—I think whoever it was must have been hiding in that area there.'

Chief-Inspector Davy looked where she pointed. At this end of Bertram's Hotel there was an old-fashioned area below the level of the street, with a gate and some steps

BERTRAMS HOTEL

down to it. Since it gave only on some store-rooms it was not much used. But a man could have hidden there easily enough.

'You didn't see him?'

'Not properly. He rushed past me like a shadow. It was all thick fog.'

Davy nodded.

The girl began to sob hysterically.

'But who could possibly want to kill me? Why should anyone want to kill me? That's the second time. I don't understand . . . why . . .'

One arm round the girl, Chief-Inspector Davy fumbled in his pocket with the other hand.

The shrill notes of a police whistle penetrated the mist.

III

In the lounge of Bertram's Hotel, Miss Gorringe had looked up sharply from the desk.

One or two of the visitors had looked up also. The older and deafer did not look up.

Henry, about to lower a glass of old brandy to a table, stopped poised with it still in his hand.

Miss Marple sat forward, clutching the arms of her chair. A retired admiral said decisively,

'Accident! Cars collided in the fog, I expect.'

The swing doors from the street were pushed open. Through them came what seemed like an outsize policeman, looking a good deal larger than life.

He was supporting a girl in a pale fur coat. She seemed hardly able to walk. The policeman looked round for help with some embarrassment.

Miss Gorringe came out from behind the desk, prepared to cope. But at that moment the lift came down. A tall figure emerged, and the girl shook herself free from the policeman's support, and ran frantically across the lounge.

'Mother,' she cried. 'Oh *Mother, Mother . . .*' and threw herself, sobbing, into Bess Sedgwick's arms.

CHAPTER XXI

Chief-Inspector Davy settled himself back in his chair and looked at the two women sitting opposite him. It was past midnight. Police officials had come and gone. There had been doctors, fingerprint men, an ambulance to remove the body; and now everything had narrowed to this one room dedicated for the purposes of the Law by Bertram's Hotel. Chief-Inspector Davy sat one side of the table. Bess Sedgwick and Elvira sat the other side. Against the wall a policeman sat unobtrusively writing. Detective-Sergeant Wadell sat near the door.

Father looked thoughtfully at the two women facing him. Mother and daughter. There was, he noted, a strong superficial likeness between them. He could understand how for one moment in the fog he had taken Elvira Blake for Bess Sedgwick. But now, looking at them, he was more struck by the points of difference than the points of resemblance. They were not really alike save in colouring, yet the impression persisted that here he had a positive and a negative version of the same personality. Everything about Bess Sedgwick was positive. Her vitality, her energy, her magnetic attraction. He admired Lady Sedgwick. He always had admired her. He had admired her courage and had always been excited over her exploits; had said, reading his Sunday papers: 'She'll never get away with *that*,' and invariably she had got away with it! He had not thought it possible that she would reach journey's end and she had reached journey's end. He admired particularly the indestructible quality of her. She had had one air crash, several car crashes, had been thrown badly twice from her horse, but at the end of it here she was. Vibrant, alive, a personality one could not ignore for a moment. He took off his hat to her mentally. Some day, of course, she would come a cropper. You could only bear a charmed life for so long. His eyes went from mother to daughter. He wondered. He wondered very much.

In Elvira Blake, he thought, everything had been driven inward. Bess Sedgwick had got through life by imposing her will on it. Elvira, he guessed, had a different way of getting through life. She submitted, he thought. She obeyed. She smiled in compliance and behind that, he thought, she slipped away through your fingers. 'Sly,' he said to himself, appraising that fact. 'That's the only way she can manage, I expect. She can never brazen things out or impose herself. That's why, I expect, the people who've looked after her have never had the least idea of what she might be up to.'

He wondered what she had been doing slipping along the street to Bertram's Hotel on a late foggy evening. He was going to ask her presently. He thought it highly probable that the answer he would get would not be the true one. 'That's the way,' he thought, 'that the poor child defends herself.' Had she come here to meet her mother or to find her mother? It was perfectly possible, but he didn't think so. Not for a moment. Instead he thought of the big sports car tucked away round the corner—the car with the number plate FAN 2266. Ladislaus Malinowski must be somewhere in the neighbourhood since his car was there.

'Well,' said Father, addressing Elvira in his most kindly

and father-like manner, 'well, and how are you feeling now?'

'I'm quite all right,' said Elvira.

'Good. I'd like you to answer a few questions if you feel up to it; because, you see, time is usually the essence of these things. You were shot at twice and a man was killed. We want as many clues as we can get to the person who killed him.'

'I'll tell you everything I can, but it all came so suddenly. And you can't *see* anything in a fog. I've no idea myself who it could have been—or even what he looked like. That's what was so frightening.'

'You said this was the second time somebody had tried to kill you. Does that mean there was an attempt on your life before?'

'Did I say that? I can't remember.' Her eyes moved uneasily. 'I don't think I said that.'

'Oh, but you did, you know,' said Father.

'I expect I was just being—being hysterical.'

'No,' said Father, 'I don't think you were. I think you meant just what you said.'

'I might have been imagining things,' said Elvira. Her eyes shifted again.

Bess Sedgwick moved. She said quietly:

'You'd better tell him, Elvira.'

Elvira shot a quick, uneasy look at her mother.

'You needn't worry,' said Father, reassuringly. 'We know quite well in the police force that girls don't tell their mothers or their guardians everything. We don't take those things too seriously, but we've got to *know* about them, because, you see, it all helps.'

Bess Sedgwick said,

'Was it in Italy?'

'Yes,' said Elvira.

Father said: 'That's where you've been at school, isn't it, or to a finishing place or whatever they call it nowadays?'

'Yes. I was at Contessa Martinelli's. There were about eighteen or twenty of us.'

'And you thought that somebody tried to kill you. How was that?'

'Well, a big box of chocolates and sweets and things came for me. There was a card with it written in Italian in a flowery hand. The sort of thing they say, you know, "To the bellissima Signorina." Something like that. And my friends and I—well—we laughed about it a bit, and wondered who'd sent it.'

'Did it come by post?'

'No. No, it couldn't have come by post. It was just there in my room. Someone must have put it there.'

'I see. Bribed one of the servants, I suppose. I am to take it that you didn't let the Contessa whoever-it-was in on this?'

A faint smile appeared on Elvira's face. 'No. No. We certainly didn't. Anyway we opened the box and they were lovely chocolates. Different kinds, you know, but there were some violet creams. That's the sort of chocolate that has a crystallized violet on top. My favourite. So of course I ate one or two of those first. And then afterwards, in the night, I felt terribly ill. I didn't think it was the chocolates, I just thought it was something perhaps that I'd eaten at dinner.'

'Anybody else ill?'

'No. Only me. Well, I was very sick and all that, but I felt all right by the end of the next day. Then a day or two later I ate another of the same chocolates, and the same thing happened. So I talked to Bridget about it. Bridget was my special friend. And we looked at the chocolates, and we found that the violet creams had got a sort of hole in the bottom that had been filled up again, so we thought that someone had put some poison in and they'd only put it in the violet creams so that I would be the one who ate them.'

'Nobody else was ill?'

'No.'

'So presumably nobody else ate the violet creams?'

'No. I don't think they could have. You see, it was my present and they knew I liked the violet ones, so they'd leave them for me.'

'The chap took a risk, whoever he was,' said Father. 'The whole place might have been poisoned.'

'It's absurd,' said Lady Sedgwick sharply. 'Utterly absurd! I never heard of anything so crude.'

Chief-Inspector Davy made a slight gesture with his hand. 'Please,' he said, then he went on to Elvira: 'Now I find that very interesting, Miss Blake. And you still didn't tell the Contessa?'

'Oh no, we didn't. She'd have made a terrible fuss."

'What did you do with the chocolates?'

'We threw them away,' said Elvira. 'They were lovely chocolates,' she added, with a tone of slight grief.

'You didn't try and find out who sent them?'

Elvira looked embarrassed.

'Well, you see, I thought it might have been Guido.'

'Yes?' said Chief-Inspector Davy, cheerfully. 'And who is Guido?'

'Oh, Guido . . .' Elvira paused. She looked at her mother.

'Don't be stupid,' said Bess Sedgwick. 'Tell Chief-Inspector Davy about Guido, whoever he is. Every girl of your age has a Guido in her life. You met him out there, I suppose?'

'Yes. When we were taken to the opera. He spoke to me there. He was nice. Very attractive. I used to see him sometimes when we went to classes. He used to pass me notes.'

'And I suppose,' said Bess Sedgwick, 'that you told a lot of lies, and made plans with some friends and you managed to get out and meet him? Is that it?'

Elvira looked relieved by this short cut to confession.

'Yes. Bridget and I sometimes went out together. Sometimes Guido managed to—'

'What was Guido's other name?'

'I don't know,' said Elvira. 'He never told me.'

Chief-Inspector Davy smiled at her.

'You mean you're not going to tell? Never mind. I dare say we'll be able to find out quite all right without your help, if it should really matter. But why should you think that this young man, who was presumably fond of you, should want to kill you?'

'Oh, because he used to threaten things like that. I mean, we used to have rows now and then. He'd bring some of his friends with him, and I'd pretend to like them better than him, and then he'd get very, very wild and angry. He said I'd better be careful what I did. I couldn't give him up just like that! That if I wasn't faithful to him he'd kill me! I just thought he was being melodramatic and theatrical.' Elvira smiled suddenly and unexpectedly. 'But it was all rather fun. I didn't think it was *real* or *serious*.'

'Well,' said Chief-Inspector Davy, 'I don't think it *does* seem very likely that a young man such as you describe would really poison chocolates and send them to you.'

'Well, I don't think so really either,' said Elvira, 'but it must have been him because I can't see that there's anyone else. It worried me. And then, when I came back here, I got a note—' She stopped.

'What sort of a note?'

'It just came in an envelope and was printed. It said, '*Be on your guard. Somebody wants to kill you*".'

Chief-Inspector Davy's eyebrows went up.

'Indeed? Very curious. Yes, very curious. And it worried you. You were frightened?'

'Yes. I began to—to wonder who could possibly want me out of the way. That's why I tried to find out if I was really very rich.'

'Go on.'

'And the other day in London something else happened. I was in the tube and there were a lot of people on the platform. I thought someone tried to push me on to the line.'

'My dear child!' said Bess Sedgwick. 'Don't romance.'

Again Father made that slight gesture of his hand.

'Yes,' said Elvira apologetically. 'I expect I *have* been imagining it all but—I don't know—I mean, after what happened this evening it seems, doesn't it, as though it might all be true?' She turned suddenly to Bess Sedgwick, speaking with urgency, '*Mother*! *You* might know. *Does* anyone want to kill me? *Could* there be anyone? Have I got an enemy?'

'Of course you've not got an enemy,' said Bess Sedgwick, impatiently. 'Don't be an idiot. Nobody wants to kill you. Why should they?'

'Then who shot at me tonight?'

'In that fog,' said Bess Sedgwick, 'you might have been mistaken for someone else. That's possible, don't you think?' she said, turning to Father.

'Yes, I think it might be quite possible,' said Chief-Inspector Davy.

Bess Sedgwick was looking at him very intently. He almost fancied the motion of her lips saying 'later.'

'Well,' he said cheerfully, 'we'd better get down to some more facts now. Where had you come from tonight? What were you doing walking along Pond Street on such a foggy evening.'

'I came up for an Art class at the Tate this morning. Then I went to lunch with my friend Bridget. She lives in Onslow Square. We went to a film and when we came out, there was this fog—quite thick and getting worse, and I thought perhaps I'd better not drive home.'

'You drive a car, do you?'

'Yes. I took my driving test last summer. Only, I'm not a very good driver and I hate driving in fog. So Bridget's mother said I could stay the night, so I rang up Cousin Mildred—that's where I live in Kent—'

Father nodded.

'—and I said I was going to stay up over-night. She said that was very wise.'

'And what happened next?' asked Father.

'And then the fog seemed lighter suddenly. You know how patchy fogs are. So I said I would drive down to Kent after all. I said goodbye to Bridget and started off. But then it began to come down again. I didn't like it very much. I ran into a very thick patch of it and I lost my way and I didn't know where I was. Then after a bit I realized I was at Hyde Park Corner and I thought "I really *can't* go down to Kent in this." At first, I thought I'd go back to Bridget's but then I remembered how I'd lost my way already. And then I realized that I was quite close to this nice hotel where Uncle Derek took me, when I came back from Italy, and I thought, "I'll go there and I'm sure they can find me a room." That was fairly easy, I found a place to leave the car and then I walked back up the street towards the hotel.'

'Did you meet anyone or did you hear anyone walking near you?'

'It's funny you saying that, because I did think I heard someone walking behind me. Of course, there must be lots of people walking about in London. Only in a fog like this, it gives you a nervous feeling. I waited and listened but I didn't hear any footsteps and I thought I'd imagined them. I was quite close to the hotel by then.'

'And then?'

'And then quite suddenly there was a shot. As I told you, it seemed to go right past my ear. The commissionaire man who stands outside the hotel came running down towards me and he pushed me behind him and then—then—the other shot came . . . He—he fell down and I screamed.' She was shaking now. Her mother spoke to her.

'Steady, girl,' said Bess in a low, firm voice. 'Steady now.' It was the voice Bess Sedgwick used for her horses and it was quite as efficacious when used on her daughter. Elvira blinked at her, drew herself up a little, and became calm again.

'Good girl,' said Bess.

'And then *you* came,' said Elvira to Father. 'You blew your whistle, you told the policeman to take me into the hotel. And as soon as I got in, I saw—I saw Mother.' She turned and looked at Bess Sedgwick.

'And that brings us more or less up to date,' said Father. He shifted his bulk a little in the chair.

'Do you know a man called Ladislaus Malinowski?' he asked. His tone was even, casual, without any direct inflection. He did not look at the girl, but he was aware, since his ears were functioning at full attention, of a quick little gasp she gave. His eyes were not on the daughter but on the mother.

'No,' said Elvira, having waited just a shade too long to say it. 'No, I don't.'

'Oh,' said Father. 'I thought you might. I thought he might have been here this evening.'

'Oh? Why should he be here?'

'Well, his car is here,' said Father. 'That's why I thought he might be.'

'I don't know him,' said Elvira.

'My mistake,' said Father. 'You do, of course?' he turned his head towards Bess Sedgwick.

'Naturally,' said Bess Sedgwick. 'Known him for many years.' She added, smiling slightly, 'He's a madman, you know. Drives like an angel or a devil—he'll break his neck one of these days. Had a bad smash eighteen months ago.'

'Yes, I remember reading about it,' said Father. 'Not racing again yet, is he?'

'No, not yet. Perhaps he never will.'

'Do you think I could go to bed now?' asked Elvira, plaintively. 'I'm—really terribly tired.'

'Of course. You must be,' said Father. 'You've told us all you can remember?'

'Oh. Yes.'

'I'll go up with you,' said Bess.

Mother and daughter went out together.

'*She* knows him all right,' said Father.

'Do you really think so?' asked Sergeant Wadell.

'I know it. She had tea with him in Battersea Park only a day or two ago.'

'How did you find that out?'

'Old lady told me—distressed. Didn't think he was a nice friend for a young girl. He isn't of course.'

'Especially if he and the mother—' Wadell broke off delicately. 'It's pretty general gossip—'

'Yes. May be true, may not. Probably *is*.'

'In that case which one is he really after?'

Father ignored that point. He said:

'I want him picked up. I want him badly. His car's here —just round the corner.'

'Do you think he might be actually staying in this hotel?'

'Don't think so. It wouldn't fit into the picture. He's not supposed to be here. *If* he came here, he came to meet the girl. She definitely came to meet him, I'd say.'

The door opened and Bess Sedgwick reappeared.

'I came back,' she said, 'because I wanted to speak to you.'

She looked from him to the other two men.

'I wonder if I could speak to you alone? I've given you all the information I have, such as it is; but I would like a word or two with you in private.'

'I don't see any reason why not,' said Chief-Inspector Davy. He motioned with his head, and the young detective-constable took his note-book and went out. Wadell went with him. 'Well?' said Chief-Inspector Davy.

Lady Sedgwick sat down again opposite him.

'That silly story about poisoned chocolates,' she said. 'It's nonsense. Absolutely ridiculous. I don't believe anything of the kind ever happened.'

'You don't, eh?'

'Do you?'

Father shook his head doubtfully. 'You think your daughter cooked it up?'

'Yes. But why?'

'Well, if you don't know why,' said Chief-Inspector Davy, 'how should I know? She's your daughter. Presumably you know her better than I do.'

'I don't know her at all,' said Bess Sedgwick bitterly. 'I've not seen her or had anything to do with her since she was two years old, when I ran away from my husband.'

'Oh yes. I know all that. I find it curious. You see, Lady Sedgwick, courts usually give the mother, even if she is a guilty party in a divorce, custody of a young child if she asks for it. Presumably then you didn't ask for it? You didn't want it.'

'I thought it—better not.'

'Why?'

'I didn't think it was—safe for her.'

'On moral grounds?'

'No. Not on moral grounds. Plenty of adultery nowadays. Children have to learn about it, have to grow up with it. No. It's just that *I* am not really a safe person to be with. The life I'd lead wouldn't be a safe life. You can't help the way you're born. I was born to live dangerously. I'm not law-abiding or conventional. I thought it would be better for Elvira, happier, to have a proper English conventional bringing-up. Shielded, looked after . . .'

'But minus a mother's love?'

'I thought if she learned to love me it might bring sorrow to her. Oh, you mayn't believe me, but that's what I felt.'

'I see. Do you still think you were right?'

'No,' said Bess. 'I don't. I think now I may have been

entirely wrong.'

'*Does* your daughter know Ladislaus Malinowski?'

'I'm sure she doesn't. She said so. You heard her.'

'I heard her, yes.'

'Well, then?'

'She was afraid, you know, when she was sitting here. In our profession we get to know fear when we meet up with it. She was afraid—why? Chocolates or no chocolates, her life has been attempted. That tube story may be true enough—'

'It was ridiculous. Like a thriller—'

'Perhaps. But that sort of thing does happen, Lady Sedgwick. Oftener than you'd think. Can you give me any idea who might want to kill your daughter?'

'Nobody—nobody at all!'

She spoke vehemently.

Chief-Inspector Davy sighed and shook his head.

CHAPTER XXII

CHIEF-INSPECTOR DAVY waited patiently until Mrs Melford had finished talking. It had been a singularly unprofitable interview. Cousin Mildred had been incoherent, unbelieving and generally feather-headed. Or that was Father's private view. Accounts of Elvira's sweet manners, nice nature, troubles with her teeth, odd excuses told through the telephone, had led on to serious doubts whether Elvira's friend Bridget was really a suitable friend for her. All these matters had been presented to the Chief-Inspector in a kind of general hasty pudding. Mrs Melford knew nothing, had heard nothing, had seen nothing and had apparently deduced very little.

A short telephone call to Elvira's guardian, Colonel Luscombe, had been even more unproductive, though fortunately less wordy. 'More Chinese monkeys,' he muttered to his sergeant as he put down the receiver. 'See no evil, hear no evil, speak no evil.

'The trouble is that everyone who's had anything to do with this girl has been far too nice—if you get my meaning. Too many nice people who don't know anything about evil. Not like my old lady.'

'The Bertram's Hotel one?'

'Yes, that's the one. She's had a long life of experience in noticing evil, fancying evil, suspecting evil and going forth to do battle with evil. Let's see what we can get out of girl friend Bridget.'

The difficulties in this interview were represented first, last, and most of the time by Bridget's mamma. To talk to Bridget without the assistance of her mother took all Chief-Inspector Davy's adroitness and cajolery. He was, it must be admitted, ably seconded by Bridget. After a certain amount of stereotyped questions and answers and expressions of horror on the part of Bridget's mother at hearing of Elvira's narrow escape from death, Bridget said, 'You know it's time for that committee meeting, Mum. You said it was very important.'

'Oh dear, dear,' said Bridget's mother.

'You know they'll get into a frightful mess without you, Mummy.'

'Oh they will, they certainly will. But perhaps I ought—'

'Now that's quite all right, Madam,' said Chief-Inspector Davy, putting on his kindly old father look. 'You don't want to worry. Just you get off. I've finished all the important things. You've told me really everything I wanted to know. I've just one or two routine inquiries about people in Italy which I think your daughter, Miss Bridget, might be able to help me with.'

'Well, if you think you could manage, Bridget—'

'Oh, I can manage, Mummy,' said Bridget.

Finally, with a great deal of fuss, Bridget's mother went off to her committee.

'Oh dear,' said Bridget, sighing, as she came back after closing the front door. 'Really! I do think mothers are *difficult*.'

'So they tell me,' said Chief-Inspector Davy. 'A lot of young ladies I come across have a lot of trouble with their mothers.'

'I'd have thought you'd put it the other way round,' said Bridget.

'Oh I do, I do,' said Davy. 'But that's not how the young ladies see it. Now you can tell me a little more.'

'I couldn't really speak frankly in front of Mummy,' explained Bridget. 'But I do feel, of course, that it is really important that you should know as much as possible about all this. I do know Elvira was terribly worried about something and *afraid*. She wouldn't exactly admit she was in danger, but she was.'

'I thought that might have been so. Of course I didn't like to ask you too much in front of your mother.'

'Oh no,' said Bridget, 'we don't want *Mummy* to hear about it. She gets in such a frightful state about things and she'd go and *tell* everyone. I mean, if Elvira doesn't want things like this to be known . . .'

'First of all,' said Chief-Inspector Davy, 'I want to know about a box of chocolates in Italy. I gather there was some idea that a box was sent to her which might have been poisoned.'

Bridget's eyes opened wide. 'Poisoned,' she said. 'Oh no. I don't think so. At least . . .'

'There was something?'

'Oh yes. A box of chocolates came and Elvira did eat a lot of them and she was rather sick that night. Quite ill.'

'But she didn't suspect poison?'

'No. At least—oh yes, she did say that someone was trying to poison one of us and we looked at the chocolates to see, you know, if anything had been injected into them.'

'And had it?'

'No, it hadn't,' said Bridget. 'At least, not as far as we could see.'

'But perhaps your friend, Miss Elvira, might still have thought so?'

'Well, she might—but she didn't *say* any more.'

'But you think she was afraid of someone?'

'I didn't think so at the time or notice anything. It was only here, later.'

'What about this man, Guido?'

Bridget giggled.

'He had a terrific crush on Elvira,' she said.

'And you and your friend used to meet him places?'

'Well, I don't mind telling *you*,' said Bridget. 'After all you're the police. It isn't important to you, that sort of thing, and I expect you understand. Countess Martinelli was frightfully strict—or thought she was. And of course we had all sorts of dodges and things. We all stood in with each other. You know.'

'And told the right lies, I suppose?'

'Well, I'm afraid so,' said Bridget. 'But what can one do when anyone is so suspicious?'

'So you did meet Guido and all that. And used he to threaten Elvira?'

'Oh, not seriously, I don't think.'

'Then perhaps there was someone else she used to meet?'

'Oh—that—well, I don't know.'

'Please tell me, Miss Bridget. It might be—vital, you know.'

'Yes. Yes I can see that. Well there was *someone*. I don't know who it was, but there was someone else—she really minded about. She was deadly serious. I mean it was a really *important* thing.'

'She used to meet him?'

'I think so. I mean she'd *say* she was meeting Guido but it wasn't always Guido. It was this other man.'

'Any idea who it was?'

'No.' Bridget sounded a little uncertain.

'It wouldn't be a racing motorist called Ladislaus Malinowski?'

Bridget gaped at him.

'So you *know*?'

'Am I right?'

'Yes—I think so. She'd got a photograph of him torn out of a paper. She kept it under her stockings.'

'That might have been just a pin-up hero, mightn't it?'

'Well it *might*, of course, but I don't think it was.'

'Did she meet him here in this country, do you know?'

'I don't know. You see I don't know really what she's been doing since she came back from Italy.'

'She came up to London to the dentist,' Davy prompted her. 'Or so she said. Instead she came to you. She rang up Mrs Melford with some story about an old governess.'

A faint giggle came from Bridget.

'That wasn't true, was it?' said the Chief-Inspector, smiling. 'Where did she really go?'

Bridget hesitated and then said, 'She went to Ireland.'

'She went to Ireland, did she? Why?'

'She wouldn't tell me. She said there was something she had to find out.'

'Do you know where she went in Ireland?'

'Not exactly. She mentioned a name. Bally something. Ballygowlan, I think it was.'

'I see. You're sure she went to Ireland?'

'I saw her off at Kensington Airport. She went by Aer Lingus.'

'She came back when?'

'The following day.'

'Also by air?'

'Yes.'

'You're quite sure, are you, that she came back by air?'

'Well—I suppose she did!'

'Had she taken a return ticket?'

'No. No, she didn't. I remember.'

'She might have come back another way, mightn't she?'

'Yes, I suppose so.'

'She might have come back for instance by the Irish Mail?'

'She didn't say she had.'

'But she didn't *say* she'd come by air, did she?'

'No,' Bridget agreed. 'But why should she come back by boat and train instead of by air?'

'Well, if she had found out what she wanted to know and had had nowhere to stay, she might think it would be easier to come back by the Night Mail.'

'Why, I suppose she *might*.'

Davy smiled faintly.

'I don't suppose you young ladies,' he said, 'think of going anywhere except in terms of flying, do you, nowadays?'

'I suppose we don't really,' agreed Bridget.

'Anyway, she came back to England. Then what happened? Did she come to you or ring you up?'

'She rang up.'

'What time of day?'

'Oh, in the morning some time. Yes, it must have been about eleven or twelve o'clock, I think.'

'And she said, what?'

'Well, she just asked if everything was all right.'

'And was it?'

'No, it wasn't, because, you see, Mrs Melford had rung up and Mummy had answered the phone and things had been very difficult and I hadn't known what to say. So Elvira said she would not come to Onslow Square, but that she'd ring up her cousin Mildred and try to fix up some story or other.'

'And that's all you can remember?'

'That's all,' said Bridget, making certain reservations. She thought of Mr Bollard and the bracelet. That was certainly a thing she was not going to tell Chief-Inspector Davy. Father knew quite well that something was being kept from him. He could only hope that it was not something pertinent to his inquiry. He asked again:

'You think your friend was really frightened of someone or something?'

'Yes I do.'

'Did she mention it to you or did you mention it to her?'

'Oh, I asked her outright. At first she said no and then she admitted that she *was* frightened. And I know she was,' went on Bridget violently. 'She was in danger. She was quite sure of it. But I don't know why or how or anything about it.'

'Your surety on this point relates to that particular morning, does it, the morning she had come back from Ireland?'

'Yes. Yes, that's when I was so sure about it.'

'On the morning when she *might* have come back on the Irish Mail?'

'I don't think it's very likely that she did. Why don't you ask her?'

'I probably shall do in the end. But I don't want to call attention to that point. Not at the moment. It might just possibly make things more dangerous for her.'

Bridget opened round eyes.

'What do you mean?'

'You may not remember it, Miss Bridget, but that was the night, or rather the early morning, of the Irish Mail robbery.'

'Do you mean that Elvira was in *that* and never told me a thing about it?'

'I agree it's unlikely,' said Father. 'But it just occurred to me that she might have seen something or someone, or some incident might have occurred connected with the Irish Mail. She might have seen someone she knew, for instance, and that might have put her in danger.'

'Oh!' said Bridget. She thought it over. 'You mean—someone she knew was mixed up in the robbery.'

Chief-Inspector Davy got up.

'I think that's all,' he said. 'Sure there's nothing more you can tell me? Nowhere where your friend went that day? Or the day before?'

Again visions of Mr Bollard and the Bond Street shop rose before Bridget's eyes.

'No,' she said.

'I think there is something you haven't told me,' said Chief-Inspector Davy.

Bridget grasped thankfully at a straw.

'Oh, I forgot,' she said. 'Yes. I mean she did go to some lawyers. Lawyers who were trustees, to find out something.'

'Oh, she went to some lawyers who were her trustees. I don't suppose you know their name?'

'Their name was Egerton—Forbes Egerton and Something,' said Bridget. 'Lots of names. I think that's more or less right.'

'I see. And she wanted to find out something, did she?'

'She wanted to know how much money she'd got,' said Bridget.

Inspector Davy's eyebrows rose.

'Indeed!' he said. 'Interesting. Why didn't she know herself?'

'Oh, because people never told her anything about money,' said Bridget. 'They seem to think it's bad for you to know actually how much money you have.'

'And she wanted to know badly, did she?'

'Yes,' said Bridget. 'I think she thought it was important.'

'Well, thank you,' said Chief-Inspector Davy. 'You've helped me a good deal.'

CHAPTER XXIII

RICHARD EGERTON looked again at the official card in front of him, then up into the Chief-Inspector's face.

'Curious business,' he said.

'Yes, sir,' said Chief-Inspector Davy, 'a very curious business.'

'Bertram's Hotel,' said Egerton, 'in the fog. Yes, it was a bad fog last night. I suppose you get a lot of that sort of thing in fogs, don't you? Snatch and grab—handbags—that sort of thing?'

'It wasn't quite like that,' said Father. 'Nobody attempted to snatch anything from Miss Blake.'

'Where did the shot come from?'

'Owing to the fog we can't be sure. She wasn't sure herself. But we think—it seems the best idea—that the man may have been standing in the area.'

'He shot at her twice, you say?'

'Yes. The first shot missed. The commissionaire rushed along from where he was standing outside the hotel door and shoved her behind him just before the second shot.'

'So that he got hit instead, eh?'

'Yes.'

'Quite a brave chap.'

'Yes. He was brave,' said the Chief-Inspector. 'His military record was very good. An Irishman.'

'What's his name?'

'Gorman. Michael Gorman.'

'Michael Gorman.' Egerton frowned for a minute. 'No,' he said. 'For a moment I thought the name meant something.'

'It's a very common name, of course. Anyway, he saved the girl's life.'

'And why exactly have you come to me, Chief-Inspector?'

'I hoped for a little information. We always like full information, you know, about the victim of a murderous assault.'

'Oh, naturally, naturally. But really, I've only seen Elvira twice since she was a child.'

'You saw her when she came to call upon you about a week ago, didn't you?'

'Yes, that's quite right. What exactly do you want to know? If it's anything about her personally, who her friends were or about boy-friends, or lovers' quarrels—all that sort of thing—you'd do better to go to one of the women. There's a Mrs Carpenter who brought her back from Italy, I believe, and there's Mrs Melford with whom she lives in Sussex.'

'I've seen Mrs Melford.'

'Oh.'

'No good. Absolutely no good at all, sir. And I don't so much want to know about the girl personally—after all, I've seen her for myself and I've heard what she can tell me—or rather what she's willing to tell me—'

At a quick movement of Egerton's eyebrows he saw that the other had appreciated the point of the word 'willing'.

'I've been told that she was worried, upset, afraid about something, and convinced that her life was in danger. Was that your impression when she came to see you?'

'No,' said Egerton, slowly, 'no, I wouldn't go as far as that; though she did say one or two things that struck me as curious.'

'Such as?'

'Well, she wanted to know who would benefit if she were to die suddenly.'

'Ah,' said Chief-Inspector Davy, 'so she had that possibility in her mind, did she? That she might die suddenly. Interesting.'

'She'd got something in her head but I didn't know what it was. She also wanted to know how much money she had—or would have when she was twenty-one. That, perhaps, is more understandable.'

'It's a lot of money I believe.'

'It's a very large fortune, Chief-Inspector.'

'Why do you think she wanted to know?'

'About the money?'

'Yes, and about who would inherit it?'

'I don't know,' said Egerton. 'I don't know at all. She also brought up the subject of marriage—'

'Did you form the impression that there was a man in the case?'

'I've no evidence—but—yes, I did think just that. I felt sure there was a boy-friend somewhere in the offing. There usually is! Luscombe—that's Colonel Luscombe, her guardian, doesn't seem to know anything about a boy friend. But then dear old Derek Luscombe wouldn't. He was quite upset when I suggested that there was such a thing in the background and probably an unsuitable one at that.'

'He is unsuitable,' said Chief-Inspector Davy.

'Oh. Then you know who he is?'

'I can have a very good guess at it. Ladislaus Malinowski.'

'The racing motorist? Really! A handsome daredevil. Women fall for him easily. I wonder how he came across Elvira. I don't see very well where their orbits would meet except—yes, I believe he was in Rome a couple of months ago. Possible she met him there.'

'Very possibly. Or she could have met him through her mother?'

'What, through Bess? I wouldn't say that was at all likely.'

Davy coughed.

'Lady Sedgwick and Malinowski are said to be close friends, sir.'

'Oh yes, yes, I know that's the gossip. May be true, may not. They are close friends—thrown together constantly by their way of life. Bess has had her affairs, of course; though, mind you, she's not the nymphomaniac type. People are ready enough to say that about a woman, but it's not true in Bess's case. Anyway, as far as I know, Bess and her daughter are practically not even acquainted with each other.'

'That's what Lady Sedgwick told me. And you agree?'

Egerton nodded.

'What other relatives has Miss Blake got?'

'For all intents and purposes, none. Her mother's two brothers were killed in the war—and she was old Coniston's only child. Mrs Melford, though the girl calls her "Cousin Mildred," is actually a cousin of Colonel Luscombe's. Luscombe's done his best for the girl in his conscientious old-fashioned way—but it's difficult . . . for a man.'

'Miss Blake brought up the subject of marriage, you say?

There's no possibility, I suppose, that she may actually already *be* married—'

'She's well under age—she'd have to have the assent of her guardian and trustees.'

'Technically, yes. But they don't always wait for that,' said Father.

'I know. Most regrettable. One has to go through all the machinery of making them Wards of Court, and all the rest of it. And even that has its difficulties.'

'And once they're married, they're married,' said Father. 'I suppose, if she *were* married, and died suddenly, her husband would inherit?'

'This idea of marriage is most unlikely. She has been most carefully looked after and . . .' He stopped, reacting to Chief-Inspector Davy's cynical smile.

However carefully Elvira had been looked after, she seemed to have succeeded in making the acquaintance of the highly unsuitable Ladislaus Manilowski.

He said dubiously, 'Her mother bolted, it's true.'

'Her mother bolted, yes—that's what she would do—but Miss Blake's a different type. She's just as set on getting her own way, but she'd go about it differently.'

'You don't really think—'

'I don't think anything—*yet*,' said Chief-Inspector Davy.

CHAPTER XXIV

Ladislaus Malinowski looked from one to the other of the two police officers and flung back his head and laughed.

'It is very amusing!' he said. 'You look solemn as owls. It is ridiculous that you should ask me to come here and wish to ask me questions. You have nothing against me, nothing.'

'We think you may be able to assist us in our inquiries, Mr Malinowski.' Chief-Inspector Davy spoke with official smoothness. 'You own a car, Mercedes-Otto, registration number FAN 2266.'

'Is there any reason why I should not own such a car?'

'No reason at all, sir. There's just a little uncertainty as to the correct number. Your car was on a motor road, M7, and the registration plate on that occasion was a different one.'

'Nonsense. It must have been some other car.'

'There aren't so many of that make. We have checked up on those there are.'

'You believe everything, I suppose, that your traffic police tell you! It is laughable! Where was all this?'

'The place where the police stopped you and asked to see your licence is not very far from Bedhampton. It was on the night of the Irish Mail robbery.'

'You really do amuse me,' said Ladislaus Malinowski.

'You have a revolver?'

'Certainly, I have a revolver and an automatic pistol. I

have proper licences for them.'

'Quite so. They are both still in your possession?'

'Certainly.'

'I have already warned you, Mr Malinowski.'

'The famous policeman's warning! Anything you say will be taken down and used against you at your trial.'

'That's not quite the wording,' said Father mildly. 'Used, yes. Against, no. You don't want to qualify that statement of yours?'

'No, I do not.'

'And you are sure you don't want your solicitor here?'

'I do not like solicitors.'

'Some people don't. Where are those firearms now?'

'I think you know very well where they are, Chief-Inspector. The small pistol is in the pocket of my car, the Mercedes-Otto whose registered number is, as I have said, FAN 2266. The revolver is in a drawer in my flat.'

'You're quite right about the one in the drawer in your flat,' said Father, 'but the other—the pistol—is not in your car.'

'Yes, it is. It is in the left hand pocket.'

Father shook his head. 'It may have been once. It isn't now. Is this it, Mr Malinowski?'

He passed a small automatic pistol across the table. Ladislaus Malinowski, with an air of great surprise, picked it up.

'Ah-ha, yes. This is it. So it was *you* who took it from my car?'

'No,' said Father, 'we didn't take it from your car. It was not in your car. We found it somewhere else.'

'Where did you find it?'

'We found it,' said Father, 'in an area in Pond Street

which—as you no doubt know—is a street near Park Lane. It could have been dropped by a man walking down that street—or running perhaps.'

Ladislaus Malinowski shrugged his shoulders. 'That is nothing to do with me—I did not put it there. It was in my car a day or two ago. One does not continually look to see if a thing is still where one has put it. One assumes it will be.'

'Do you know, Mr Malinowski, that this is the pistol which was used to shoot Michael Gorman on the night of November 26th?'

'Michael Gorman? I do not know a Michael Gorman.'

'The commissionaire from Bertram's Hotel.'

'Ah yes, the one who was shot. I read about it. And you say *my* pistol shot him? Nonsense!'

'It's not nonsense. The ballistic experts have examined it. You know enough of firearms to be aware that their evidence is reliable.'

'You are trying to frame me. I know what you police do!'

'I think you know the police of this country better than that, Mr Malinowski.'

'Are you suggesting that I shot Michael Gorman?'

'So far we are only asking for a statement. No charge has been made.'

'But this is what you think—that I shot that ridiculous dressed-up military figure. Why should I? I didn't owe him money, I had no grudge against him.'

'It was a young lady who was shot at. Gorman ran to protect her and received the second bullet in his chest.'

'A young lady?'

'A young lady whom I think you know. Miss Elvira Blake.'

'Do you say someone tried to shoot Elvira with *my* pistol?'

He sounded incredulous.

'It could be that you had had a disagreement.'

'You mean that I quarrelled with Elvira and shot her? What madness! Why should I shoot the girl I am going to marry?'

'Is that part of your statement? That you are going to marry Miss Elvira Blake?'

Just for a moment or two Ladislaus hesitated. Then he said, shrugging his shoulders,

'She is still very young. It remains to be discussed.'

'Perhaps she had promised to marry you, and then—she changed her mind. There was *someone* she was afraid of. Was it you, Mr Malinowski?'

'Why should *I* want her to die? I am in love with her and want to marry her or if I do not want to marry her I need not marry her. It is as simple as that. So why should I kill her?'

'There aren't many people close enough to her to want to kill her.' Davy waited a moment and then said, almost casually: 'There's her mother, of course.'

'What!' Malinowski sprang up. '*Bess*? Bess kill her own daughter? You are mad! Why should Bess kill Elvira?'

'Possibly because, as next of kin, she might inherit an enormous fortune.'

'Bess? You mean Bess would kill for money? She has plenty of money from her American husband. Enough, anyway.'

'Enough is not the same as a great fortune,' said Father. 'People do do murder for a large fortune, mothers have been known to kill their children, and children have killed their mothers.'

'I tell you, you are mad!'

'You say that you may be going to marry Miss Blake. Perhaps you have already married her? If so, then *you* would be the one to inherit a vast fortune.'

'What more crazy, stupid things can you say! No, I am not married to Elvira. She is a pretty girl. I like her, and she is in love with me. Yes, I admit it. I met her in Italy. We had fun—but that is all. No more, do you understand?'

'Indeed? Just now, Mr Malinowski, you said quite definitely that she was the girl you were going to marry.'

'Oh that.'

'Yes—that. Was it true?'

'I said it because—it sounded more respectable that way. You are so—prudish in this country—'

'That seems to me an unlikely explanation.'

'You do not understand anything at all. The mother and I—we are lovers—I did not wish to say so—so I suggest instead that the daughter and I—we are engaged to be married. That sounds very English and proper.'

'It sounds to me even more far-fetched. You're rather badly in need of money, aren't you, Mr Malinowski?'

'My dear Chief-Inspector, I am always in need of money. It is very sad.'

'And yet a few months ago I understand you were flinging money about in a very carefree way.'

'Ah. I had had a lucky flutter. I am a gambler. I admit it.'

'I find that quite easy to believe. Where did you have this "flutter"?'

'That I do not tell. You can hardly expect it.'

'I don't expect it.'

'Is that all you have to ask me?'

'For the moment, yes. You have identified the pistol as yours. That will be very helpful.'

'I don't understand—I can't conceive—' he broke off and stretched out his hand. 'Give it me please.'

'I'm afraid we'll have to keep it for the present, so I'll write you out a receipt for it.'

He did so and handed it to Malinowski.

The latter went out slamming the door.

'Temperamental chap,' said Father.

'You didn't press him on the matter of the false number plate and Bedhampton?'

'No. I wanted him rattled. But not too badly rattled. We'll give him one thing to worry about at a time— And he *is* worried.'

'The Old Man wanted to see you, sir, as soon as you were through.'

Chief-Inspector Davy nodded and made his way to Sir Ronald's room.

'Ah! Father. Making progress?'

'Yes. Getting along nicely—quite a lot of fish in the net. Small fry mostly. But we're closing in on the big fellows. Everything's in train—'

'Good show, Fred,' said the A.C.

CHAPTER XXV

MISS MARPLE got out of her train at Paddington and saw the burly figure of Chief-Inspector Davy standing on the platform waiting for her.

He said, 'Very good of you, Miss Marple,' put his hand under her elbow and piloted her through the barrier to where a car was waiting. The driver opened the door, Miss Marple got in, Chief-Inspector Davy followed her and the car drove off.

'Where are you taking me, Chief-Inspector Davy?'

'To Bertram's Hotel.'

'Dear me, Bertram's Hotel again. Why?'

'The official reply is: because the police think you can assist them in their inquiries.'

'That sounds familiar, but surely rather sinister? So often the prelude to an arrest, is it not?'

'I am not going to arrest you, Miss Marple.' Father smiled. 'You have an alibi.'

Miss Marple digested this in silence. Then she said, 'I see.'

They drove to Bertram's Hotel in silence. Miss Gorringe looked up from the desk as they entered, but Chief-Inspector Davy piloted Miss Marple straight to the lift.

'Second floor.'

The lift ascended, stopped, and Father led the way along the corridor.

As he opened the door of No. 18 Miss Marple said,

'This is the same room I had when I was staying here before.'

'Yes,' said Father.

Miss Marple sat down in the arm-chair.

'A very comfortable room,' she observed, looking round with a slight sigh.

'They certainly know what comfort is here,' Father agreed.

'You look tired, Chief-Inspector,' said Miss Marple unexpectedly.

'I've had to get around a bit. As a matter of fact I've just got back from Ireland.'

'Indeed. From Ballygowlan?'

'Now how the devil did *you* know about Ballygowlan? I'm sorry—I beg your pardon.'

Miss Marple smiled forgiveness.

'I suppose Michael Gorman happened to tell you he came from there—was that it?'

'No, not exactly,' said Miss Marple.

'Then how, if you'll excuse me asking you, *did* you know?'

'Oh dear,' said Miss Marple, 'it's really very embarrassing. It was just something I—happened to overhear.'

'Oh, I see.'

'I wasn't eavesdropping. It was in a public room—at least technically a public room. Quite frankly, I enjoy listening to people talking. One does. Especially when one is old and doesn't get about very much. I mean, if people are talking near you, you listen.'

'Well, that seems to me quite natural,' said Father.

'Up to a point, yes,' said Miss Marple. 'If people do not

choose to lower their voices, one must assume that they are prepared to be overheard. But of course matters may develop. The situation sometimes arises when you realize that though it *is* a public room, other people talking do not realize that there is anyone else in it. And then one has to decide what to do about it. Get up and cough, or just stay quite quiet and hope they won't realize you've been there. Either way is embarrassing.'

Chief-Inspector Davy glanced at his watch.

'Look here,' he said, 'I want to hear more about this—but I've got Canon Pennyfather arriving at any moment. I must go and collect him. You don't mind?'

Miss Marple said she didn't mind. Chief-Inspector Davy left the room.

II

Canon Pennyfather came through the swing doors into the hall of Bertram's Hotel. He frowned slightly, wondering what it was that seemed a little different about Bertram's today. Perhaps it had been painted or done up in some way? He shook his head. That was not it, but there was *something*. It did not occur to him that it was the difference between a six foot commissionaire with blue eyes and dark hair and a five foot seven commissionaire with sloping shoulders, freckles and a sandy thatch of hair bulging out under his commissionaire's cap. He just knew something was different. In his usual vague way he wandered up to the desk. Miss Gorringe was there and greeted him.

'Canon Pennyfather. How nice to see you. Have you come to fetch your baggage? It's all ready for you. If you'd only let us know we could have sent it to you to any address you like.'

'Thank you,' said Canon Pennyfather, 'thank you very much. You're always most kind, Miss Gorringe. But as I had to come up to London anyway today I thought I might as well call for it.'

'We were so worried about you,' said Miss Gorringe. 'Being missing, you know. Nobody able to find you. You had a car accident, I hear?'

'Yes,' said Canon Pennyfather. 'Yes. People drive much too fast nowadays. Most dangerous. Not that I can remember much about it. It affected my head. Concussion, the doctor says. Oh well, as one is getting on in life, one's memory—' he shook his head sadly. 'And how are you, Miss Gorringe?'

'Oh, I'm very well,' said Miss Gorringe.

At that moment it struck Canon Pennyfather that Miss Gorringe also was different. He peered at her, trying to analyse where the difference lay. Her hair? That was the same as usual. Perhaps even a little frizzier. Black dress, large locket, cameo brooch. All there as usual. But there was a difference. Was she perhaps a little thinner? Or was it— yes, surely, she looked *worried*. It was not often that Canon Pennyfather noticed whether people looked worried, he was not the kind of man who noticed emotion in the faces of others, but it struck him today, perhaps because Miss Gorringe had so invariably presented exactly the same countenance to guests for so many years.

'You've not been ill, I hope?' he asked solicitously. 'You look a little thinner.'

'Well, we've had a good deal of worry, Canon Pennyfather.'

'Indeed. Indeed. I'm sorry to hear it. Not due to my disappearance, I hope?'

'Oh no,' said Miss Gorringe. 'We were worried, of course, about that, but as soon as we heard that you were all right —' She broke off and said, 'No. No—it's this—well, perhaps you haven't read about it in the papers. Gorman, our outside porter, got killed.'

'Oh yes,' said Canon Pennyfather. 'I remember now. I did see it mentioned in the paper—that you had had a murder here.'

Miss Gorringe shuddered at this blunt mention of the word murder. The shudder went all up her black dress.

'Terrible,' she said, 'terrible. Such a thing has *never* happened at Bertram's. I mean, we're not the sort of hotel where murders happen.'

'No, no, indeed,' said Canon Pennyfather quickly. 'I'm sure you're not. I mean it would never have occurred to me that anything like that could happen *here*.'

'Of course it wasn't *inside* the hotel,' said Miss Gorringe, cheering up a little as this aspect of the affair struck her. 'It was outside in the street.'

'So really nothing to do with you at all,' said the Canon, helpfully.

That apparently was not quite the right thing to say.

'But it was connected with Bertram's. We had to have the police here questioning people, since it was our commissionaire who was shot.'

'So that's a new man you have outside. D'you know, I thought somehow things looked a little strange.'

'Yes, I don't know that he's very satisfactory. I mean, not quite the style we're used to here. But of course we had to get someone quickly.'

'I remember all about it now,' said Canon Pennyfather, assembling some rather dim memories of what he had read in the paper a week ago. 'But I thought it was a *girl* who was shot.'

'You mean Lady Sedgwick's daughter? I expect you remember seeing her here with her guardian, Colonel Luscombe. Apparently she was attacked by someone in the fog. I expect they wanted to snatch her bag. Anyway they fired a shot at her and then Gorman, who of course had been a soldier and was a man with a lot of presence of mind, rushed down, got in front of her and got shot himself, poor fellow.'

'Very sad, very sad,' said the Canon, shaking his head.

'It makes everything terribly difficult,' complained Miss Gorringe. 'I mean, the police constantly in and out. I suppose that's to be expected, but we don't *like* it here, though I must say Chief-Inspector Davy and Sergeant Wadell are very respectable looking. Plain clothes, and very good style, not the sort with boots and macintoshes like one sees on films. Almost like one of *us*.'

'Er—yes,' said Canon Pennyfather.

'Did you have to go to hospital?' inquired Miss Gorringe.

'No,' said the Canon, 'some very nice people, really good Samaritans—a market gardener, I believe—picked me up and his wife nursed me back to health. I'm most grateful, most grateful. It is refreshing to find that there is still human kindness in the world. Don't you think so?'

Miss Gorringe said she thought it was very refreshing. 'After all one reads about the increase in crime,' she added, 'all those dreadful young men and girls holding up banks and robbing trains and ambushing people.' She looked up and said, 'There's Chief-Inspector Davy coming down the stairs now. I think he wants to speak to you.'

'I don't know why he should want to speak to me,' said Canon Pennyfather, puzzled. 'He's already been to see me, you know,' he said, 'At Chadminster. He was very disappointed, I think, that I couldn't tell him anything useful.'

'You couldn't?'

The Canon shook his head sorrowfully.

'I couldn't remember. The accident took place somewhere near a place called Bedhampton and really I don't understand *what* I can have been doing there. The Chief-Inspector kept asking me why I was there and I couldn't tell him. Very odd, isn't it? He seemed to think I'd been driving a car from somewhere near a railway station to a vicarage.'

'That sounds very possible,' said Miss Gorringe.

'It doesn't seem possible at all,' said Canon Pennyfather. 'I mean, why should I be driving about in a part of the world that I don't really know?'

Chief-Inspector Davy had come up to them.

'So here you are, Canon Pennyfather,' he said. 'Feeling quite yourself again?'

'Oh, I feel quite well now,' said the Canon, 'but rather inclined to have headaches still. And I've been told not to do too much. But I still don't seem to remember what I ought to remember and the doctor says it may never come back.'

'Oh well,' said Chief-Inspector Davy, 'we mustn't give up hope.' He led the Canon away from the desk. 'There's a little experiment I want you to try,' he said. 'You don't mind helping me, do you?'

III

When Chief-Inspector Davy opened the door of Number 18 Miss Marple was still sitting in the arm-chair by the window.

'A good many people in the street today,' she observed. 'More than usual.'

'Oh well—this is a way through to Berkeley Square and Shepherd's Market.'

'I didn't mean only passers-by. Men doing things—road repairs, a telephone repair van—a meat trolley—a couple of private cars—'

'And what—may I ask—do you deduce from that?'

'I didn't say that I deduced anything.'

Father gave her a look. Then he said,

'I want you to help me.'

'Of course. That is why I am here. What do you want me to do?'

'I want you to do exactly what you did on the night of November 19th. You were asleep—you woke up—possibly awakened by some unusual noise. You switched on the light, looked at the time, got out of bed, opened the door and looked out. Can you repeat those actions?'

'Certainly,' said Miss Marple. She got up and went across to the bed.

'Just a moment.'

Chief-Inspector Davy went and tapped on the connecting walls of the next room.

'You'll have to do that louder,' said Miss Marple. 'This place is very well built.'

The Chief-Inspector redoubled the force of his knuckles.

'I told Canon Pennyfather to count ten,' he said, looking at his watch. 'Now then, off you go.'

Miss Marple touched the electric lamp, looked at an imaginary clock, got up, walked to the door, opened it and looked out. To her right, just leaving his room, walking to the top of the stairs, was Canon Pennyfather. He arrived at the top of the stairs and started down them. Miss Marple gave a slight catch of her breath. She turned back.

'Well?' said Chief-Inspector Davy.

'The man I saw that night can't have been Canon Pennyfather,' said Miss Marple. 'Not if that's Canon Pennyfather now.'

'I thought you said—'

'I know. He looked like Canon Pennyfather. His hair and his clothes and everything. But he didn't walk the same way. I think—I think he must have been a younger man. I'm sorry, very sorry, to have misled you, but it wasn't Canon Pennyfather that I saw that night. I'm quite sure of it.'

'You really are quite sure this time, Miss Marple.'

'Yes,' said Miss Marple. 'I'm sorry,' she added again, 'to have misled you.'

'You were very nearly right. Canon Pennyfather did come back to the hotel that night. Nobody saw him come in—but that wasn't remarkable. He came in after midnight. He came up the stairs, he opened the door of his room next door and he went in. What he saw or what happened next we don't know, because he can't or won't tell us. If there was only some way we could jog his memory . . .'

'There's that German word of course,' said Miss Marple, thoughtfully.

'What German word?'

'Dear me, I've forgotten it now, but—'

There was a knock at the door.

'May I come in?' said Canon Pennyfather. He entered. 'Was it satisfactory?'

'Most satisfactory,' said Father. 'I was just telling Miss Marple—you know Miss Marple?'

'Oh yes,' said Canon Pennyfather, really slightly uncertain as to whether he did or not.

'I was just telling Miss Marple how we have traced your movements. You came back to the hotel that night after midnight. You came upstairs and you opened the door of your room and went in—' He paused.

Miss Marple gave an exclamation.

'I remember now,' she said, 'what that German word is. *Doppelganger*!'

Canon Pennyfather uttered an exclamation. 'But of course,' he said, 'of *course*! How could I have forgotten? You're quite right, you know. After that film, *The Walls of Jericho* I came back here and I came upstairs and I opened my room and I saw—extraordinary, I distinctly saw *myself* sitting in a chair facing me. As you say, dear lady, a *doppelganger*. How very remarkable! And then—let me see—' He raised his eyes, trying to think.

'And then,' said Father, 'startled out of their lives to see you, when they thought you were safely in Lucerne, somebody hit you on the head.'

CHAPTER XXVI

Canon Pennyfather had been sent on his way in a taxi to the British Museum. Miss Marple had been ensconced in the lounge by the chief-inspector. Would she mind waiting for him there for about ten minutes? Miss Marple had not minded. She welcomed the opportunity to sit and look around her and think.

Bertram's Hotel. So many memories . . . The past fused itself with the present. A French phrase came back to her, *Plus ça change, plus c'est la même chose*. She reversed the wording. *Plus c'est la même chose, plus ça change*. Both true, she thought.

She felt sad—for Bertram's Hotel and for herself. She wondered what Chief-Inspector Davy wanted of her next. She sensed in him the excitement of purpose. He was a man whose plans were at last coming to fruition. It was Chief-Inspector Davy's D-Day.

The life of Bertram's went on as usual. No, Miss Marple decided, *not* as usual. There was a difference, though she could not have defined where the difference lay. An underlying uneasiness, perhaps?

The doors swung open once more and this time the big bovine-looking countryman came through them and across to where Miss Marple sat.

'All set?' he inquired genially.

'Where are you taking me now?'

'We're going to pay a call on Lady Sedgwick.'

'Is she staying here?'

'Yes. With her daughter.'

Miss Marple rose to her feet. She cast a glance round her and murmured: 'Poor Bertram's.'

'What do you mean—poor Bertram's?'

'I think you know quite well what I mean.'

'Well—looking at it from your point of view, perhaps I do.'

'It is always sad when a work of art has to be destroyed.'

'You call this place a work of art?'

'Certainly I do. So do you.'

'I see what you mean,' admitted Father.

'It is like when you get ground elder really badly in a border. There's nothing else you can do about it—except dig the whole thing up.'

'I don't know much about gardens. But change the metaphor to dry rot and I'd agree.'

They went up in the lift and along a passage to where Lady Sedgwick and her daughter had a corner suite.

Chief-Inspector Davy knocked on the door, a voice said Come in, and he entered with Miss Marple behind him.

Bess Sedgwick was sitting in a high-backed chair near the window. She had a book on her knee which she was not reading.

'So it's you again, Chief-Inspector.' Her eyes went past him towards Miss Marple and she looked slightly surprised.

'This is Miss Marple,' explained Chief-Inspector Davy. 'Miss Marple—Lady Sedgwick.'

'I've met you before,' said Bess Sedgwick. 'You were with Selina Hazy the other day, weren't you? Do sit down,' she added. Then she turned towards Chief-Inspector Davy again. 'Have you any news of the man who shot at Elvira?'

'Not actually what you'd call *news*.'

'I doubt if you ever will have. In a fog like that, predatory creatures come out and prowl around looking for women walking alone.'

'True up to a point,' said Father. 'How is your daughter?'

'Oh, Elvira is quite all right again.'

'You've got her here with you?'

'Yes. I rang up Colonel Luscombe—her guardian. He was delighted that I was willing to take charge.' She gave a sudden laugh. 'Dear old boy. He's always been urging a mother-and-daughter reunion act!'

'He may be right at that,' said Father.

'Oh no, he isn't. Just at the moment, yes, I think it is the best thing.' She turned her head to look out of the window and spoke in a changed voice. 'I hear you've arrested a friend of mine—Ladislaus Malinowski. On what charge?'

'Not *arrested*,' Chief-Inspector Davy corrected her. 'He's just assisting us with our inquiries.'

'I've sent my solicitor to look after him.'

'Very wise,' said Father approvingly. 'Anyone who's having a little difficulty with the police is very wise to have a solicitor. Otherwise they may so easily say the wrong thing.'

'Even if completely innocent?'

'Possibly it's even more necessary in that case,' said Father.

'You're quite a cynic, aren't you? What are you questioning him about, may I ask? Or mayn't I?'

'For one thing we'd like to know just exactly what his movements were on the night when Michael Gorman died.'

Bess Sedgwick sat up sharply in her chair.

'Have you got some ridiculous idea that *Ladislaus* fired

those shots at Elvira? They didn't even know each other.'

'He could have done it. His car was just round the corner.'

'Rubbish,' said Lady Sedgwick robustly.

'How much did that shooting business the other night upset you, Lady Sedgwick?'

She looked faintly surprised.

'Naturally I was upset when my daughter had a narrow escape of her life. What do you expect?'

'I didn't mean that. I mean how much did the death of Michael Gorman upset you?'

'I was very sorry about it. He was a brave man.'

'Is that all?'

'What more would you expect me to say?'

'You knew him, didn't you?'

'Of course. He worked here.'

'You knew him a little better than that, though, didn't you?'

'What do you mean?'

'Come, Lady Sedgwick. He was your husband, wasn't he?'

She did not answer for a moment or two, though she displayed no signs of agitation or surprise.

'You know a good deal, don't you, Chief-Inspector?' She sighed and sat back in her chair. 'I hadn't seen him for—let me see—a great many years. Twenty—more than twenty. And then I looked out of a window one day, and suddenly recognized Micky.'

'And he recognized you?'

'Quite surprising that we did recognize each other,' said Bess Sedgwick. 'We were only together for about a week. Then my family caught up with us, paid Micky off, and took me home in disgrace.'

She sighed.

'I was very young when I ran away with him. I knew very little. Just a fool of a girl with a head full of romantic notions. He was a hero to me, mainly because of the way he rode a horse. He didn't know what fear was. And he was handsome and gay with an Irishman's tongue! I suppose really *I* ran away with *him*! I doubt if he'd have thought of it himself! But I was wild and headstrong and madly in love!' She shook her head. 'It didn't last long . . . The first twenty-four hours were enough to disillusion me. He drank and he was coarse and brutal. When my family turned up and took me back with them, I was thankful. I never wanted to see him or hear of him again.'

'Did your family know that you were married to him?'

'No.'

'You didn't tell them?'

'I didn't think I *was* married.'

'How did that come about?'

'We were married in Ballygowlan, but when my people turned up, Micky came to me and told me the marriage had been a fake. He and his friends had cooked it up between them, he said. By that time it seemed to me quite a natural thing for him to have done. Whether he wanted the money that was being offered him, or whether he was afraid he'd committed a breach of law by marrying me when I wasn't of age, I don't know. Anyway, I didn't doubt for a moment that what he said was true—not then.'

'And later?'

She seemed lost in her thoughts. 'It wasn't until—oh, quite a number of years afterwards, when I knew a little more of life, and of legal matters, that it suddenly occurred to me that probably I was married to Micky Gorman after all!'

'In actual fact, then, when you married Lord Coniston, you committed bigamy.'

'And when I married Johnnie Sedgwick, and again when I married my American husband, Ridgeway Becker.' She looked at Chief-Inspector Davy and laughed with what seemed like genuine amusement.

'So much bigamy,' she said. 'It really does seem very ridiculous.'

'Did you never think of getting a divorce?'

She shrugged her shoulders. 'It all seemed like a silly dream. Why rake it up? I'd told Johnnie, of course.' Her voice softened and mellowed as she said his name.

'And what did he say?'

'He didn't care. Neither Johnnie nor I were ever very law-abiding.'

'Bigamy carries certain penalties, Lady Sedgwick.'

She looked at him and laughed.

'Who was ever going to worry about something that had happened in Ireland years ago? The whole thing was over and done with. Micky had taken his money and gone off. Oh don't you understand? It seemed just a silly little incident. An incident I wanted to forget. I put it aside with the things—the very many things—that don't matter in life.'

'And then,' said Father, in a tranquil voice, 'one day in November, Michael Gorman turned up again and blackmailed you?'

'Nonsense! Who said he blackmailed me?'

Slowly Father's eyes went round to the old lady sitting quietly, very upright, in her chair.

'You.' Bess Sedgwick stared at Miss Marple. 'What can

you know about it?'

Her voice was more curious than accusing.

'The arm-chairs in this hotel have very high backs,' said Miss Marple. 'Very comfortable they are. I was sitting in one in front of the fire in the writing-room. Just resting before I went out one morning. You came in to write a letter. I suppose you didn't realize there was anyone else in the room. And so—I heard your conversation with this man Gorman.'

'You listened?'

'Naturally,' said Miss Marple. 'Why not? It was a public room. When you threw up the window and called to the man outside, I had no idea that it was going to be a private conversation.'

Bess stared at her for a moment, then she nodded her head slowly.

'Fair enough,' she said. 'Yes, I see. But all the same you misunderstood what you heard. Micky didn't blackmail me. He might have thought of it—but I warned him off before he could try!' Her lips curled up again in that wide generous smile that made her face so attractive. 'I frightened him off.'

'Yes,' agreed Miss Marple. 'I think you probably did. You threatened to shoot him. You handled it—if you won't think it impertinent of me to say so—very well indeed.'

Bess Sedgwick's eyebrows rose in some amusement.

'But I wasn't the only person to hear you,' Miss Marple went on.

'Good gracious! Was the whole hotel listening?'

'The other arm-chair was also occupied.'

'By whom?'

Miss Marple closed her lips. She looked at Chief-Inspector Davy, and it was almost a pleading glance. 'If it *must* be done, *you* do it,' the glance said, 'but I can't . . .'

'Your daughter was in the other chair,' said Chief-Inspector Davy.

'Oh, no!' The cry came out sharply. 'Oh *no*. Not Elvira! I see—yes, I see. She must have thought—'

'She thought seriously enough of what she had overheard to go to Ireland and search for the truth. It wasn't difficult to discover.'

Again Bess Sedgwick said softly: 'Oh no . . .' And then: 'Poor child! . . . Even now, she's never asked me a thing. She's kept it all to herself. Bottled it up inside herself. If she'd only told me I could have explained it all to her—showed her how it didn't matter.'

'She mightn't have agreed with you there,' said Chief-Inspector Davy. 'It's a funny thing, you know,' he went on, in a reminiscent, almost gossipy manner, looking like an old farmer discussing his stock and his land, 'I've learnt after a great many years' trial and error—I've learned to distrust a pattern when it's simple. Simple patterns are often too good to be true. The pattern of this murder the other night was like that. Girl says someone shot at her and missed. The commissionaire came running to save her, and copped it with a second bullet. That may be all true enough. That may be the way the girl saw it. But actually behind the appearances, things might be rather different.

'You said pretty vehemently just now, Lady Sedgwick, that there could be no reason for Ladislaus Malinowski to attempt your daughter's life. Well, I'll agree with you. I don't think there was. He's the sort of young man who might have a row with a woman, pull out a knife and stick it into her. But I don't think he'd hide in an area, and wait cold-bloodedly to shoot her. But supposing he wanted to shoot *someone else*. Screams and shots—but what actually has happened is that *Michael Gorman* is dead. Suppose that was actually what was *meant* to happen. Malinowski plans it very carefully. He chooses a foggy night, hides in the area and waits until your daughter comes up the street. He knows she's coming because he has managed to arrange it that way. He fires a shot. It's not meant to hit the girl. He's careful not to let the bullet go anywhere near her, but *she* thinks it's aimed at her all right. She screams. The porter from the hotel, hearing the shot and the scream, comes rushing down the street *and then Malinowski shoots the person he's come to shoot. Michael Gorman.*'

'I don't believe a word of it! Why on earth should Ladislaus want to shoot Micky Gorman?'

'A little matter of blackmail, perhaps,' said Father.

'Do you mean that Micky was blackmailing *Ladislaus*? What about?'

'Perhaps,' said Father, 'about the things that go on at Bertram's Hotel. Michael Gorman might have found out quite a lot about that.'

'Things that go on at Bertram's Hotel? What *do* you mean?'

'It's been a good racket,' said Father. 'Well planned, beautifully executed. But nothing lasts for ever. Miss Marple here asked me the other day what was wrong with this place. Well, I'll answer that question now. Bertram's Hotel is to all intents and purposes the headquarters of one of the best and biggest crime syndicates that's been known for years.'

CHAPTER XXVII

THERE WAS silence for about a minute and a half. Then Miss Marple spoke.

'How *very* interesting,' she said conversationally.

Bess Sedgwick turned on her. 'You don't seem surprised, Miss Marple.'

'I'm not. Not really. There were so many curious things that didn't seem quite to fit in. It was all too good to be true—if you know what I mean. What they call in theatrical circles, a beautiful performance. But it *was* a performance—not real.

'And there were a lot of little things, people claiming a friend or an acquaintance—and turning out to be wrong.'

'These things happen,' said Chief-Inspector Davy, 'but they happened too often. Is that right, Miss Marple?'

'Yes,' agreed Miss Marple. 'People like Selina Hazy do make that kind of mistake. But there were so many other people doing it too. One couldn't help *noticing* it.'

'She notices a lot,' said Chief-Inspector Davy, speaking to Bess Sedgwick as though Miss Marple was his pet performing dog.

Bess Sedgwick turned on him sharply.

'What did you mean when you said this place was the headquarters of a Crime Syndicate? I should have said that Bertram's Hotel was the most respectable place in the world.'

'Naturally,' said Father. 'It would have to be. A lot of money, time, and thought has been spent on making it just what it is. The genuine and the phony are mixed up very cleverly. You've got a superb actor manager running the show in Henry. You've got that chap, Humfries, wonderfully plausible. He hasn't got a record in this country but he's been mixed up in some rather curious hotel dealings abroad. There are some very good character actors playing various parts here. I'll admit, if you like, that I can't help feeling a good deal of admiration for the whole set-up. It has cost this country a mint of money. It's given the CID and the provincial police forces constant headaches. Every time we seemed to be getting somewhere, and put our finger on some particular incident—it turned out to be the kind of incident that had nothing to do with anything else. But we've gone on working on it, a piece there, a piece here. A garage where stacks of number plates were kept, transferable at a moment's notice to certain cars. A firm of furniture vans, a butcher's van, a grocer's van, even one or two phony postal vans. A racing driver with a racing car covering incredible distances in incredibly few minutes, and at the other end of the scale an old clergyman jogging along in his old Morris Oxford. A cottage with a market gardener in it who lends first aid if necessary and who is in touch with a useful doctor. I needn't go into it all. The ramifications seem unending. That's one half of it. The foreign visitors who come to Bertram's are the other half. Mostly from America, or from the Dominions. Rich people above suspicion, coming here with a good lot of luxury luggage, leaving here with a good lot of luxury luggage which looks the same but isn't. Rich tourists arriving in France and not worried unduly by the Customs because the Customs don't worry tourists when they're bringing money into the country. Not the same tourists too many times. The pitcher mustn't go to the well too often. None of it's going to be easy to prove or to tie up, but it will all tie up in the end. We've made a beginning. The Cabots, for instance—'

'What about the Cabots?' asked Bess sharply.

'You remember them? Very nice Americans. Very nice indeed. They stayed here last year and they've been here again this year. They wouldn't have come a third time. Nobody ever comes here more than twice on the same racket. Yes, we arrested them when they arrived at Calais. Very well made job, that wardrobe case they had with them. It had over three hundred thousand pounds neatly stashed. Proceeds of the Bedhampton train robbery. Of course, that's only a drop in the ocean.

'Bertram's Hotel, let me tell you, is the headquarters of the whole thing! Half the staff are in on it. Some of the guests are in on it. Some of the guests are who they say they are—some are not. The real Cabots, for instance, are in Yucatan just now. Then there was the identification racket. Take Mr Justice Ludgrove. A familiar face, bulbous nose and a wart. Quite easy to impersonate. Canon Pennyfather. A mild country clergyman, with a great white thatch of hair and notable absent-minded behaviour. His mannerisms, his way of peering over his spectacles—all very easily imitated by a good character actor.'

'But what was the use of all that?' asked Bess.

'Are you really asking me? Isn't it obvious? Mr Justice Ludgrove is seen near the scene of a bank hold-up. Someone recognizes him, mentions it. We go into it. It's all a mistake. He was somewhere else at the time. But it wasn't for a while that we realized that these were all what is sometimes called "deliberate mistakes". Nobody's bothered about the man who had looked so like him. And doesn't look particularly like him really. He takes off his make-up and stops acting his part. The whole thing brings about confusion. At one time we had a High Court judge, an Archdeacon, an Admiral, a Major-General, all seen near the scene of a crime.

'After the Bedhampton train robbery at least four vehicles were concerned before the loot arrived in London. A racing car driven by Malinowski took part in it, a false Metal Box lorry, an old-fashioned Daimler with an admiral in it, and an old clergyman with a thatch of white hair in a Morris Oxford. The whole thing was a splendid operation, beautifully planned.

'And then one day the gang had a bit of bad luck. That muddle-headed old ecclesiastic, Canon Pennyfather, went off to catch his plane on the wrong day, they turned him away from the air station, he wandered out into Cromwell Road, went to a film, arrived back here after midnight, came up to his room of which he had the key in his pocket, opened the door, and walked in to get the shock of his life when he saw what appeared to be *himself* sitting in a chair facing him! The last thing the gang expected was to see the real Canon Pennyfather, supposed to be safely in Lucerne, walk in! His double was just getting ready to start off to play his part at Bedhampton when in walked the real man. They didn't know what to do but there was a quick reflex action from one member of the party. Humfries, I suspect. He hit the old man on the head, and he went down unconscious. Somebody, I think, was angry over that. Very angry. However, they examined the old boy, decided he was only knocked out, and would probably come round later and they went on with their plans. The false Canon Pennyfather left his room, went out of the hotel, and drove to the scene of activities where he was to play his part in the relay race. What they did with the real Canon Pennyfather I don't know. I can only guess. I presume he too was moved later that night, driven down in a car, taken to the market gardener's cottage which was at a spot not too far from where the train was to be held up and where a doctor could attend to him. Then, if reports came through about Canon Pennyfather having been seen in that neighbourhood, it would all fit in. It must have been an anxious moment for all concerned until he regained consciousness and they found that at least three days had been knocked out of his remembrance.'

'Would they have killed him otherwise?' asked Miss Marple.

'No,' said Father. 'I don't think they would have killed him. Someone wouldn't have let that happen. It has seemed very clear all along that whoever ran this show had an objection to murder.'

'It sounds fantastic,' said Bess Sedgwick. 'Utterly fantastic! And I don't believe you have any evidence whatever to link Ladislaus Malinowski with this rigmarole.'

'I've got plenty of evidence against Ladislaus Malinowski,' said Father. 'He's careless, you know. He hung around here when he shouldn't have. On the first occasion he came to establish connection with your daugher. They had a code arranged.'

'Nonsense. She told you herself that she didn't know him.'

'She may have told me that but it wasn't true. She's in love with him. She wants the fellow to marry her.'

'I don't believe it!'

'You're not in a position to know,' Chief-Inspector Davy pointed out. 'Malinowski isn't the sort of person who tells all his secrets and your daughter you don't know at all. You admitted as much. You were angry, weren't you, when you found out Malinowski had come to Bertram's Hotel.'

'Why should I be angry?'

'*Because you're the brains of the show*,' said Father. 'You and Henry. The financial side was run by the Hoffman brothers. They made all the arrangements with the continental banks and accounts and that sort of thing, but the boss of the syndicate, the brains that run it, and plan it, are your brains, Lady Sedgwick.'

Bess looked at him and laughed. 'I never heard anything so ridiculous!' she said.

'Oh no, it's not ridiculous at all. You've got brains, courage and daring. You've tried most things; you thought you'd turn your hand to crime. Plenty of excitement in it, plenty of risk. It wasn't the money that attracted you, I'd say, it was the fun of the whole thing. But you wouldn't stand for murder, or for undue violence. There were no killings, no brutal assaults, only nice quiet scientific taps on the head if necessary. You're a very interesting woman, you know. One of the few really interesting great criminals.'

There was silence for some few minutes. Then Bess Sedgwick rose to her feet.

'I think you must be mad.' She put her hand out to the telephone.

'Going to ring up your solicitor? Quite the right thing to do before you say too much.'

With a sharp gesture she slammed the receiver back on the hook.

'On second thoughts I hate solicitors . . . All right. Have

it your own way. Yes, I ran this show. You're quite correct when you say it was fun. I loved every minute of it. It was fun scooping money from banks, trains and post offices and so-called security vans! It was fun planning and deciding; glorious fun and I'm glad I had it. The pitcher goes to the well once too often? That's what you said just now, wasn't it? I suppose it's true. Well, I've had a good run for my money! But you're wrong about Ladislaus Malinowski shooting Michael Gorman! He didn't. *I did.*' She laughed a sudden high, excited laugh. 'Never mind what it was he did, what he threatened . . . I told him I'd shoot him—Miss Marple heard me—and I *did* shoot him. I did very much what you suggested Ladislaus did. I hid in that area. When Elvira passed, I fired one shot wild, and when she screamed and Micky came running down the street, I'd got him where I wanted him, and I let him have it! I've got keys to all the hotel entrances, of course. I just slipped in through the area door and up to my room. It never occurred to me you'd trace the pistol to Ladislaus—or would even suspect him. I'd pinched it from his car without his knowing. But not, I can assure you, with any idea of throwing suspicion on *him*.'

She swept round on Miss Marple. 'You're a witness to what I've said, remember. *I killed Gorman.*'

'Or perhaps you are saying so because you're in love with Malinowski,' suggested Davy.

'I'm not.' Her retort came sharply. 'I'm his good friend, that's all. Oh yes, we've been lovers in a casual kind of way, but I'm not in love with him. In all my life, I've only loved one person—John Sedgwick.' Her voice changed and softened as she pronounced the name.

'But Ladislaus is my friend. I don't want him railroaded

for something he didn't do. *I killed Michael Gorman.* I've said so, and Miss Marple has heard me . . . And now, dear Chief-Inspector Davy—' Her voice rose excitedly, and her laughter rang out—'*Catch me if you can.*'

With a sweep of her arm, she smashed the window with the heavy telephone set, and before Father could get to his feet, she was out of the window and edging her way rapidly along the narrow parapet. With surprising quickness in spite of his bulk, Davy had moved to the other window and flung up the sash. At the same time he blew the whistle he had taken from his pocket.

Miss Marple, getting to her feet with rather more difficulty a moment or two later, joined him. Together they stared out along the façade of Bertram's Hotel.

'She'll fall. She's climbing up a drainpipe,' Miss Marple exclaimed. 'But why *up*?'

'Going to the roof. It's her only chance and she knows it. Good God, look at her. Climbs like a cat. She looks like a fly on the side of the wall. The risks she's taking!'

Miss Marple murmured, her eyes half closing, 'She'll fall. She can't do it . . .'

The woman they were watching disappeared from sight. Father drew back a little into the room.

Miss Marple asked,

'Don't you want to go and—?'

Father shook his head. 'What good am I with my bulk? I've got my men posted ready for something like this. They know what to do. In a few minutes we shall know . . . I wouldn't put it past her to beat the lot of them! She's a woman in a thousand, you know.' He sighed. 'One of the wild ones. Oh, we've some of them in every generation. You can't tame them, you can't bring them into the community and make them live in law and order. They go their own way. If they're saints they go and tend lepers or something, or get themselves martyred in jungles. If they're bad lots they commit the atrocities that you don't like hearing about. And sometimes—they're just wild! They'd have been all right, I suppose, born in another age when it was everyone's hand for himself, everyone fighting to keep life in their veins. Hazards at every turn, danger all round them, and they themselves perforce dangerous to others. That world would have suited them; they'd have been at home in it. This one doesn't.'

'Did you know what she was going to do?'

'Not really. That's one of her gifts. The unexpected. She must have thought this out, you know. She knew what was coming. So she sat looking at us—keeping the ball rolling—and thinking. Thinking and planning hard. I expect—ah—' He broke off as there came the sudden roar of a car's exhaust, the screaming of wheels, and the sound of a big racing engine. He leaned out. 'She's made it, she's got to her car.'

There was more screaming as the car came round the corner on two wheels, a great roar, and the beautiful white monster came tearing up the street.

'She'll kill someone,' said Father, 'she'll kill a lot of people . . . even if she doesn't kill herself.'

'I wonder,' said Miss Marple.

'She's a good driver, of course. A damn' good driver. Whoof, that was a near one!'

They heard the roar of the car racing away with the horn blaring, heard it grow fainter. Heard cries, shouts, the sound of brakes, cars hooting and pulling up and finally a great scream of tyres and a roaring exhaust and—

'She's crashed,' said Father.

He stood there very quietly waiting with the patience that was characteristic of his whole big patient form. Miss Marple stood silent beside him. Then, like a relay race, word came down along the street. A man on the pavement opposite looked up at Chief-Inspector Davy and made rapid signs with his hands.

'She's had it,' said Father heavily. 'Dead! Went about ninety miles an hour into the park railings. No other casualties bar a few slight collisions. Magnificent driving. Yes, she's dead.' He turned back into the room and said heavily, 'Well, she told her story first. You heard her.'

'Yes,' said Miss Marple. 'I heard her.' There was a pause. 'It wasn't true, of course,' said Miss Marple quietly.

Father looked at her. 'You didn't believe her, eh?'

'Did you?'

'No,' said Father. 'No, it wasn't the right story. She thought it out so that it would meet the case exactly, but it wasn't true. She didn't shoot Michael Gorman. D'you happen to know who did?'

'Of course I know,' said Miss Marple. 'The girl.'

'Ah! When did you begin to think that?'

'I always wondered,' said Miss Marple.

'So did I,' said Father. 'She was full of fear that night. And the lies she told were poor lies. But I couldn't see a motive at first.'

'That puzzled me,' said Miss Marple. 'She had found out her mother's marriage was bigamous, but would a girl do murder for that? Not nowadays! I suppose—there was a money side to it?'

'Yes, it was money,' said Chief-Inspector Davy. 'Her

father left her a colossal fortune. When she found out that her mother was married to Michael Gorman she realized that the marriage to Coniston hadn't been legal. She thought that meant that the money wouldn't come to her because, though she was his daughter, she wasn't legitimate. She was wrong, you know. We had a case something like that before. Depends on the terms of a will. Coniston left it quite clearly to her, naming her by name. She'd get it all right, but she didn't know that. And she wasn't going to let go of the cash.'

'Why did she need it so badly?'

Chief-Inspector Davy said grimly, 'To buy Ladislaus Malinowski. He would have married her for her money. He wouldn't have married her without it. She wasn't a fool, that girl. She knew that. But she wanted him on any terms. She was desperately in love with him.'

'I know,' said Miss Marple. She explained: 'I saw her face that day in Battersea Park . . .'

'She knew that with the money she'd get him, and without the money she'd lose him,' said Father. 'And so she planned a cold-blooded murder. She didn't hide in the area, of course. There was nobody in the area. She just stood by the railings and fired a shot and screamed, and when Michael Gorman came racing down the street from the hotel, she shot him at close quarters. Then she went on screaming. She was a cool hand. She'd no idea of incriminating young Ladislaus. She pinched his pistol because it was the only way she could get hold of one easily; and she never dreamed that he would be suspected of the crime, or that he would be anywhere in the neighbourhood that night. She thought it would be put down to some thug taking advantage of the fog. Yes, she was a cool hand. But she was afraid that night—afterwards! And her mother was afraid for her . . .'

'And now—what will you do?'

'I know she did it,' said Father, 'but I've no evidence. Maybe she'll have beginner's luck . . . Even the law seems to go on the principle now of allowing a dog to have one bite—translated into human terms. An experienced counsel could make great play with the sob stuff—so young a girl, unfortunate upbringing—and she's beautiful, you know.'

'Yes,' said Miss Marple. 'The children of Lucifer are often beautiful— And as we know, they flourish like the green bay tree.'

'But, as I tell you, it probably won't even come to that—there's no evidence—take yourself—you'll be called as a witness—a witness to what her mother said—to her mother's confession of the crime.'

'I know,' said Miss Marple. 'She impressed it on me, didn't she? She chose death for herself, at the price of her daughter going free. She forced it on me as a dying request . . .'

The connecting door to the bedroom opened. Elvira Blake came through. She was wearing a straight shift dress of pale blue. Her fair hair fell down each side of her face. She looked like one of the angels in an early primitive Italian painting. She looked from one to the other of them. She said,

'I heard a car and a crash and people shouting . . . Has there been an accident?'

'I'm sorry to tell you, Miss Blake,' said Chief-Inspector Davy formally, 'that your mother is dead.'

Elvira gave a little gasp. 'Oh no,' she said. It was a faint uncertain protest.

'Before she made her escape,' said Chief-Inspector Davy, 'because it *was* an escape—she confessed to the murder of Michael Gorman.'

'You mean—she said—that it was *she*—'

'Yes,' said Father. 'That is what she *said*. Have you anything to add?'

Elvira looked for a long time at him. Very faintly she shook her head.

'No,' she said, 'I haven't anything to add.'

Then she turned and went out of the room.

'Well,' said Miss Marple. 'Are you going to let her get away with it?'

There was a pause, then Father brought down his fist with a crash on the table.

'No,' he roared— 'No, by God I'm not!'

Miss Marple nodded her head slowly and gravely.

'May God have mercy on her soul,' she said.

A Caribbean Mystery

To my old friend
JOHN CRUIKSHANK ROSE
with happy memories of my visit
to the West Indies

CONTENTS

CHAPTER I

MAJOR PALGRAVE TELLS A STORY

"Take all this business about Kenya," said Major Palgrave. "Lots of chaps gabbing away who know nothing about the place! Now *I* spent fourteen years of my life there. Some of the best years of my life, too——"

Old Miss Marple inclined her head.

It was a gentle gesture of courtesy. Whilst Major Palgrave proceeded with the somewhat uninteresting recollections of a lifetime, Miss Marple peacefully pursued her own thoughts. It was a routine with which she was well acquainted. The locale varied. In the past, it had been predominantly India. Majors, Colonels, Lieutenant-Generals—and a familiar series of words: *Simla. Bearers. Tigers. Chota Hazri—Tiffin. Khitmagars*, and so on. With Major Palgrave the terms were slightly different. *Safari. Kikuyu. Elephants. Swahili.* But the pattern was essentially the same. An elderly man who needed a listener so that he could, in memory, relive days in which he had been happy. Days when his back had been straight, his eyesight keen, his hearing acute. Some of these talkers had been handsome soldierly old boys, some again had been regrettably unattractive; and Major Palgrave, purple of face, with a glass eye, and the general appearance of a stuffed frog, belonged in the latter category.

Miss Marple had bestowed on all of them the same gentle charity. She had sat attentively, inclining her head from time to time in gentle agreement, thinking her own thoughts and enjoying what there was to enjoy : in this case the deep blue of a Caribbean Sea.

So kind of dear Raymond,—she was thinking gratefully, so really and truly kind . . . Why he should take so much trouble about his old aunt, she really did not know. Conscience, perhaps; family feeling? Or possibly he was truly fond of her . . .

She thought, on the whole, that he *was* fond of her—he always had been—in a slightly exasperated and contemptuous way! Always trying to bring her up to date. Sending her books to read. Modern novels. So difficult—all about such unpleasant people, doing such very odd things and not, apparently, even enjoying them. " Sex " as a word had not been much mentioned in Miss Marple's young days; but there had been plenty of it—not talked about so much—but enjoyed far more than nowadays, or so it seemed to her. Though usually labelled Sin, she couldn't help feeling that that was preferable to what it seemed to be nowadays—a kind of Duty.

Her glance strayed for a moment to the book on her lap lying open at page twenty-three which was as far as she had got (and indeed as far as she felt like getting!).

'" Do you mean that you've had no sexual experience at ALL? " demanded the young man incredulously. " At *nineteen*? But you *must.* It's vital."

The girl hung her head unhappily, her straight greasy hair fell forward over her face.

" I know," she muttered, " I know."

He looked at her, stained old jersey, the bare feet, the dirty toe nails, the smell of rancid fat . . . He wondered why he found her so maddeningly attractive.

Miss Marple wondered too! And really! To have sex experience urged on you exactly as though it was an iron tonic! Poor young things . . .

" My dear Aunt Jane, why must you bury your head in the sand like a very delightful ostrich? All bound up in this idyllic rural life of yours. REAL LIFE—that's what matters."

Thus Raymond—and his Aunt Jane had looked properly abashed—and said "Yes," she was afraid she *was* rather old-fashioned.

Though really rural life was far from idyllic. People like Raymond were so ignorant. In the course of her duties in a country parish, Jane Marple had acquired quite a comprehensive knowledge of the facts of rural life. She had no urge to *talk* about them, far less to *write* about them—but she knew them. Plenty of sex, natural and unnatural. Rape, incest, perversions of all kinds. (Some kinds, indeed, that even the clever young men from Oxford who wrote books didn't seem to have heard about.)

Miss Marple came back to the Caribbean and took up the thread of what Major Palgrave was saying . . .

" A very unusual experience," she said encouragingly. " *Most* interesting."

" I could tell you a lot more. Some of the things, of course, not fit for a lady's ears——"

With the ease of long practice, Miss Marple dropped her eyelids in a fluttery fashion, and Major Palgrave continued his bowdlerised version of tribal customs whilst Miss Marple resumed her thoughts of her affectionate nephew.

Raymond West was a very successful novelist and made a large income, and he conscientiously and kindly did all he could to alleviate the life of his elderly aunt. The preceding winter she had had a bad go of pneumonia, and medical opinion had advised sunshine. In lordly fashion Raymond had suggested a trip to the West Indies. Miss Marple had demurred—at the expense, the distance, the difficulties of travel, and at abandoning her house in St. Mary Mead. Raymond had dealt with everything. A friend who was writing a book wanted a quiet place in the country. " He'll look after the house all right. He's very house proud. He's a queer. I mean——"

He had paused, slightly embarrassed—but surely even dear old Aunt Jane must have heard of queers.

He went on to deal with the next points. Travel was

nothing nowadays. She would go by air—another friend, Diana Horrocks, was going out to Trinidad and would see Aunt Jane was all right as far as there, and at St. Honoré she would stay at the Golden Palm Hotel which was run by the Sandersons. Nicest couple in the world. They'd see she was all right. He'd write to them straightaway.

As it happened the Sandersons had returned to England. But their successors, the Kendals, had been very nice and friendly and had assured Raymond that he need have no qualms about his aunt. There was a very good doctor on the island in case of emergency and they themselves would keep an eye on her and see to her comfort.

They had been as good as their word, too. Molly Kendal was an ingenuous blonde of twenty odd, always apparently in good spirits. She had greeted the old lady warmly and did everything to make her comfortable. Tim Kendal, her husband, lean, dark and in his thirties, had also been kindness itself.

So there she was, thought Miss Marple, far from the rigours of the English climate, with a nice little bungalow of her own, with friendly smiling West Indian girls to wait on her, Tim Kendal to meet her in the dining-room and crack a joke as he advised her about the day's menu, and an easy path from her bungalow to the sea front and the bathing beach where she could sit in a comfortable basket chair and watch the bathing. There were even a few elderly guests for company. Old Mr

Rafiel, Dr Graham, Canon Prescott and his sister, and her present cavalier Major Palgrave.

What more could an elderly lady want?

It is deeply to be regretted, and Miss Marple felt guilty even admitting it to herself, but she was not as satisfied as she ought to be.

Lovely and warm, yes—and *so* good for her rheumatism—and beautiful scenery, though perhaps—a trifle monotonous? So *many* palm trees. Everything the same every day—never anything *happening*. Not like St. Mary Mead where something was always happening. Her nephew had once compared life in St. Mary Mead to scum on a pond, and she had indignantly pointed out that smeared on a slide under the microscope there would be plenty of life to be observed. Yes, indeed, in St. Mary Mead, there was always something going on. Incident after incident flashed through Miss Marple's mind, the mistake in old Mrs Linnett's cough mixture—that very odd behaviour of young Polegate—the time when Georgy Wood's mother had come down to see him—(but *was* she his mother—?) the real cause of the quarrel between Joe Arden and his wife. So many interesting human problems—giving rise to endless pleasurable hours of speculation. If only there were something here that she could—well—get her teeth into.

With a start she realised that Major Palgrave had abandoned Kenya for the North West Frontier and was relating his experiences as a subaltern. Unfortunately he was asking her with great earnestness: " Now don't you agree? "

Long practice had made Miss Marple quite an adept at dealing with that one.

" I don't really feel that I've got sufficient experience to judge. I'm afraid I've led rather a sheltered life."

" And so you should, dear lady, so you should," cried Major Palgrave gallantly.

" You've had such a very varied life," went on Miss Marple, determined to make amends for her former pleasurable inattention.

" Not bad," said Major Palgrave, complacently. " Not bad at all." He looked round him appreciatively. " Lovely place, this."

" Yes, indeed," said Miss Marple and was then unable to stop herself going on: " Does anything ever happen here, I wonder? "

Major Palgrave stared.

" Oh rather. Plenty of scandals—eh what? Why, I could tell you——"

But it wasn't really scandals Miss Marple wanted. Nothing to get your teeth into in scandals nowadays. Just men and women changing partners, and calling attention to it, instead of trying decently to hush it up and be properly ashamed of themselves.

" There was even a murder here a couple of years ago. Man called Harry Western. Made a big splash in the papers. Daresay you remember it."

Miss Marple nodded without enthusiasm. It had

not been her kind of murder. It had made a big splash mainly because everyone concerned had been very rich. It had seemed likely enough that Harry Western had shot the Count de Ferrari, his wife's lover, and equally likely that his well-arranged alibi had been bought and paid for. Everyone seemed to have been drunk, and there was a fine scattering of dope addicts. Not really interesting people, thought Miss Marple—although no doubt very spectacular and attractive to *look* at. But definitely not *her* cup of tea.

" And if you ask me, that wasn't the only murder about that time." He nodded and winked. " I had my suspicions—oh!—well——"

Miss Marple dropped her ball of wool, and the Major stooped and picked it up for her.

" Talking of murder," he went on. " I once came across a very curious case—not exactly personally."

Miss Marple smiled encouragingly.

" Lot of chaps talking at the club one day, you know, and a chap began telling a story. Medical man he was. One of his cases. Young fellow came and knocked him up in the middle of the night. His wife had hanged herself. They hadn't got a telephone, so after the chap had cut her down and done what he could, he'd got out his car and hared off looking for a doctor. Well, she wasn't dead but pretty far gone. Anyway, she pulled through. Young fellow seemed devoted to her. Cried like a child. He'd noticed that she'd been odd for some time, fits of depression and all that. Well, that was that. Everything seemed all right. But actually, about a month later, the wife took an overdose of sleeping stuff and passed out. Sad case."

Major Palgrave paused, and nodded his head several times. Since there was obviously more to come Miss Marple waited.

" And that's that, you might say. Nothing there. Neurotic woman, nothing out of the usual. But about a year later, this medical chap was swapping yarns with a fellow medico, and the other chap told him about a woman who'd tried to drown herself, husband got her out, got a doctor, they pulled her round—and then a few weeks later she gassed herself.

" Well, a bit of a coincidence—eh? Same sort of story. My chap said—' I had a case rather like that. Name of Jones (or whatever the name was)—What was your man's name? ' ' Can't remember. Robinson I think. Certainly not Jones.'

" Well, the chaps looked at each other and said it was pretty odd. And then my chap pulled out a snapshot. He showed it to the second chap. ' That's the fellow,' he said—' I'd gone along the next day to check up on the particulars, and I noticed a magnificent species of hibiscus just by the front door, a variety I'd never seen before in this country. My camera was in the car and I took a photo. Just as I snapped the shutter the husband came out of the front door so I got him as well. Don't think he realised it. I asked him about the hibiscus but he couldn't tell me its name.' Second medico looked at the snap. He said: 'It's a bit out of focus—But I could swear—at any rate I'm almost sure—*it's the same man.*'

"Don't know if they followed it up. But if so they didn't get anywhere. Expect Mr Jones or Robinson covered his tracks too well. But queer story, isn't it? Wouldn't think things like that could happen."

"Oh yes, I would," said Miss Marple placidly. "Practically every day."

"Oh, come, come. That's a bit fantastic."

"If a man gets a formula that works—he won't stop. He'll go on."

"Brides in the bath—eh?"

"That kind of thing, yes."

"Doctor let me have that snap just as a curiosity——"

Major Palgrave began fumbling through an over-stuffed wallet murmuring to himself: "Lots of things in here—don't know why I keep all these things . . ."

Miss Marple thought she did know. They were part of the Major's stock-in-trade. They illustrated his repertoire of stories. The story he had just told, or so she suspected, had not been originally like that—it had been worked up a good deal in repeated telling.

The Major was still shuffling and muttering—"Forgotten all about *that* business. Good-looking woman *she* was, you'd never suspect—Now *where*—Ah—that takes my mind back—what tusks! I must show you——"

He stopped—sorted out a small photographic print and peered down at it.

" Like to see the picture of a murderer? "

He was about to pass it to her when his movement was suddenly arrested. Looking more like a stuffed frog than ever, Major Palgrave appeared to be staring fixedly over her right shoulder—from whence came the sound of approaching footsteps and voices.

" Well, I'm damned—I mean——" He stuffed everything back into his wallet and crammed it into his pocket.

His face went an even deeper shade of purplish red— He exclaimed in a loud, artificial voice.

" As I was saying—I'd like to have shown you those elephant tusks—Biggest elephant I've ever shot— Ah, hallo! " His voice took on a somewhat spurious hearty note.

" Look who's here! The great quartette—Flora and Fauna— What luck have you had to-day—Eh? "

The approaching footsteps resolved themselves into four of the hotel guests whom Miss Marple already knew by sight. They consisted of two married couples and though Miss Marple was not as yet acquainted with their surnames, she knew that the big man with the upstanding bush of thick grey hair was addressed as " Greg ", that the golden blonde woman, his wife, was known as Lucky—and that the other married couple, the dark lean man and the handsome but rather weather-beaten woman, were Edward and Evelyn.

They were botanists, she understood, and also interested in birds.

"No luck at all," said Greg—"At least no luck in getting what we were after."

"Don't know if you know Miss Marple? Colonel and Mrs. Hillingdon and Greg and Lucky Dyson."

They greeted her pleasantly and Lucky said loudly that she'd die if she didn't have a drink at once or sooner.

Greg hailed Tim Kendal who was sitting a little way away with his wife poring over account books.

"Hi, Tim. Get us some drinks." He addressed the others. "Planters Punch?"

They agreed.

"Same for you, Miss Marple?"

Miss Marple said Thank you, but she would prefer fresh lime.

"Fresh lime it is," said Tim Kendal "and five Planters Punches."

"Join us, Tim?"

"Wish I could. But I've got to fix up these accounts. Can't leave Molly to cope with everything. Steel band to-night, by the way."

"Good," cried Lucky. "Damn it," she winced, "I'm all over thorns. Ouch! Edward deliberately rammed me into a thorn bush!"

"Lovely pink flowers," said Hillingdon.

"And lovely long thorns. Sadistic brute, aren't you, Edward?"

"Not like me," said Greg, grinning. "Full of the milk of human kindness."

Evelyn Hillingdon sat down by Miss Marple and started talking to her in an easy pleasant way.

Miss Marple put her knitting down on her lap. Slowly and with some difficulty, owing to rheumatism in the neck, she turned her head over her right shoulder to look behind her. At some little distance there was the large bungalow occupied by the rich Mr Rafiel. But it showed no sign of life.

She replied suitably to Evelyn's remarks (really, how kind people were to her!) but her eyes scanned thoughtfully the faces of the two men.

Edward Hillingdon looked a nice man. Quiet but with a lot of charm . . . And Greg—big, boisterous, happy-looking. He and Lucky were Canadian or American, she thought.

She looked at Major Palgrave, still acting a *bonhomie* a little larger than life.

Interesting . . .

CHAPTER II

MISS MARPLE MAKES COMPARISONS

It was very gay that evening at the Golden Palm Hotel.

Seated at her little corner table, Miss Marple looked round her in an interested fashion. The dining-room was a large room open on three sides to the soft warm scented air of the West Indies. There were small table lamps, all softly coloured. Most of the women were in evening dress; light cotton prints out of which bronzed shoulders and arms emerged. Miss Marple herself had been urged by her nephew's wife, Joan, in the sweetest way possible, to accept " a small cheque ".

" Because, Aunt Jane, it will be rather hot out there, and I don't expect you have any very thin clothes."

Jane Marple had thanked her and had accepted the cheque. She came of the age when it was natural for the old to support and finance the young, but also for the middle-aged to look after the old. She could not, however, force herself to buy anything very *thin*! At her age she seldom felt more than pleasantly warm even in the hottest weather, and the temperature of St. Honoré was not really what is referred to as " tropical heat ". This evening she was attired in the best traditions of the provincial gentlewomen of England—grey lace.

Not that she was the only elderly person present. There were representatives of all ages in the room. There were elderly tycoons with young third or fourth wives. There were middle-aged couples from the North of England. There was a gay family from Caracas complete with children. The various countries of South America were well represented, all chattering loudly in Spanish or Portuguese. There was a solid English background of two clergymen, one doctor and one retired judge. There was even a family of Chinese. The dining-room service was mainly done by women, tall black girls of proud carriage, dressed in crisp white; but there was an experienced Italian head waiter in charge, and a French wine waiter, and there was the attentive eye of Tim Kendal watching over everything, pausing here and there to have a social word with people at their tables. His wife seconded him ably. She was a good-looking girl. Her hair was a natural golden blonde and she had a wide generous mouth that laughed easily. It was very seldom that Molly Kendal was out of temper. Her staff worked for her enthusiastically, and she adapted her manner carefully to suit her different guests. With the elderly men she laughed and flirted ; she congratulated the younger women on their clothes.

" Oh what a smashing dress you've got on to-night,

Mrs Dyson. I'm so jealous I could tear it off your back." But she looked very well in her own dress, or so Miss Marple thought; a white sheath, with a pale green embroidered silk shawl thrown over her shoulders. Lucky was fingering the shawl. "Lovely colour! I'd like one like it." "You can get them at the shop here," Molly told her and passed on. She did not pause by Miss Marple's table. Elderly ladies she usually left to her husband. "The old dears like a man much better," she used to say.

Tim Kendal came and bent over Miss Marple.

"Nothing special you want, is there?" he asked. "Because you've only got to tell me—and I could get it specially cooked for you. Hotel food, and semi-tropical at that, isn't quite what you're used to at home, I expect?"

Miss Marple smiled and said that that was one of the pleasures of coming abroad.

"That's all right, then. But if there *is* anything——"

"Such as?"

"Well—" Tim Kendal looked a little doubtful—"Bread and butter pudding?" he hazarded.

Miss Marple smiled and said that she thought she could do without bread and butter pudding very nicely for the present.

She picked up her spoon and began to eat her passion fruit sundae with cheerful appreciation.

Then the steel band began to play. The steel bands were one of the main attractions of the islands. Truth to tell, Miss Marple could have done very well without them. She considered that they made a hideous noise, unnecessarily loud. The pleasure that everyone else took in them was undeniable, however, and Miss Marple, in the true spirit of her youth, decided that as they had to be, she must manage somehow to learn to like them. She could hardly request Tim Kendal to conjure up from somewhere the muted strains of the "Blue Danube." (So graceful—waltzing.) Most peculiar, the way people danced nowadays. Flinging themselves about, seeming quite *contorted*. Oh well, young people must enjoy—— Her thoughts were arrested. Because, now she came to think of it, very few of these people *were* young. Dancing, lights, the music of a band (even a steel band) all that surely was for *youth*. But where was youth? Studying, she supposed, at universities, or doing a job—with a fortnight's holiday a year. A place like this was too far away and too expensive. This gay and carefree life was all for the thirties and the forties—and the old men who were trying to live up (or down) to their young wives. It seemed, somehow, a *pity*.

Miss Marple sighed for youth. There was Mrs Kendal, of course. She wasn't more than twenty-two or three, probably, and she seemed to be enjoying herself—but even so, it was a *job* she was doing.

At a table nearby Canon Prescott and his sister were sitting. They motioned to Miss Marple to join them for coffee and she did so. Miss Prescott was a thin severe-looking woman, the Canon was a round, rubicund man, breathing geniality.

Coffee was brought, and chairs were pushed a little way away from the tables. Miss Prescott opened a work bag and took out some frankly hideous table mats that she was hemming. She told Miss Marple all about the day's events. They had visited a new Girls' School in the morning. After an afternoon's rest, they had walked through a cane plantation to have tea at a *pension* where some friends of theirs were staying.

Since the Prescotts had been at the Golden Palm longer than Miss Marple, they were able to enlighten her as to some of her fellow guests.

That very old man, Mr Rafiel. He came every year. Fantastically rich! Owned an enormous chain of supermarkets in the North of England. The young woman with him was his secretary, Esther Walters—a widow. (Quite all *right*, of course. Nothing improper. After all, he was nearly eighty!)

Miss Marple accepted the propriety of the relationship with an understanding nod and the Canon remarked:

" A very nice young woman; her mother, I understand, is a widow and lives in Chichester."

" Mr Rafiel has a valet with him, too. Or rather a kind of Nurse Attendant—he's a qualified masseur, I believe. Jackson, his name is. Poor Mr Rafiel is practically paralysed. So sad—with all that money, too."

" A generous and cheerful giver," said Canon Prescott approvingly.

People were regrouping themselves round about, some going farther from the steel band, others crowding up to it. Major Palgrave had joined the Hillingdon-Dyson quartette.

" Now those people——" said Miss Prescott, lowering her voice quite unnecessarily since the steel band easily drowned it.

" Yes, I was going to ask you about them."

" They were here last year. They spend three months every year in the West Indies, going round the different islands. The tall thin man is Colonel Hillingdon and the dark woman is his wife—they are botanists. The other two, Mr and Mrs Gregory Dyson—they're American. He writes on butterflies, I believe. And all of them are interested in birds."

" So nice for people to have open-air hobbies," said Canon Prescott genially.

" I don't think they'd like to hear you call it hobbies, Jeremy," said his sister. " They have articles printed in the *National Geographic* and in the *Royal Horticultural Journal*. They take themselves very seriously."

A loud outburst of laughter came from the table they had been observing. It was loud enough to overcome the steel band. Gregory Dyson was leaning back in his chair and thumping the table, his wife was protesting, and Major Palgrave emptied his glass and seemed to be applauding.

They hardly qualified for the moment as people who took themselves seriously.

" Major Palgrave should not drink so much," said Miss Prescott acidly. " He has blood pressure."

A fresh supply of Planters Punches were brought to the table.

" It's so nice to get people sorted out," said Miss Marple. " When I met them this afternoon I wasn't sure which was married to which."

There was a slight pause. Miss Prescott coughed a small dry cough, and said—" Well, as to that——"

" Joan," said the Canon in an admonitory voice. " Perhaps it would be wise to say no more."

" Really, Jeremy, I wasn't going to say *anything*. Only that last year, for some reason or other—I really don't know *why*—we got the idea that Mrs Dyson was Mrs Hillingdon until someone told us she wasn't."

" It's odd how one gets impressions, isn't it? " said Miss Marple innocently. Her eyes met Miss Prescott's for a moment. A flash of womanly understanding passed between them.

A more sensitive man than Canon Prescott might have felt that he was *de trop*.

Another signal passed between the women. It said as clearly as if the words had been spoken: " *Some other time* . . ."

" Mr Dyson calls his wife ' Lucky '. Is that her real name or a nickname? " asked Miss Marple.

" It can hardly be her real name, I should think."

" I happened to ask him," said the Canon. " He said he called her Lucky because she was his good luck piece. If he lost her, he said, he'd lose his luck. Very nicely put, I thought."

" He's very fond of joking," said Miss Prescott.

The Canon looked at his sister doubtfully.

The steel band outdid itself with a wild burst of cacophony and a troupe of dancers came racing on to the floor.

Miss Marple and the others turned their chairs to watch. Miss Marple enjoyed the dancing better than the music; she liked the shuffling feet and the rhythmic sway of the bodies. It seemed, she thought, very *real.* It had a kind of power of understatement.

To-night, for the first time, she began to feel slightly at home in her new environment. . . . Up to now, she had missed what she usually found so easily, points of resemblance in the people she met, to various people known to her personally. She had, possibly, been dazzled by the gay clothes and the exotic colouring; but soon, she felt, she would be able to make some interesting comparisons.

Molly Kendal, for instance, was like that nice girl whose name she couldn't remember, but who was a conductress on the Market Basing bus. Helped you in, and never rang the bus on until she was sure you'd sat down safely. Tim Kendal was just a little like the head waiter at the Royal George in Medchester. Self-confident, and yet, at the same time, worried. (He had had an ulcer, she remembered.) As for Major Palgrave, he was indistinguishable from General Leroy, Captain Flemming, Admiral Wicklow and Commander Richardson. She went on to someone more interesting. Greg for instance? Greg was difficult because he was American. A dash of Sir George Trollope, perhaps, always so full of jokes at the Civil Defence meetings—or perhaps Mr Murdoch the butcher. Mr Murdoch had had rather a bad reputation, but some people said it was just gossip, and that Mr Murdoch himself liked to encourage the rumours! 'Lucky' now? Well, that was easy—Marleen at the Three Crowns. Evelyn Hillingdon? She couldn't fit Evelyn in precisely. In appearance she fitted many roles—tall thin weather-beaten Englishwomen were plentiful. Lady Caroline Wolfe, Peter Wolfe's first wife, who had committed suicide? Or there was Leslie James—that quiet woman who seldom showed what she felt and who had sold up her house and left without ever telling anyone she was going. Colonel Hillingdon? No immediate clue there. She'd have to get to know him a little first. One of those quiet men with good manners. You never knew what they were thinking about. Sometimes they surprised you. Major Harper, she remembered, had quietly cut his throat one day. Nobody had ever known why. Miss Marple thought that she did know—but she'd never been quite sure. . . .

Her eyes strayed to Mr Rafiel's table. The principal thing known about Mr Rafiel was that he was incredibly rich, he came every year to the West Indies, he was semi-paralysed and looked like a wrinkled old bird of prey. His clothes hung loosely on his shrunken form. He might have been seventy or eighty, or even ninety. His eyes were shrewd and he was frequently rude, but people seldom took offence, partly because he was so rich, and partly because of his overwhelming personality which hypnotised you into feeling that somehow, Mr Rafiel had the right to be rude if he wanted to.

With him sat his secretary, Mrs Walters. She had corn-coloured hair, and a pleasant face. Mr Rafiel was frequently very rude to her, but she never seemed to notice it—She was not so much subservient, as oblivious. She behaved like a well-trained hospital nurse. Possibly, thought Miss Marple, she had been a hospital nurse.

A young man, tall and good-looking, in a white jacket, came to stand by Mr Rafiel's chair. The old man looked up at him, nodded, then motioned him to a chair. The young man sat down as bidden. " Mr Jackson, I presume," said Miss Marple to herself—" His valet-attendant."

She studied Mr Jackson with some attention.

II

In the bar, Molly Kendal stretched her back, and

slipped off her high-heeled shoes. Tim came in from the terrace to join her. They had the bar to themselves for the moment.

"Tired, darling?" he asked.

"Just a bit. I seem to be feeling my feet to-night."

"Not too much for you, is it? All this? I know it's hard work." He looked at her anxiously.

She laughed. "Oh Tim, don't be ridiculous. I love it here. It's gorgeous. The kind of dream I've always had, come true."

"Yes, it would be all right—if one was just a guest. But running the show—that's work."

"Well, you can't have anything for nothing, can you?" said Molly Kendal reasonably.

Tim Kendal frowned.

"You think it's going all right? A success? We're making a go of it?"

"Of course we are."

"You don't think people are saying, 'It's not the same as when the Sandersons were here'."

"Of course *someone* will be saying that—they always do! But only some old stick-in-the-mud. I'm sure that we're far better at the job than they were. We're more glamorous. You charm the old pussies and manage to look as though you'd like to make love to the desperate forties and fifties, and I ogle the old gentlemen and make them feel sexy dogs—or play the sweet little daughter the sentimental ones would love to have had. Oh, we've got it all taped splendidly."

Tim's frown vanished.

" As long as *you* think so. I get scared. We've risked everything on making a job of this. I chucked my job——"

" And quite right to do so," Molly put in quickly. " It was soul-destroying."

He laughed and kissed the tip of her nose.

" I tell you we've got it taped," she repeated. " Why do you always worry? "

" Made that way, I suppose. I'm always thinking—suppose something should go wrong."

" What sort of thing——"

" Oh I don't know. Somebody might get drowned."

" Not they. It's one of the safest of all the beaches. And we've got that hulking Swede always on guard."

" I'm a fool," said Tim Kendal. He hesitated—and then said, " You—haven't had any more of those dreams, have you? "

" That was shellfish," said Molly, and laughed.

CHAPTER III

A DEATH IN THE HOTEL

Miss Marple had her breakfast brought to her in bed as usual. Tea, a boiled egg, and a slice of paw-paw.

The fruit on the island, thought Miss Marple, was rather disappointing. It seemed always to be paw-paw. If she could have a nice apple now—but apples seemed to be unknown.

Now that she had been here a week, Miss Marple had cured herself of the impulse to ask what the weather was like. The weather was always the same—fine. No interesting variations.

" The many splendoured weather of an English day " she murmured to herself and wondered if it was a quotation, or whether she had made it up.

There were, of course, hurricanes, or so she understood. But hurricanes were not weather in Miss Marple's sense of the word. They were more in the nature of an Act of God. There was rain, short violent rainfall that lasted five minutes and stopped abruptly. Everything and everyone was wringing wet, but in another five minutes they were dry again.

The black West Indian girl smiled and said Good

Morning as she placed the tray on Miss Marple's knees. Such lovely white teeth and so happy and smiling. Nice natures, all these girls, and a pity they were so averse to getting married. It worried Canon Prescott a good deal. Plenty of christenings, he said, trying to console himself, but no weddings.

Miss Marple ate her breakfast and decided how she would spend her day. It didn't really take much deciding. She would get up at her leisure, moving slowly because it was rather hot and her fingers weren't as nimble as they used to be. Then she would rest for ten minutes or so, and she would take her knitting and walk slowly along towards the hotel and decide where she would settle herself. On the terrace overlooking the sea? Or should she go on to the bathing beach to watch the bathers and the children? Usually it was the latter. In the afternoon, after her rest, she might take a drive. It really didn't matter very much.

To-day would be a day like any other day, she said to herself.

Only, of course, it wasn't.

Miss Marple carried out her programme as planned and was slowly making her way along the path towards the hotel when she met Molly Kendal. For once that sunny young woman was not smiling. Her air of distress was so unlike her that Miss Marple said immediately:

" My dear, is anything wrong? "

Molly nodded. She hesitated and then said: " Well,

you'll have to know—everyone will have to know. It's Major Palgrave. He's dead."

"Dead?"

"Yes. He died in the night."

"Oh dear, I *am* sorry."

"Yes, it's horrid having a death here. It makes everyone depressed. Of course—he *was* quite old."

"He seemed quite well and cheerful yesterday," said Miss Marple, slightly resenting this calm assumption that everyone of advanced years was liable to die at any minute.

"He seemed quite healthy," she added.

"He had high blood pressure," said Molly.

"But surely there are things one takes nowadays—some kind of pill. Science is so wonderful."

"Oh yes, but perhaps he forgot to take his pills, or took too many of them. Like insulin, you know."

Miss Marple did not think that diabetes and high blood pressure were at all the same kind of thing. She asked:

"What does the doctor say?"

"Oh, Dr Graham, who's practically retired now, and lives in the hotel, took a look at him, and the local people came officially, of course, to give a death certificate, but it all seems quite straightforward. This kind of thing is quite liable to happen when you have high blood pressure, especially if you overdo the alcohol, and Major Palgrave was really very naughty that way. Last night, for instance."

" Yes, I noticed," said Miss Marple.

" He probably forgot to take his pills. It is bad luck for the old boy—but people can't live for ever, can they? But it's terribly worrying—for me and Tim, I mean. People might suggest it was something in the food."

" But surely the symptoms of food poisoning and of blood pressure are *quite* different? "

" Yes. But people do *say* things so easily. And if people decided the food was bad—and left—or told their friends——"

" I really don't think you need worry," said Miss Marple kindly. " As you say, an elderly man like Major Palgrave—he must have been over seventy—is quite liable to die. To most people it will seem quite an ordinary occurrence—sad, but not out of the way at all."

" If only," said Molly unhappily, " it hadn't been so *sudden*."

Yes, it had been very sudden, Miss Marple thought as she walked slowly on. There he had been last night, laughing and talking in the best of spirits with the Hillingdons and the Dysons.

The Hillingdons and the Dysons. . . . Miss Marple walked more slowly still . . . Finally she stopped abruptly. Instead of going to the bathing beach she settled herself in a shady corner of the terrace. She took out her knitting and the needles clicked rapidly as though they were trying to match the speed of her thoughts. *She didn't like it—no she didn't like it. It came so pat.*

She went over the occurrences of yesterday in her mind.

Major Palgrave and his stories . . .

That was all as usual and one didn't need to listen very closely . . . Perhaps, though, it would have been better if she had.

Kenya—he had talked about Kenya and then India —the North West Frontier—and then—for some reason they had got on to murder— And even *then* she hadn't really been listening . . .

Some famous case that had taken place out here— that had been in the newspapers—

It was after that—when he picked up her ball of wool—that he had begun telling her about a snap-shot—*A snapshot of a murderer*—that is what he had said.

Miss Marple closed her eyes and tried to remember just exactly how that story had gone.

It had been rather a confused story—told to the Major in his Club—or in somebody else's club—told him by a doctor—who had heard it from another doctor—and one doctor had taken a snapshot of some-one coming through a front door—someone who was a murderer—

Yes, that was it—the various details were coming back to her now—

And he had offered to show her that snapshot—

He had got out his wallet and begun hunting through its contents—talking all the time—

And then still talking, he had looked up—had looked—not at her—but at something behind her—behind her right shoulder to be accurate. And he had stopped talking, his face had gone purple—and he had started stuffing back everything into his wallet with slightly shaky hands and had begun talking in a loud unnatural voice about elephant tusks!

A moment or two later the Hillingdons and the Dysons had joined them. . . .

It was then that she had turned her head over her right shoulder to look . . . But there had been nothing and nobody to see. To her left, some distance away, in the direction of the hotel, there had been Tim Kendal and his wife ; and beyond them a family group of Venezuelans. But Major Palgrave had not been looking in that direction . . .

Miss Marple meditated until lunch time.

After lunch she did not go for a drive.

Instead she sent a message to say that she was not feeling very well, and to ask if Dr Graham would be kind enough to come and see her.

CHAPTER IV

MISS MARPLE SEEKS MEDICAL ATTENTION

Dr Graham was a kindly elderly man of about sixty-five. He had practised in the West Indies for many years, but was now semi-retired, and left most of his work to his West Indian partners. He greeted Miss Marple pleasantly and asked her what the trouble was. Fortunately at Miss Marple's age, there was always some ailment that could be discussed with slight exaggerations on the patient's part. Miss Marple hesitated between " her shoulder " and " her knee ", but finally decided upon the knee. Miss Marple's knee, as she would have put it to herself, was always with her.

Dr Graham was exceedingly kindly but he refrained from putting into words the fact that at her time of life such troubles were only to be expected. He prescribed for her one of the brands of useful little pills that form the basis of a doctor's prescriptions. Since he knew by experience that many elderly people could be lonely when they first came to St. Honoré, he remained for a while gently chatting.

" A very nice man," thought Miss Marple to herself,

" and I really feel rather ashamed of having to tell him lies. But I don't quite see what else I can do."

Miss Marple had been brought up to have a proper regard for truth and was indeed by nature a very truthful person. But on certain occasions, when she considered it her duty so to do, she could tell lies with a really astonishing verisimilitude.

She cleared her throat, uttered an apologetic little cough, and said, in an old ladyish and slightly twittering manner:

"There is something, Dr Graham, I would like to ask you. I don't really like mentioning it—but I don't quite see what else I am to do—although of course it's *quite* unimportant really. But you see, it's important to *me*. And I hope you will understand and not think what I am asking is tiresome or—or unpardonable in any way."

To this opening Dr Graham replied kindly: " Something is worrying you? Do let me help."

" It's connected with Major Palgrave. *So* sad about his dying. It was quite a shock when I heard it this morning."

" Yes," said Dr Graham, " it was very sudden, I'm afraid. He seemed in such good spirits yesterday." He spoke kindly, but conventionally. To him, clearly, Major Palgrave's death was nothing out of the way. Miss Marple wondered whether she was really making something out of nothing. Was this suspicious habit of mind growing on her? Perhaps she could no longer trust her own judgment. Not that it was judgment really, only suspicion. Anyway she was in for it now! She must go ahead.

"We were sitting talking together yesterday afternoon," she said. "He was telling me about his very varied and interesting life. So many strange parts of the globe."

"Yes indeed," said Dr Graham, who had been bored many times by the Major's reminiscences.

"And then he spoke of his family, boyhood rather, and I told him a little about my own nephews and nieces and he listened very sympathetically. And I showed him a snapshot I had with me of one of my nephews. Such a dear boy—at least not exactly a boy now, but always a boy to *me* if you understand."

"Quite so," said Dr Graham, wondering how long it would be before the old lady was going to come to the point.

"I had handed it to him and he was examining it when quite suddenly those people—those very nice people—who collect wild flowers and butterflies, Colonel and Mrs Hillingdon I think the name is——"

"Oh yes? The Hillingdons and the Dysons."

"Yes, that's right. They came suddenly along laughing and talking. They sat down and ordered drinks and we all talked together. Very pleasant it was. But without thinking, Major Palgrave must have put back my snapshot into his wallet and returned it to his pocket. I wasn't paying very much attention at the time but I remembered afterward and I said to myself —' I mustn't forget to ask the Major to give me back my picture of Denzil.' I *did* think of it last night while the dancing and the band was going on, but I didn't like to interrupt him just then, because they were having such a merry party together and I thought ' I will remember to ask him for it in the morning '. Only this morning——" Miss Marple paused—out of breath.

" Yes, yes," said Dr Graham, " I quite understand. And you—well, naturally you want the snapshot back. Is that it? "

Miss Marple nodded her head in eager agreement.

" Yes. That's it. You see, it is the only one I have got and I haven't got the negative. And I would hate to lose that snapshot, because poor Denzil died some five or six years ago and he was my favourite nephew. This is the only picture I have to remind me of him. I wondered—I hoped—it is rather tiresome of me to ask—whether you could possibly manage to get hold of it for me? I don't really know who else to ask, you see. I don't know who'll attend to all his belongings and things like that. It is all so difficult. They would think it such a nuisance of me. You see, they don't understand. Nobody could quite understand what this snapshot means to me."

" Of course, of course," said Dr Graham. " I quite understand. A most natural feeling on your part. Actually, I am meeting the local authorities shortly— the funeral is to-morrow, and someone will be coming from the Administrator's office to look over his papers and effects before communicating with the next of kin —all that sort of thing— If you could describe this snapshot."

" It was just the front of a house," said Miss Marple. " And someone—Denzil, I mean—was just coming out of the front door. As I say it was taken by one of my other nephews who is very keen on flower shows—and he was photographing a hibiscus, I think, or one of those beautiful—something like antipasto—lilies. Denzil just happened to come out of the front door at that time. It wasn't a very good photograph of him—just a trifle blurred— But I liked it and have always kept it."

" Well," said Dr Graham, " that seems clear enough. I think we'll have no difficulty in getting back your picture for you, Miss Marple."

He rose from his chair. Miss Marple smiled up at him.

" You are very kind, Dr Graham, very kind *indeed.* You do understand, don't you? "

" Of course I do, of course I do," said Dr Graham, shaking her warmly by the hand. " Now don't you worry. Exercise that knee every day gently but not too much, and I'll send you round these tablets. Take one three times a day."

CHAPTER V

MISS MARPLE MAKES A DECISION

The funeral service was said over the body of the late Major Palgrave on the following day. Miss Marple attended in company with Miss Prescott. The Canon read the service—after that life went on as usual.

Major Palgrave's death was already only an incident, a slightly unpleasant incident, but one that was soon forgotten. Life here was sunshine, sea, and social pleasures. A grim visitor had interrupted these activities, casting a momentary shadow, but the shadow was now gone. After all, nobody had known the deceased very well. He had been rather a garrulous elderly man of the club-bore type, always telling you personal reminiscences that you had no particular desire to hear. He had had little to anchor himself to any particular part of the world. His wife had died many years ago. He had had a lonely life and a lonely death. But it had been the kind of loneliness that spends itself in living amongst people, and in passing the time that way not unpleasantly. Major Palgrave might have been a lonely man, he had also been quite a cheerful one. He had enjoyed himself in his own particular way. And now he was dead, buried, and nobody cared very much, and in another week's time nobody would even remember him or spare him a passing thought.

The only person who could possibly be said to miss him was Miss Marple. Not indeed out of any personal affection, but he represented a kind of life that she knew. As one grew older, so she reflected to herself, one got more and more into the habit of listening; listening possibly without any great interest, but there had been between her and the Major the gentle give and take of two old people. It had had a cheerful, human quality. She did not actually mourn Major Palgrave but she missed him.

On the afternoon of the funeral, as she was sitting knitting in her favourite spot, Dr Graham came and joined her. She put her needles down and greeted him. He said at once, rather apologetically:

"I am afraid I have rather disappointing news, Miss Marple."

"Indeed? About my——"

"Yes. We haven't found that precious snapshot of yours. I'm afraid that will be a disappointment to you."

"Yes. Yes it is. But of course it does not *really* matter. It was a sentimentality. I do realise that now. It wasn't in Major Palgrave's wallet?"

"No. Nor anywhere else among his things. There were a few letters and newspaper clippings and odds and ends, and a few old photographs, but no sign of a snapshot such as you mentioned."

"Oh dear," said Miss Marple. "Well, it can't be helped... Thank you very much, Dr Graham, for the trouble you've taken."

"Oh it was no trouble, indeed. But I know quite well from my own experience how much family trifles mean to one, especially as one is getting older."

The old lady was really taking it very well, he thought. Major Palgrave, he presumed, had probably come across the snapshot when taking something out of his wallet, and not even realising how it had come there, had torn it up as something of no importance. But of course it was of great importance to this old lady. Still, she seemed quite cheerful and philosophical about it.

Internally, however, Miss Marple was far from being either cheerful or philosophical. She wanted a little time in which to think things out, but she was also determined to use her present opportunities to the fullest effect.

She engaged Dr Graham in conversation with an eagerness which she did not attempt to conceal. That kindly man, putting down her flow of talk to the natural loneliness of an old lady, exerted himself to divert her mind from the loss of the snapshot, by conversing easily and pleasantly about life in St. Honoré, and the various interesting places perhaps Miss Marple might like to visit. He hardly knew himself how the conversation drifted back to Major Palgrave's decease.

"It seems so sad," said Miss Marple, "to think of

anyone dying like this away from home. Though I gather, from what he himself told me, that he had no immediate family. It seems he lived by himself in London."

" He travelled a fair amount, I believe," said Dr Graham. " At any rate in the winters. He didn't care for our English winters. Can't say I blame him."

" No, indeed," said Miss Marple. " And perhaps he had some special reason like a weakness of the lungs or something which made it necessary for him to winter abroad? "

" Oh no, I don't think so."

" He had high blood pressure, I believe. So sad nowadays. One hears so much of it."

" He spoke about it to you, did he? "

" Oh no. No, *he* never mentioned it. It was somebody else who told me."

" Ah, really."

" I suppose," went on Miss Marple, " that death was to be expected under those circumstances."

" Not necessarily," said Dr Graham. " There are methods of controlling blood pressure nowadays."

" His death *seemed* very sudden—but I suppose *you* weren't surprised."

" Well I wasn't particularly surprised in a man of that age. But I certainly didn't expect it. Frankly, he always seemed to me in very good form, but I hadn't ever attended him professionally. I'd never taken his blood pressure or anything like that."

"Does one know—I mean, does a doctor know—when a man has high blood pressure just by looking at him?" Miss Marple inquired with a kind of dewy innocence.

"Not just by looking," said the doctor, smiling. "One has to do a bit of testing."

"Oh I see. That dreadful thing when you put a rubber band round somebody's arm and blow it up—I dislike it *so* much. But my doctor said that my blood pressure was really very good for my age."

"Well that's good hearing," said Dr Graham.

"Of course, the Major *was* rather fond of Planters Punch," said Miss Marple thoughtfully.

"Yes. Not the best thing with blood pressure—alcohol."

"One takes tablets, doesn't one, or so I have heard?"

"Yes. There are several on the market. There was a bottle of one of them in his room—Serenite."

"How wonderful science is nowadays," said Miss Marple. "Doctors can do so much, can't they?"

"We all have one great competitor," said Dr Graham. "Nature, you know. And some of the good old-fashioned home remedies come back from time to time."

"Like putting cobwebs on a cut?" said Miss Marple. "We always used to do that when I was a child."

"Very sensible," said Dr Graham.

"And a linseed poultice on the chest and rubbing in camphorated oil for a bad cough."

" I see you know it all! " said Dr Graham laughing. He got up. " How's the knee? Not been too troublesome? "

" No, it seems much, much better."

" Well, we won't say whether that's Nature or my pills," said Dr Graham. " Sorry I couldn't have been of more help to you."

" But you have been most kind—I am really ashamed of taking up your time— Did you say that there were no photographs in the Major's wallet? "

" Oh yes—a very old one of the Major himself as quite a young man on a polo pony—and one of a dead tiger— He was standing with his foot on it. Snaps of that sort—memories of his younger days— But I looked very carefully, I assure you, and the one you describe of your nephew was definitely not there——"

" Oh I'm sure you looked carefully—I didn't mean that—I was just interested— We all tend to keep such very odd things——"

" Treasures from the past," said the doctor smiling. He said good-bye and departed.

Miss Marple remained looking thoughtfully at the palm trees and the sea. She did not pick up her knitting again for some minutes. She had a fact now. She had to think about that fact and what it meant. The snapshot that the Major had brought out of his wallet and replaced so hurriedly was *not there after he died.* It was not the sort of thing the Major would throw away. He had replaced it in his wallet and it ought to have been in his wallet after his death. Money might have been stolen, but no-one would want to steal a snapshot. Unless, that is, they had a special reason for so doing. . . .

Miss Marple's face was grave. She had to take a decision. Was she, or was she not, going to allow Major Palgrave to remain quietly in his grave? Might it not be better to do just that? She quoted under her breath. " Duncan is dead. After Life's fitful fever he sleeps well! " Nothing could hurt Major Palgrave now. He had gone where danger could not touch him. Was it just a coincidence that he should have died on that particular night? Or was it just possibly *not* a coincidence? Doctors accepted the deaths of elderly men so easily. Especially since in his room there had been a bottle of the tablets that people with high blood pressure had to take every day of their lives. But if someone had taken the snapshot from the Major's wallet, that same person could have put that bottle of tablets in the Major's room. She herself never remembered *seeing* the Major take tablets; he had never spoken about his blood pressure to her. The only thing he had ever said about his health was the admission-- " Not as young as I was ". He had been occasionally a little short of breath, a trifle asthmatic, nothing else. But someone had mentioned that Major Palgrave had high blood pressure—Molly? Miss Prescott? She couldn't remember.

Miss Marple sighed, then admonished herself in

words, though she did not speak those words aloud.

"Now, Jane, what are you suggesting or thinking? Are you, perhaps, just making the whole thing up? Have you *really* got anything to build on?"

She went over, step by step, as nearly as she could, the conversation between herself and the Major on the subject of murder and murderers.

"Oh dear," said Miss Marple. "Even if—really, I *don't* see how I *can* do anything about it——"

But she knew that she meant to try.

CHAPTER VI

IN THE SMALL HOURS

Miss Marple woke early. Like many old people she slept lightly and had periods of wakefulness which she used for the planning of some action or actions to be carried out on the next or following days. Usually, of course, these were of a wholly private or domestic nature, of little interest to anybody but herself. But this morning Miss Marple lay thinking soberly and constructively of murder, and what, if her suspicions were correct, she could do about it. It wasn't going to be easy. She had one weapon and one weapon only, and that was conversation.

Old ladies were given to a good deal of rambling conversation. People were bored by this, but certainly did not suspect them of ulterior motives. It would not be a case of asking direct questions. (Indeed, she would have found it difficult to know what questions to ask!) It would be a question of finding out a little more about certain people. She reviewed these certain people in her mind.

She could find out, possibly, a little more about Major Palgrave, but would that really help her? She doubted if it would. If Major Palgrave had been killed it was not because of secrets in his life or to inherit his money or for revenge upon him. In fact, although he was the victim, it was one of those rare cases where a greater knowledge of the victim does not help you or lead you in any way to his murderer. The point, it seemed to her, and the sole point, was that Major Palgrave talked too much!

She had learnt one rather interesting fact from Dr Graham. He had had in his wallet various photographs; one of himself in company with a polo pony, one of a dead tiger, also one or two other shots of the same nature. Now why did Major Palgrave carry these about with him? Obviously, thought Miss Marple, with long experience of old Admirals, Brigadier-Generals and mere Majors behind her, because he had certain stories which he enjoyed telling to people. Starting off with " Curious thing happened once when I was out tiger shooting in India . . ." Or a reminiscence of himself and a polo pony. Therefore this story about a suspected murderer would in due course be illustrated by the production of the snapshot from his wallet.

He had been following that pattern in his conversation with her. The subject of murder having come up, and to focus interest on his story, he had done what he no doubt usually did, produced his snapshot and said something in the nature of " Wouldn't think this chap was a murderer, would you? "

The point was that it had been a *habit* of his. This murderer story was one of his regular repertoire. If any reference to murder came up, then away went the Major, full steam ahead.

In that case reflected Miss Marple, he might *already* have told his story to someone else here. Or to more than one person— If that were so, then she herself might learn from that person what the further details of the story had been, possibly what the person in the snapshot had looked like.

She nodded her head in satisfaction— That would be a beginning.

And, of course, there were the people she called in her mind the " Four Suspects ". Though really, since Major Palgrave had been talking about a *man*—there were only two. Colonel Hillingdon or Mr Dyson, very unlikely looking murderers, but then murderers so often *were* unlikely. Could there have been anyone else? She had seen no-one when she turned her head to look. There was the bungalow of course. Mr Rafiel's bungalow. Could somebody have come out of the bungalow and gone in again before she had had time to turn her head? If so, it could only have been the valet-attendant. What was his name? Oh yes, Jackson. Could it have been *Jackson* who had come out of the door? That would have been the same pose as the photograph. *A man coming out of a door.* Recognition might have struck suddenly. Up till then, Major Palgrave would not have looked at Arthur Jackson, valet-attendant, with any interest. His roving and curious eye was essentially a snobbish eye—Arthur Jackson was not a *pukka sahib*—Major Palgrave would not have glanced at him twice.

Until, perhaps, he had had the snapshot in his hand, and had looked over Miss Marple's right shoulder and had seen a man coming out of a door . . . ?

Miss Marple turned over on her pillow—Programme for to-morrow—or rather for to-day—Further investigation of the Hillingdons, the Dysons and Arthur Jackson, valet-attendant.

II

Dr Graham also woke early. Usually he turned over and went to sleep again. But to-day he was uneasy and sleep failed to come. This anxiety that made it so difficult to go to sleep again was a thing he had not suffered from for a long time. What was causing this anxiety? Really, he couldn't make it out. He lay there thinking it over. Something to do with—something to do with—yes, Major Palgrave. Major Palgrave's death? He didn't see, though, what there could be to make him uneasy there. Was it something that that twittery old lady had said? Bad luck for her about her snapshot. She'd taken it very well. But now what was it she had said, what chance word of hers had it been, that had given him this funny feeling of uneasiness?

After all, there was nothing *odd* about the Major's death. Nothing at all. At least he supposed there was nothing at all.

It was quite clear that in the Major's state of health—a faint check came in his thought process. Did he really know much *about* Major Palgrave's state of health? Everybody *said* that he'd suffered from high blood pressure. But he himself had never had any conversation with the Major about it. But then he'd never had much conversation with Major Palgrave anyway. Palgrave was an old bore and he avoided old bores. Why on earth should he have this idea that perhaps everything *mightn't* be all right? Was it that old woman? But after all she hadn't *said* anything. Anyway, it was none of his business. The local authorities were quite satisfied. There had been that bottle of Serenite tablets, and the old boy had apparently talked to people about his blood pressure quite freely.

Dr Graham turned over in bed and soon went to sleep again.

III

Outside the hotel grounds, in one of a row of shanty cabins beside a creek, the girl Victoria Johnson rolled over and sat up in bed. The St. Honoré girl was a magnificent creature with a torso of black marble such as a sculptor would have enjoyed. She ran her fingers through her dark, tightly curling hair. With her foot she nudged her sleeping companion in the ribs.

"Wake up, man."

The man grunted and turned.

"What you want? It's not morning."

"Wake up, man. I want to talk to you."

The man sat up, stretched, showed a wide mouth and beautiful teeth.

"What's worrying you, woman?"

"That Major man who died. Something I don't like. Something wrong about it."

"Ah, what d'you want to worry about that? He was old. He died."

"Listen, man. It's them pills. Them pills the doctor asked me about."

"Well, what about them? He took too many maybe."

"No. It's not that. Listen." She leant towards him, talking vehemently. He yawned and lay down again.

"There's nothing in that. What're you talking about?"

"All the same, I'll speak to Mrs Kendal about it in the morning. I think there's something wrong there somewhere."

"Shouldn't bother," said the man who, without benefit of ceremony, she considered as her present husband. "Don't let's look for trouble," he said and rolled over on his side yawning.

CHAPTER VII

MORNING ON THE BEACH

It was mid morning on the beach below the hotel.

Evelyn Hillingdon came out of the water and dropped on the warm golden sand. She took off her bathing cap and shook her dark head vigorously. The beach was not a very big one. People tended to congregate there in the mornings and about 11.30 there was always something of a social reunion. To Evelyn's left in one of the exotic-looking modern basket chairs lay Señora de Caspearo, a handsome woman from Venezuela. Next to her was old Mr Rafiel who was by now the doyen of the Golden Palm Hotel and held the sway that only an elderly invalid of great wealth could attain. Esther Walters was in attendance on him. She usually had her shorthand notebook and pencil with her in case Mr Rafiel should suddenly think of urgent business cables which must be got off at once. Mr Rafiel in beach attire was incredibly desiccated, his bones draped with festoons of dry skin. Though looking like a man on the point of death, he had looked exactly the same for at least the last eight years—or so it was said in the islands. Sharp blue eyes peered out of his wrinkled cheeks, and his principal pleasure in life was denying robustly anything that anyone else said.

Miss Marple was also present. As usual she sat and knitted and listened to what went on, and very occasionally joined in the conversation. When she did so, everyone was surprised because they had usually forgotten that she was there! Evelyn Hillingdon looked at her indulgently, and thought that she was a nice old pussy.

Señora de Caspearo rubbed some more oil on her long beautiful legs and hummed to herself. She was not a woman who spoke much. She looked discontentedly at the flask of sun oil.

" This is not so good as Frangipanio," she said, sadly. " One cannot get it here. A pity." Her eyelids drooped again.

" Are you going in for your dip now, Mr Rafiel? " asked Esther Walters.

" I'll go in when I'm ready," said Mr Rafiel, snappishly.

" It's half past eleven," said Mrs Walters.

" What of it? " said Mr Rafiel. " Think I'm the kind of man to be tied by the clock? Do this at the hour, do this at twenty minutes past, do that at twenty to—bah! "

Mrs Walters had been in attendance on Mr Rafiel long enough to have adopted her own formula for dealing with him. She knew that he liked a good space of time in which to recover from the exertion of bathing

and she had therefore reminded him of the time, allowing a good ten minutes for him to rebut her suggestion and then be able to adopt it without seeming to do so.

"I don't like these espadrilles," said Mr Rafiel raising a foot and looking at it. "I told that fool Jackson so. The man never pays attention to a word I say."

"I'll fetch you some others, shall I, Mr Rafiel?"

"No, you won't, you'll sit here and keep quiet. I hate people rushing about like clucking hens."

Evelyn shifted slightly in the warm sand, stretching out her arms.

Miss Marple, intent on her knitting—or so it seemed—stretched out a foot, then hastily she apologised.

"I'm so sorry, so very sorry, Mrs Hillingdon. I'm afraid I kicked you."

"Oh, it's quite all right," said Evelyn. "This beach gets rather crowded."

"Oh, please don't move. Please. I'll move my chair a little back so that I won't do it again."

As Miss Marple resettled herself, she went on talking in a childish and garrulous manner.

"It still seems so wonderful to be *here*! I've never been to the West Indies before, you know. I thought it was the kind of place I never should come to and here I am. All by the kindness of my dear nephew. I suppose you know this part of the world very well, don't you, Mrs Hillingdon?"

" I have been in this island once or twice before and of course in most of the others."

" Oh yes. Butterflies isn't it, and wild flowers? You and your—your friends—or are they relations? "

" Friends. Nothing more."

" And I suppose you go about together a great deal because of your interests being the same? "

" Yes. We've travelled together for some years now."

" I suppose you must have had some rather exciting adventures sometimes? "

" I don't think so," said Evelyn. Her voice was unaccentuated, slightly bored. " Adventures always seem to happen to other people." She yawned.

" No dangerous encounters with snakes or with wild animals or with natives gone berserk? "

(' What a fool I sound,') thought Miss Marple.

" Nothing worse than insect bites," Evelyn assured her.

" Poor Major Palgrave, you know, was bitten by a snake once," said Miss Marple, making a purely fictitious statement.

" Was he? "

" Did he never tell you about it? "

" Perhaps. I don't remember."

" I suppose you knew him quite well, didn't you? "

" Major Palgrave? No, hardly at all."

" He always had so many interesting stories to tell."

" Ghastly old bore," said Mr Rafiel. " Silly fool, too. He needn't have died if he'd looked after himself properly."

" Oh come now, Mr Rafiel," said Mrs Walters.

" I know what I'm talking about. If you look after your health properly you're all right anywhere. Look at me. The doctors gave *me* up years ago. All right, I said, I've got my own rules of health and I shall keep to them. And here I am."

He looked round proudly.

It did indeed seem rather a miracle that he should be there.

" Poor Major Palgrave had high blood pressure," said Mrs Walters.

" Nonsense," said Mr Rafiel.

" Oh, but he did," said Evelyn Hillingdon. She spoke with sudden, unexpected authority.

" Who says so? " said Mr Rafiel. " Did he tell you so? "

" Somebody said so."

" He looked very red in the face," Miss Marple contributed.

" Can't go by that," said Mr Rafiel. " And anyway he *didn't* have high blood pressure because he told me so."

" What do you mean, he told you so? " said Mrs Walters. " I mean, you can't exactly tell people you *haven't* got a thing."

" Yes you can. I said to him once when he was

downing all those Planters Punches, and eating too much, I said, ' You ought to watch your diet and your drink. You've got to think of your blood pressure at your age.' And he said he'd nothing to look out for in that line, that his blood pressure was very good for his age."

" But he took some stuff for it, I believe," said Miss Marple, entering the conversation once more. " Some stuff called—oh, something like—was it Serenite? "

" If you ask me," said Evelyn Hillingdon, " I don't think he ever liked to admit that there could be anything the matter with him or that he could be ill. I think he was one of those people who are afraid of illness and therefore deny there's ever anything wrong with them."

It was a long speech for her. Miss Marple looked thoughtfully down at the top of her dark head.

" The trouble is," said Mr Rafiel dictatorially " everybody's too fond of knowing other people's ailments. They think everybody over fifty is going to die of hypertension or coronary thrombosis or one of those things—poppycock! If a man says there's nothing much wrong with him I don't suppose there is. A man ought to know about his own health. What's the time? Quarter to twelve? I ought to have had my dip long ago. Why can't you remind me about these things, Esther? "

Mrs Walters made no protest. She rose to her feet and with some deftness assisted Mr Rafiel to his.

Together they went down the beach, she supporting him carefully. Together they stepped into the sea.

Señora de Caspearo opened her eyes and murmured: " How ugly are old men! Oh how they are ugly! They should all be put to death at forty, or perhaps thirty-five would be better. Yes? "

Edward Hillingdon and Gregory Dyson came crunching down the beach.

" What's the water like, Evelyn? "

" Just the same as always."

" Never much variation, is there? Where's Lucky? "

" I don't know," said Evelyn.

Again Miss Marple looked down thoughtfully at the dark head.

" Well, now I give my imitation of a whale," said Gregory. He threw off his gaily patterned Bermuda shirt and tore down the beach, flinging himself, puffing and panting, into the sea, doing a fast crawl. Edward Hillingdon sat down on the beach by his wife. Presently he asked, " Coming in again? "

She smiled—put on her cap—and they went down the beach together in a much less spectacular manner.

Señora de Caspearo opened her eyes again.

" I think at first those two they are on their honeymoon, he is so charming to her, but I hear they have been married eight—nine years. It is incredible, is it not? "

" I wonder where Mrs Dyson is? " said Miss Marple.

" That Lucky? She is with some man."

" You—you think so? "

" It is certain," said Señora de Caspearo. " She is that type. But she is not so young any longer—Her husband—already his eyes go elsewhere—He makes passes—here, there, all the time. I know."

" Yes," said Miss Marple, " I expect you would know."

Señora de Caspearo shot a surprised glance at her. It was clearly not what she had expected from that quarter.

Miss Marple, however, was looking at the waves with an air of gentle innocence.

II

" May I speak to you, ma'am, Mrs Kendal? "

" Yes, of course," said Molly. She was sitting at her desk in the office.

Victoria Johnson tall, and buoyant in her crisp white uniform came in farther and shut the door behind her with a somewhat mysterious air.

" I like to tell you something, please, Mrs Kendal."

" Yes, what is it. Is anything wrong? "

" I don't know that. Not for sure. It's the old gentleman who died. The Major gentleman. He die in his sleep."

" Yes, yes. What about it? "

" There was a bottle of pills in his room. Doctor, he asked me about them."

" Yes? "

" The doctor said—' Let me see what he has here on the bathroom shelf,' and he looked, you see. He see there was tooth powder and indigestion pills and aspirin and cascara pills, and then these pills in a bottle called Serenite."

" Yes," repeated Molly yet again.

" And the doctor looked at them. He seemed quite satisfied, and nodded his head. But I get to thinking afterwards. Those pills weren't there before. I've not seen them in his bathroom before. The others, yes. The tooth powder and the aspirin and the after shave lotion and all the rest. But those pills, those Serenite pills, I never noticed them before."

" So you think——" Molly looked puzzled.

" I don't know what to think," said Victoria. " I just think it's not right, so I think I better tell you about it. Perhaps you tell doctor? Perhaps it means something. Perhaps *someone* put those pills there so he take them and he died."

" Oh, I don't think that's likely at all," said Molly.

Victoria shook her dark head. " You never know. People do bad things."

Molly glanced out of the window. The place looked like an earthly paradise. With its sunshine, its sea, its coral reef, its music, its dancing, it seemed a Garden of Eden. But even in the Garden of Eden, there had been a shadow—the shadow of the Serpent—*Bad things*—how hateful to hear those words.

" I'll make inquiries, Victoria," she said sharply. " Don't worry. And above all don't go starting a lot of silly rumours."

Tim Kendal came in, just as Victoria was, somewhat unwillingly, leaving.

" Anything wrong, Molly? "

She hesitated—but Victoria might go to him— She told him what the girl had said.

" I don't see what all this rigmarole—what *were* these pills anyway? "

" Well, I don't really know, Tim. Dr Robertson when he came said they—were something to do with blood pressure, I think."

" Well, that would be all right, wouldn't it? I mean, he *had* high blood pressure, and he *would* be taking things for it, wouldn't he? People do. I've seen them, lots of times."

" Yes," Molly hesitated, " but Victoria seemed to think that he might have taken one of these pills and it would have killed him."

" Oh darling, that is a bit *too* melodramatic! You mean that somebody might have changed his blood pressure pills for something else, and that they poisoned him? "

" It does sound absurd," said Molly apologetically, " when you say it like that. But that seemed to be what Victoria thought! "

" Silly girl! We *could* go and ask Dr Graham about it, I suppose he'd know. But really it's such nonsense that it's not worth bothering him."

" That's what I think."

" What on earth made the girl think anybody would have changed the pills. You mean, put different pills into the same bottle? "

" I didn't quite gather," said Molly, looking rather helpless. " Victoria seemed to think that was the first time that Serenite bottle had been there."

" Oh but that's nonsense," said Tim Kendal. " He had to take those pills all the time to keep his blood pressure down." And he went off cheerfully to consult with Fernando the *maître d'hôtel.*

But Molly could not dismiss the matter so lightly. After the stress of lunch was over she said to her husband:

" Tim—I've been thinking— If Victoria is going around talking about this perhaps we ought just to ask someone about it? "

" My dear girl! Robertson and all the rest of them came and looked at everything and asked all the questions they wanted at the time."

"Yes, but you know how they work themselves up, these girls—"

" Oh, all right! I'll tell you what—we'll go and ask Graham—he'll know."

Dr Graham was sitting on his loggia with a book. The young couple came in and Molly plunged into her recital. It was a little incoherent and Tim took over.

"Sounds rather idiotic," he said apologetically, "but as far as I can make out, this girl has got it into her head that someone put some poison tablets in the —what's the name of the stuff—Sera—something. bottle."

"But why should she get this idea into her head?" asked Dr Graham. "Did she see anything or hear anything or—I mean, why should she think so?"

"I don't know," said Tim rather helplessly. "Was it a different bottle? Was that it, Molly?"

"No," said Molly. "I think what she said was that there was a bottle there labelled—Seven—Seren——"

"Serenite," said the doctor. "That's quite right. A well-known preparation. He'd been taking it regularly."

"Victoria said she'd never seen it in his room before."

"Never seen it in his room before?" said Graham sharply. "What does she mean by that?"

"Well, that's what she *said*. She said there were all sorts of things on the bathroom shelf. You know, tooth powder, aspirin and after shave and—oh—she rattled them off gaily. I suppose she's always cleaning them and so she knows them all off by heart. But this one— the Serenite—she hadn't seen it there until the day after he died."

"That's very odd," said Dr Graham, rather sharply. "Is she sure?"

The unusual sharpness of his tone made both of the Kendals look at him. They had not expected Dr Graham to take up quite this attitude.

" She sounded sure," said Molly slowly.

" Perhaps she just wanted to be sensational," suggested Tim.

" I think perhaps," said Dr Graham, " I'd better have a few words with the girl myself."

Victoria displayed a distinct pleasure at being allowed to tell her story.

" I don't want to get in no trouble," she said. " *I* didn't put that bottle there and I don't know who did."

" But you think it *was* put there? " asked Graham.

" Well, you see, Doctor, it *must* have been put there if it wasn't there before."

" Major Palgrave could have kept it in a drawer—or a dispatch-case, something like that."

Victoria shook her head shrewdly.

" Wouldn't do that if he was taking it all the time, would he? "

" No," said Graham reluctantly. " No, it was stuff he would have to take several times a day. You never saw him taking it or anything of that kind? "

" He didn't have it there before. I just thought—word got round as that stuff had something to do with his death, poisoned his blood or something, and I thought maybe he had an enemy put it there so as to kill him."

" Nonsense, my girl," said the doctor robustly. " Sheer nonsense."

Victoria looked shaken.

" You say as this stuff was medicine, good medicine?" she asked doubtfully.

" Good medicine, and what is more, *necessary* medicine," said Dr Graham. " So you needn't worry, Victoria. I can assure you there was nothing wrong with that medicine. It was the proper thing for a man to take who had his complaint."

" Surely you've taken a load off my mind," said Victoria. She showed white teeth at him in a cheerful smile.

But the load was not taken off Dr Graham's mind. That uneasiness of his that had been so nebulous was now becoming tangible.

CHAPTER VIII

A TALK WITH ESTHER WALTERS

" This place isn't what it used to be," said Mr Rafiel, irritably, as he observed Miss Marple approaching the spot where he and his secretary were sitting. " Can't move a step without some old hen getting under your feet. What do old ladies want to come to the West Indies for? "

" Where do you suggest they should go? " asked Esther Walters.

" To Cheltenham," said Mr Rafiel promptly. " Or Bournemouth," he offered, " or Torquay or Llandrindod Wells. Plenty of choice. They like it there—they're quite happy."

" They can't often afford to come to the West Indies, I suppose," said Esther. " It isn't everyone who is as lucky as you are."

" That's right," said Mr Rafiel. " Rub it in. Here am I, a mass of aches and pains and disjoints. You grudge me any alleviation! And you don't do any work— Why haven't you typed out those letters yet? "

" I haven't had time."

" Well, get on with it, can't you? I bring you out

here to do a bit of work, not to sit about sunning yourself and showing off your figure."

Some people would have considered Mr Rafiel's remarks quite insupportable but Esther Walters had worked for him for some years and she knew well enough that Mr Rafiel's bark was a great deal worse than his bite. He was a man who suffered almost continual pain, and making disagreeable remarks was one of his ways of letting off steam. No matter what he said she remained quite imperturbable.

" Such a lovely evening, isn't it? " said Miss Marple, pausing beside them.

" Why not? " said Mr Rafiel. " That's what we're here for, isn't it? "

Miss Marple gave a tinkly little laugh.

" You're so severe—of course the weather *is* a very English subject of conversation—one forgets— Oh dear—this is the wrong coloured wool." She deposited her knitting bag on the garden table and trotted towards her own bungalow.

"Jackson! " yelled Mr Rafiel.

Jackson appeared.

" Take me back inside," said Mr Rafiel. " I'll have my massage now before that chattering hen comes back. Not that massage does me a bit of good," he added. Having said which, he allowed himself to be deftly helped to his feet and went off with the masseur beside him into his bungalow.

Esther Walters looked after them and then turned

her head as Miss Marple came back with a ball of wool to sit down near her.

"I hope I'm not disturbing you?" said Miss Marple.

"Of course not," said Esther Walters, "I've got to go off and do some typing in a minute, but I'm going to enjoy another ten minutes of the sunset first."

Miss Marple sat down and in a gentle voice began to talk. As she talked, she summed up Esther Walters. Not at all glamorous, but could be attractive looking if she tried. Miss Marple wondered why she didn't try. It could be, of course, because Mr Rafiel would not have liked it, but Miss Marple didn't think Mr Rafiel would really mind in the least. He was so completely taken up with himself that so long as he was not personally neglected, his secretary might have got herself up like a houri in Paradise without his objecting. Besides, he usually went to bed early and in the evening hours of steel bands and dancing, Esther Walters might easily have—Miss Marple paused to select a word in her mind, at the same time conversing cheerfully about her visit to Jamestown.— Ah yes, *blossomed*. Esther Walters might have blossomed in the evening hours.

She led the conversation gently in the direction of Jackson.

On the subject of Jackson Esther Walters was rather vague.

"He's very competent," she said. "A fully trained masseur."

"I suppose he's been with Mr Rafiel a long time?"

" Oh no—about nine months, I think——"

" Is he married? " Miss Marple hazarded.

" Married? I don't think so," said Esther slightly surprised. " He's never mentioned it if so——

" No," she added. " Definitely *not* married, I should say." And she showed amusement.

Miss Marple interpreted that by adding to it in her own mind the following sentence—" At any rate he doesn't behave as though he were married."

But then, how many married men there were who behaved as though they weren't married! ! Miss Marple could think of a dozen examples!

" He's quite good looking," she said thoughtfully.

" Yes—I suppose he is," said Esther without interest.

Miss Marple considered her thoughtfully. Uninterested in men? The kind of woman, perhaps, who was only interested in one man— A widow, they had said.

She asked—" Have you worked for Mr Rafiel long? "

" Four or five years. After my husband died, I had to take a job again. I've got a daughter at school and my husband left me very badly off."

" Mr Rafiel must be a difficult man to work for? " Miss Marple hazarded.

" Not really, when you get to know him. He flies into rages and is very contradictory. I think the real trouble is he gets tired of people. He's had five different valet-attendants in two years. He likes having someone new to bully. But he and I have always got on very well."

"Mr Jackson seems a very obliging young man?"

"He's very tactful and resourceful," said Esther. "Of course, he's sometimes a little——" She broke off.

Miss Marple considered. "Rather a difficult position sometimes?" she suggested.

"Well, yes. Neither one thing nor the other. However—" she smiled—"I think he manages to have quite a good time."

Miss Marple considered this also. It didn't help her much. She continued her twittering conversation and soon she was hearing a good deal about that nature-loving quartet, the Dysons and the Hillingdons.

"The Hillingdons have been here for the last three or four years at least," said Esther, "but Gregory Dyson has been here much longer than that. He knows the West Indies very well. He came here, originally, I believe, with his first wife. She was delicate and had to go abroad in the winters, or go somewhere warm, at any rate."

"And she died? Or was it divorce?"

"No. She died. Out here, I believe. I don't mean this particular island but one of the West Indies islands. There was some sort of trouble, I believe, some kind of scandal or other. He never talks about her. Somebody else told me about it. They didn't, I gather, get on very well together."

"And then he married this wife. 'Lucky'." Miss Marple said the word with faint dissatisfaction as if to say 'Really, a most incredible name!'

"I believe she was a relation of his first wife."

"Have they known the Hillingdons a great many years?"

"Oh, I think only since the Hillingdons came out here. Three or four years, not more."

"The Hillingdons seem very pleasant," said Miss Marple. "Quiet, of course."

"Yes. They're both quiet."

"Everyone says they're very devoted to each other," said Miss Marple. The tone of her voice was quite non-committal but Esther Walters looked at her sharply.

"But you don't think they are?" she said.

"You don't really think so yourself, do you, my dear?"

"Well, I've wondered sometimes . . ."

"Quiet men, like Colonel Hillingdon," said Miss Marple "are often attracted to flamboyant types." And she added, after a significant pause "Lucky—such a curious name. Do you think Mr Dyson has any idea of—of what might be going on?"

'Old scandal-monger', thought Esther Walters. 'Really, these old women!'

She said rather coldly, "I've no idea."

Miss Marple shifted to another subject. "It's very sad about poor Major Palgrave isn't it?" she said.

Esther Walters agreed, though in a somewhat perfunctory fashion.

" The people I'm really sorry for are the Kendals," she said.

" Yes, I suppose it is really rather unfortunate when something of that kind happens in a hotel."

" People come here, you see, to enjoy themselves, don't they? " said Esther. " To forget about illnesses and deaths and income tax and frozen pipes and all the rest of it. They don't like—" she went on, with a sudden flash of an entirely different manner—" any reminders of mortality."

Miss Marple laid down her knitting. " Now that is very well put, my dear," she said, " very well put indeed. Yes, it is as you say."

" And you see they're quite a young couple," went on Esther Walters. " They only just took over from the Sandersons six months ago and they're terribly worried about whether they're going to succeed or not, because they haven't had much experience."

" And you think this might be really disadvantageous to them? "

" Well, no, I don't, frankly," said Esther Walters. " I don't think people remember anything for more than a day or two, not in this atmosphere of ' we've-all-come-out-here-to-enjoy-ourselves-let's-get-on-with-it '. I think a death just gives them a jolt for about twenty-four hours or so and then they don't think of it again once the funeral is over. Not unless they're reminded of it, that is. I've told Molly so, but of course she is a worrier."

"Mrs Kendal is a worrier? She always seems so carefree."

"I think a lot of that is put on," said Esther slowly. "Actually, I think she's one of those anxious sort of people who can't help worrying all the time that things *may* go wrong."

"I should have thought *he* worried more than she did."

"No, I don't think so. I think she's the worrier and he worries because she worries if you know what I mean."

"That is interesting," said Miss Marple.

"I think Molly wants desperately to try and appear very gay and to be enjoying herself. She works at it very hard but the effort exhausts her. Then she has these odd fits of depression. She's not—well not really well-balanced."

"Poor child," said Miss Marple. "There certainly are people like that, and very often outsiders don't suspect it."

"No, they put on such a good show, don't they? However," Esther added, "I don't think Molly has really anything to worry about in this case. I mean, people are dying of coronary thrombosis or cerebral hæmorrhage or things of that kind all the time nowadays. Far more than they used to, as far as I can see. It's only food poisoning or typhoid or something like that, that makes people get het up."

" Major Palgrave never mentioned to *me* that he had high blood pressure," said Miss Marple. " Did he to you? "

" He said so to somebody—I don't know who—It may have been to Mr Rafiel. I know Mr Rafiel says just the opposite—but then he's like that! Certainly Jackson mentioned it to me once. He said the Major ought to be more careful over the alcohol he took."

" I see," said Miss Marple, thoughtfully. She went on: " I expect you found him rather a boring old man? He told a lot of stories and I expect repeated himself a good deal."

" That's the worst of it," said Esther. " You do hear the same story again and again unless you can manage to be quick enough to fend it off."

" Of course *I* didn't mind so much," said Miss Marple, " because I'm used to that sort of thing. If I get stories told to me rather often, I don't really mind hearing them again because I've usually forgotten them."

" There is that," said Esther and laughed cheerfully.

" There was one story he was very fond of telling," said Miss Marple, " about a murder. I expect he told you that, didn't he? "

Esther Walters opened her handbag and started searching through it. She drew out her lipstick saying, " I thought I'd lost it." Then she asked, " I beg your pardon, what did you say? "

" I asked if Major Palgrave told you his favourite murder story? "

" I believe he did, now I come to think of it. Something about someone who gassed themselves, wasn't it? Only really it was the *wife* who gassed him. I mean she'd given him a sedative of some kind and then stuck his head in the gas oven. Was that it? "

" I don't think that was exactly it," said Miss Marple. She looked at Esther Walters thoughtfully.

" He told such a lot of stories," said Esther Walters, apologetically, " and as I said, one didn't always listen."

" He had a snapshot," said Miss Marple, " that he used to show people."

" I believe he did . . . I can't remember what it was now. Did he show it to you? "

" No," said Miss Marple. " He didn't show it to me. We were interrupted——"

CHAPTER IX

MISS PRESCOTT AND OTHERS

" The story *I* heard," began Miss Prescott, lowering her voice, and looking carefully around.

Miss Marple drew her chair a little closer. It had been some time before she had been able to get together with Miss Prescott for a heart-to-heart chat. This was owing to the fact that clergymen are very strong family men so that Miss Prescott was nearly always accompanied by her brother, and there was no doubt that Miss Marple and Miss Prescott found it less easy to take their back hair down in a good gossip when the jovial Canon was of their company.

" It seems," said Miss Prescott, " though of course I don't want to talk any scandal and I really know *nothing* about it——"

" Oh, I *quite* understand," said Miss Marple.

" It seems there was some scandal when his first wife was still alive! Apparently this woman, Lucky—such a name!—who I think was a cousin of his first wife, came out here and joined them and I think did some work with him on flowers or butterflies or whatever it was. And people talked a lot because they got on so well together—if you know what I mean."

" People do *notice* things so much, don't they," said Miss Marple.

" And then of course, when his wife died rather suddenly——"

" She died here, on this island? "

" No. No, I think they were in Martinique or Tobago at the time."

" I see."

" But I gathered from some other people who were there at the time, and who came on here and talked about things, that the doctor wasn't very satisfied."

" Indeed," said Miss Marple, with interest.

" It was only *gossip*," of course, " but—well, Mr Dyson certainly married again *very quickly*." She lowered her voice again. " Only a *month* I believe."

" Only a month," said Miss Marple.

The two women looked at each other. " It seemed—unfeeling," said Miss Prescott.

" Yes," said Miss Marple. " It certainly did." She added delicately, " Was there—any money? "

" I don't really know. He makes his little joke—perhaps you've heard him—about this wife being his ' lucky piece '——"

" Yes, I've heard him," said Miss Marple.

" And some people think that means that he was lucky to marry a rich wife. Though, of course," said Miss Prescott with the air of one being entirely fair, " she's very good-looking too, if you care for that type.

And I think myself that it was the *first* wife who had the money."

"Are the Hillingdons well off?"

"Well, I think they're *well off*. I don't mean fabulously rich, I just mean well off. They have two boys at Public School and a very nice place in England, I believe, and they travel most of the winter."

The Canon appearing at this moment to suggest a brisk walk, Miss Prescott rose to join her brother. Miss Marple remained sitting there.

A few minutes later Gregory Dyson passed her striding along towards the hotel. He waved a cheerful hand as he passed.

"Penny for your thoughts," he called out.

Miss Marple smiled gently, wondering how he would have reacted if she had replied:

"I was wondering if you were a murderer."

It really seemed most probable that he was. It all fitted in so nicely— This story about the death of the first Mrs Dyson— Major Palgrave had certainly been talking about a wife killer—with special reference to the "Brides in the bath Case."

Yes—it fitted—the only objection was that it fitted almost too well. But Miss Marple reproved herself for this thought— Who was she to demand Murders Made to Measure?

A voice made her jump—a somewhat raucous one.

"Seen Greg any place, Miss—er——"

Lucky, Miss Marple thought, was not in a good temper.

" He passed by just now—going towards the hotel."

" I'll bet! " Lucky uttered an irritated ejaculation and hurried on.

" Forty, if she's a day, and looks it this morning," thought Miss Marple.

Pity invaded her—Pity for the Luckys of the world—who were so vulnerable to Time—

At the sound of a noise behind her, she turned her chair round—

Mr Rafiel, supported by Jackson, was making his morning appearance and coming out of his bungalow—

Jackson settled his employer in his wheel chair and fussed round him. Mr Rafiel waved his attendant away impatiently and Jackson went off in the direction of the hotel.

Miss Marple lost no time—Mr Rafiel was never left alone for long—Probably Esther Walters would come and join him. Miss Marple wanted a word alone with Mr Rafiel and now, she thought, was her chance. She would have to be quick about what she wanted to say. There could be no leading up to things. Mr Rafiel was not a man who cared for the idle twittering conversation of old ladies. He would probably retreat again into his bungalow, definitely regarding himself the victim of persecution. Miss Marple decided to plump for downrightness.

She made her way to where he was sitting, drew up a chair, sat down, and said:

" I want to ask you something, Mr Rafiel."

" All right, all right," said Mr Rafiel, " let's have it. What do you want—a subscription, I suppose? Missions in Africa or repairing a church, something of that kind? "

" Yes," said Miss Marple. " I am interested in several objects of that nature, and I shall be delighted if you will give me a subscription for them. But that wasn't actually what I was going to ask you. What I was going to ask you was if Major Palgrave ever told you a story about a murder."

" Oho," said Mr Rafiel. " So he told it to you too, did he? And I suppose you fell for it, hook line and sinker."

" I didn't really know what to think," said Miss Marple. " What exactly did he tell you? "

" He prattled on," said Mr Rafiel, " about a lovely creature, Lucrezia Borgia reincarnated. Beautiful, young, golden-haired, everything."

" Oh," said Miss Marple slightly taken aback, " and who did she murder? "

" Her husband, of course," said Mr Rafiel, " who do you think? "

" Poison? "

" No, I think she gave him a sleeping draught and then stuck him in a gas oven. Resourceful female. Then she said it was suicide. She got off quite lightly.

Diminished responsibility or something. That's what it's called nowadays if you're a good-looking woman, or some miserable young hooligan whose mother's been too fond of him. Bah! "

" Did the Major show you a snapshot? "

" What—a snapshot of the woman? No. Why should he? "

" Oh——" said Miss Marple.

She sat there, rather taken aback. Apparently Major Palgrave spent his life telling people not only about tigers he had shot and elephants he had hunted but also about murderers he had met. Perhaps he had a whole repertoire of murder stories. One had to face it—She was startled by Mr Rafiel suddenly giving a roar of " Jackson! " There was no response.

" Shall I find him for you? " said Miss Marple rising.

" You won't find him. Tom-catting somewhere, that's what he does. No good, that fellow. Bad character. But he suits me all right."

" I'll go and look for him," said Miss Marple.

Miss Marple found Jackson sitting on the far side of the hotel terrace having a drink with Tim Kendal.

" Mr Rafiel is asking for you," she said.

Jackson made an expressive grimace, drained his glass, and rose to his feet.

" Here we go again," he said. " No peace for the wicked— Two telephone calls and a special diet order—I thought that might give me a quarter of an hour's alibi— Apparently not! Thank you, Miss Marple. Thanks for the drink, Mr Kendal."

He strode away.

"I feel sorry for that chap," said Tim. "I have to stand him a drink now and then, just to cheer him up— Can I offer you something, Miss Marple— How about fresh lime? I know you're fond of that."

"Not just now, thank you— I suppose looking after someone like Mr Rafiel must always be rather exacting. Invalids are frequently difficult——"

"I didn't mean only that— It's very well paid and you expect to put up with a good deal of crotchetiness—old Rafiel's not really a bad sort. I meant more that——" he hesitated.

Miss Marple looked inquiring.

"Well—how shall I put it—it's difficult for him socially. People are so damned snobbish—there's no one here of his class. He's better than a servant—and below the average visitor—or they think he is. Rather like the Victorian governess. Even the secretary woman, Mrs Walters—feels she's a cut above him. Makes things difficult." Tim paused, then said with feeling: "It's really awful the amount of social problems there are in a place like this."

Dr Graham passed them— He had a book in his hand. He went and sat at a table overlooking the sea.

"Dr Graham looks rather worried," remarked Miss Marple.

"Oh! We're all worried."

" You too? Because of Major Palgrave's death? "

" I've left off worrying about that. People seem to have forgotten it—taken it in their stride. No—it's my wife—Molly— Do you know anything about dreams?"

" Dreams? " Miss Marple was surprised.

" Yes—bad dreams—nightmares, I suppose. Oh, we all get that sort of thing sometimes. But Molly—she seems to have them nearly all the time. They frighten her. Is there anything one can do about them? Take for them? She's got some sleeping pills, but she says they make it worse—she struggles to wake up and can't."

" What are the dreams about? "

" Oh, something or someone chasing her— Or watching her and spying on her—she can't shake off the feeling even when she's awake."

" Surely a doctor——"

" She's got a thing against doctors. Won't hear of it— Oh well—I daresay it will all pass off— But we were so happy. It was all such fun— And now, just lately— Perhaps old Palgrave's death upset her. She seems like a different person since . . ."

He got up.

" Must get on with the daily chores—are you sure you won't have that fresh lime? "

Miss Marple shook her head.

She sat there, thinking. Her face was grave and anxious.

She glanced over at Dr Graham.

Presently she came to a decision.

She rose and went across to his table.

" I have got to apologise to you, Dr Graham," she said.

" Indeed? " The doctor looked at her in kindly surprise. He pulled forward a chair and she sat down.

" I am afraid I have done the most disgraceful thing," said Miss Marple. " I told you, Dr Graham, a deliberate lie."

She looked at him apprehensively.

Dr Graham did not look at all shattered, but he did look a little surprised.

" Really? " he said. " Ah well, you mustn't let that worry you too much."

What had the dear old thing been telling lies about, he wondered; her age? Though as far as he could remember she hadn't mentioned her age. " Well, let's hear about it," he said, since she clearly wished to confess.

" You remember my speaking to you about a snapshot of my nephew, one that I showed to Major Palgrave, and that he didn't give back to me? "

" Yes, yes, of course I remember. Sorry we couldn't find it for you."

" There wasn't any such thing," said Miss Marple, in a small, frightened voice.

" I beg your pardon? "

" There wasn't any such thing. I made up that story, I'm afraid."

"You made it up?" Dr Graham looked slightly annoyed. "Why?"

Miss Marple told him. She told him quite clearly, without twittering. She told him about Major Palgrave's murder story and how he'd been about to show her this particular snapshot and his sudden confusion and then she went on to her own anxiety and to her final decision to try somehow to obtain a view of it.

"And really, I couldn't see *any* way of doing so without telling you something that was quite untrue," she said, "I do hope you will forgive me."

"You thought that what he had been about to show you was a picture of a murderer?"

"That's what he said it was," said Miss Marple. "At least he said it was given him by this acquaintance who had told him the story about a man who was a murderer."

"Yes, yes. And—excuse me—you believed him?"

"I don't know if I really believed him or not at the time," said Miss Marple. "But then, you see, the next day he died."

"Yes," said Dr Graham, struck suddenly by the clarity of that one sentence. *The next day he died. . . .*

"And the snapshot had disappeared."

Dr Graham looked at her. He didn't know quite what to say.

"Excuse me, Miss Marple," he said at last, "but is what you're telling me now—is it really true this time?"

" I don't wonder your doubting me," said Miss Marple. " I should, in your place. Yes, it is true what I am telling you now, but I quite realise that you have only my word for it. Still, even if you don't believe me, I thought I ought to tell you."

" Why? "

" I realised that you ought to have the fullest information possible— In case——"

" In case what? "

" In case you decided to take any steps about it."

CHAPTER X

A DECISION IN JAMESTOWN

Dr Graham was in Jamestown, in the Adminstrator's office; sitting at a table opposite his friend Daventry, a grave young man of thirty-five.

" You sounded rather mysterious on the phone, Graham," said Daventry. " Anything special the matter? "

" I don't know," said Dr Graham, " but I'm worried."

Daventry looked at the other's face, then he nodded as drinks were brought in. He spoke lightly of a fishing expedition he had made lately. Then when the servant had gone away, he sat back in his chair and looked at the other man.

" Now then," he said, " let's have it."

Dr Graham recounted the facts that had worried him. Daventry gave a slow long whistle.

" I see. You think maybe there's something funny about old Palgrave's death? You're no longer sure that it was just natural causes? Who certified the death? Robertson, I suppose. He didn't have any doubts, did he? "

" No, but I think he may have been influenced in

giving the certificate by the fact of the Serenite tablets in the bathroom. He asked me if Palgrave had mentioned that he suffered from hypertension, and I said No, I'd never had any medical conversation with him myself, but apparently he had talked about it to other people in the hotel. The whole thing—the bottle of tablets, and what Palgrave had said to people—it all fitted in—no earthly reason to suspect anything else. It was a perfectly natural inference to make—but I think now it may not have been correct. If it had been my business to give the certificate, I'd have given it without a second thought. The appearances are quite consistent with his having died from that cause. I'd never have thought about it since if it hadn't been for the odd disappearance of that snapshot . . ."

" But look here, Graham," said Daventry, " if you will allow me to say so, aren't you relying a little too much on a rather fanciful story told you by an elderly lady. You know what these elderly ladies are like. They magnify some small detail and work the whole thing up."

" Yes, I know," said Dr Graham, unhappily. " I know that. I've said to myself that it may be so, that it probably *is* so. But I can't quite convince myself. She was so very clear and detailed in her statement."

" The whole thing seems wildly improbable to me," said Daventry. " Some old lady tells a story about a snapshot that ought not to be there—no I'm getting mixed myself—I mean the other way about don't I?—

but the only thing you've really got to go on is that a chambermaid says that a bottle of pills which the authorities had relied on for evidence, wasn't in the Major's room the day before his death. But there are a hundred explanations for that. He might always have carried those pills about in his pocket."

" It's possible, I suppose, yes."

" Or the chambermaid may have made a mistake and she simply hadn't noticed them before——"

" That's possible, too."

" Well, then."

Graham said slowly:

" The girl was very positive."

" Well, the St. Honoré people are very excitable, you know. Emotional. Work themselves up easily. Are you thinking that she knows—a little more than she has said? "

" I think it might be so," said Dr Graham slowly.

" You'd better try and get it out of her, if so. We don't want to make an unnecessary fuss—unless we've something definite to go on. If he didn't die of blood pressure, what do you think it was? "

" There are too many things it might be nowadays," said Dr Graham.

" You mean things that don't leave recognisable traces? "

" Not everyone," said Dr Graham dryly, " is so considerate as to use arsenic."

" Now let's get things quite clear—what's the suggestion? That a bottle of pills was substituted for the real ones? And that Major Palgrave was poisoned in that way? "

" No—it's not like that. That's what the girl—Victoria Something thinks— But she's got it all wrong— If it was decided to get rid of the Major—quickly—he would have been given something—most likely in a drink of some kind. Then to make it appear a natural death, a bottle of the tablets prescribed to relieve blood pressure was put in his room. And the rumour was put about that he suffered from high blood pressure."

" Who put the rumour about? "

" I've tried to find out—with no success— It's been too cleverly done. A says ' I *think* B told me '— B, asked, says ' No, I didn't say so but I do remember C mentioning it one day '. C says ' Several people talked about it—one of them, I think, was A '. And there we are, back again."

" Someone was clever? "

" Yes. As soon as the death was discovered, everybody seemed to be talking about the Major's high blood pressure and repeating round what other people had said."

" Wouldn't it have been simpler just to poison him and let it go at that? "

" No. That might have meant inquiry—possibly an autopsy— This way, a doctor would accept the death and give a certificate—as he did."

" What do you want me to do? Go to the C.I.D? Suggest they dig the chap up? It'd make a lot of stink——"

" It could be kept quite quiet."

" Could it? In St. Honoré? Think again! The grapevine would be on to it before it had happened. All the same," Daventry sighed— " I suppose we'll have to do something. But if you ask me, it's all a mare's nest!"

" I devoutly hope it is," said Dr Graham.

CHAPTER XI

EVENING AT THE GOLDEN PALM

Molly rearranged a few of the table decorations in the dining-room, removed an extra knife, straightened a fork, reset a glass or two, stood back to look at the effect and then walked out on to the terrace outside. There was no one about just at present and she strolled to the far corner and stood by the balustrade. Soon another evening would begin. Chattering, talking, drinking, all so gay and carefree, the sort of life she had longed for and, up to a few days ago, had enjoyed so much. Now even Tim seemed anxious and worried. Natural, perhaps, that he should worry a little. It was important that this venture of theirs should turn out all right. After all, he had sunk all he had in it.

But that, thought Molly, is not *really* what's worrying him. It's *me*. But I don't see, said Molly to herself, why he should worry about *me*. Because he did worry about her. That she was quite sure of. The questions he put, the quick nervous glance he shot at her from time to time. But why? thought Molly. " I've been very careful," she summed up things in her mind. She didn't understand it really herself. She couldn't remember when it had begun. She wasn't even very sure what it was. She'd begun to be frightened of people. She didn't know why. What could they do to her? What should they want to do to her?

She nodded her head, then started violently as a hand touched her arm. She spun round to find Gregory Dyson, slightly taken aback, looking apologetic.

" Ever so sorry. Did I startle you, little girl? "

Molly hated being called ' little girl '. She said quickly and brightly: " I didn't hear you coming, Mr Dyson, so it made me jump."

" Mr Dyson? We're very formal to-night. Aren't we all one great happy family here? Ed and me and Lucky and Evelyn and you and Tim and Esther Walters and old Rafiel. All the lot of us one happy family."

'He's had plenty to drink already,' thought Molly. She smiled at him pleasantly.

" Oh! I come over the heavy hostess sometimes," she said, lightly. " Tim and I think it's more polite not to be too handy with Christian names."

" Aw! we don't want any of that stuffed-shirt business. Now then, Molly my lovely, have a drink with me."

" Ask me later," said Molly. " I have a few things to get on with."

" Now don't run away." His arm fastened round her arm. " You're a lovely girl, Molly. I hope Tim appreciates his good luck."

" Oh, I see to it that he does," said Molly cheerfully.

" I could go for you, you know, in a big way." He

leered at her—" though I wouldn't let my wife hear me say so."

" Did you have a good trip this afternoon? "

" I suppose so. Between you and me I get a bit fed up sometimes. You can get tired of the birds and butterflies. What say you and I go for a little picnic on our own one day? "

" We'll have to see about that," said Molly gaily. " I'll be looking forward to it."

With a light laugh she escaped, and went back into the bar.

" Hallo, Molly," said Tim, " you seem in a hurry. Who's that you've been with out there? "

He peered out.

" Gregory Dyson."

" What does he want? "

" Wanted to make a pass at me," said Molly.

" Blast him," said Tim.

" Don't worry," said Molly, " I can do all the blasting necessary."

Tim started to answer her, caught sight of Fernando and went over to him shouting out some directions. Molly slipped away through the kitchen, out through the kitchen door and down the steps to the beach.

Gregory Dyson swore under his breath. Then he walked slowly back in the direction of his bungalow. He had nearly got there when a voice spoke to him from the shadow of one of the bushes. He turned his head, startled. In the gathering dusk he thought for a moment that it was a ghostly figure that stood there. Then he laughed. It had looked like a faceless apparition but that was because, though the dress was white, the face was black.

Victoria stepped out of the bushes on to the path.

" Mr Dyson, please? "

" Yes. What is it? "

Ashamed of being startled, he spoke with a touch of impatience.

" I brought you this, sir." She held out her hand. In it was a bottle of tablets. " This belongs to you, doesn't it. Yes? "

" Oh, my bottle of Serenite tablets. Yes, of course. Where did you find it ? "

" I found it where it had been put. In the gentleman's room."

" What do you mean—in the gentleman's room? "

" The gentleman who is dead," she added gravely. " I do not think he sleeps very well in his grave."

" Why the devil not? " asked Dyson.

Victoria stood looking at him.

" I still don't know what you're talking about. You mean you found this bottle of tablets in Major Palgrave's bungalow? "

" That is right, yes. After the doctor and the Jamestown people go away, they give me all the things in his bathroom to throw away. The toothpaste and the lotions, and all the other things—including this."

" Well, why didn't you throw it away? "

" Because these are yours. You missed them. You remember, you asked about them? "

" Yes—well—yes, I did. I—I thought I'd just mislaid them."

" No, you did not mislay them. They were taken from your bungalow and put in Major Palgrave's bungalow."

" How do you know? " He spoke roughly.

" I know. I saw." She smiled at him in a sudden flash of white teeth. " Someone put them in the dead gentleman's room. Now I give them back to you."

" Here—wait. What do you mean? What—who did you see? "

She hurried away, back into the darkness of the bushes. Greg made as to move after her and then stopped. He stood stroking his chin.

" What's the matter, Greg? Seen a ghost? " asked Mrs Dyson, as she came along the path from their bungalow.

" Thought I had for a minute or two."

" Who was that you were talking to? "

" The coloured girl who does our place. Victoria, her name is, isn't it? "

" What did she want? Making a pass at you? "

" Don't be stupid, Lucky. That girl's got some idiotic idea into her head."

" Idea about what? "

" You remember I couldn't find my Serenite the other day? "

" You said you couldn't."

" What do you mean ' I said I couldn't '? "

" Oh, for heck's sake, have you got to take me up on everything? "

" I'm sorry," said Greg. " Everybody goes about being so damn' mysterious" He held out his hand with the bottle in it. " That girl brought them back to me."

" Had she pinched them? "

" No. She—found them somewhere I think."

" Well, what of it? What's the mystery about? "

" Oh nothing," said Greg. " She just riled me, that's all."

" Look here, Greg, what is this stuff all about? Come along and have a drink before dinner."

II

Molly had gone down to the beach. She pulled out one of the old basket chairs, one of the more rickety ones that were seldom used. She sat in it for a while looking at the sea, then suddenly she dropped her head in her hands and burst into tears. She sat there sobbing unrestrainedly for some time. Then she heard a rustle close by her and glanced up sharply to see Mrs Hillingdon looking down at her.

" Hallo, Evelyn, I didn't hear you. I—I'm sorry."

" What's the matter, child? " said Evelyn. " Something gone wrong? " She pulled another chair forward and sat down. " Tell me."

" There's nothing wrong," said Molly. " Nothing at all."

" Of course there is. You wouldn't sit and cry here for nothing. Can't you tell me? Is it—some trouble between you and Tim? "

" Oh *no*."

" I'm glad of that. You always look so happy together."

" Not more than you do," said Molly. " Tim and I always think how wonderful it is that you and Edward should seem so happy together after being married so many years."

" Oh, that," said Evelyn. Her voice was sharp as she spoke but Molly hardly noticed.

" People bicker so," she said, " and have such rows. Even if they're quite fond of each other they still seem to have rows and not to mind a bit whether they have them in public or not."

" Some people like living that way," said Evelyn. " It doesn't really mean anything."

" Well, I think it's horrid," said Molly.

" So do I, really," said Evelyn.

" But to see you and Edward——"

" Oh it's no good, Molly. I can't let you go on thinking things of that kind. Edward and I—" she paused. " If you want to know the truth, we've hardly said a word to each other in private for the last three years."

" What! " Molly stared at her, appalled. " I—I can't believe it."

" Oh, we both put up quite a good show," said Evelyn. " We're neither of us the kind that like having rows in public. And anyway there's nothing really to have a row about."

" But what went wrong? " asked Molly.

" Just the usual."

" What do you mean by the usual? Another——"

" Yes, another woman in the case, and I don't suppose it will be difficult for you to guess who the woman is."

" Do you mean Mrs Dyson—Lucky? "

Evelyn nodded.

" I know they always flirt together a lot," said Molly, " but I thought that was just . . ."

" Just high spirits? " said Evelyn. " Nothing behind it? "

" But why—" Molly paused and tried again. " But didn't you—oh I mean, well I suppose I oughtn't to ask."

" Ask anything you like," said Evelyn. " I'm tired of never saying a word, tired of being a well-bred happy wife. Edward just lost his head completely about Lucky. He was stupid enough to come and tell me about it. It made him feel better I suppose. Truthful. Honourable. All that sort of stuff. It didn't occur to him to think that it wouldn't make *me* feel better."

" Did he want to leave you? "

Evelyn shook her head. " We've got two children, you know," she said. " Children whom we're both very fond of. They're at school in England. We didn't want to break up the home. And then of course, Lucky didn't want a divorce either. Greg's a very rich man. His first wife left a lot of money. So we agreed to live and let live—Edward and Lucky in happy immorality, Greg in blissful ignorance, and Edward and I just good friends." She spoke with scalding bitterness.

" How—how can you bear it? "

" One gets used to anything. But sometimes——"

" Yes? " said Molly.

" Sometimes I'd like to kill that woman."

The passion behind her voice startled Molly.

" Don't let's talk any more about me," said Evelyn. " Let's talk about you. I want to know what's the matter."

Molly was silent for some moments and then she said, " It's only—it's only that I think there's something wrong about me."

" Wrong? What do you mean? "

Molly shook her head unhappily. " I'm frightened," she said. " I'm terribly frightened."

" Frightened of what? "

" Everything," said Molly. " It's—growing on me. Voices in the bushes, footsteps—or things that people say. As though someone were watching me all the time, spying on me. Somebody hates me. That's what I keep feeling. Somebody hates me."

" My dear child." Evelyn was shocked and startled. " How long has this been going on? "

" I don't know. It came—it started by degrees. And there have been other things too."

" What sort of things? "

" There are times," said Molly slowly, " that I can't account for, that I can't remember."

" Do you mean you have blackouts—that sort of thing."

" I suppose so. I mean sometimes it's—oh, say it's five o'clock—and I can't remember anything since about half past one or two."

" Oh my dear, but that's just that you've been asleep. Had a doze."

" No," said Molly, " it's not like that at all. Because you see, at the end of the time it's not as though I'd just dozed off. I'm in a different *place*. Sometimes I'm wearing different clothes and sometimes I seem to have been doing things—even saying things to people, talking to someone, and not remembering that I've done so."

Evelyn looked shocked. " But, Molly, my dear, if this is so, then you ought to see a doctor."

" I won't see a doctor! I don't want to. I wouldn't go *near* a doctor."

Evelyn looked sharply down into her face, then she took the girl's hand in hers.

" You may be frightening yourself for nothing, Molly. You know there are all kinds of nervous disorders that aren't really serious at all. A doctor would soon reassure you."

" He mightn't. He might say that there was something really wrong with me."

" Why should there be anything wrong with you? "

" Because—" Molly spoke and then was silent,—"—no reason, I suppose," she said.

" Couldn't your family—haven't you any family, any mother or sisters or someone who could come out here? "

" I don't get on with my mother. I never have. I've got sisters. They're married but I suppose—I suppose they could come if I wanted them. But I don't want them. I don't want anyone—anyone except Tim."

" Does Tim know about this? Have you told him? "

" Not really," said Molly. " But he's anxious about me and he watches me. It's as though he were trying to—to help me or to shield me. But if he does that it means I want shielding, doesn't it? "

" I think a lot of it may be imagination but I still think you ought to see a doctor."

" Old Dr Graham? He wouldn't be any good."

" There are other doctors on the island."

" It's all right, really," said Molly. " I just—mustn't think of it. I expect, as you say, it's all imagination. Good gracious, it's getting frightfully late. I ought to be on duty now in the dining-room. I—I must go back."

She looked sharply and almost offensively at Evelyn Hillingdon, and then hurried off. Evelyn stared after her.

CHAPTER XII

OLD SINS CAST LONG SHADOWS

" I think as I am on to something, man."

" What's that you say, Victoria? "

" I think I'm on to something. It may mean money. Big money."

" Now look, girl, you be careful, you'll not tangle yourself up in something. Maybe I'd better tackle what it is."

Victoria laughed, a deep rich chuckle.

" You wait and see," she said. " I know how to play this hand. It's money, man, it's big money. Something I see, and something I guess. I think I guess right."

And again the soft rich chuckle rolled out on the night.

II

" Evelyn . . ."

" Yes? "

Evelyn Hillingdon spoke mechanically, without interest. She did not look at her husband.

" Evelyn, would you mind if we chucked all this and went home to England? "

She had been combing her short dark hair. Now her hands came down from her head sharply. She turned towards him.

" You mean—but we've only just come. We've not been out here in the islands for more than three weeks."

" I know. But—would you mind? "

Her eyes searched him incredulously.

" You really want to go back to England. Back home? "

" Yes."

" Leaving—Lucky."

He winced.

" You've known all the time, I suppose, that—that it was still going on? "

" Pretty well. Yes."

" You've never said anything."

" Why should I? We had the whole thing out years ago. Neither of us wanted to make a break. So we agreed to go our separate ways—but keep up the show in public." Then she added before he could speak, " But why are you so set on going back to England *now*? "

" Because I'm at breaking point. I can't stick it any longer, Evelyn. I can't." The quiet Edward Hillingdon was transformed. His hands shook, he swallowed, his calm unemotional face seemed distorted by pain.

" For God's sake, Edward, what's the *matter*? "

" Nothing's the matter except that I want to get out of here——"

" You fell wildly in love with Lucky. And now you've got over it. Is that what you're telling me? "

" Yes. I don't suppose you'll ever feel the same."

" Oh let's not go into that now! I want to understand what's upsetting you so much, Edward."

" I'm not particularly upset."

" But you are. Why? "

" Isn't it obvious? "

" No, it isn't," said Evelyn. " Let's put it in plain concrete terms. You've had an affair with a woman. That happens often enough. And now it's over. Or isn't it over? Perhaps it isn't over on *her* side. Is that it? Does Greg know about it? I've often wondered."

" I don't know," said Edward. " He's never said anything. He always seems friendly enough."

" Men can be extraordinarily obtuse," said Evelyn thoughtfully. " Or else— Perhaps Greg has got an outside interest of his own! "

" He's made passes at you, hasn't he? " said Edward. " Answer me—I know he has——"

" Oh yes," said Evelyn, carelessly, " but he makes passes at everybody. That's just Greg. It doesn't ever really mean much, I imagine. It's just part of the Greg he-man act."

" Do you care for him, Evelyn? I'd rather know the truth."

" Greg? I'm quite fond of him—he amuses me. He's a good friend."

" And that's all? I wish I could believe you."

" I can't really see how it can possibly matter to you," said Evelyn dryly.

" I suppose I deserve that."

Evelyn walked to the window, looked out across the veranda and came back again.

" I wish you would tell me what's *really* upsetting you, Edward."

" I've told you."

" I wonder."

" You can't understand, I suppose, how extraordinary a temporary madness of this kind can seem to you after you've got over it."

" I can try, I suppose. But what's worrying me now is that Lucky seems to have got some kind of stranglehold upon you. She's not just a discarded mistress. She's a tigress with claws. You *must* tell me the truth, Edward. It's the only way if you want me to stand by you."

Edward said in a low voice: " If I don't get away from her soon—I shall kill her."

" Kill Lucky? Why? "

" Because of what she made me do . . ."

" What did she make you do? "

" I helped her to commit a murder——"

The words were out— There was silence— Evelyn stared at him.

" Do you know what you are saying? "

" Yes. I didn't know I was doing it. There were things she asked me to get for her—at the chemist's. I didn't know—I hadn't the least idea what she wanted them for— She got me to copy out a prescription she had . . ."

" When was this? "

" Four years ago. When we were in Martinique. When—when Greg's wife——"

" You mean Greg's first wife—Gail? You mean Lucky poisoned her? "

" Yes—and I helped her. When I realised——"

Evelyn interrupted him.

" When you realised what had happened, Lucky pointed out to you that *you* had written out the prescription, that *you* had got the drugs, that you and she were in it together? Is that right? "

" Yes. She saig she had done it out of pity—that Gail was suffering—that she had begged Lucky to get something that would end it all."

" A mercy killing! I see. And you believed *that*? "

Edward Hillingdon was silent a moment—then he said:

" No—I didn't really—not deep down—I accepted it because I *wanted* to believe it—because I was infatuated with Lucky."

" And afterwards—when she married Greg—did you still believe it? "

" I'd made myself believe it by then."

" And Greg—how much did he know about it all? "

" Nothing at all."

" That I find hard to believe! "

Edward Hillingdon broke out—

" Evelyn, I've *got* to get free of it all! That woman taunts me still with what I did. She knows I don't care for her any longer. Care for her?— I've come to hate her— But she makes me feel I'm tied to her—by the thing we did together——"

Evelyn walked up and down the room—then she stopped and faced him.

" The entire trouble with you, Edward, is that you are ridiculously sensitive—and also incredibly suggestible. That devil of a woman has got you just where she wants you by playing on your sense of guilt— And I'll tell you this in plain Bible terms, the guilt that weighs on you is the guilt of adultery—not murder— You were guilt-stricken about your affair with Lucky—and then she made a cat's-paw of you for her murder scheme, and managed to make you feel you shared her guilt. You *don't*."

" Evelyn " . . . He stepped towards her—

She stepped back a minute—and looked at him searchingly.

" Is this all true, Edward— *Is* it? Or are you making it up? "

" Evelyn! Why on earth should I do such a thing? "

" I don't know," said Evelyn Hillingdon slowly— " It's just perhaps—because I find it hard to trust—

anybody. And because— Oh! I don't know— I've got, I suppose, so that I don't know the truth when I hear it."

" Let's chuck all this— Go back home to England."

" Yes— We will— But not now."

" Why not? "

" We must carry on as usual—just for the present. It's important. Do you understand, Edward? Don't let Lucky have an inkling of what we're up to——"

CHAPTER XIII

EXIT VICTORIA JOHNSON

The evening was drawing to a close. The steel band was at last relaxing its efforts. Tim stood by the dining-room looking over the terrace. He extinguished a few lights on tables that had been vacated.

A voice spoke behind him. " Tim, can I speak to you a moment? "

Tim Kendal started.

" Hallo, Evelyn, is there anything I can do for you? "

Evelyn looked round.

" Come to this table here, and let's sit down a minute."

She led the way to a table at the extreme end of the terrace. There were no other people near them.

" Tim, you must forgive me talking to you, but I'm worried about Molly."

His face changed at once.

" What about Molly? " he said stiffly.

" I don't think she's awfully well. She seems upset."

" Things do seem to upset her rather easily just lately."

" She ought to see a doctor, I think."

" Yes, I know, but she doesn't want to. She'd hate it."

" Why? "

" Eh? What d'you mean? "

" I said why? Why should she hate seeing a doctor?"

" Well," said Tim rather vaguely, " People do sometimes, you know. It's—well, it sort of makes them feel frightened about themselves."

" You're worried about her yourself, aren't you, Tim? "

" Yes. Yes, I am rather."

" Isn't there anyone of her family who could come out here to be with her? "

" No. That'd make things worse, far worse."

" What *is* the trouble—with her family, I mean? "

" Oh, just one of those things. I suppose she's just highly strung and—she didn't get on with them—particularly her mother. She never has. They're—they're rather an odd family in some ways and she cut loose from them. Good thing she did, I think."

Evelyn said hesitantly—" She seems to have had blackouts, from what she told me, and to be frightened of people. Almost like persecution mania."

" Don't say that," said Tim angrily. " Persecution mania! People always say that about people. Just because she—well—maybe she's a bit nervy. Coming out here to the West Indies. All the dark faces. You know, people are rather queer, sometimes, about the West Indies and coloured people."

" Surely not girls like Molly? "

" Oh, how does one know the things people are frightened of? There are people who can't be in the room with cats. And other people who faint if a caterpillar drops on them."

" I hate suggesting it—but don't you think perhaps she ought to see a—well, a psychiatrist? "

" *No!* " said Tim explosively. " I won't have people like that monkeying about with her. I don't believe in them. They make people worse. If her mother had left psychiatrists alone . . ."

" So there *was* trouble of that kind in her family—was there? I mean a history of—" she chose the word carefully—" instability."

" I don't want to talk about it— I took her away from it all and she was all right, quite all right. She has just got into a nervous state. . . . But these things aren't hereditary. Everybody knows that nowadays. It's an exploded idea. Molly's perfectly sane. It's just that—oh! I believe it was that wretched old Palgrave dying that started it all off."

" I see," said Evelyn thoughtfully. " But there was nothing really to worry anyone in Major Palgrave's death, was there? "

" No of course there wasn't. But it's a kind of shock when somebody dies suddenly."

He looked so desperate and defeated that Evelyn's heart smote her. She put her hand on his arm.

" Well, I hope you know what you're doing, Tim,

but if I could help in any way—I mean if I could go with Molly to New York—I could fly with her there or Miami or somewhere where she could get really first-class medical advice."

" It's very good of you, Evelyn, but Molly's all right. She's getting over it, anyway."

Evelyn shook her head in doubt. She turned away slowly and looked along the line of the terrace. Most people had gone by now to their bungalows. Evelyn was walking towards her table to see if she'd left anything behind there, when she heard Tim give an exclamation. She looked up sharply. He was staring towards the steps at the end of the terrace and she followed his gaze. Then she too caught her breath.

Molly was coming up the steps from the beach. She was breathing with deep, sobbing breaths, her body swayed to and fro as she came, in a curious directionless run. Tim cried,

" *Molly!* What's the matter? "

He ran towards her and Evelyn followed him. Molly was at the top of the steps now and she stood there, both hands behind her back. She said in sobbing breaths:

" I found her. . . . She's there in the bushes . . . There in the bushes . . . And look at my hands—look at my *hands*." She held them out and Evelyn caught her breath as she saw the queer dark stains. They looked dark in the subdued lighting but she knew well enough that their real colour was red.

" What's happened, Molly? " cried Tim.

" Down there," said Molly. She swayed on her feet. " In the bushes . . ."

Tim hesitated, looked at Evelyn, then shoved Molly a little towards Evelyn and ran down the steps. Evelyn put her arm round the girl.

" Come. Sit down, Molly. Here. You'd better have something to drink."

Molly collapsed in a chair and leaned forward on the table, her forehead on her crossed arms. Evelyn did not question her any more. She thought it better to leave her time to recover.

" It'll be all right, you know," said Evelyn gently. " It'll be all right."

" I don't know," said Molly. " I don't know what happened. I don't know anything. I can't remember. I—" she raised her head suddenly. " What's the matter with me? What's the *matter* with me? "

" It's all right, child. It's all right."

Tim was coming slowly up the steps. His face was ghastly. Evelyn looked up at him, raising her eyebrows in a query.

" It's one of our girls," he said. " What's-her-name—Victoria. Somebody's put a knife in her."

CHAPTER XIV

INQUIRY

Molly lay on her bed. Dr Graham and Dr Robertson, the West Indian police doctor stood on one side—Tim on the other. Robertson had his hand on Molly's pulse— He nodded to the man at the foot of the bed, a slender dark man in police uniform, Inspector Weston of the St. Honoré Police Force.

" A bare statement—no more," the doctor said.

The other nodded.

" Now, Mrs Kendal—just tell us how you came to find this girl."

For a moment or two it was as though the figure on the bed had not heard. Then she spoke in a faint, faraway voice.

" In the bushes—white. . . ."

" You saw something white—and you looked to see what it was? Is that it? "

" Yes—white—lying there—I tried—tried to lift—she—it—blood—blood all over my hands."

She began to tremble.

Dr Graham shook his head at them. Robertson whispered—" She can't stand much more."

"What were you doing on the beach path, Mrs Kendal?"

"Warm—nice—by the sea——"

"You knew who the girl was?"

"Victoria—nice—nice girl—laughs—she used to laugh—oh! and now she won't— She won't ever laugh again. I'll never forget it—I'll never forget it——" Her voice rose hysterically.

"Molly—don't." It was Tim.

"Quiet—Quiet—." Dr Robertson spoke with a soothing authority— "Just relax—relax— Now just a small prick—"

He withdrew the hypodermic.

"She'll be in no fit condition to be questioned for at least twenty-four hours," he said—"I'll let you know when."

II

The big handsome negro looked from one to the other of the men sitting at the table.

"Ah declare to God," he said. "That's all I know. I don't know nothing but what Ah've told you."

The perspiration stood out on his forehead. Daventry sighed. The man presiding at the table, Inspector Weston of the St. Honoré C.I.D., made a gesture of dismissal. Big Jim Ellis shuffled out of the room.

"It's not all he knows, of course," Weston said. He

had the soft Island voice. " But it's all we shall learn from him."

" You think he's in the clear himself? " asked Daventry.

" Yes. They seem to have been on good terms together."

" They weren't married? "

A faint smile appeared on Lieutenant Weston's lips. " No," he said, " they weren't married. We don't have so many marriages on the Island. They christen the children, though. He's had two children by Victoria."

" Do you think he was in it, whatever it was, with her? "

" Probably not. I think he'd have been nervous of anything of that kind. And I'd say, too, that what she did know wasn't very much."

" But enough for blackmail? "

" I don't know that I'd even call it that. I doubt if the girl would even understand that word. Payment for being discreet isn't thought of as blackmail. You see, some of the people who stay here are the rich playboy lot and their morals won't bear much investigation." His voice was slightly scathing.

" We get all kinds, I agree," said Daventry. " A woman, maybe, doesn't want it known that she's sleeping around, so she gives a present to the girl who waits on her. It's tacitly understood that the payment's for discretion."

" Exactly."

" But this," objected Daventry, " wasn't anything of *that* kind. It was murder."

" I should doubt, though, if the girl knew it was serious. She saw something, some puzzling incident. something to do presumably with this bottle of pills. It belonged to Mr Dyson, I understand. We'd better see him next."

Gregory came in with his usual hearty air.

" Here I am," he said, " what can I do to help? Too bad about this girl. She was a nice girl. We both liked her. I suppose it was some sort of quarrel or other with a man, but she seemed quite happy and no signs of being in trouble about anything. I was kidding her only last night."

" I believe you take a preparation, Mr Dyson, called Serenite? "

" Quite right. Little pink tablets."

" You have them on prescription from a physician? "

" Yes. I can show it to you if you like. Suffer a bit from high blood pressure, like so many people do nowadays."

" Very few people seem to be aware of that fact."

" Well, I don't go talking about it. I—well, I've always been well and hearty and I never like people who talk about their ailments all the time."

" How many of the pills do you take? "

" Two, three times a day."

" Do you have a fairly large stock with you? "

" Yes. I've got about half a dozen bottles. But

they're locked up, you know, in a suitcase. I only keep out one, the one that's in current use."

" And you missed this bottle a short time ago, so I hear? "

" Quite right."

" And you asked this girl, Victoria Johnson, whether she'd seen it? "

" Yes, I did."

" And what did she say? "

" She said the last time she'd seen it was on the shelf in our bathroom. She said she'd look around."

" And after that? "

" She came and returned the bottle to me some time later. She said was this the bottle that was missing? "

" And you said? "

" I said ' that's it, all right, where did you find it? ' And she said it was in old Major Palgrave's room. I said ' how on earth did it get there? ' "

" And what did she answer to that? "

" She said she didn't know, but——" he hesitated.

" Yes, Mr Dyson? "

" Well, she gave me the feeling that she did know a little more than she was saying, but I didn't pay much attention. After all, it wasn't very important. As I say, I've got other bottles of the pills with me. I thought perhaps I'd left it around in the restaurant or somewhere and old Palgrave picked it up for some reason. Perhaps he put it in his pocket meaning to return it to me, then forgot."

" And that's all you know about it, Mr Dyson? "

" That's all I know. Sorry to be so unhelpful. Is it important? Why? "

Weston shrugged his shoulders. " As things are, anything may be important."

" I don't see where pills come in. I thought you'd want to know about what my movements were when this wretched girl was stabbed. I've written them all down as carefully as I can."

Weston looked at him thoughtfully.

" Indeed? That was very helpful of you, Mr Dyson."

" Save everybody trouble, I thought," said Greg. He shoved a piece of paper across the table.

Weston studied it and Daventry dew his chair a little closer and looked over his shoulder.

" That seems very clear," said Weston, after a moment or two. " You and your wife were together changing for dinner in your bungalow until ten minutes to nine. You then went along to the terrace where you had drinks with Señora de Caspearo. At quarter past nine Colonel and Mrs Hillingdon joined you and you went in to dine. As far as you can remember, you went off to bed at about half past eleven."

" Of course," said Greg. " I don't know what time the girl was actually killed——? "

There was a faint semblance of a question in the words. Lieutenant Weston, however, did not appear to notice it.

"Mrs Kendal found her, I understand? Must have been a very nasty shock for her."

"Yes. Dr Robertson had to give her a sedative."

"This was quite late, wasn't it, when most people had trundled off to bed?"

"Yes."

"Had she been dead long? When Mrs Kendal found her, I mean?"

"We're not quite certain of the exact time yet," said Weston smoothly.

"Poor little Molly. It must have been a nasty shock for her. Matter of fact, I didn't notice *her* about last night. Thought she might have had a headache or something and was lying down."

"When was the last time you *did* see Mrs Kendal?"

"Oh, quite early, before I went to change. She was playing about with some of the table decorations and things. Rearranging the knives."

"I see."

"She was quite cheerful then," said Greg. "Kidding and all that. She's a great girl. We're all very fond of her. Tim's a lucky fellow."

"Well, thank you, Mr Dyson. You can't remember anything more than you've told us about what the girl Victoria said when she returned the tablets?"

"No . . . It was just as I say. Asked me were these the tablets I'd been asking for. Said she'd found them in old Palgrave's room."

" She'd no idea who put them there? "

" Don't think so—can't remember, really."

" Thank you, Mr Dyson."

Gregory went out.

" Very thoughtful of him," said Weston, gently tapping the paper with his fingernail, " to be so anxious to want us to know for sure exactly where he was last night."

" A little over-anxious do you think? " asked Daventry.

" That's very difficult to tell. There are people, you know, who are naturally nervous about their own safety, about being mixed up with anything. It isn't necessarily because they have any guilty knowledge. On the other hand it might be just that."

" What about opportunity? Nobody's really got much of an alibi, what with the band and the dancing and the coming and going. People are getting up, leaving their tables, coming back. Women go to powder their noses. Men take a stroll. Dyson could have slipped away. Anybody could have slipped away. But he does seem rather anxious to prove that *he* didn't." He looked thoughtfully down at the paper. " So Mrs Kendal was rearranging knives on the table," he said. " I rather wonder if he dragged that in on purpose."

" Did it sound like it to you? "

The other considered. " I think it's possible."

Outside the room where the two men were sitting,

a noise had arisen. A high voice was demanding admittance shrilly.

"I've got something to tell. I've got something to tell. You take me in to where the gentlemen are. You take me in to where the policeman is."

A uniformed policeman pushed open the door.

"It's one of the cooks here," he said, "very anxious to see you. Says he's got something you ought to know."

A frightened dark man in a cook's cap pushed past him and came into the room. It was one of the minor cooks. A Cuban, not a native of St. Honoré.

"I tell you something. I tell you," he said. "She come through my kitchen, she did, and she had a knife with her. A knife, I tell you. She had a knife in her hand. She come through my kitchen and out the door. Out into the garden. I saw her."

"Now calm down," said Daventry, "calm down. Who are you talking about?"

"I tell you who I'm talking about. I'm talking about the boss's wife. Mrs Kendal. I'm talking about her. She have a knife in her hand and she go out into the dark. Before dinner that was—and *she didn't come back.*"

CHAPTER XV

INQUIRY CONTINUED

" Can we have a word with you, Mr Kendal? "

" Of course." Tim looked up from his desk. He pushed some papers aside and indicated chairs. His face was drawn and miserable. " How are you getting on? Got any forwarder? There seems to be a doom in this place. People are wanting to leave, you know, asking about air passages. Just when it seemed everything was being a success. Oh lord, you don't know what it means, this place, to me and to Molly. We staked everything on it."

" It's very hard on you, I know," said Inspector Weston. " Don't think that we don't sympathise."

" If it all could be cleared up quickly," said Tim. " This wretched girl Victoria—Oh! I oughtn't to talk about her like that. She was quite a good sort, Victoria was. But—but there must be some quite simple reason, some—kind of intrigue, or love affair she had. Perhaps her husband——"

" Jim Ellis wasn't her husband, and they seemed a settled sort of couple."

" If it could only be cleared up *quickly*," said Tim

again. " I'm sorry. You wanted to talk to me about something, ask me something."

" Yes. It was about last night. According to medical evidence Victoria was killed some time between 10.30 p.m. and midnight. Alibis under the circumstances that prevail here, are not very easy to prove. People are moving about, dancing, walking away from the terrace, coming back. It's all very difficult."

" I suppose so. But does that mean that you definitely consider Victoria was killed by one of the guests here? "

" Well, we have to examine that possibility, Mr Kendal. What I want to ask you particularly about, is a statement made by one of your cooks."

" Oh? Which one? What does he say? "

" He's a Cuban, I understand."

" We've got two Cubans and a Puerto Rican."

" This man Enrico states that your wife passed through the kitchen on her way from the dining-room, and went out into the garden and that she was carrying a knife."

Tim stared at him.

" Molly, carrying a knife? Well, why shouldn't she? I mean—why—you don't think—what are you trying to suggest? "

" I am talking of the time before people had come into the dining-room. It would be, I suppose, some time about 8.30. You yourself were in the dining-room talking to the head waiter, Fernando, I believe."

"Yes." Tim cast his mind back. "Yes, I remember."

"And your wife came in from the terrace?"

"Yes, she did," Tim agreed. "She always went out to look over the tables. Sometimes the boys set things wrong, forgot some of the cutlery, things like that. Very likely that's what it was. She may have been re-arranging cutlery or something. She might have had a spare knife or a spoon, something like that in her hand."

"And she came from the terrace into the dining-room. Did she speak to you?"

"Yes, we had a word or two together."

"What did she say? Can you remember?"

"I think I asked her who she'd been talking to. I heard her voice out there."

"And who did she say she'd been talking to?"

"Gregory Dyson."

"Ah. Yes. That is what *he* said."

Tim went on, "He'd been making a pass at her, I understand. He was a bit given to that kind of thing. It annoyed me and I said 'Blast him' and Molly laughed and said she could do all the blasting that needed to be done. Molly's a very clever girl that way. It's not always an easy position, you know. You can't offend guests, and so an attractive girl like Molly has to pass things off with a laugh and a shrug. Gregory Dyson finds it difficult to keep his hands off any good-looking woman."

"Had there been any altercation between them?"

"No, I don't think so. I think, as I say, she just laughed it off as usual."

" You can't say definitely whether she had a knife in her hand or not? "

" I can't remember—I'm almost sure she didn't—In fact quite sure she didn't."

" But you said just now . . ."

" Look here, what I meant was that if she was in the dining-room or in the kitchen it's quite likely she might have picked up a knife or had one in her hand. Matter of fact I can remember quite well, she came in from the dining-room and she had *nothing* in her hand. *Nothing at all*. That's definite."

" I see," said Weston.

Tim looked at him uneasily.

" What on earth is this you're getting at? What did that damn' fool Enrico—Manuel—whichever it was—say? "

" He said your wife came out into the kitchen, that she looked upset, that she had a knife in her hand."

" He's just dramatising."

" Did you have any further conversation with your wife during dinner or after? "

" No, I don't think I did really. Matter of fact I was rather busy."

" Was your wife there in the dining-room during the meal? "

" I—oh—yes, we always move about among the guests and things like that. See how things are going on."

" Did you speak to her at all? "

" No, I don't think I did . . . We're usually fairly busy. We don't always notice what the other one's doing and we certainly haven't got time to talk to each other."

" Actually you don't remember speaking to her until she came up the steps three hours later, after finding the body? "

" It was an awful shock for her. It upset her terribly."

" I know. A very unpleasant experience. How did she come to be walking along the beach path? "

" After the stress of dinner being served, she often does go for a turn. You know, get away from the guests for a minute or two, get a breather."

" When she came back, I understand you were talking to Mrs Hillingdon."

" Yes. Practically everyone else had gone to bed."

" What was the subject of your conversation with Mrs Hillingdon? "

" Nothing particular. Why? What's she been saying? "

" So far she hasn't said anything. We haven't asked her."

" We were just talking of this and that. Molly, and hotel running, and one thing and another."

" And then—your wife came up the steps of the terrace and told you what had happened? "

" Yes."

" There was blood on her hands? "

" Of course there was! She'd bent over the girl, tried to lift her, couldn't understand what had happened, what was the matter with her. Of course there was blood on her hands! Look here, what the hell are you suggesting? You *are* suggesting something? "

" Please calm down," said Daventry. " It's all a great strain on you I know, Tim, but we have to get the facts clear. I understand your wife hasn't been feeling very well lately? "

" Nonsense—she's all right. Major Palgrave's death upset her a bit. Naturally. She's a sensitive girl."

" We shall have to ask her a few questions as soon as she's fit enough," said Weston.

" Well, you can't now. The doctor gave her a sedative and said she wasn't to be disturbed. I won't have her upset and brow-beaten, d'you hear? "

" We're not going to do any brow-beating," said Weston. " We've just got to get the facts clear. We won't disturb her at present, but as soon as the doctor allows us, we'll have to see her." His voice was gentle—inflexible.

Tim looked at him, opened his mouth, but said nothing.

II

Evelyn Hillingdon, calm and composed as usual, sat down in the chair indicated. She considered the few questions asked her, taking her time over it. Her dark, intelligent eyes looked at Weston thoughtfully.

"Yes," she said, "I was talking to Mr Kendal on the terrace when his wife came up the steps and told us about the murder."

"Your husband wasn't there?"

"No, he had gone to bed."

"Had you any special reason for your conversation with Mr Kendal?"

Evelyn raised her finely pencilled eyebrows— It was a definite rebuke.

She said coldly:

"What a very odd question. No—there was nothing special about our conversation."

"Did you discuss the matter of his wife's health?"

Again Evelyn took her time.

"I really can't remember," she said at last.

"Are you sure of that?"

"Sure that I can't remember? What a curious way of putting it—one talks about so many things at different times."

"Mrs Kendal has not been in good health lately, I understand."

"She looked quite all right—a little tired perhaps. Of course running a place like this means a lot of worries, and she is quite inexperienced. Naturally, she gets flustered now and then."

"Flustered." Weston repeated the word. "That was the way you would describe it?"

" It's an old-fashioned word, perhaps, but just as good as the modern jargon we use for everything—A ' virus infection ' for a bilious attack—an ' anxiety neurosis ' for the minor bothers of daily life——"

Her smile made Weston feel slightly ridiculous. He thought to himself that Evelyn Hillingdon was a clever woman. He looked at Daventry whose face remained unmoved and wondered what he thought.

" Thank you, Mrs Hillingdon," said Weston.

III

" We don't want to worry you, Mrs Kendal, but we have to have your account of just how you came to find this girl. Dr Graham says you are sufficiently recovered to talk about it now."

" Oh yes," said Molly, " I'm really quite all right again." She gave them a small nervous smile. " It was just the shock— It *was* rather awful, you know."

" Yes, indeed it must have been—I understand you went for a walk after dinner."

" Yes—I—often do."

Her eyes shifted, Daventry noticed, and the fingers of her hands twined and untwined about each other.

" What time would that have been, Mrs Kendal? " asked Weston.

" Well, I don't really know—we don't go much by the time."

"The steel band was still playing?"

"Yes—at least—I think so—I can't really remember."

"And you walked—which way?"

"Oh, along the beach path."

"To the left or the right?"

"Oh! First one way—and then the other—I—I—really didn't notice."

"Why didn't you notice, Mrs Kendal?"

She frowned.

"I suppose I was—well—thinking of things."

"Thinking of anything particular?"

"No—No—Nothing particular— Just things that had to be done—seen to—in the hotel." Again that nervous twining and untwining of fingers. "And then—I noticed something white—in a clump of hibiscus bushes—and I wondered what it was. I stopped and—and pulled—" She swallowed convulsively— "And it was her—Victoria—all huddled up—and I tried to raise her head up and I got—blood—on my hands."

She looked at them and repeated wonderingly as though recalling something impossible:

"Blood—on my hands."

"Yes—Yes— A very dreadful experience. There is no need for you to tell us more about that part of it—How long had you been walking, do you think, when you found her——"

"I don't know—I have no idea."

" An hour? Half an hour? Or more than an hour——"

" I don't know," Molly repeated.

Daventry asked in a quiet everyday voice:

" Did you take a knife with you on your—walk? "

" A knife? " Molly sounded surprised. " Why should I take a knife? "

" I only ask because one of the kitchen staff mentioned that you had a knife in your hand when you went out of the kitchen into the garden."

Molly frowned.

" But I didn't go out of the kitchen—oh you mean earlier—before dinner—I—I don't *think* so——"

" You had been rearranging the cutlery on the tables, perhaps."

" I have to, sometimes. They lay things wrong—not enough knives—or too many. The wrong number of forks and spoons—that sort of thing."

" And did that happen on this particular evening? "

" It may have done—something like that— It's really automatic. One doesn't think, or remember——"

" So you may have gone out of the kitchen that evening carrying a knife in your hand? "

" I don't think I did—I'm sure I didn't—" She added— " Tim was there—he would know. Ask him."

" Did you like this girl—Victoria—was she good at her work? " asked Weston.

" Yes—she was a very nice girl."

" You had had no dispute with her? "

" Dispute? No."

" She had never threatened you—in any way? "

" Threatened me? What do you mean? "

" It doesn't matter— You have no idea of who could have killed her? No idea at all? "

" None." She spoke positively.

" Well, thank you, Mrs Kendal." He smiled. " It wasn't so terrible, was it? "

" That's all? "

" That's all for now."

Daventry got up, opened the door for her, and watched her go out.

" Tim would know," he quoted as he returned to his chair. " And Tim says definitely that she *didn't* have a knife."

Weston said gravely:

" I think that that is what any husband would feel called upon to say."

" A table knife seems a very poor type of knife to use for murder."

" But it was a *steak* knife, Mr Daventry. Steaks were on the menu that evening. Steak knives are kept sharp."

" I really can't bring myself to believe that that girl we've just been talking to is a red-handed murderess, Weston."

" It is not necessary to believe it yet. It could be

that Mrs Kendal went out into the garden before dinner, clasping a knife she had taken off one of the tables because it was superfluous—she might not even have noticed she was holding it, and she could have put it down somewhere—or dropped it— It could have been found and used by someone else— I, too, think her an unlikely murderess."

"All the same," said Daventry thoughtfully, "I'm pretty sure she is not telling all she knows. Her vagueness over time is odd—where was she—what was she doing out there? Nobody, so far, seems to have noticed her in the dining-room that evening."

"The husband was about as usual—but not the wife——"

"You think she went to meet someone—Victoria Johnson?"

"Perhaps—or perhaps she saw whoever it was who did go to meet Victoria."

"You're thinking of Gregory Dyson?"

"We know he was talking to Victoria earlier— He may have arranged to meet her again later—everyone moved around freely on the terrace, remember—dancing, drinking—in and out of the bar."

"No alibi like a steel band," said Daventry wryly.

CHAPTER XVI

MISS MARPLE SEEKS ASSISTANCE

If anybody had been there to observe the gentle-looking elderly lady who stood meditatively on the loggia outside her bungalow, they would have thought she had nothing more on her mind than deliberation on how to arrange her time that day— An expedition, perhaps, to Castle Cliff—a visit to Jamestown—a nice drive and lunch at Pelican Point—or just a quiet morning on the beach—

But the gentle old lady was deliberating quite other matters—she was in militant mood.

"*Something has got to be done,*" said Miss Marple to herself.

Moreover, she was convinced that there was no time to be lost— There was urgency.

But who was there that she could convince of that fact? Given time, she thought she could find out the truth by herself.

She had found out a good deal. But not enough—not nearly enough. And time was short.

She realised, bitterly, that here on this Paradise of an island, she had none of her usual allies.

She thought regretfully of her friends in England—

Sir Henry Clithering—always willing to listen indulgently—his godson Dermot, who in spite of his increased status at Scotland Yard, was still ready to believe that when Miss Marple voiced an opinion there was usually something behind it.

But would that soft-voiced native police officer pay any attention to an old lady's urgency? Dr Graham? But Dr Graham was not what she needed—too gentle and hesitant, certainly not a man of quick decisions and rapid actions.

Miss Marple, feeling rather like a humble deputy of the Almighty, almost cried aloud her need in Biblical phrasing.

Who will go for me?

Whom shall I send?

The sound that reached her ears a moment later was not instantly recognised by her as an answer to prayer—far from it— At the back of her mind it registered only as a man possibly calling his dog.

" Hi! "

Miss Marple, lost in perplexity, paid no attention.

" Hi! " The volume thus increased, Miss Marple looked vaguely round.

" HI! " called Mr Rafiel impatiently. He added— " You—there——"

Miss Marple had not at first realised that Mr Rafiel's " Hi You " was addressed to her. It was not a method that anyone had ever used before to summon her. It was certainly not a gentlemanly mode of address. Miss

Marple did not resent it, because people seldom did resent Mr Rafiel's somewhat arbitrary method of doing things. He was a law unto himself and people accepted him as such. Miss Marple looked across the intervening space between her bungalow and his. Mr Rafiel was sitting outside on his loggia and he beckoned her.

" You were calling me? " she asked.

" Of course I was calling you," said Mr Rafiel. " Who did you think I was calling—a cat? Come over here."

Miss Marple looked round for her handbag, picked it up, and crossed the intervening space.

" I can't come to you unless someone helps me," explained Mr Rafiel, " so you've got to come to me."

" Oh yes," said Miss Marple, " I quite understand *that*."

Mr Rafiel pointed to an adjacent chair. " Sit down," he said, " I want to talk to you. Something damned odd is going on in this island."

" Yes, indeed," agreed Miss Marple, taking the chair as indicated. By sheer habit she drew her knitting out of her bag.

" Don't start knitting again," said Mr Rafiel, " I can't stand it. I hate women knitting. It irritates me."

Miss Marple returned her knitting to her bag. She did this with no undue air of meekness, rather with the air of one who makes allowances for a fractious patient.

" There's a lot of chit-chat going on," said Mr Rafiel,

" and I bet you're in the forefront of it. You and the parson and his sister."

" It is, perhaps, only natural that there should be chit-chat," said Miss Marple with spirit, " given the circumstances."

" This Island girl gets herself knifed. Found in the bushes. *Might* be ordinary enough. That chap she was living with might have got jealous of another man —or he's got himself another girl and she got jealous and they had a row. Sex in the tropics. That sort of stuff. What do you say? "

" No," said Miss Marple, shaking her head.

" The authorities don't think so, either."

" They would say more to you," pointed out Miss Marple, " than they would say to me."

" All the same, I bet you know more about it than I do. You've listened to the tittle-tattle."

" Certainly I have," said Miss Marple.

" Nothing much else to do, have you, except listen to tittle-tattle? "

" It is often informative and useful."

" D'you know," said Mr Rafiel, studying her attentively, " I made a mistake about you. I don't often make mistakes about people. There's a lot more to you than I thought there was. All these rumours about Major Palgrave and the stories he told. You think he was bumped off, don't you? "

" I very much fear so," said Miss Marple.

" Well, he was," said Mr Rafiel.

Miss Marple drew a deep breath. " That is definite, is it? " she asked.

" Yes, it's definite enough. I had it from Daventry. I'm not breaking a confidence because the facts of the autopsy will have to come out. You told Graham something, he went to Daventry, Daventry went to the Administrator, the C.I.D. were informed, and between them they agreed that things looked fishy, so they dug up old Palgrave and had a look."

" And they found? " Miss Marple paused interrogatively.

" They found he'd had a lethal dose of something that only a doctor could pronounce properly. As far as I remember it sounds vaguely like di-flor, hexagonal-ethylcarbenzol. That's not the right name. But that's roughly what it *sounds* like. The police doctor put it that way so that nobody should know, I suppose, what it really *was*. The stuff's probably got some quite simple nice easy name like Evipan or Veronal or Easton's Syrup or something of that kind. This is its official name to baffle laymen with. Anyway, a sizeable dose of it, I gather, would produce death, and the signs would be much the same as those of high blood pressure aggravated by over indulgence in alcohol on a gay evening. In fact, it all looked perfectly natural and nobody questioned it for a moment. Just said ' poor old chap ' and buried him quick. Now they wonder if he ever had high blood pressure at all. Did he ever say he had to you? "

" No."

" Exactly! And yet everyone seems to have taken it as a fact."

" Apparently he told people he had."

" It's like seeing ghosts," said Mr Rafiel. " You never meet the chap who's seen the ghost himself. It's always the second cousin of his aunt, or a friend, or a friend of a friend. But leave that for a moment. They thought he had blood pressure, because there was a bottle of tablets controlling blood pressure found in his room but—and now we're coming to the point—I gather that this girl who was killed went about saying that that bottle was put there by somebody else, and that *actually* it belonged to that fellow Greg."

" Mr Dyson *has* got blood pressure. His wife mentioned it," said Miss Marple.

" So it was put in Palgrave's room to suggest that he suffered from blood pressure and to make his death seem natural."

" Exactly," said Miss Marple. " And the story was put about, very cleverly, that he had frequently mentioned to people that he had high blood pressure. But you know, it's very easy to put about a story. Very easy. I've seen a lot of it in my time."

" I bet you have," said Mr Rafiel.

" It only needs a murmur here and there," said Miss Marple. " You don't say it of your own knowledge, you just say that Mrs B. told you that Colonel C. told her. It's always at second hand or third hand or fourth hand and it's very difficult to find out who was the original whisperer. Oh yes, it can be done. And the people you say it to go on and repeat it to others as if they know it of their own knowledge."

" Somebody's been clever," said Mr Rafiel thoughtfully.

" Yes," said Miss Marple, " I think somebody's been quite clever."

" This girl saw something, or knew something and tried blackmail, I suppose," said Mr Rafiel.

" She mayn't have thought of it as blackmail," said Miss Marple. " In these large hotels, there are often things the maids know that some people would rather not have repeated. And so they hand out a larger tip or a little present of money. The girl possibly didn't realise at first the importance of what she knew."

" Still, she got a knife in her back all right," said Mr Rafiel brutally.

" Yes. Evidently someone couldn't afford to let her talk."

" Well? Let's hear what you think about it all."

Miss Marple looked at him thoughtfully.

" Why should you think I know any more than you do, Mr Rafiel?"

" Probably you don't," said Mr Rafiel, " but I'm interested to hear your ideas about what you do know."

" But why?"

" There's not very much to do out here," said Mr Rafiel, " except make money."

Miss Marple looked slightly surprised.

" Make money? Out here? "

" You can send out half a dozen cables in code every day if you like," said Mr Rafiel. " That's how I amuse myself."

" Take-over bids? " Miss Marple asked doubtfully, in the tone of one who speaks a foreign language.

" That kind of thing," agreed Mr Rafiel. " Pitting your wits against other people's wits. The trouble is it doesn't occupy enough time, so I've got interested in this business. It's aroused my curiosity. Palgrave spent a good deal of his time talking to you. Nobody else would be bothered with him, I expect. What did he say? "

" He told me a good many stories," said Miss Marple.

" I know he did. Damn' boring, most of them. And you hadn't only got to hear them once. If you got anywhere within range you heard them three or four times over."

" I know," said Miss Marple. " I'm afraid that does happen when gentlemen get older."

Mr Rafiel looked at her very sharply.

" I don't tell stories," he said. " Go on. It started with one of Palgrave's stories, did it? "

" He said he knew a murderer," said Miss Marple. " There's nothing really special about that," she added in her gentle voice, " because I suppose it happens to nearly everybody."

" I don't follow you," said Mr Rafiel.

"I don't mean specifically," said Miss Marple, "but surely, Mr Rafiel, if you cast over in your mind your recollections of various events in your life, hasn't there nearly always been an occasion when somebody has made some careless reference such as 'Oh yes I knew the So-and-So's quite well—he died very suddenly and they always say his wife did him in, but I daresay that's just gossip'. You've heard people say something like that, haven't you?"

"Well, I suppose so—yes, something of the kind. But not—well, not seriously."

"Exactly," said Miss Marple, "but Major Palgrave was a very serious man. I think he enjoyed telling this story. He said he had a snapshot of the murderer. He was going to show it to me but—actually—he didn't."

"Why?"

"Because he saw something," said Miss Marple. "Saw someone, I suspect. His face got very red and he shoved back the snapshot into his wallet and began talking on another subject."

"Who did he see?"

"I've thought about that a good deal," said Miss Marple. "I was sitting outside my bungalow, and he was sitting nearly opposite me and—whatever he saw, he saw over my right shoulder."

"Someone coming along the path then from behind you on the right, the path from the creek and the car park——"

"Yes."

"*Was* anyone coming along the path?"

"Mr and Mrs Dyson and Colonel and Mrs Hillingdon."

"Anybody else?"

"Not that I can find out. Of course, your bungalow would also be in his line of vision. . . ."

"Ah. Then we include—shall we say—Esther Walters and my chap, Jackson. Is that right? Either of them, I suppose, *might* have come out of the bungalow and gone back inside again without your seeing them."

"They might have," said Miss Marple, "I didn't turn my head at once."

"The Dysons, the Hillingdons, Esther, Jackson. One of them's a murderer. Or of course, myself," he added; obviously as an afterthought.

Miss Marple smiled faintly.

"And he spoke of the murderer as a *man*?"

"Yes."

"Right. That cuts out Evelyn Hillingdon, Lucky and Esther Walters. So your murderer, allowing that all this far-fetched nonsense is true, your murderer is Dyson, Hillingdon or my smooth-tongued Jackson."

"Or yourself," said Miss Marple.

Mr Rafiel ignored this last point.

"Don't say things to irritate me," he said. "I'll tell you the first thing that strikes me, and which you don't seem to have thought of. *If* it's one of those three, why the devil didn't old Palgrave recognise him before?

Dash it all, they've all been sitting round looking at each other for the last two weeks. That doesn't seem to make sense."

" I think it could," said Miss Marple.

" Well, tell me how."

" You see, in Major Palgrave's story he hadn't seen this man *himself* at any time. It was a story told to him by a doctor. The doctor gave him the snapshot as a curiosity. Major Palgrave may have looked at the snapshot fairly closely at the time but after that he'd just stack it away in his wallet and keep it as a souvenir. Occasionally, perhaps, he'd take it out and show it to someone he was telling the story to. And another thing, Mr Rafiel, we don't know how long ago this happened. He didn't give me any indication of that when he was telling the story. I mean this may have been a story he's been telling to people for *years*. Five years—ten years—longer still perhaps. Some of his tiger stories go back about twenty years."

" They would! " said Mr Rafiel.

" So I don't suppose for a moment that Major Palgrave would recognise the face in the snapshot if he came across the man casually. What I think happened, what I'm almost sure *must* have happened, is that as he told his story he fumbled for the snapshot, took it out, looked down at it studying the face and then looked up to see *the same face*, or one with a strong resemblance coming towards him from a distance of about ten or twelve feet away."

" Yes," said Mr Rafiel consideringly, " Yes, that's possible."

" He was taken aback," said Miss Marple, " and he shoved it back in his wallet and began to talk loudly about something else."

" He couldn't have been sure," said Mr Rafiel, shrewdly.

" No," said Miss Marple, " he couldn't have been sure. But of course afterwards he would have studied the snapshot very carefully and would have looked at the man and tried to make up his mind whether it was just a likeness or whether it could actually be the same person."

Mr Rafiel reflected a moment or two, then he shook his head.

" There's something wrong here. The motive's inadequate. Absolutely inadequate. He was speaking to you loudly, was he? "

" Yes," said Miss Marple, " quite loudly. He always did."

" True enough. Yes, he did shout. So whoever was approaching would hear what he said? "

" I should imagine you could hear it for quite a good radius round."

Mr Rafiel shook his head again. He said, " It's fantastic, too fantastic. Anybody would laugh at such a story. Here's an old booby telling a story about another story somebody told him, and showing a snapshot, and all of it centring round a murder which had taken place years ago! Or at any rate, a year or two. How on earth can *that* worry the man in question. No evidence, just a bit of hearsay, a story at third hand. He could even admit a likeness, he could say: 'Yes, I *do* look rather like that fellow, don't I! Ha, ha!' Nobody's going to take old Palgrave's identification seriously. Don't tell me so, because I won't believe it. No, the chap, if it *was* the chap, had nothing to fear—nothing whatever. It's the kind of accusation he can just laugh off. Why on earth should he proceed to murder old Palgrave? It's absolutely unnecessary. You must see that."

"Oh I do see that," said Miss Marple. "I couldn't agree with you more. That's what makes me uneasy. So very uneasy that I really couldn't sleep last night."

Mr Rafiel stared at her. "Let's hear what's on your mind," he said quietly.

"I may be entirely wrong," said Miss Marple hesitantly.

"Probably you are," said Mr Rafiel with his usual lack of courtesy, "but at any rate let's hear what you've thought up in the small hours."

"There could be a very powerful motive if——"

"If what?"

"If there was going to be—quite soon—*another murder*."

Mr Rafiel stared at her. He tried to pull himself up a little in his chair.

"Let's get this clear," he said.

"I am so bad at explaining." Miss Marple spoke

rapidly and rather incoherently. A pink flush rose to her cheeks. " Supposing there was a murder planned. If you remember, the story Major Palgrave told me concerned a man whose wife died under suspicious circumstances. Then, after a certain lapse of time, there was another murder under exactly the same circumstances. A man of a different name had a wife who died in much the same way and the doctor who was telling it recognised him as the same man, although he'd changed his name. Well, it does look, doesn't it, as though this murderer might be the kind of murderer who made a habit of the thing? "

" You mean like Smith, *Brides in the Bath*, that kind of thing. Yes."

" As far as I can make out," said Miss Marple, " and from what I have heard and read, a man who does a wicked thing like this and gets away with it the first time, is, alas, *encouraged.* He thinks it's easy, he thinks he's clever. And so he repeats it. And in the end, as you say, like Smith and the Brides in the Bath, it becomes a *habit.* Each time in a different place and each time the man changes his name. But the crimes themselves are all very much alike. So it seems to me, although I may be quite wrong——"

" But you don't think you are wrong, do you? " Mr Rafiel put in shrewdly.

Miss Marple went on without answering. "—that if that *were* so and if this—this person had got things all lined up for a murder out here, for getting rid of *another* wife, say, and if this is crime three or four, well then, the Major's story *would* matter because the murderer couldn't afford to have any similarity pointed out. If you remember, that was exactly the way Smith got caught. The circumstances of a crime attracted the attention of somebody who compared it with a newspaper clipping of some other case. So you do see, don't you, that if this wicked person has got a crime planned, arranged, and shortly about to take place, he couldn't afford to let Major Palgrave go about telling this story and showing that snapshot."

She stopped and looked appealingly at Mr Rafiel.

" So you see he had to do something very quickly, as quickly as possible."

Mr Rafiel spoke, " In fact, that very same night, eh? "

" Yes," said Miss Marple.

" Quick work," said Mr Rafiel, " but it could be done. Put the tablets in old Palgrave's room, spread the blood pressure rumour about and add a little of our fourteen syllable drug to a Planters Punch. Is that it? "

" Yes— But that's all over—we needn't worry about it. It's the *future.* It's now. With Major Palgrave out of the way and the snapshot destroyed, ***this man will go on with his murder as planned.***"

Mr Rafiel whistled.

" You've got it all worked out, haven't you? "

Miss Marple nodded. She said in a most unaccustomed voice, firm and almost dictatorial, " And we've got to stop it. *You've* got to stop it, Mr Rafiel."

" Me? " said Mr Rafiel, astonished, " why me? "

" Because you're rich and important," said Miss Marple, simply. " People will take notice of what you say or suggest. They wouldn't listen to me for a moment. They would say that I was an old lady imagining things."

" They might at that," said Mr Rafiel. " More fools if they did. I must say, though, that nobody would think you had any brains in your head to hear your usual line of talk. Actually, you've got a logical mind. Very few women have." He shifted himself uncomfortably in his chair. " Where the hell's Esther or Jackson? " he said. " I need resettling. No, it's no good your doing it. You're not strong enough. I don't know what they mean, leaving me alone like this."

" I'll go and find them."

" No, you won't. You'll stay here—and thrash this out. Which of them is it? The egregious Greg? The quiet Edward Hillingdon or my fellow Jackson? It's got to be one of the three, hasn't it? "

CHAPTER XVII

MR RAFIEL TAKES CHARGE

" I don't know," said Miss Marple.

" What do you mean? What have we been talking about for the last twenty minutes? "

" It has occurred to me that I may have been wrong."

Mr Rafiel stared at her.

" Scatty after all! " he said disgustedly. " And you sounded so sure of yourself."

" Oh, I am sure—about the *murder*. It's the *murderer* I'm not sure about. You see I've found out that Major Palgrave had more than one murder story—you told me yourself he'd told you one about a kind of Lucrezia Borgia——"

" So he did—at that. But that was quite a different kind of story."

" I know. And Mrs Walters said he had one about someone being gassed in a gas oven——"

" But the story he told you——"

Miss Marple allowed herself to interrupt—a thing that did not often happen to Mr Rafiel.

She spoke with desperate earnestness and only moderate incoherence.

" Don't you see—it's so difficult to be *sure*. The whole point is that—so often—one doesn't *listen*. Ask Mrs Walters—she said the same thing—you listen to begin with—and then your attention flags—your mind wanders—and suddenly you find you've missed a bit. I just wonder if possibly there may have been a gap —a very small one—between the story he was telling me—about a *man*—and the moment when he was getting out his wallet and saying—'Like to see a picture of a murderer'. "

" But you thought it was a picture of the man he had been talking about? "

" I thought so—yes. It never occurred to me that it mightn't have been. But now—how can I be *sure*? "

Mr Rafiel looked at her very thoughtfully. . . .

" The trouble with you is," he said, " that you're too conscientious. Great mistake— Make up your mind and don't shilly shally. You didn't shilly shally to begin with. If you ask me, in all this chit-chat you've been having with the parson's sister and the rest of them, you've got hold of something that's unsettled you."

" Perhaps you're right."

" Well, cut it out for the moment. Let's go ahead with what you had to begin with. Because, nine times out of ten, one's original judgments are right—or so I've found. We've got three suspects. Let's take 'em out and have a good look at them. Any preference? "

"I really haven't," said Miss Marple, "all three of them seem so very unlikely."

"We'll take Greg first," said Mr Rafiel. "Can't stand the fellow. Doesn't make him a murderer, though. Still, there *are* one or two points against him. Those blood pressure tablets belonged to him. Nice and handy to make use of."

"That would be a little obvious, wouldn't it?" Miss Marple objected.

"I don't know that it would," said Mr Rafiel. "After all, the main thing was to do something *quickly*, and he'd got the tablets. Hadn't much time to go looking round for tablets that somebody else might have. Let's say it's Greg. All right. *If* he wanted to put his dear wife Lucky out of the way—(Good job, too, I'd say. In fact I'm in sympathy with him) I can't actually see his motive. From all accounts he's rich. Inherited money from his first wife who had pots of it. He qualifies on that as a possible wife murderer all right. But that's over and done with. He got away with it. But Lucky was his first wife's poor relation. No money there, so if he wants to put *her* out of the way it must be in order to marry somebody else. Any gossip going around about that?"

Miss Marple shook her head.

"Not that I have heard. He—er—has a very gallant manner with *all* the ladies."

"Well, that's a nice, old-fashioned way of putting

it," said Mr Rafiel. "All right, he's a stoat. He makes passes. Not enough! We want more than that. Let's go on to Edward Hillingdon. Now there's a dark horse, if ever there was one."

"He is not, I think, a happy man," offered Miss Marple.

Mr Rafiel looked at her thoughtfully.

"Do you think a murderer ought to be a happy man?"

Miss Marple coughed.

"Well, they usually have been in my experience."

"I don't suppose your experience has gone very far," said Mr Rafiel.

In this assumption, as Miss Marple could have told him, he was wrong. But she forbore to contest his statement. Gentlemen, she knew, did not like to be put right in their facts.

"I rather fancy Hillingdon myself," said Mr Rafiel. "I've an idea that there is something a bit odd going on between him and his wife. You noticed it at all?"

"Oh yes," said Miss Marple, "I have noticed it. Their behaviour is perfect in public, of course, but that one would expect."

"You probably know more about those sort of people than I would," said Mr Rafiel. "Very well, then, everything is in perfectly good taste but it's a probability that, in a gentlemanly way, Edward Hillingdon is contemplating doing away with Evelyn Hillingdon. Do you agree?"

"If so," said Miss Marple, "there must be another woman."

"But what woman?"

Miss Marple shook her head in a dissatisfied manner.

"I can't help feeling—I really can't—that it's not all quite as simple as that."

"Well, who shall we consider next—Jackson? We leave me out of it."

Miss Marple smiled for the first time.

"And why do we leave you out of it, Mr Rafiel?"

"Because if you want to discuss the possibilities of my being a murderer you'd have to do it with somebody else. Waste of time talking about it to me. And anyway, I ask you, am I cut out for the part? Helpless, hauled out of bed like a dummy, dressed, wheeled about in a chair, shuffled along for a walk. What earthly chance have *I* of going and murdering anyone?"

"Probably as good a chance as anyone else," said Miss Marple vigorously.

"And how do you make that out?"

"Well, you would agree yourself, I think, that you have brains?"

"Of course I've got brains," declared Mr Rafiel. "A good deal more than anybody else in this community, I'd say."

"And having brains," went on Miss Marple, "would enable you to overcome the physical difficulties of being a murderer."

" It would take some doing! "

" Yes," said Miss Marple, " it would take some doing. But then, I think, Mr. Rafiel, you would enjoy that."

Mr Rafiel stared at her for quite a long time and then he suddenly laughed.

" You've got a nerve! " he said. " Not quite the gentle fluffy old lady you look, are you? So you really think I'm a murderer? "

" No," said Miss Marple, " I do not."

" And why? "

" Well, really, I think just *because* you have got brains. Having brains, you can get most things you want without having recourse to murder. Murder is stupid."

" And anyway who the devil should I want to murder? "

" That would be a very interesting question," said Miss Marple. " I have not yet had the pleasure of sufficient conversation with you to evolve a theory as to that."

Mr Rafiel's smile broadened.

" Conversations with you might be dangerous," he said.

" Conversations are always dangerous, if you have something to hide," said Miss Marple.

" You may be right. Let's get on to Jackson. What do you think of Jackson? "

" It is difficult for me to say. I have not had the opportunity really of *any* conversation with him."

" So you've no views on the subject? "

" He reminds me a little," said Miss Marple reflectively, " of a young man in the Town Clerk's office near where I live, Jonas Parry."

" And? " Mr Rafiel asked and paused.

" He was not," said Miss Marple, " very satisfactory."

" Jackson's not wholly satisfactory either. He suits me all right. He's first class at his job, and he doesn't mind being sworn at. He knows he's damn' well paid and so he puts up with things. I wouldn't employ him in a position of trust, but I don't have to trust him. Maybe his past is blameless, maybe it isn't. His references were all right but I discern—shall I say, a note of reserve. Fortunately, I'm not a man who has any guilty secrets, so I'm not a subject for blackmail."

" No secrets? " said Miss Marple, thoughtfully. " Surely, Mr Rafiel, you have business secrets? "

" Not where Jackson can get at them. No. Jackson is a smooth article, one might say, but I really don't see him as a murderer. I'd say that wasn't his line at all."

He paused a minute and then said suddenly, " Do you know, if one stands back and takes a good look at all this fantastic business, Major Palgrave and his ridiculous stories and all the rest of it, the *emphasis* is entirely wrong. *I'm* the person who ought to be murdered."

Miss Marple looked at him in some surprise.

" Proper type casting," explained Mr Rafiel. " Who's the victim in murder stories? Elderly men with lots of money."

" And lots of people with a good reason for wishing him out of the way, so as to get that money," said Miss Marple. " Is that true also? "

" Well——" Mr Rafiel considered, " I can count up to five or six men in London who wouldn't burst into tears if they read my obituary in *The Times*. But they wouldn't go so far as to do anything to bring about my demise. After all, why should they? I'm expected to die any day. In fact the bug—blighters are astonished that I've lasted so long. The doctors are surprised too."

" You have of course, a great will to live," said Miss Marple.

" You think that's odd, I suppose," said Mr Rafiel.

Miss Marple shook her head.

" Oh no," she said, " I think it's quite natural. Life is more worth living, more full of interest when you are likely to lose it. It shouldn't be, perhaps, but it is. When you're young and strong and healthy, and life stretches ahead of you, living isn't really important at all. It's young people who commit suicide easily, out of despair from love, sometimes from sheer anxiety and worry. But old people know how valuable life is and how interesting."

" Hah! " said Mr Rafiel, snorting. " Listen to a couple of old crocks."

" Well, what I said is true, isn't it? " demanded Miss Marple.

" Oh, yes," said Mr Rafiel, " it's true enough. But don't you think I'm right when I say that I ought to be cast as the victim? "

" It depends on who has reason to gain by your death," said Miss Marple.

" Nobody, really," said Mr Rafiel. " Apart, as I've said, from my competitors in the business world who, as I have also said, can count comfortably on my being out of it before very long. I'm not such a fool as to leave a lot of money divided up among my relations. Precious little they'd get of it after the Government had taken practically the lot. Oh no, I've attended to all that years ago. Settlements, trusts and all the rest of it."

" Jackson, for instance, wouldn't profit by your death? "

" He wouldn't get a penny," said Mr Rafiel cheerfully. " I pay him double the salary that he'd get from anyone else. That's because he has to put up with my bad temper; and he knows quite well that he will be the loser when I die."

" And Mrs Walters? "

" The same goes for Esther. She's a good girl. First-class secretary, intelligent, good-tempered, understands my ways, doesn't turn a hair if I fly off the handle, couldn't care less if I insult her. Behaves like a nice nursery governess in charge of an outrageous and obstreperous child. She irritates me a bit sometimes, but who doesn't? There's nothing outstanding about her. She's rather a commonplace young woman in many ways, but I couldn't have anyone who suited me better. She's had a lot of trouble in her life. Married a man who wasn't much good. I'd say she never had much judgment when it came to men. Some women haven't. They fall for anyone who tells them a hard luck story. Always convinced that all the man needs is proper female understanding. That, once married to her, he'll pull up his socks and make a go of life! But of course that type of man never does. Anyway, fortunately her unsatisfactory husband died; drank too much at a party one night and stepped in front of a bus. Esther had a daughter to support and she went back to her secretarial job. She's been with me five years. I made it quite clear to her from the start that she need have no expectations from me in the event of my death. I paid her from the start a very large salary, and that salary I've augmented by as much as a quarter as much again each year. However decent and honest people are, one should never trust *anybody*—that's why I told Esther quite clearly that she'd nothing to hope for from my death. Every year I live she'll get a bigger salary. If she puts most of that aside every year—and that's what I think she has done—she'll be quite a well-to-do woman by the time I kick the bucket. I've made myself responsible for her daughter's schooling and

I've put a sum in trust for the daughter which she'll get when she comes of age. So Mrs Esther Walters is very comfortably placed. My death, let me tell you, would mean a serious financial loss to her." He looked very hard at Miss Marple. " She fully realises all that. She's very sensible, Esther is."

" Do she and Jackson get on? " asked Miss Marple.

Mr Rafiel shot a quick glance at her.

" Noticed something, have you? " he said. " Yes, I think Jackson's done a bit of tom-catting around, with an eye in her direction, especially lately. He's a good-looking chap, of course, but he hasn't cut any ice in that direction. For one thing, there's class distinction. She's just a cut above him. Not very much. If she was *really* a cut above him it wouldn't matter, but the lower middle class—they're very particular. Her mother was a school teacher and her father a bank clerk. No, she won't make a fool of herself about Jackson. Dare say he's after her little nest egg, but he won't get it."

" Hush—she's coming now! " said Miss Marple.

They both looked at Esther Walters as she came along the hotel path towards them.

" She's quite a good-looking girl, you know," said Mr Rafiel, " but not an atom of glamour. I don't know why, she's quite nicely turned out."

Miss Marple sighed, a sigh that any woman will give however old at what might be considered wasted opportunities. What was lacking in Esther had been called by so many names during Miss Marple's span of existence. 'Not really attractive to men.' 'No S.A.' 'Lacks Come-hither in her eye.' Fair hair, good complexion, hazel eyes, quite a good figure, pleasant smile, but lacking that something that makes a man's head turn when he passes a woman in the street.

"She ought to get married again," said Miss Marple, lowering her voice.

"Of course she ought. She'd make a man a good wife."

Esther Walters joined them and Mr Rafiel said, in a slightly artificial voice,

"So there you are at last! What's been keeping you?"

"Everyone seemed to be sending cables this morning," said Esther. "What with that, and people trying to check out——"

"Trying to check out, are they? A result of this murder business?"

"I suppose so. Poor Tim Kendal is worried to death."

"And well he might be. Bad luck for that young couple, I must say."

"I know. I gather it was rather a big undertaking for them to take on this place. They've been worried about making a success of it. They were doing very well, too."

"They were doing a good job," agreed Mr Rafiel

" He's very capable and a damned hard worker. She's a very nice girl—attractive too. They've both worked like blacks, though that's an odd term to use out here, for blacks don't work themselves to death at all, so far as I can see. Was looking at a fellow shinning up a coconut tree to get his breakfast, then he goes to sleep for the rest of the day. Nice life."

He added, " We've been discussing the murder here."

Esther Walters looked slightly startled. She turned her head towards Miss Marple.

" I've been wrong about her," said Mr Rafiel, with characteristic frankness. " Never been much of a one for the old pussies. All knitting wool and tittle-tattle. But this one's got something. Eyes and ears, and she uses them."

Esther Walters looked apologetically at Miss Marple, but Miss Marple did not appear to take offence.

" That's really meant to be a compliment, you know," Esther explained.

" I quite realise that," said Miss Marple. " I realise, too, that Mr Rafiel is privileged, or thinks he is."

" What do you mean—privileged? " asked Mr Rafiel.

" To be rude if you want to be rude," said Miss Marple.

" Have I been rude? " said Mr Rafiel, surprised. " I'm sorry if I've offended you."

" You haven't offended me," said Miss Marple, " I make allowances."

" Now, don't be nasty. Esther, get a chair and bring it here. Maybe you can help."

Esther walked a few steps to the balcony of the bungalow and brought over a light basket chair.

" We'll go on with our consultation," said Mr Rafiel. " We started with old Palgrave, deceased, and his eternal stories."

" Oh dear," sighed Esther. " I'm afraid I used to escape from him whenever I could."

" Miss Marple was more patient," said Mr Rafiel. " Tell me, Esther, did he ever tell you a story about a murderer? "

" Oh yes," said Esther. " Several times."

" What was it exactly? Let's have *your* recollection."

" Well——" Esther paused to think. " The trouble is," she said apologetically, " I didn't really listen very closely. You see, it was rather like that terrible story about the lion in Rhodesia which used to go on and on. One did get rather in the habit of not listening."

" Well, tell us what you *do* remember."

" I think it arose out of some murder case that had been in the papers. Major Palgrave said that he'd had an experience not every person had had. He'd actually met a murderer face to face."

" Met? " Mr Rafiel exclaimed. " Did he actually use the word ' Met '? "

Esther looked confused.

" I think so." She was doubtful. " Or he may have said, ' I can point you out a murderer '."

" Well, which was it? There's a difference."

" I can't really be sure . . . I *think* he said he'd show me a picture of someone."

" That's better."

" And then he talked a lot about Lucrezia Borgia."

" Never mind Lucrezia Borgia. We know all about her."

" He talked about poisoners and that Lucrezia was very beautiful and had red hair. He said there were probably far more women poisoners going about the world than anyone knew."

" That I fear is *quite* likely," said Miss Marple.

" And he talked about poison being a woman's weapon."

" Seems to have been wandering from the point a bit," said Mr Rafiel.

" Well, of course, he always did wander from the point in his stories. And then one used to stop listening and just say ' Yes ' and ' Really? ' and ' You don't say so '."

" What about this picture he was going to show you? "

" I don't remember. It may have been something he'd seen in the paper——"

" He didn't actually show you a snapshot? "

" A snapshot? No." She shook her head. " I'm

quite sure of that. He did say that she was a good-looking woman, and you'd never think she was a murderer to look at her."

"She?"

"There you are," exclaimed Miss Marple. "It makes it all so confusing."

"He was talking about a woman?" Mr Rafiel asked.

"Oh yes."

"The snapshot was a snapshot of a woman?"

"Yes."

"It can't have been!"

"But it was," Esther persisted. "He said 'She's here in this island. I'll point her out to you, and then I'll tell you the whole story'."

Mr Rafiel swore. In saying what he thought of the late Major Palgrave he did not mince his words.

"The probabilities are," he finished, "that not a word of anything he said was true!"

"One does begin to wonder," Miss Marple murmured.

"So there we are," said Mr Rafiel. "The old booby started telling you hunting tales. Pig sticking, tiger shooting, elephant hunting, narrow escapes from lions. One or two of them might have been fact. Several of them were fiction, and others had happened to somebody else! Then he gets on to the subject of murder and he tells one murder story to cap another murder story. And what's more he tells them all as if they'd happened to *him*. Ten to one most of them were a hash up of what he'd read in the paper, or seen on T.V."

He turned accusingly on Esther. "You admit that you weren't listening closely. Perhaps you misunderstood what he was saying."

"I'm certain he was talking about a woman," said Esther obstinately, "because of course I wondered who it was."

"Who do you think it was?" asked Miss Marple.

Esther flushed and looked slightly embarrassed.

"Oh, I didn't really—I mean, I wouldn't like to——"

Miss Marple did not insist. The presence of Mr Rafiel, she thought, was inimical to her finding out exactly what suppositions Esther Walters had made. That could only be cosily brought out in a tête-à-tête between two women. And there was, of course, the possibility that Esther Walters was lying. Naturally, Miss Marple did not suggest this aloud. She registered it as a possibility but she was not inclined to believe in it. For one thing she did not think that Esther Walters was a liar (though one never knew) and for another, she could see no point in such a lie.

"But *you* say," Mr Rafiel was now turning upon Miss Marple, "*you* say that he told you this yarn about a murderer and that he then said he had a picture of him which he was going to show you."

"I thought so, yes."

" You thought so? You were sure enough to begin with! "

Miss Marple retorted with spirit.

" It is never easy to repeat a conversation and be entirely accurate in what the other party to it has said. One is always inclined to jump at what you think they *meant*. Then, afterwards, you put actual words into their mouths. Major Palgrave told me this story, yes. He told me that the man who told it to him, this doctor, had shown him a snapshot of the murderer; but if I am to be quite honest I must admit that what he actually said to me was ' Would you like to see a snapshot of a murderer? ' and naturally I assumed that it was the same snapshot he had been talking about. That it was the snapshot of that particular murderer. But I have to admit that it is possible—only remotely possible, but still possible—that by an association of ideas in his mind he leaped from the snapshot he had been shown in the past, to a snapshot he had taken recently of someone here whom he was convinced was a murderer."

" Women! " snorted Mr Rafiel, in exasperation, " You're all the same, the whole blinking lot of you! Can't be accurate. You're never exactly *sure* of what a thing was. And now," he added irritably, " where does *that* leave us? " He snorted. " Evelyn Hillingdon, or Greg's wife, Lucky? The whole thing is a mess."

There was a slight apologetic cough. Arthur

Jackson was standing at Mr Rafiel's elbow. He had come so noiselessly that nobody had noticed him.

"Time for your massage, sir," he said.

Mr Rafiel displayed immediate temper.

"What do you mean by sneaking up on me in that way and making me jump? I never heard you."

"Very sorry, sir."

"I don't think I'll have any massage to-day. It never does me a damn' bit of good."

"Oh come sir, you mustn't say that." Jackson was full of professional cheerfulness. "You'd soon notice it if you left it off."

He wheeled the chair deftly round.

Miss Marple rose to her feet, smiled at Esther and went down to the beach.

CHAPTER XVIII

WITHOUT BENEFIT OF CLERGY

The beach was rather empty this morning. Greg was splashing in the water in his usual noisy style, Lucky was lying on her face on the beach with a sun-tanned back well oiled and her blonde hair splayed over her shoulders. The Hillingdons were not there. Señora de Caspearo, with an assorted bag of gentlemen in attendance was lying face upwards and talking deep-throated, happy Spanish. Some French and Italian children were playing at the water's edge and laughing. Canon and Miss Prescott were sitting in beach chairs observing the scene. The Canon had his hat tilted forward over his eyes and seemed half asleep. There was a convenient chair next to Miss Prescott and Miss Marple made for it and sat down.

" Oh dear," she said, with a deep sigh.

" I know," said Miss Prescott.

It was their joint tribute to violent death.

" That poor girl," said Miss Marple.

" Very sad," said the Canon. " Most deplorable."

" For a moment or two," said Miss Prescott, " we really thought of leaving, Jeremy and I. But then we decided against it. It would not really be fair, I felt, on the Kendals. After all, it's not *their* fault— It might have happened anywhere."

" In the midst of life we are in death," said the Canon solemnly.

" It's very important, you know," said Miss Prescott, " that they should make a go of this place. They have sunk all their capital in it."

" A very sweet girl," said Miss Marple, " but not looking at all well lately."

" Very nervy," agreed Miss Prescott. " Of course her family——" she shook her head.

" I really think, Joan," said the Canon in mild reproof, " that there are some things——"

" Everybody knows about it," said Miss Prescott. " Her family live in our part of the world. A great-aunt—most peculiar—and one ot her uncles took off all his clothes in one of the tube stations. Green Park, I believe it was."

" Joan, that is a thing that should *not* be repeated."

" Very sad," said Miss Marple, shaking her head, " though I believe not an uncommon form of madness. I know when we were working for the Armenian relief, a most respectable elderly clergyman was afflicted the same way. They telephoned his wife and she came along at once and took him home in a cab, wrapped in a blanket."

" Of course, Molly's immediate family's all right," said Miss Prescott. " She never got on very well with her mother, but then so few girls seem to get on with their mothers nowadays."

"Such a pity," said Miss Marple, shaking her head, "because really a young girl needs her mother's knowledge of the world and experience."

"Exactly," said Miss Prescott with emphasis. "Molly, you know, took up with some man—*quite* unsuitable, I understand."

"It so often happens," said Miss Marple.

"Her family disapproved, naturally. *She* didn't tell them about it. They heard about it from a complete outsider. Of course her mother said she must bring him along so that they met him properly. This, I understand, the girl refused to do. She said it was humiliating to him. Most insulting to be made to come and meet her family and be looked over. Just as though you were a horse, she said."

Miss Marple sighed. "One does need so much *tact* when dealing with the young," she murmured.

"Anyway there it was! They forbade her to see him."

"But you can't *do* that nowadays," said Miss Marple. "Girls have jobs and they meet people whether anyone forbids them or not."

"But then, very fortunately," went on Miss Prescott, "she met Tim Kendal, and the other man sort of faded out of the picture. I can't *tell* you how relieved the family was."

"I hope they didn't show it too plainly," said Miss

Marple. "That so often puts girls off from forming suitable attachments."

"Yes, indeed."

"One remembers oneself——" murmured Miss Marple, her mind going back to the past. A young man she had met at a croquet party. He had seemed so nice—rather gay, almost *Bohemian* in his views. And then he had been unexpectedly warmly welcomed by her father. He had been suitable, eligible; he had been asked freely to the house more than once, and Miss Marple had found that, after all, he was *dull*. Very dull.

The Canon seemed safely comatose and Miss Marple advanced tentatively to the subject she was anxious to pursue.

"Of course you know so much about this place," she murmured. "You have been here several years running, have you not?"

"Well, last year and two years before that. We like St. Honoré very much. Always such nice people here. Not the flashy, ultra-rich set."

"So I suppose you know the Hillingdons and the Dysons well!"

"Yes, fairly well."

Miss Marple coughed and lowered her voice slightly.

"Major Palgrave told me such an interesting story," she said.

"He had a great repertoire of stories, hadn't he? Of course he had travelled very widely. Africa, India, even China I believe."

" Yes indeed," said Miss Marple. " But I didn't mean one of *those* stories. This was a story concerned with—well, with one of the people I have just mentioned."

" Oh! " said Miss Prescott. Her voice held meaning.

" Yes. Now I wonder——" Miss Marple allowed her eyes to travel gently round the beach to where Lucky lay sunning her back. " Very beautifully tanned, isn't she," remarked Miss Marple. " And her hair. Most attractive. Practically the same colour as Molly Kendal's, isn't it? "

" The only difference," said Miss Prescott, " is that Molly's is natural and Lucky's comes out of a bottle! "

" Really, Joan," the Canon protested, unexpectedly awake again. " Don't you think that is *rather* an uncharitable thing to say? "

" It's not uncharitable," said Miss Prescott, acidly. " Merely a *fact*."

" It looks very nice to *me*," said the Canon.

" Of course. That's why she does it. But I assure you, my dear Jeremy, it wouldn't deceive any *woman* for a moment. Would it? " She appealed to Miss Marple.

" Well, I'm afraid—" said Miss Marple, " of course I haven't the experience that you have—but I'm afraid—yes I should say definitely *not natural*. The appearance at the roots every fifth or sixth day——" She looked at Miss Prescott and they both nodded with quiet female assurance.

The Canon appeared to be dropping off again.

"Major Palgrave told me a really extraordinary story," murmured Miss Marple, "about—well I couldn't quite make out. I am a little deaf sometimes. He appeared to be saying or hinting——" she paused.

"I know what you mean. There was a great deal of talk at the time——"

"You mean at the time that——"

"When the first Mrs Dyson died. Her death was quite unexpected. In fact, everybody thought she was a *malade imaginaire*—a hypochondriac. So when she had this attack and died so unexpectedly, well, of course, people did talk."

"There wasn't—any—trouble at the time?"

"The doctor was puzzled. He was quite a young man and he hadn't had much experience. He was what I call one of those antibiotics-for-all men. You know, the kind that doesn't bother to look at the patient much, or worry what's the matter with him. They just give them some kind of pill out of a bottle and if they don't get better, then they try a different pill. Yes, I believe he *was* puzzled, but it seemed she had had gastric trouble before. At least her husband said so, and there seemed no reason for believing anything was *wrong*."

"But you yourself think——"

"Well, I always try to keep an open mind, but one does *wonder*, you know. And what with various things people said——"

"Joan!" The Canon sat up. He looked belligerent.

"I don't like—I really don't like to hear this kind of ill-natured gossip being repeated. We've always set our faces against that kind of thing. See no evil, hear no evil, speak no evil—and what is more, *think* no evil! That should be the motto of every Christian man and woman."

The two women sat in silence. They were rebuked, and in deference to their training they deferred to the criticism of a man. But inwardly they were frustrated, irritated and quite unrepentant. Miss Prescott threw a frank glance of irritation towards her brother. Miss Marple took out her knitting and looked at it. Fortunately for them Chance was on their side.

"*Mon père,*" said a small shrill voice. It was one of the French children who had been playing at the water's edge. She had come up unnoticed, and was standing by Canon Prescott's chair.

"*Mon père,*" she fluted.

"Eh? Yes, my dear? *Oui, qu'est-ce qu'il y a, ma petite?*"

The child explained. There had been a dispute about who should have the water-wings next and also other matters of seaside etiquette. Canon Prescott was extremely fond of children, especially small girls. He was always delighted to be summoned to act as arbiter in their disputes. He rose willingly now and accompanied the child to the water's edge. Miss Marple and Miss Prescott breathed deep sighs and turned avidly towards each other.

" Jeremy, of course rightly, is very against ill-natured gossip," said Miss Prescott, " but one cannot really ignore what people are saying. And there was, as I say, a great deal of talk at the time."

" Yes? " Miss Marple's tone urged her forward.

" This young woman, you see, Miss Greatorex I think her name was then, I can't remember now, was a kind of cousin and she looked after Mrs Dyson. Gave her all her medicines and things like that." There was a short, meaningful pause. " And of course there had, I understand"—Miss Prescott's voice was lowered —" been goings-on between Mr Dyson and Miss Greatorex. A lot of people had noticed them. I mean things like that are quickly observed in a place like this. Then there was some curious story about some stuff that Edward Hillingdon got for her at a chemist."

" Oh, Edward Hillingdon came into it? "

" Oh yes, he was very much attracted. People noticed it. And Lucky—Miss Greatorex—played them off against each other. Gregory Dyson and Edward Hillingdon. One has to face it, she has always been an attractive woman."

" Though not as young as she was," Miss Marple replied.

" Exactly. But she was always very well turned out and made up. Of course not so flamboyant when she was just the poor relation. She always *seemed* very devoted to the invalid. But, well, you see how it was."

" What was this story about the chemist—how did that get known? "

" Well, it wasn't in Jamestown, I think it was when they were in Martinique. The French, I believe, are more lax than we are in the matter of drugs— This chemist talked to someone, and the story got around— Well, you know how these things happen."

Miss Marple did. None better.

" He said something about Colonel Hillingdon asking for something and not seeming to know what it was he was asking for. Consulting a piece of paper, you know, on which it was written down. Anyway, as I say, there was *talk*."

" But I don't see quite why Colonel Hillingdon——" Miss Marple frowned in perplexity.

" I suppose he was just being used as a *cat's-paw*. Anyway, Gregory Dyson married again in an almost indecently short time. Barely a month later, I understand."

They looked at each other.

" But there was no *real* suspicion? " Miss Marple asked.

" Oh no, it was just—well, *talk*. Of course there may have been absolutely nothing in it."

" Major Palgrave thought there was."

" Did he say so to you? "

" I wasn't really listening very closely," confessed Miss Marple. " I just wondered if—er—well, if he'd said the same things to you? "

"He did point her out to me one day," said Miss Prescott.

"Really? He actually pointed her out?"

"Yes. As a matter of fact, I thought at first it was Mrs Hillingdon he was pointing out. He wheezed and chuckled a bit and said 'Look at that woman over there. In my opinion that's a woman who's done murder and got away with it.' I was very shocked, of course. I said, 'surely you're joking, Major Palgrave,' and he said 'Yes, yes, dear lady, let's call it joking.' The Dysons and the Hillingdons were sitting at a table quite near to us, and I was afraid they'd overhear. He chuckled and said 'Wouldn't care to go to a drink party and have a certain person mix me a cocktail. Too much like supper with the Borgias.'"

"How *very* interesting," said Miss Marple. "Did he mention a—a photograph?"

"I don't remember. . . . Was it some newspaper cutting?"

Miss Marple, about to speak, shut her lips. The sun was momentarily obscured by a shadow. Evelyn Hillingdon paused beside them.

"Good morning," she said.

"I was wondering where you were," said Miss Prescott, looking up brightly.

"I've been to Jamestown, shopping."

"Oh, I see."

Miss Prescott looked round vaguely and Evelyn Hillingdon said:

"Oh, I didn't take Edward with me. Men hate shopping."

"Did you find anything of interest?"

"It wasn't that sort of shopping. I just had to go to the chemist."

With a smile and a slight nod she went on down the beach.

"Such nice people, the Hillingdons," said Miss Prescott, "though she's not really very easy to know, is she? I mean, she's always very pleasant and all that, but one never seems to get to know her any better."

Miss Marple agreed thoughtfully.

"One never knows what she is thinking," said Miss Prescott.

"Perhaps that is just as well," said Miss Marple.

"I beg your pardon?"

"Oh nothing really, only that I've always had the feeling that perhaps her thoughts might be rather disconcerting."

"Oh," said Miss Prescott, looking puzzled. "I see what you mean." She went on with a slight change of subject. "I believe they have a very charming place in Hampshire, and a boy—or is it two boys—who have just gone—or one of them—to Winchester."

"Do you know Hampshire well?"

"No. Hardly at all. I believe their house is somewhere near Alton."

" I see." Miss Marple paused and then said, " And where do the Dysons live? "

" California," said Miss Prescott. " When they are at home, that is. They are great travellers."

" One really knows so little about the people one meets when one is travelling," said Miss Marple. " I mean—how shall I put it— One only knows, doesn't one, what they choose to tell you about themselves. For instance, you don't *really* know that the Dysons live in California."

Miss Prescott looked startled.

" I'm sure Mr Dyson mentioned it."

" Yes. Yes, exactly. That's what I mean. And the same thing perhaps with the Hillingdons. I mean when you say that they live in Hampshire, you're really repeating what *they* told *you*, aren't you? "

Miss Prescott looked slightly alarmed. " Do you mean that they don't live in Hampshire? " she asked.

" No, no, not for one moment," said Miss Marple, quickly apologetic. "I was only using them as an instance as to what one knows or doesn't know about people." She added, " *I* have told you that I live at St. Mary Mead, which is a place, no doubt, of which you have never heard. But you don't, if I may say so, know it of your *own* knowledge, do you? "

Miss Prescott forbore from saying that she really couldn't care less *where* Miss Marple lived. It was somewhere in the country and in the south of England and that is all she knew. " Oh, I do see what you mean," she agreed hastily, " and I know that one can't possibly be too careful when one is abroad."

" I didn't exactly mean *that*," said Miss Marple.

There were some odd thoughts going through Miss Marple's mind. Did she really know, she was asking herself, that Canon Prescott and Miss Prescott were really Canon Prescott and Miss Prescott? They said so. There was no evidence to contradict them. It would really be easy, would it not, to put on a dog-collar, to wear the appropriate clothes, to make the appropriate conversation. If there was a motive . . .

Miss Marple was fairly knowledgeable about the clergy in her part of the world, but the Prescotts came from the north. Durham, wasn't it? She had no doubt they were the Prescotts, but still, it came back to the same thing—one believed what people said to one.

Perhaps one ought to be on one's guard against that. Perhaps. . . . She shook her head thoughtfully.

CHAPTER XIX

USES OF A SHOE

Canon Prescott came back from the water's edge slightly short of breath (playing with children is always exhausting).

Presently he and his sister went back to the hotel, finding the beach a little too hot.

" But," said Señora de Caspearo scornfully as they walked away— " How can a beach be too hot? It is nonsense that— And look what she wears—her arms and her neck are all covered up. Perhaps it is as well, that. Her skin it is hideous, like a plucked chicken! "

Miss Marple drew a deep breath. Now or never was the time for conversation with Señora de Caspearo. Unfortunately she did not know what to say. There seemed to be no common ground on which they could meet.

" You have children, Señora? " she inquired.

" I have three angels," said Señora de Caspearo, kissing her fingertips.

Miss Marple was rather uncertain as to whether this meant that Señora de Caspearo's offspring were in Heaven or whether it merely referred to their characters.

One of the gentlemen in attendance made a remark in Spanish and Señora de Caspearo flung back her head appreciatively and laughed loudly and melodiously.

"You understand what he said?" she inquired of Miss Marple.

"I'm afraid not," said Miss Marple apologetically.

"It is just as well. He is a wicked man."

A rapid and spirited interchange of Spanish badinage followed.

"It is infamous—infamous," said Señora de Caspearo, reverting to English with sudden gravity, "that the police do not let us go from this island. I storm, I scream, I stamp my foot—but all they say is No—No. You know how it will end—we shall all be killed."

Her bodyguard attempted to reassure her.

"But yes—I tell you it is unlucky here. I knew it from the first— That old Major, the ugly one—he had the Evil Eye—you remember? His eyes they crossed— It is bad, that! I make the Sign of the Horns every time when he looks my way." She made it in illustration. "Though since he is cross-eyed I am not always sure when he does look my way——"

"He had a glass eye," said Miss Marple in an explanatory voice. "An accident, I understand, when he was quite young. It was not his fault."

"I tell you he brought bad luck— I say it is the evil eye he had."

Her hand shot out again in the well-known Latin

gesture—the first finger and the little finger sticking out, the two middle ones doubled in. "Anyway," she said cheerfully, "he is dead—I do not have to look at him any more. I do not like to look at things that are ugly."

It was, Miss Marple thought, a somewhat cruel epitaph on Major Palgrave.

Farther down the beach Gregory Dyson had come out of the sea. Lucky had turned herself over on the sand. Evelyn Hillingdon was looking at Lucky, and her expression, for some reason, made Miss Marple shiver.

"Surely I can't be cold—in this hot sun," she thought.

What was the old phrase—"*A goose walking over your grave*——"

She got up and went slowly back to her bungalow.

On the way she passed Mr Rafiel and Esther Walters coming down the beach. Mr Rafiel winked at her. Miss Marple did not wink back. She looked disapproving.

She went into her bungalow and lay down on her bed. She felt old and tired and worried.

She was quite certain that there was no time to be lost—no time—to—be lost. . . . It was getting late. . . . The sun was going to set—the sun—one must always look at the sun through smoked glass— Where was that piece of smoked glass that someone had given her? . . .

No, she wouldn't need it after all. A shadow had

come over the sun blotting it out. A shadow. Evelyn Hillingdon's shadow— No, not Evelyn Hillingdon— The Shadow (what were the words) the *Shadow of the Valley of Death*. That was it. She must—what was it? Make the Sign of the Horns—to avert the Evil Eye —Major Palgrave's Evil Eye.

Her eyelids flickered open—she had been asleep. But there *was* a shadow—someone peering in at her window.

The shadow moved away—and Miss Marple saw who it was—It was Jackson.

'Impertinence—peering in like that,' she thought —and added parenthetically 'Just like Jonas Parry.'

The comparison reflected no credit on Jackson.

Then she wondered *why* Jackson had been peering into her bedroom. To see if she was there? Or to note that she was there, but was asleep.

She got up, went into the bathroom and peered cautiously through the window.

Arthur Jackson was standing by the door of the bungalow next door. Mr Rafiel's bungalow. She saw him give a rapid glance round and then slip quickly inside. Interesting, thought Miss Marple. Why did he have to look round in that furtive manner. Nothing in the world could have been more natural than his going into Mr Rafiel's bungalow since he himself had a room at the back of it. He was always going in and out of it on some errand or other. So why that quick, guilty glance round? 'Only one reason,' said Miss Marple answering her own question,

' he wanted to be sure that nobody was observing him enter at this particular moment because of something he was going to do in there.'

Everybody, of course, was on the beach at this moment except those who had gone for expeditions. In about twenty minutes or so, Jackson himself would arrive on the beach in the course of his duties to aid Mr Rafiel to take his sea dip. If he wanted to do anything in the bungalow unobserved, now was a very good time. He had satisfied himself that Miss Marple was asleep on her bed, he had satisfied himself that there was nobody near at hand to observe his movements. Well, she must do her best to do exactly that.

Sitting down on her bed, Miss Marple removed her neat sandal shoes and replaced them with a pair of plimsolls. Then she shook her head, removed the plimsolls, burrowed in her suitcase and took out a pair of shoes the heel on one of which she had recently caught on a hook by the door. It was now in a slightly precarious state and Miss Marple adroitly rendered it even more precarious by attention with a nail file. Then she emerged with due precaution from her door walking in stockinged feet. With all the care of a Big Game Hunter approaching up-wind of a herd of antelope, Miss Marple gently circumnavigated Mr Rafiel's bungalow.

Cautiously she manœuvred her way around the corner of the house. She put on one of the shoes she was carrying, gave a final wrench to the heel of the other, sank gently to her knees and lay prone under the window. If Jackson heard anything, if he came to the window to look out, an old lady would have had a fall owing to the heel coming off her shoe. But evidently Jackson had heard nothing.

Very, very gently Miss Marple raised her head. The windows of the bungalow were low. Shielding herself slightly with a festoon of creeper she peered inside. . . .

Jackson was on his knees before a suitcase. The lid of the suitcase was up and Miss Marple could see that it was a specially fitted affair containing compartments filled with various kinds of papers. Jackson was looking through the papers, occasionally drawing documents out of long envelopes. Miss Marple did not remain at her observation post for long. All she wanted was to know what Jackson was doing. She knew now. Jackson was snooping. Whether he was looking for something in particular, or whether he was just indulging his natural instincts, she had no means of judging. But it confirmed her in her belief that Arthur Jackson and Jonas Parry had strong affinities in other things than facial resemblance.

Her problem was now to withdraw. Very carefully she dropped down again and crept along the flower-bed until she was clear of the window. She returned to her bungalow and carefully put away the shoe and the heel that she had detached from it. She looked at them with affection. A good device which she could use on another day if necessary. She resumed her own sandal shoes, and went thoughtfully down to the beach again.

Choosing a moment when Esther Walters was in the water, Miss Marple moved into the chair Esther had vacated.

Greg and Lucky were laughing and talking with Señora de Caspearo and making a good deal of noise.

Miss Marple spoke very quietly, almost under her breath, without looking at Mr Rafiel.

" Do you know that Jackson snoops?"

" Doesn't surprise me," said Mr Rafiel. " Caught him at it, did you?"

" I managed to observe him through a window. He had one of your suitcases open and was looking through your papers."

" Must have managed to get hold of a key to it. Resourceful fellow. He'll be disappointed though. Nothing he gets hold of in that way will do him a mite of good."

" He's coming down now," said Miss Marple, glancing up towards the hotel.

" Time for that idiotic sea dip of mine."

He spoke again—very quietly.

" As for you—don't be too enterprising. We don't want to be attending *your* funeral next. Remember your age, and be careful. There's somebody about who isn't too scrupulous, remember."

CHAPTER XX

NIGHT ALARM

Evening came— The lights came up on the terrace— People dined and talked and laughed, albeit less loudly and merrily than they had a day or two ago— The steel band played.

But the dancing ended early. People yawned—went off to bed— The lights went out— There was darkness and stillness— The Golden Palm Tree slept. . . .

" Evelyn, Evelyn! " The whisper came sharp and urgent.

Evelyn Hillingdon stirred and turned on her pillow.

" *Evelyn.* Please wake up."

Evelyn Hillingdon sat up abruptly. Tim Kendal was standing in the doorway. She stared at him in surprise.

" Evelyn, *please*, could you come? It's—Molly. She's ill. I don't know what's the matter with her. I think she must have taken something."

Evelyn was quick, decisive.

" All right, Tim. I'll come. You go back to her. I'll be with you in a moment."

Tim Kendal disappeared. Evelyn slipped out of bed, threw on a dressing-gown and looked across at the other bed. Her husband, it seemed, had not been awakened. He lay there, his head turned away, breathing quietly. Evelyn hesitated for a moment, then decided not to disturb him. She went out of the door and walked rapidly to the main building and beyond it to the Kendals' bungalow. She caught up with Tim in the doorway.

Molly lay in bed. Her eyes were closed and her breathing was clearly not natural. Evelyn bent over her, rolled up an eyelid, felt her pulse and then looked at the bedside table. There was a glass there which had been used. Beside it was an empty phial of tablets. She picked it up.

" They were her sleeping pills," said Tim, " but that bottle was half full yesterday or the day before. I think she—must have taken the lot."

" Go and get Dr Graham," said Evelyn, " and on the way knock them up and tell them to make strong coffee. Strong as possible. Hurry."

Tim dashed off. Just outside the doorway he collided with Edward Hillingdon.

" Oh, sorry, Edward."

" What's happening here? " demanded Hillingdon. " What's going on? "

" It's Molly. Evelyn's with her. I must get hold of the doctor. I suppose I ought've gone to him first but I—I wasn't sure and I thought Evelyn would know. Molly would have hated it if I'd fetched a doctor when it wasn't necessary."

He went off, running. Edward Hillingdon looked after him for a moment and then he walked into the bedroom.

" What's happening? " he said. " Is it serious? "

" Oh, there you are, Edward. I wondered if you'd woken up. This silly child has been taking things."

" Is it bad? "

" One can't tell without knowing how much she's taken. I shouldn't think it was too bad if we get going in time. I've sent for coffee. If we can get some of that down her——"

" But why should she do such a thing? You don't think——" He stopped.

" What don't I think ? " asked Evelyn.

" You don't think it's because of the inquiry—the police—all that? "

" It's possible, of course. That sort of thing could be very alarming to a nervous type."

" Molly never used to seem a nervous type."

" One can't really tell," said Evelyn. " It's the most unlikely people sometimes who lose their nerve."

" Yes, I remember . . ." Again he stopped.

" The truth is," said Evelyn, " that one doesn't really know anything about anybody." She added, " Not even the people who are nearest to you. . . ."

" Isn't that going a little too far, Evelyn—exaggerating too much? "

"I don't think it is. When you think of people, it is in the image you have made of them for yourself."

"I know you," said Edward Hillingdon quietly.

"You think you do."

"No. I'm sure." He added, "And you're sure of me."

Evelyn looked at him then turned back to the bed. She took Molly by the shoulders and shook her.

"We ought to be doing something, but I suppose it's better to wait until Dr Graham comes— Oh, I think I hear them."

II

"She'll do now." Dr Graham stepped back, wiped his forehead with a handkerchief and breathed a sigh of relief.

"You think she'll be all right, sir?" Tim demanded anxiously.

"Yes, yes. We got to her in good time. Anyway, she probably didn't take enough to kill her. A couple of days and she'll be as right as rain but she'll have a rather nasty day or two first." He picked up the empty bottle. "Who gave her these things anyway?"

"A doctor in New York. She wasn't sleeping well."

"Well, well. I know all we medicos hand these things out freely nowadays. Nobody tells young women who can't sleep to count sheep, or get up and eat a biscuit, or write a couple of letters and then go back to bed. Instant remedies, that's what people demand nowadays. Sometimes I think it's a pity we give them to them. You've got to learn to put up with things in life. All very well to stuff a comforter into a baby's mouth to stop it crying. Can't go on doing that all a person's life." He gave a small chuckle. "I bet you, if you asked Miss Marple what she does if she can't sleep, she'd tell you she counted sheep going under a gate." He turned back to the bed where Molly was stirring. Her eyes were open now. She looked at them without interest or recognition. Dr Graham took her hand.

"Well, well, my dear, and what have you been doing to yourself?"

She blinked but did not reply.

"Why did you do it, Molly, why? Tell me why?" Tim took her other hand.

Still her eyes did not move. If they rested on anyone it was on Evelyn Hillingdon. There might have been even a faint question in them but it was hard to tell. Evelyn spoke as though there had been the question.

"Tim came and fetched me," she said.

Her eyes went to Tim, then shifted to Dr Graham.

"You're going to be all right now," said Dr Graham, "but don't do it again."

"She didn't mean to do it," said Tim quietly.

"I'm sure she didn't mean to do it. She just wanted a good night's rest. Perhaps the pills didn't work at first and so she took more of them. Is that it, Molly?"

Her head moved very faintly in a negative motion.

"You mean—you took them on purpose?" said Tim.

Molly spoke then. "Yes," she said.

"But why, Molly, why?"

The eyelids faltered. "Afraid." The word was just heard.

"Afraid? Of what?"

But her eyelids closed down.

"Better let her be," said Dr Graham. Tim spoke impetuously.

"Afraid of what? The police? Because they've been hounding you, asking you questions? I don't wonder. Anyone might feel frightened. But it's just their way, that's all. Nobody thinks for one moment——" he broke off.

Dr Graham made him a decisive gesture.

"I want to go to sleep," said Molly.

"The best thing for you," said Dr Graham.

He moved to the door and the others followed him.

"She'll sleep all right," said Graham.

"Is there anything I ought to do?" asked Tim. He had the usual, slightly apprehensive attitude of a man in illness.

"I'll stay if you like," said Evelyn kindly.

" Oh no. No, that's quite all right," said Tim.

Evelyn went back towards the bed. " Shall I stay with you, Molly? "

Molly's eyes opened again. She said, " No," and then after a pause, " just Tim."

Tim came back and sat down by the bed.

" I'm here, Molly," he said and took her hand. " Just go to sleep. I won't leave you."

She sighed faintly and her eyes closed.

The doctor paused outside the bungalow and the Hillingdons stood with him.

" You're sure there's nothing more I can do? " asked Evelyn.

" I don't think so, thank you, Mrs Hillingdon. She'll be better with her husband now. But possibly to-morrow—after all, he's got this hotel to run—I think someone should be with her."

" D'you think she might—try again? " asked Hillingdon.

Graham rubbed his forehead irritably.

" One never knows in these cases. Actually, it's most unlikely. As you've seen for yourselves, the restorative treatment is extremely unpleasant. But of course one can never be absolutely certain. She may have more of this stuff hidden away somewhere."

" I should never have thought of suicide in connection with a girl like Molly," said Hillingdon.

Graham said dryly, " It's not the people who are always talking of killing themselves, threatening to do so, who do it. They dramatise themselves that way and let off steam."

"Molly always seemed such a happy girl. I think perhaps"—Evelyn hesitated—"I ought to tell you, Dr Graham."

She told him then about her interview with Molly on the beach the night that Victoria had been killed. Graham's face was very grave when she had finished.

"I'm glad you've told me, Mrs Hillingdon. There are very definite indications there of some kind of deep-rooted trouble. Yes. I'll have a word with her husband in the morning."

III

"I want to talk to you seriously, Kendal, about your wife."

They were sitting in Tim's office. Evelyn Hillingdon had taken his place by Molly's bedside and Lucky had promised to come and, as she expressed it, 'spell her' later. Miss Marple had also offered her services. Poor Tim was torn between his hotel commitments and his wife's condition.

"I can't understand it," said Tim, "I can't understand Molly any longer. She's changed. Changed out of all seeming."

"I understand she's been having bad dreams?"

"Yes. Yes, she complained about them a good deal."

" For how long? "

" Oh, I don't know. About—oh I suppose a month—perhaps longer. She—we—thought they were just—well, nightmares, you know."

" Yes, yes, I quite understand. But what's a much more serious sign is the fact that she seems to have felt afraid of someone. Did she complain about that to you? "

" Well, yes. She said once or twice that—oh, people were following her."

" Ah! Spying on her?"

" Yes, she did use that term once. She said they were her enemies and they'd followed her here."

" Did she have enemies, Mr Kendal? "

" No. Of course she didn't."

" No incident in England, anything you know about before you were married? "

" Oh no, nothing of that kind. She didn't get on with her family very well, that was all. Her mother was rather an eccentric woman, difficult to live with perhaps, but. . . ."

" Any signs of mental instability in her family? "

Tim opened his mouth impulsively, then shut it again. He pushed a fountain pen about on the desk in front of him.

The doctor said:

" I must stress the fact that it would be better to tell me, Tim, if that is the case."

" Well, yes, I believe so. Nothing serious, but I

believe there was an aunt or something who was a bit batty. But that's nothing. I mean—well you get that in almost any family."

"Oh yes, yes, that's quite true. I'm not trying to alarm you about that, but it just might show a tendency to—well to break down or imagine things if any stress arose."

"I don't really know very much," said Tim. "After all, people don't pour out all their family histories to you, do they?"

"No, no. Quite so. She had no former friend—she was not engaged to anyone, anyone who might have threatened her or made jealous threats? That sort of thing?"

"I don't know. I don't think so. Molly *was* engaged to some other man before I came along. Her parents were very against it, I understand, and I think she really stuck to the chap more out of opposition and defiance than anything else." He gave a sudden half-grin. "You know what it is when you're young. If people cut up a fuss it makes you much keener on whoever it is."

Dr Graham smiled too. "Ah yes, one often sees that. One should never take exception to one's children's objectionable friends. Usually they grow out of them naturally. This man, whoever he was, didn't make threats of any kind against Molly?"

"No, I'm sure he didn't. She would have told me. She said herself she just had a silly adolescent craze on him, mainly because he had such a bad reputation."

"Yes, yes. Well, that doesn't sound serious. Now there's another thing. Apparently your wife has had what she describes as blackouts. Brief passages of time during which she can't account for her actions. Did you know about that, Tim?"

"No," said Tim slowly. "No. I didn't. She never told me. I did notice, you know, now you mention it, that she seemed rather vague sometimes and . . ." He paused, thinking. "Yes, that explains it. I couldn't understand how she seemed to have forgotten the simplest things, or sometimes not to seem to know what time of day it was. I just thought she was absent-minded, I suppose."

"What it amounts to, Tim, is just this. I advise you most strongly to take your wife to see a good specialist."

Tim flushed angrily.

"You mean a mental specialist, I suppose?"

"Now, now, don't be upset by labels. A neurologist, a psychologist, someone who specialises in what the layman calls nervous breakdowns. There's a good man in Kingston. Or there's New York of course. There is something that is causing these nervous terrors of your wife's. Something perhaps for which she hardly knows the reason herself. Get advice about her, Tim. Get advice as soon as possible."

He clapped his hand on the young man's shoulder and got up.

" There's no immediate worry. Your wife has good friends and we'll all be keeping an eye on her."

" She won't—you don't think she'll try it again? "

" I think it most unlikely," said Dr Graham.

" You can't be sure," said Tim.

" One can never be sure," said Dr Graham, " that's one of the first things you learn in my profession." Again he laid a hand on Tim's shoulder. " Don't worry too much."

" That's easy to say," said Tim as the doctor went out of the door. "Don't worry, indeed! What does he think I'm made of? "

CHAPTER XXI

JACKSON ON COSMETICS

" You're sure you don't mind, Miss Marple? " said Evelyn Hillingdon.

" No, indeed, my dear," said Miss Marple. " I'm only too delighted to be of use in any way. At my age, you know, one feels very useless in the world. Especially when I am in a place like this, just enjoying myself. No duties of any kind. No, I'll be delighted to sit with Molly. You go along on your expedition. Pelican Point, wasn't it? "

" Yes," said Evelyn. " Both Edward and I love it. I never get tired of seeing the birds diving down, catching up the fish. Tim's with Molly now. But he's got things to do and he doesn't seem to like her being left alone."

" He's quite right," said Miss Marple. " I wouldn't in his place. One never knows, does one? when anyone has attempted anything of that kind— Well, go along, my dear."

Evelyn went off to join a little group that was waiting for her. Her husband, the Dysons and three or four other people. Miss Marple checked her knitting requirements, saw that she had all she wanted with her, and walked over towards the Kendals' bungalow.

As she came up on to the loggia she heard Tim's voice through the half-open french window.

" If you'd only tell me *why* you did it, Molly. What made you? Was it anything I did? There must be some reason. If you'd only tell me."

Miss Marple paused. There was a little pause inside before Molly spoke. Her voice was flat and tired.

" I don't know, Tim, I really don't know. I suppose —something came over me."

Miss Marple tapped on the window and walked in.

" Oh there you are, Miss Marple. It is very good of you."

" Not at all," said Miss Marple. " I'm delighted to be of any help. Shall I sit here in this chair? You're looking much better, Molly. I'm so glad."

" I'm all right," said Molly. " Quite all right. Just—oh, just sleepy."

" I shan't talk," said Miss Marple. " You just lie quiet and rest. I'll get on with my knitting."

Tim Kendal threw her a grateful glance and went out. Miss Marple established herself in her chair.

Molly was lying on her left side. She had a half-stupefied, exhausted look. She said in a voice that was almost a whisper:

" It's very kind of you, Miss Marple. I—I think I'll go to sleep."

She half turned away on her pillows and closed her eyes. Her breathing grew more regular though it was still far from normal. Long experience of nursing made Miss Marple almost automatically straighten the sheet and tuck it under the mattress on her side of the bed. As she did so her hand encountered something hard and rectangular under the mattress. Rather surprised she took hold of this and pulled it out. It was a book. Miss Marple threw a quick glance at the girl in the bed, but she lay there utterly quiescent. She was evidently asleep. Miss Marple opened the book. It was, she saw, a current work on nervous diseases. It came open naturally at a certain place which gave a description of the onset of persecution mania and various other manifestations of schizophrenia and allied complaints.

It was not a highly technical book, but one that could be easily understood by a layman. Miss Marple's face grew very grave as she read. After a minute or two she closed the book and stayed thinking. Then she bent forward and with some care replaced the book where she had found it, under the mattress.

She shook her head in some perplexity. Noiselessly she rose from her chair. She walked the few steps towards the window, then turned her head sharply over her shoulder. Molly's eyes were open but even as Miss Marple turned the eyes shut again. For a minute or two Miss Marple was not quite certain whether she might not have imagined that quick, sharp glance. Was Molly then only pretending to be asleep? That might be natural enough. She might feel that Miss Marple would start talking to her if she showed herself awake. Yes, that could be all it was.

Was she reading into that glance of Molly's a kind of slyness that was somehow innately disagreeable? One doesn't know, Miss Marple thought to herself, one really doesn't know.

She decided that she would try to manage a little talk with Dr Graham as soon as it could be managed. She came back to her chair by the bed. She decided after about five minutes or so that Molly was really asleep. No one could have lain so still, could have breathed so evenly. Miss Marple got up again. She was wearing her plimsolls to-day. Not perhaps very elegant, but admirably suited to this climate and comfortable and roomy for the feet.

She moved gently round the bedroom, pausing at both of the windows, which gave out in two different directions.

The hotel grounds seemed quiet and deserted. Miss Marple came back and was standing a little uncertainly before regaining her seat, when she thought she heard a faint sound outside. Like the scrape of a shoe on the loggia? She hesitated a moment then she went to the window, pushed it a little farther open, stepped out and turned her head back into the room as she spoke.

" I shall be gone only a very short time, dear," she said, " just back to my bungalow, to see where I could possibly have put that pattern. I was so sure I had brought it with me. You'll be quite all right till I come back, won't you? " Then turning her head back, she nodded to herself. " Asleep, poor child. A good thing."

She went quietly along the loggia, down the steps and turned sharp right to the path there. Passing along between the screen of some hibiscus bushes an observer might have been curious to see that Miss Marple veered sharply on to the flower-bed, passed round to the back of the bungalow and entered it again through the second door there. This led directly into a small room that Tim sometimes used as an unofficial office and from that into the sitting-room.

Here there were wide curtains semi-drawn to keep the room cool. Miss Marple slipped behind one of them. Then she waited. From the window here she had a good view of anyone who approached Molly's bedroom. It was some few minutes, four or five, before she saw anything.

The neat figure of Jackson in his white uniform went up the steps of the loggia. He paused for a minute at the balcony there, and then appeared to be giving a tiny discreet tap on the door of the window that was ajar. There was no response that Miss Marple could hear. Jackson looked around him, a quick furtive glance, then he slipped inside the open doors. Miss

Marple moved to the door which led directly into the bedroom. She did not go through it but applied her eye to the hinge.

Jackson had walked into the room. He approached the bed and looked down for a minute on the sleeping girl. Then he turned away and walked not to the sitting-room door but to the far door which led into the adjoining bathroom. Miss Marple's eyebrows rose in slight surprise. She reflected a minute or two, then walked out into the passageway and into the bathroom by the other door.

Jackson spun round from examining the shelf over the wash-basin. He looked taken aback, which was not surprising.

"Oh," he said, "I—I didn't. . . ."

"Mr Jackson," said Miss Marple, in great surprise.

"I thought you'd be here somewhere," said Jackson.

"Did you want anything?" inquired Miss Marple.

"Actually," said Jackson, "I was just looking at Mrs Kendal's brand of face cream."

Miss Marple appreciated the fact that as Jackson was standing with a jar of face cream in his hand he had been adroit in mentioning the fact at once.

"Nice smell," he said, wrinkling up his nose. "Fairly good stuff, as these preparations go. The cheaper brands don't suit every skin. Bring it out in a rash as likely as not. The same thing with face powders sometimes."

" You seem to be very knowledgeable on the subject," said Miss Marple.

" Worked in the pharmaceutical line for a bit," said Jackson. " One learns to know a good deal about cosmetics there. Put stuff in a fancy jar, package it expensively, and it's astonishing what you could rook women for."

" Is that what you——? " Miss Marple broke off deliberately.

" Well no, I didn't come in here to talk about cosmetics," Jackson agreed.

' You've not had much time to think up a lie,' thought Miss Marple to herself. ' Let's see what you'll come out with.'

" Matter of fact," said Jackson, " Mrs Walters lent her lipstick to Mrs Kendal the other day. I came in to get it back for her. I tapped on the window and then I saw Mrs Kendal was fast asleep, so I thought it would be quite all right if I just walked across into the bathroom and looked for it."

" I see," said Miss Marple. " And did you find it? "

Jackson shook his head. " Probably in one of her handbags," he said lightly. " I won't bother. Mrs Walters didn't make a point of it. She only just mentioned it casually." He went on, surveying the toilet preparations: " Doesn't have very much, does she? Ah well, doesn't need it at her age. Good natural skin."

" You must look at women with quite a different eye from ordinary men," said Miss Marple, smiling pleasantly.

" Yes. I suppose various jobs do alter one's angle."

" You know a good deal about drugs? "

" Oh yes. Good working acquaintance with them. If you ask me, there are too many of them about nowadays. Too many tranquillisers and pep pills and miracle drugs and all the rest of it. All right if they're given on prescription, but there are too many of them you can get without prescription. Some of them can be dangerous."

" I suppose so," said Miss Marple. " Yes, I suppose so."

" They have a great effect, you know, on behaviour. A lot of this teenage hysteria you get from time to time. It's not natural causes. The kids've been taking things. Oh, there's nothing new about it. It's been known for ages. Out in the East—not that I've ever been there—all sorts of funny things used to happen. You'd be surprised at some of the things women gave their husbands. In India, for example, in the bad old days, a young wife who married an old husband. Didn't want to get rid of him, I suppose, because she'd have been burnt on the funeral pyre, or if she wasn't burnt she'd have been treated as an outcast by the family. No catch to have been a widow in India in those days. But she could keep an elderly husband under drugs, make him semi-imbecile, give him hallucinations, drive him more or less off his head." He shook his head. " Yes, lot of dirty work."

He went on: "And witches, you know. There's a lot of interesting things known now about witches. Why did they always confess, why did they admit so readily that they *were* witches, that they had flown on broomsticks to the Witches' Sabbath."

" Torture," said Miss Marple.

" Not always," said Jackson. " Oh yes, torture accounted for a lot of it, but they came out with some of those confessions almost before torture was mentioned. They didn't so much confess as boast about it. Well, they rubbed themselves with ointments, you know. Anointing they used to call it. Some of the preparations, belladonna, atropine, all that sort of thing; if you rub them on the skin they give you hallucinations of levitation, of flying through the air. They thought it all was genuine, poor devils. And look at the Assassins—medieval people, out in Syria, the Lebanon, somewhere like that. They fed them Indian hemp, gave them hallucinations of paradise and houris, and endless time. They were told that that was what would happen to them after death, but to attain it they had to go and do a ritual killing. Oh, I'm not putting it in fancy language, but that's what it came to."

" What it came to," said Miss Marple, " is in essence the fact that people are highly credulous."

" Well yes, I suppose you could put it like that."

" They believe what they are told," said Miss

Marple. " Yes indeed, we're all inclined to do that," she added. Then she said sharply, " Who told you these stories about India, about the doping of husbands with datura," and she added sharply, before he could answer, " Was it Major Palgrave? "

Jackson looked slightly surprised. " Well—yes, as a matter of fact, it was. He told me a lot of stories like that. Of course most of it must have been before his time, but he seemed to know all about it."

" Major Palgrave was under the impression that he knew a lot about everything," said Miss Marple. " He was often inaccurate in what he told people." She shook her head thoughtfully. " Major Palgrave," she said, " has a lot to answer for."

There was a slight sound from the adjoining bedroom. Miss Marple turned her head sharply. She went quickly out of the bathroom into the bedroom. Lucky Dyson was standing just inside the window.

" I—oh! I didn't think you were here, Miss Marple."

" I just stepped into the bathroom for a moment," said Miss Marple, with dignity and a faint air of Victorian reserve.

In the bathroom, Jackson grinned broadly. Victorian modesty always amused him.

" I just wondered if you'd like me to sit with Molly for a bit," said Lucky. She looked over towards the bed. " She's asleep, isn't she? "

" I think so," said Miss Marple. " But it's really

quite all right. You go and amuse yourself, my dear. I thought you'd gone on that expedition? "

" I was going," said Lucky, " but I had such a filthy headache that at the last moment I cried off. So I thought I might as well make myself useful."

" That was very nice of you," said Miss Marple. She reseated herself by the bed and resumed her knitting, " but I'm *quite* happy here."

Lucky hesitated for a moment or two and then turned away and went out. Miss Marple waited a moment then tiptoed back into the bathroom, but Jackson had departed, no doubt through the other door. Miss Marple picked up the jar of face cream he had been holding, and slipped it into her pocket.

CHAPTER XXII

A MAN IN HER LIFE?

Getting a little chat in a natural manner with Dr Graham was not so easy as Miss Marple had hoped. She was particularly anxious not to approach him directly since she did not want to lend undue importance to the questions that she was going to ask him.

Tim was back, looking after Molly and Miss Marple had arranged that she should relieve him there during the time that dinner was served and he was needed in the dining-room. He had assured her that Mrs Dyson was quite willing to take that on, or even Mrs Hillingdon, but Miss Marple said firmly that they were both young women who liked enjoying themselves and that she herself preferred a light meal early and so that would suit everybody. Tim once again thanked her warmly. Hovering rather uncertainly round the hotel and on the pathway which connected with various bungalows, among them Dr Graham's, Miss Marple tried to plan what she was going to do next.

She had a lot of confused and contradictory ideas in her head and if there was one thing that Miss Marple did not like, it was to have confused and contradictory ideas. This whole business had started out clearly enough. Major Palgrave with his regrettable capacity for telling stories, his indiscretion that had obviously been overheard and the corollary, his death within twenty-four hours. Nothing difficult about *that*, thought Miss Marple.

But afterwards, she was forced to admit, there was nothing *but* difficulty. Everything pointed in too many different directions at once. Once admit that you didn't believe a word that anybody had said to you, that nobody could be trusted, and that many of the persons with whom she had conversed here had had regrettable resemblances to certain persons at St. Mary Mead, and where did that lead you?

Her mind was increasingly focused on the victim. Someone was going to be killed and she had the increasing feeling that she ought to know quite well who that someone was. There had been *something*. Something she had heard? Noticed? Seen?

Something someone had told her that had a bearing on the case. Joan Prescott? Joan Prescott had said a lot of things about a lot of people. Scandal? Gossip? What exactly *had* Joan Prescott said?

Gregory Dyson, Lucky—Miss Marple's mind hovered over Lucky. Lucky, she was convinced with a certainty born of her natural suspicions, had been actively concerned in the death of Gregory Dyson's first wife. Everything pointed to it. Could it be that the predestined victim over whom she was worrying was Gregory Dyson? That Lucky intended to try her luck again with another husband, and for that reason wanted not only freedom but the handsome inheritance that she would get as Gregory Dyson's widow?

'But really,' said Miss Marple to herself, 'this is all pure conjecture. I'm being stupid. I know I'm being stupid. The truth must be quite plain, if one could just clear away the litter. Too much litter, that's what's the matter.'

"Talking to yourself?" said Mr Rafiel.

Miss Marple jumped. She had not noticed his approach. Esther Walters was supporting him and he was coming slowly down from his bungalow to the terrace.

"I really didn't notice you, Mr Rafiel."

"Your lips were moving. What's become of all this urgency of yours?"

"It's still urgent," said Miss Marple, "only I can't just see what must be perfectly plain——"

"I'm glad it's as simple as that— Well, if you want any help, count on me."

He turned his head as Jackson approached them along the path.

"So there you are, Jackson. Where the devil have you been? Never about when I want you."

"Sorry, Mr Rafiel."

Dexterously he slipped his shoulder under Mr Rafiel's. "Down to the terrace, sir?"

" You can take me to the bar," said Mr Rafiel. " All right, Esther, you can go now and change into your evening togs. Meet me on the terrace in half an hour."

He and Jackson went off together. Mrs Walters dropped into the chair by Miss Marple. She rubbed her arm gently.

" He *seems* a very light weight," she observed, " but at the moment my arm feels quite numb. I haven't seen you this afternoon at all, Miss Marple."

" No, I've been sitting with Molly Kendal," Miss Marple explained. " She seems really very much better."

" If you ask me there was never very much wrong with her," said Esther Walters.

Miss Marple raised her eyebrows. Esther Walters's tone had been decidedly dry.

" You mean—you think her suicide attempt . . ."

" I don't think there *was* any suicide attempt," said Esther Walters. " I don't believe for a moment she took a real overdose and I think Dr Graham knows that perfectly well."

" Now you interest me very much," said Miss Marple. " I wonder why you say that? "

" Because I'm almost certain that it's the case. Oh, it's a thing that happens very often. It's a way, I suppose, of calling attention to oneself," went on Esther Walters.

" ' You'll be sorry when I'm dead '? " quoted Miss Marple.

" That sort of thing," agreed Esther Walters, " though I don't think that was the motive in this particular instance. That's the sort of thing you feel like when your husband's playing you up and you're terribly fond of him."

" You don't think Molly Kendal is fond of her husband? "

" Well," said Esther Walters, " do you? "

Miss Marple considered. " I have," she said, " more or less assumed it." She paused a moment before adding, " perhaps wrongly."

Esther was smiling her rather wry smile.

" I've heard a little about her, you know. About the whole business."

" From Miss Prescott? "

" Oh," said Esther, " from one or two people. There's a man in the case. Someone she was keen on. Her people were dead against him."

" Yes," said Miss Marple, " I did hear that."

" And then she married Tim. Perhaps she was fond of him in a way. But the other man didn't give up. I've wondered once or twice if he didn't actually follow her out here."

" Indeed. But—who? "

" I've no idea who," said Esther, " and I should imagine that they've been very careful."

" You think she cares for this other man? "

Esther shrugged her shoulders. " I dare say he's a bad lot," she said, " but that's very often the kind who knows how to get under a woman's skin and stay there."

" You never heard what kind of a man—what he did—anything like that? "

Esther shook her head. " No. People hazard guesses, but you can't go by that type of thing. He may have been a married man. That may have been why her people disliked it, or he may have been a real bad lot. Perhaps he drank. Perhaps he tangled with the law—I don't know. But she cares for him still. That I know positively."

" You've seen something, heard something? " Miss Marple hazarded.

" I know what I'm talking about," said Esther. Her voice was harsh and unfriendly.

" These murders——" began Miss Marple.

" Can't you forget murders? " said Esther. " You've got Mr Rafiel now all tangled up in them. Can't you just—let them be? You'll never find out any more, I'm sure of that."

Miss Marple looked at her.

" You think you know, don't you? " she said.

" I think I do, yes. I'm fairly sure."

" Then oughtn't you to tell what you know—do something about it? "

" Why should I? What good would it do? I couldn't prove anything. What would happen anyway? People get let off nowadays so easily. They call it diminished responsibility and things like that.

A few years in prison and you're out again, as right as rain."

"Supposing, because you don't tell what you know, somebody else gets killed—another victim?"

Esther shook her head with confidence. "That won't happen," she said.

"You can't be sure of it."

"I am sure. And in any case I don't see who——" She frowned. "Anyway," she added, almost inconsequently, "perhaps it *is*—diminished responsibility. Perhaps you can't help it—not if you are really mentally unbalanced. Oh, I don't know. By far the best thing would be if she went off with whoever it is, then we could all forget about things."

She glanced at her watch, gave an exclamation of dismay and got up.

"I must go and change."

Miss Marple sat looking after her. Pronouns, she thought, were always puzzling and women like Esther Walters were particularly prone to strew them about haphazard. Was Esther Walters for some reason convinced that a *woman* had been responsible for the deaths of Major Palgrave and Victoria? It sounded like it. Miss Marple considered.

"Ah, Miss Marple, sitting here all alone—and not even knitting?"

It was Dr Graham for whom she had sought so long and so unsuccessfully. And here he was prepared of his own accord to sit down for a few minutes' chat.

He wouldn't stay long, Miss Marple thought, because he too was bent on changing for dinner, and he usually dined fairly early. She explained that she had been sitting by Molly Kendal's bedside that afternoon.

" One can hardly believe she has made such a good recovery so quickly," she said.

" Oh well," said Dr Graham, " it's not very surprising. She didn't take a very heavy overdose, you know."

" Oh, I understood she'd taken quite a half-bottle full of tablets."

Dr Graham was smiling indulgently.

" No," he said, " I don't think she took that amount. I dare say she meant to take them, then probably at the last moment she threw half of them away. People, even when they think they want to commit suicide, often don't *really* want to do it. They manage not to take a full overdose. It's not always deliberate deceit, it's just the subconscious looking after itself."

" Or, I suppose it might be deliberate. I mean, wanting it to appear that . . ." Miss Marple paused.

" It's possible," said Dr Graham.

" If she and Tim had had a row, for instance? "

" They don't have rows, you know. They seem very fond of each other. Still, I suppose it can always happen once. No, I don't think there's very much wrong with her now. She could really get up and go about as usual. Still, it's safer to keep her where she is for a day or two——"

He got up, nodded cheerfully and went off towards

the hotel. Miss Marple sat where she was a little while longer.

Various thoughts passed through her mind— The book under Molly's mattress— The way Molly had feigned sleep—

Things Joan Prescott and, later, Esther Walters, had said . . .

And then she went back to the beginning of it all—to Major Palgrave—

Something struggled in her mind. Something about Major Palgrave—

Something that if she could only remember—

CHAPTER XXIII

THE LAST DAY

'*And the evening and the morning were the last day*,' said Miss Marple to herself.

Then, slightly confused, she sat upright again in her chair. She had dozed off, an incredible thing to do because the steel band was playing and anyone who could doze off during the steel band— Well, it showed, thought Miss Marple, that she was getting used to this place! What was it she had been saying? Some quotation that she'd got wrong. Last day? *First* day. That's what it ought to be. This wasn't the first day. Presumably it wasn't the last day either.

She sat upright again. The fact was that she was extremely tired. All this anxiety, this feeling of having been shamefully inadequate in some way. . . . She remembered unpleasantly once more that queer sly look that Molly had given her from under her half-closed eyelids. What had been going on in that girl's head? How different, thought Miss Marple, everything had seemed at first. Tim Kendal and Molly, such a natural happy young couple. The Hillingdons so pleasant, so well-bred, such what is called 'nice' people. The gay hearty extrovert, Greg Dyson, and the gay strident Lucky, talking nineteen to the dozen, pleased with herself and the world . . . A quartet of people getting on so well together. Canon Prescott, that genial kindly man. Joan Prescott, an acid streak in her, but a very nice woman, and nice women have to have their gossipy distractions. They have to know what is going on, to know when two and two make four, and when it is possible to stretch them to five! There was no harm in such women. Their tongues wagged but they were kind if you were in misfortune. Mr Rafiel, a personality, a man of character, a man that you would never by any chance forget. But Miss Marple thought she knew something else about Mr Rafiel.

The doctors had often given him up, so he had said, but this time, she thought, they had been more certain in their pronouncements. Mr Rafiel knew that his days were numbered.

Knowing this with certainty, was there any action he might have been likely to take?

Miss Marple considered the question.

It might, she thought, be important.

What was it exactly he had said, his voice a little too loud, a little too sure? Miss Marple was very skilful in tones of voice. She had done so much listening in her life.

Mr Rafiel had been telling her something that wasn't true.

Miss Marple looked round her. The night air, the soft fragrance of flowers, the tables with their little lights, the women with their pretty dresses, Evelyn in a dark indigo and white print, Lucky in a white sheath, her golden hair shining. Everybody seemed gay and full of life to-night. Even Tim Kendal was smiling. He passed her table and said:

" Can't thank you enough for all you've done. Molly's practically herself again. The doc says she can get up to-morrow."

Miss Marple smiled at him and said that that was good hearing. She found it, however, quite an effort to smile. Decidedly, she was tired . . .

She got up and walked slowly back to her bungalow. She would have liked to go on thinking, puzzling, trying to remember, trying to assemble various facts and words and glances. But she wasn't able to do it. The tired mind rebelled. It said ' Sleep! You've got to go to sleep! '

Miss Marple undressed, got into bed, read a few verses of the Thomas à Kempis which she kept by her bed, then she turned out the light. In the darkness she sent up a prayer. One couldn't do everything oneself. One had to have help. ' Nothing will happen to-night,' she murmured hopefully.

II

Miss Marple woke suddenly and sat up in bed. Her

heart was beating. She switched on the light and looked at the little clock by her bedside. Two a.m. Two a.m. and outside activity of some kind was going on. She got up, put on her dressing-gown and slippers, and a woollen scarf round her head and went out to reconnoitre. There were people moving about with torches. Among them she saw Canon Prescott and went to him.

"What's happening?"

"Oh, Miss Marple? It's Mrs Kendal. Her husband woke up, found she'd slipped out of bed and gone out. We're looking for her."

He hurried on. Miss Marple walked more slowly after him. Where had Molly gone? Why? Had she planned this deliberately, planned to slip away as soon as the guard on her was relaxed, and while her husband was deep in sleep? Miss Marple thought it was probable. But why? What was the reason? Was there, as Esther Walters had so strongly hinted, some other man? If so, who could that man be? Or was there some more sinister reason?

Miss Marple walked on, looking around her, peering under bushes. Then suddenly she heard a faint call:

"Here. . . . This way. . . ."

The cry had come from some little distance beyond the hotel grounds. It must be, thought Miss Marple, near the creek of water that ran down to the sea. She went in that direction as briskly as she could.

There were not really so many searchers as it had

seemed to her at first. Most people must still be asleep in their bungalows. She saw a place on the creek bank where there were people standing. Someone pushed past her, almost knocking her down, running in that direction. It was Tim Kendal. A minute or two later she heard his voice cry out:

"Molly! My God, Molly!"

It was a minute or two before Miss Marple was able to join the little group. It consisted of one of the Cuban waiters, Evelyn Hillingdon, and two of the native girls. They had parted to let Tim through. Miss Marple arrived as he was bending over to look.

"Molly . . ." He slowly dropped on to his knees. Miss Marple saw the girl's body clearly, lying there in the creek, her face below the level of the water, her golden hair spread over the pale green embroidered shawl that covered her shoulders. With the leaves and rushes of the creek, it seemed almost like a scene from *Hamlet* with Molly as the dead Ophelia. . . .

As Tim stretched out a hand to touch her, the quiet, common-sense Miss Marple took charge and spoke sharply and authoritatively.

"Don't move her, Mr Kendal," she said. "She mustn't be moved."

Tim turned a dazed face up to her.

"But—I must—it's Molly. I must . . ."

Evelyn Hillingdon touched his shoulder.

"She's dead, Tim. I didn't move her, but I did feel her pulse."

" Dead? " said Tim unbelievingly. " Dead? You mean she's—*drowned* herself? "

" I'm afraid so. It looks like it."

" But *why*? " A great cry burst from the young man. " *Why?* She was so happy this evening. Talking about what we'd do to-morrow. Why should this terrible death wish come over her again. Why should she steal away as she did—rush out into the night, come down here and drown herself. What despair did she have—what misery—why couldn't she *tell* me anything? "

" I don't know, my dear," said Evelyn gently. " I don't know."

Miss Marple said,

" Somebody had better get Dr Graham. And someone will have to telephone the police."

" The police?" Tim uttered a bitter laugh. " What good will they be? "

" The police have to be notified in a case of suicide," said Miss Marple.

Tim rose slowly to his feet.

" I'll get Graham," he said heavily. " Perhaps—even now—he could—do something."

He stumbled away in the direction of the hotel.

Evelyn Hillingdon and Miss Marple stood side by side looking down at the dead girl.

Evelyn shook her head. " It's too late. She's quite cold. She must have been dead at least an hour—perhaps more. What a tragedy it all is. Those two always seemed so happy. I suppose she was always unbalanced."

"No," said Miss Marple. "I don't think she was unbalanced."

Evelyn looked at her curiously. "What do you mean?"

The moon had been behind a cloud, but now it came out into the open. It shone with a luminous silvery brightness on Molly's outspread hair . . .

Miss Marple gave a sudden ejaculation. She bent down, peering, then stretched out her hand and touched the golden head. She spoke to Evelyn Hillingdon, and her voice sounded quite different.

"I think," she said, "that we had better make sure."

Evelyn Hillingdon stared at her in astonishment.

"But you yourself told Tim we mustn't touch anything?"

"I know. But the moon wasn't out. I hadn't seen——"

Her finger pointed. Then, very gently, she touched the blonde hair and parted it so that the roots were exposed . . .

Evelyn gave a sharp ejaculation.

"*Lucky!*"

And then after a moment she repeated:

"Not Molly. . . . Lucky."

Miss Marple nodded. "Their hair was of much the same colour—but hers, of course, was dark at the roots because it was dyed."

" But she's wearing Molly's shawl? "

" She admired it. I heard her say she was going to get one like it. Evidently she did."

" So that's why we were—deceived. . . ."

Evelyn broke off as she met Miss Marple's eyes watching her.

" Someone," said Miss Marple, " will have to tell her husband."

There was a moment's pause, then Evelyn said:

" All right. I'll do it."

She turned and walked away through the palm trees.

Miss Marple remained for a moment motionless, then she turned her head very slightly, and said:

" Yes, Colonel Hillingdon? "

Edward Hillingdon came from the trees behind her to stand by her side.

" You knew I was there? "

" You cast a shadow," said Miss Marple.

They stood a moment in silence.

He said, more as though he were speaking to himself:

" So, in the end, she played her luck too far. . . ."

" You are, I think, glad that she is dead? "

" And that shocks you? Well, I will not deny it. I am glad she is dead."

" Death is often a solution to problems."

Edward Hillingdon turned his head slowly. Miss Marple met his eyes calmly and steadfastly.

" If you think——" he took a sharp step towards her.

There was a sudden menace in his tone.

Miss Marple said quietly:

" Your wife will be back with Mr Dyson in a moment. Or Mr Kendal will be here with Dr Graham."

Edward Hillingdon relaxed. He turned back to look down at the dead woman.

Miss Marple slipped away quietly. Presently her pace quickened.

Just before reaching her own bungalow, she paused. It was here that she had sat that day talking to Major Palgrave. It was here that he had fumbled in his wallet looking for the snapshot of a murderer. . . .

She remembered how he had looked up, and how his face had gone purple and red . . . " So ugly," as Señora de Caspearo had said. " He has the Evil Eye."

The Evil Eye . . . Eye . . . *Eye.* . . .

CHAPTER XXIV

NEMESIS

Whatever the alarms and excursions of the night, Mr Rafiel had not heard them.

He was fast asleep in bed, a faint thin snore coming from his nostrils, when he was taken by the shoulders and shaken violently.

" Eh—what—what the devil's this? "

" It's me," said Miss Marple, for once ungrammatical, " though I should put it a little more strongly than that. The Greeks, I believe, had a word for it. Nemesis, if I am not wrong."

Mr Rafiel raised himself on his pillows as far as he could. He stared at her. Miss Marple, standing there in the moonlight, her head encased in a fluffy scarf of pale pink wool, looked as unlike a figure of Nemesis as it was possible to imagine.

" So you're Nemesis, are you? " said Mr Rafiel after a momentary pause.

" I hope to be—with your help."

" Do you mind telling me quite plainly what you're talking about like this in the middle of the night."

" I think we may have to act quickly. Very

quickly. I have been foolish. Extremely foolish. I ought to have known from the very beginning what all this was about. It was so simple."

"What was simple, and what are you talking about?"

"You slept through a good deal," said Miss Marple. "A body was found. We thought at first it was the body of Molly Kendal. It wasn't, it was Lucky Dyson. Drowned in the creek."

"Lucky, eh?" said Mr Rafiel. "And drowned? In the creek. Did she drown herself or did somebody drown her?"

"Somebody drowned her," said Miss Marple.

"I see. At least I think I see. That's what you mean by saying it's so simple, is it? Greg Dyson was always the first possibility, and he's the right one. Is that it? Is that what you're thinking? And what you're afraid of is that he may get away with it."

Miss Marple took a deep breath.

"Mr Rafiel, will you trust me. We have got to stop a murder being committed."

"I thought you said it *had* been committed."

"That murder was committed in error. Another murder may be committed any moment now. There's no time to lose. We must prevent it happening. We must go at once."

"It's all very well to talk like that," said Mr Rafiel. "*We*, you say? What do you think *I* can do about it? I can't even walk without help. How can you and I set about preventing a murder? You're about a hundred and I'm a broken up old crock."

"I was thinking of Jackson," said Miss Marple. "Jackson will do what you tell him, won't he?"

"He will indeed," said Mr Rafiel, "especially if I add that I'll make it worth his while. Is that what you want?"

"Yes. Tell him to come with me and tell him to obey any orders I give him."

Mr Rafiel looked at her for about six seconds. Then he said:

"Done. I expect I'm taking the biggest risk of my life. Well, it won't be the first one." He raised his voice. "Jackson." At the same time he picked up the electric bell that lay beside his hand and pressed the button.

Hardly thirty seconds passed before Jackson appeared through the connecting door to the adjoining room.

"You called and rang, sir? Anything wrong?" He broke off, staring at Miss Marple.

"Now Jackson, do as I tell you. You will go with this lady, Miss Marple. You'll go where she takes you and you'll do exactly as she says. You'll obey every order she gives you. Is that understood?"

"I——"

"*Is that understood?*"

"Yes, sir."

"And for doing that," said Mr Rafiel, "you won't be the loser. I'll make it worth your while."

"Thank you, sir."

"Come along, Mr Jackson," said Miss Marple. She spoke over her shoulder to Mr Rafiel. "We'll tell Mrs Walters to come to you on our way. Get her to get you out of bed and bring you along."

"Bring me along where?"

"To the Kendals' bungalow," said Miss Marple. "I think Molly will be coming back there."

II

Molly came up the path from the sea. Her eyes stared fixedly ahead of her. Occasionally, under her breath, she gave a little whimper . . .

She went up the steps of the loggia, paused a moment, then pushed open the window and walked into the bedroom. The lights were on, but the room itself was empty. Molly went across to the bed and sat down. She sat for some minutes, now and again passing her hand over her forehead and frowning.

Then, after a quick surreptitious glance round, she slipped her hand under the mattress and brought out the book that was hidden there. She bent over it, turning the pages to find what she wanted.

Then she raised her head as a sound of running footsteps came from outside. With a quick guilty movement she pushed the book behind her back.

Tim Kendal, panting and out of breath, came in,

and uttered a great sigh of relief at the sight of her.

"Thank God. Where have you been, Molly? I've been searching everywhere for you."

"I went to the creek."

"You went——" he stopped.

"Yes. I went to the creek. But I couldn't wait there. I couldn't. There was someone in the water—and she was dead."

"You mean—Do you know I thought it was *you.* I've only just found out it was Lucky."

"I didn't kill her. Really, Tim, I didn't kill her. I'm sure I didn't. I mean—I'd remember if I did, wouldn't I?"

Tim sank slowly down on the end of the bed.

"You didn't— Are you sure that—? No. No, of course you didn't!" He fairly shouted the words. "Don't start thinking like that, Molly. Lucky drowned herself. Of course she drowned herself. Hillingdon was through with her. She went and lay down with her face in the water——"

"Lucky wouldn't do that. She'd never do that. But *I* didn't kill her. I swear I didn't."

"Darling, of course you didn't!" He put his arms round her but she pulled herself away.

"I hate this place. It ought to be all sunlight. It seemed to be all sunlight. But it isn't. Instead there's a shadow—a big black shadow . . . And I'm in it—and I can't get out——"

Her voice had risen to a shout.

" Hush, Molly. For God's sake, hush!" He went into the bathroom, came back with a glass.

" Look. Drink this. It'll steady you."

" I—I can't drink anything. My teeth are chattering so."

" Yes you can, darling. Sit down. Here, on the bed." He put his arm round her. He approached the glass to her lips. " There you are now. Drink it."

A voice spoke from the window.

"Jackson," said Miss Marple clearly. " Go over. Take that glass from him and hold it tightly. Be careful. He's strong and he may be pretty desperate."

There were certain points about Jackson. He was a man of training, trained to obey orders. He was a man with a great love for money, and money had been promised him by his employer, that employer being a man of stature and authority. He was also a man of extreme muscular development heightened by his training. His not to reason why, his but to do.

Swift as a flash he had crossed the room. His hand went over the glass that Tim was holding to Molly's lips, his other arm had fastened round Tim. A quick flick of the wrist and he had the glass. Tim turned on him wildly, but Jackson held him firmly.

" What the devil—let go of me. Let go of me. Have you gone mad? What are you doing?"

Tim struggled violently.

" Hold him, Jackson," said Miss Marple.

" What's going on? What's the matter here?"

Supported by Esther Walters, Mr Rafiel came through the window.

"You ask what's the matter?" shouted Tim. "Your man's gone mad, stark, staring mad, that's what's the matter. Tell him to let go of me."

"No," said Miss Marple.

Mr Rafiel turned to her.

"Speak up, Nemesis," he said. "We've got to have chapter and verse of some kind."

"I've been stupid and a fool," said Miss Marple, "but I'm not being a fool now. When the contents of that glass that he was trying to make his wife drink, have been analysed, I'll wager—yes, I'll wager my immortal soul that you'll find it's got a lethal dose of narcotic in it. It's the same pattern, you see, the same pattern as in Major Palgrave's story. A wife in a depressed state, and she tries to do away with herself, husband saves her in time. Then the second time she succeeds. Yes, it's the right pattern. Major Palgrave told me the story and he took out a snapshot and then he looked up and saw——"

"Over your right shoulder——" continued Mr Rafiel.

"No," said Miss Marple, shaking her head. "*He didn't see anything over my right shoulder.*"

"What are you talking about? You told me . . ."

"I told you wrong. I was completely wrong. I was stupid beyond belief. Major Palgrave *appeared* to me to be looking over my right shoulder, glaring, in fact, at something— But he couldn't have *seen* anything, because he was looking through his left eye and his left eye was his glass eye."

" I remember—he *had* a glass eye," said Mr Rafiel. " I'd forgotten—or I took it for granted. You mean he couldn't see anything? "

" Of course he could *see*," said Miss Marple. " He could *see* all right, but he could only see with one eye. The eye he *could* see with was his *right* eye. And so, you see, he must have been looking at something or someone not to the right of me but to the *left* of me."

" Was there anyone on the left of you? "

" Yes," said Miss Marple. " Tim Kendal and his wife were sitting not far off. Sitting at a table just by a big hibiscus bush. They were doing accounts there. So you see the Major looked up. His glass left eye was glaring over my shoulder, but what he *saw* with his other eye was a man sitting by a hibiscus bush and the face was the same, only rather older, as the face in the snapshot. Also by a hibiscus bush. Tim Kendal had heard the story the Major had been telling and he saw that the Major had recognised him. So, of course, he had to kill him. Later, he had to kill the girl, Victoria, because she'd seen him putting a bottle of tablets in the Major's room. She didn't think anything of it at first because of course it was quite natural on various occasions for Tim Kendal to go into the guests' bungalows. He might have just been returning something to it that had been left on a restaurant table. But she thought about it and then she asked him questions and so he had to get rid of her. But this is the real murder, the murder he's been planning all along. He's a wife-killer, you see."

"What damned nonsense, what——" Tim Kendal shouted.

There was a sudden cry, a wild angry cry. Esther Walters detached herself from Mr Rafiel, almost flinging him down and rushed across the room. She pulled vainly at Jackson.

"Let go of him—let go of him. It's not true. Not a word of it's true. Tim—Tim darling, it's not true. You could never kill anyone, I know you couldn't. I know you wouldn't. It's that horrible girl you married. She's been telling lies about you. They're not true. None of them are true. I believe in you. I love you and trust in you. I'll never believe a word anyone says. I'll——"

Then Tim Kendal lost control of himself.

"For God's sake, you damned bitch," he said, "shut up, can't you? D'you want to get me hanged? Shut up, I tell you. Shut that big, ugly mouth of yours."

"Poor silly creature," said Mr Rafiel softly. "So that's what's been going on, is it?"

CHAPTER XXV

MISS MARPLE USES HER IMAGINATION

" So that's what had been going on? " said Mr Rafiel.

He and Miss Marple were sitting together in a confidential manner.

" She'd been having an affair with Tim Kendal, had she? "

" Hardly an affair, I imagine," said Miss Marple, primly. " It was, I think, a romantic attachment with the prospect of marriage in the future.'

" What—after his wife was dead? "

" I don't think poor Esther Walters knew that Molly was going to die," said Miss Marple. " I just think she believed the story Tim Kendal told her about Molly having been in love with another man, and the man having followed her here, and I think she counted on Tim's getting a divorce. I think it was all quite proper and respectable. But she was very much in love with him."

" Well, that's easily understood. He was an attractive chap. But what made *him* go for her—d'you know that too? "

" *You* know, don't you? " said Miss Marple.

" I dare say I've got a pretty fair idea, but I don't

know how you should know about it. As far as that goes, I don't see how Tim Kendal could know about it."

"Well, I really think I could explain all that with a little imagination, though it would be simpler if you told me."

"I'm not going to tell you," said Mr Rafiel. "You tell me, since you're being so clever."

"Well, it seems to me possible," said Miss Marple, "that as I have already hinted to you, your man Jackson was in the habit of taking a good snoop through your various business papers from time to time."

"Perfectly possible," said Mr Rafiel, "but I shouldn't have said there was anything there that could do him much good. I took care of that."

"I imagine," said Miss Marple, "he read your will."

"Oh I see. Yes, yes, I did have a copy of my will along."

"You told me," said Miss Marple, "you told me—(as Humpty Dumpty said—very loud and clear) that you had *not* left anything to Esther Walters in your will. You had impressed that fact upon her, and also upon Jackson. It was true in Jackson's case, I should imagine. You have not left *him* anything, but you *had* left Esther Walters money, though you weren't going to let her have any inkling of the fact. Isn't that right?"

"Yes, it's quite right, but I don't know how *you* knew."

"Well, it's the way you insisted on the point," said Miss Marple. "I have a certain experience of the way people tell lies."

"I give in," said Mr Rafiel. "All right. I left Esther £50,000. It would come as a nice surprise to her when I died. I suppose that, knowing this, Tim Kendal decided to exterminate his present wife with a nice dose of something or other and marry £50,000 and Esther Walters. Possibly to dispose of her also in good time. But how did *he* know she was going to have £50,000?"

"Jackson told him, of course," said Miss Marple. "They were very friendly, those two. Tim Kendal was nice to Jackson and, quite, I should imagine, without ulterior motive. But amongst the bits of gossip that Jackson let slip I think Jackson told him that unbeknownst to herself, Esther Walters was going to inherit a fat lot of money, and he may have said that he himself hoped to induce Esther Walters to marry him though he hadn't had much success so far in taking her fancy. Yes, I think that's how it happened."

"The things you imagine always seem perfectly plausible," said Mr Rafiel.

"But I was stupid," said Miss Marple, "very stupid. Everything fitted in really, you see. Tim Kendal was a very clever man as well as being a very wicked one. He was particularly good at putting about rumours. Half the things I've been told here came from him originally, I imagine. There were stories going around about Molly wanting to marry an undesirable young man, but I rather fancy that the undesirable young man was actually Tim Kendal himself, though that wasn't the name he was using then. Her people had heard something, perhaps that his background was rather fishy. So he put on a high indignation act, refused to be taken by Molly to be 'shown off' to her people and then he brewed up a little scheme with her which they both thought great fun. She pretended to sulk and pine for him. Then a Mr Tim Kendal turned up, primed with the names of various old friends of Molly's people, and they welcomed him with open arms as being the sort of young man who would put the former delinquent one out of Molly's head. I am afraid Molly and he must have laughed over it a good deal. Anyway, he married her, and with her money he bought out the people who ran this place and they came out here. I should imagine that he ran through her money at a pretty fair rate. Then he came across Esther Walters and he saw a nice prospect of more money."

"Why didn't he bump me off?" said Mr Rafiel.

Miss Marple coughed.

"I expect he wanted to be fairly sure of Mrs Walters first. Besides—I mean . . ." She stopped, a little confused.

"Besides, he realised he wouldn't have to wait long," said Mr Rafiel, "and it would clearly be better for me to die a natural death. Being so rich. Deaths of millionaires are scrutinised rather carefully, aren't they, unlike mere wives? "

" Yes, you're quite right. Such a lot of lies as he told," said Miss Marple. " Look at the lies he got Molly herself to believe—putting that book on mental disorders in her way. Giving her drugs which would give her dreams and hallucinations. You know, your Jackson was rather clever over that. I think he recognised certain of Molly's symptoms as being the result of drugs. And he came into the bungalow that day to potter about a bit in the bathroom. That face cream he examined. He might have got some idea from the old tales of witches rubbing themselves with ointments that had belladonna in them. Belladonna in face cream could have produced just that result. Molly would have black-outs. Times she couldn't account for, dreams of flying through the air. No wonder she got frightened about herself. She had all the signs of mental illness, Jackson was on the right track. Maybe he got the idea from Major Palgrave's stories about the use of datura by Indian women on their husbands."

" Major Palgrave! " said Mr Rafiel. " Really, that man! "

" He brought about his own murder," said Miss Marple, " and that poor girl Victoria's murder, and he nearly brought about Molly's murder. But he recognised a murderer all right."

" What made you suddenly remember about his glass eye? " asked Mr Rafiel curiously.

" Something that Señora de Caspearo said. She talked some nonsense about his being ugly, and having the Evil Eye; and I said it was only a glass eye, and he couldn't help that, poor man, and she said his eyes looked different ways, they were cross-eyes—which, of course, they were. And she said it brought bad luck. I knew—I *knew* that I had heard something that day that was important. Last night, just after Lucky's death, it came to me what it was! And then I realised there was no time to waste . . ."

" How did Tim Kendal come to kill the wrong woman? "

" Sheer chance. I think his plan was this: Having convinced everybody—and that included Molly herself—that she was mentally unbalanced, and after giving her a sizeable dose of the drug he was using, he told her that between them they were going to clear up all these murder puzzles. But she had got to help him. After everyone was asleep, they would go separately and meet at an agreed spot by the creek.

" He said he had a very good idea who the murderer was, and they would trap him. Molly went off obediently—but she was confused and stupefied with the drug she had been given, and it slowed her up. Tim arrived there first and saw what he thought was Molly. Golden hair and pale green shawl. He came up behind her, put his hand over her mouth, and forced her down into the water and held her there."

"Nice fellow! But wouldn't it have been easier just to give her an overdose of narcotic?"

"Much easier, of course. But that *might* have given rise to suspicion. All narcotics and sedatives had been very carefully removed from Molly's reach, remember. And if she *had* got hold of a fresh supply, who more likely to have supplied it than her husband? But if, in a fit of despair, she went out and drowned herself whilst her innocent husband slept, the whole thing would be a romantic tragedy, and no one would be likely to suggest that she had been drowned deliberately. Besides," added Miss Marple, "murderers always find it difficult to keep things simple. They can't keep themselves from elaborating."

"You seem convinced you know all there is to be known about murderers! So you believe Tim didn't know he had killed the wrong woman?"

Miss Marple shook her head.

"He didn't even look at her face, just hurried off as quickly as he could, let an hour elapse, then started to organise a search for her, playing the part of a distracted husband."

"But what the devil was Lucky doing hanging about the creek in the middle of the night?"

Miss Marple gave an embarrassed little cough.

"It is possible, I think, that she was—er—waiting to meet someone."

"Edward Hillingdon?"

"Oh *no*," said Miss Marple. "That's all over. I wondered whether—just possibly—she might have been waiting for Jackson."

"Waiting for *Jackson*?"

"I've noticed her—look at him once or twice," murmured Miss Marple, averting her eyes.

Mr Rafiel whistled.

"My Tom Cat Jackson! I wouldn't put it past him! Tim must have had a shock later when he found he'd killed the wrong woman."

"Yes, indeed. He must have felt quite desperate. Here was Molly alive and wandering about. And the story he'd circulated so carefully about her mental condition wouldn't stand up for a moment once she got into the hands of competent mental specialists. And once she told her damning story of his having asked her to meet him at the creek, where would Tim Kendal be? He'd only one hope—to finish off Molly as quickly as possible. Then there was a very good chance that everyone would believe that Molly, in a fit of mania, had drowned Lucky, and had then, horrified by what she had done, taken her own life."

"And it was then," said Mr Rafiel, "that you decided to play Nemesis, eh?"

He leaned back suddenly and roared with laughter. "It's a damned good joke," he said. "If you knew what you looked like that night with that fluffy pink wool all round your head, standing there and saying you were Nemesis! I'll never forget it!"

EPILOGUE

The time had come and Miss Marple was waiting at the airport for her plane. Quite a lot of people had come to see her off. The Hillingdons had left already. Gregory Dyson had flown to one of the other islands and the rumour had come that he was devoting himself to an Argentinian widow. Señora de Caspearo had returned to South America.

Molly had come to see Miss Marple off. She was pale and thin but she had weathered the shock of her discovery bravely and with the help of one of Mr Rafiel's nominees whom he had wired for to England, she was carrying on with the running of the hotel.

"Do you good to be busy," Mr Rafiel observed. "Keep you from thinking. Got a good thing here."

"You don't think the murders——"

"People love murders when they're all cleared up," Mr Rafiel had assured her. "You carry on, girl, and keep your heart up. Don't distrust all men because you've met one bad lot."

"You sound like Miss Marple," Molly had said, "she's always telling me Mr. Right will come along one day."

Mr Rafiel grinned at this sentiment. So Molly was there and the two Prescotts and Mr Rafiel, of course, and Esther—an Esther who looked older and sadder and to whom Mr Rafiel was quite often unexpectedly kind. Jackson also was very much to the fore, pretending to be looking after Miss Marple's baggage. He was all smiles these days and let it be known that he had come into money.

There was a hum in the sky. The plane was arriving. Things were somewhat informal here. There was no 'taking your place by Channel 8' or Channel 9. You just walked out from the little flower-covered pavilion on to the tarmac.

"Good-bye, darling Miss Marple." Molly kissed her.

"Good-bye. Do try and come and visit us." Miss Prescott shook her warmly by the hand.

"It has been a great pleasure to know you," said the Canon. "I second my sister's invitation most warmly."

"All the best, Madam," said Jackson, "and remember any time you want any massage free, just you send me a line and we'll make an appointment."

Only Esther Walters turned slightly away when the time came for good-byes. Miss Marple did not force one upon her. Mr Rafiel came last. He took her hand.

"*Ave Caesar, nos morituri te salutamus*," he said.

"I'm afraid," said Miss Marple, "I don't know very much Latin."

"But you understand that?"

"Yes." She said no more. She knew quite well what he was telling her.

"It has been a great pleasure to know you," she said.

Then she walked across the tarmac and got into the plane.

THE END

Printed in Italy